D0122849

STRANGE
SWEET SONG

STRANGE
SWEET SONG

ADI RULE

ST. MARTIN'S GRIFFIN
NEW YORK

This is a work of fiction. All of the characters, organizations, and events portrayed in this novel are either products of the author's imagination or are used fictitiously.

STRANGE SWEET SONG. Copyright © 2014 by Adi Rule. All rights reserved. Printed in the United States of America. For information, address St. Martin's Press, 175 Fifth Avenue, New York, N.Y. 10010.

www.stmartins.com

Library of Congress Cataloging-in-Publication Data

Rule, Adi.
  Strange sweet song / Adi Rule.—First ed.
     p. cm.
  ISBN 978-1-250-04816-5 (hardcover)
  ISBN 978-1-250-03634-6 (e-book)
  1. Singers—Fiction. 2. Conservatories of music—Fiction. 3. Schools—Fiction. 4. Supernatural—Fiction. 5. Forests and forestry—Fiction.
I. Title.
  PZ7.R8875Str 2014
  [Fic]—dc23   2013032020

St. Martin's Griffin books may be purchased for educational, business, or promotional use. For information on bulk purchases, please contact Macmillan Corporate and Premium Sales Department at 1-800-221-7945, extension 5442, or write specialmarkets@macmillan.com.

First Edition: March 2014

10 9 8 7 6 5 4 3 2 1

STRANGE
SWEET SONG

One

I F YOU HAD BEEN THERE that night, the night it happened, you might not have even noticed. The strings and woodwinds shone fat and glossy in the concert hall's perfect humidity, and the brass instruments sparkled in the gentle light of the chandeliers. The music itself shimmered as well, lighting up dark places people hadn't even known were there.

You might not have noticed the small movement. It fluttered the fading sunlight stretching in through one of the high, arched windows that encircled the room like a crown. You would have been staring at the orchestra, or at the polished floor, or at the blackness inside your closed eyelids, as the music swirled around you. Had you opened your eyes or broken your fuzzy-glass gaze and looked up at the fluttering light, you would have seen the silhouette of the crow. But you wouldn't have heard it, because the crow didn't make a sound.

At least, not at first. It alighted on the ledge of the little window and folded its wings, flexing its toes as though it meant to be there awhile. Some of the windows still held their colorful panels, but the crow had chosen one through which tendrils of ivy had pushed their way, dislodging the glass with a long-forgotten drop and shatter.

The crow seemed comfortable, somehow, and not just because it was a crow adorning a remote Gothic hall surrounded by dark pine trees; not just because St. Augustine's was a natural place for a crow to be. It seemed to be *listening,* cocking its head and stretching its black neck as far into the room as it could.

At intermission, the grand piano was wheeled onto the stage, black and sleek and curvy. The crow looked at the piano with one eye and then the other and ruffled its wings. As the audience applauded, a middle-aged woman lowered herself onto the bench and placed her hands on the gleaming keys, stretching and bending her fingers. The crow twitched its own knobbly gray feet experimentally.

Then the conductor waved the orchestra to life again—a romantic piano concerto, well-known to the concertgoers, who settled in their seats and breathed.

When the woman at the piano began to play, when the first smooth, icy notes reached the small, broken window in the ceiling, the crow froze. It stared, its dingy feathers raised just a little. It was listening again, but now it listened with its whole body. As the concerto progressed, the crow remained utterly still. It might have been a stone gargoyle, except there was something too bright about its eyes. They were fixed on the woman's hands.

If you had looked, then, into the crow's eyes, if you had been a ghost or a puff of smoke and had floated up to the ceiling to look deeply into those shiny black eyes where the brilliant white keys were reflected, you would have seen a despair bigger than those eyes could hold, bigger than the hall itself.

And you would have heard the faintest hiss—an ugly, crackling hiss, as different from the pure, clear tones of the piano as it could possibly be. You might then have noticed the grubby beak was open very slightly. And you might have realized with a start that the crow was trying to *sing*.

But perhaps you *were* there. Perhaps you already know this story.

Two

S ING DA NAVELLI STARES ACROSS the moonlit quadrangle and up the snowy mountain that watches over the campus. A porter unloads baggage from her father's Mercedes. Just inside the doorway to the dormitory, a haggard young man in gray academic robes speaks to one of her father's secretaries. She is finally here, counted among the select few.

Dunhammond Conservatory. European prestige tucked away in New World mountain wilderness, surrounded by its own black forest. A scattering of mismatched buildings huddle in the shadow of St. Augustine's, the famous Gothic church synonymous with musical greatness. Until her first visit, this spring, Sing had seen St. Augustine's only in magazines. Now she is here to sing, in the place that has produced the brightest stars in classical music for a century and a half.

She drifts away from the yellow lights of campus toward the chilly northern woods. Not too far, not too deep, just the shadowy, crackling edge. The mountain snow tingles her nose as she peers into the twisted darkness. *Quand il se trouvera dans la forêt sombre . . .* She finds herself humming an all-too-familiar aria. *When he finds himself in the dark forest . . .*

When she was little, music was her nanny when her parents were gone, which was most of the time. Sure, various starched, soap-smelling women bustled around, but it was music that raised her, folding around her like a blanket—fuzzy or spiky or cold or sweet and warm. It sparked her, calmed her, made her want to get off the velvety floor and look out the window. Sing da Navelli is more music than words, inside.

Chatter from the campus drowns out the song in her mind. People are taking care of her registration, checking in, all those little details she has never had to worry about. Then it will be official. No more mediocre high school ensembles. She will spend the last of her teen years with her peers—those young musicians destined to attend the best universities and build careers like fireworks, explosive and brilliant. She is finally going to sing for real.

How can something so wonderful fill her with dread?

It would be better if Zhin were here. Zhin, Sing's first almost–best friend, who loves the violin almost as much as the soap opera world of classical music. She looked out for Sing at Stone Hill Youth Music Retreat this past summer—can it have been only a few weeks ago? They even got to do the opera together, *Osiris and Seth*. Sing loved the elaborate set with the big lotus pillars. Zhin loved the battle scene with all the shirtless baritones.

If Zhin were here, she would tell Sing what she can't quite tell herself: *You are good enough. You belong at Dunhammond Conservatory. You deserve this.*

The voice in Sing's head won't say these things. It says, *Not yet. Something is missing.* But it offers no insight when she tries, every day at the piano, to perfect her imperfect voice.

She heard some of the other singers through the wall at the spring auditions; they were good. Very good, but not out of her league. Now, across the gravel driveway, Sing hears her father speaking. *He* wouldn't let her come to DC if he didn't think she could be good enough.

It's just that, in her family, "good enough" means "the best."

Her parents could have named her Aria, or Harmonia, or Tessitura, or a hundred other clever names that would have alluded to her ancestry. But they weren't for her, these names that roll or sparkle or play or simply proclaim, *I am normal!*

No, it was Sing. A name and a command.

"Sing, must you wander off? It is time to go in." Her father is suddenly there, speaking in that calm, unwavering voice, more used to command than leisure. Instead of his native Italian, he speaks to her in English, her language. Her mother's language. "You must get to bed as soon as possible, but do not sleep too long tomorrow. When is your placement audition?"

It is a quiz. He knows the answer already. "One o'clock." Her voice feels small here, at the edge of this great forest.

"So you must be awake and singing by when?"

"Nine o'clock."

"Exactly. Eat a good breakfast. Go over your piece tonight, but don't overdo it. It is there, eh?" He taps her head lightly. "You know it very well. I have heard you sing this vocalise one hundred times, eh?" Sing nods. Her father looks back toward campus. "It is a shame we are so late in arriving. I would like to see Maestro Keppler—I so much enjoyed his interpretation of the *Little Night Music* last spring. He has not aged one day since I last saw him! And I have not the opportunity to speak with my old friend Martin."

It's just as well he won't get to speak with DC's president. Sing already feels her father tugging on the invisible marionette strings of her budding career. The conservatory's brand-new theater is evidence of his sudden interest in philanthropy toward his alma mater.

"I hope they have chosen a suitable opera for the Autumn Festival." He puts an arm around her shoulders. "Something Baroque, eh, *carina*? That would be lovely in your voice. I would like to hear it."

Something Baroque, she thinks. *Something safe. Something technical and stylized.* But in her mind she keeps hearing a different melody, a sweeping, wailing one that was born of this very forest almost one hundred fifty years ago. *Quand il se trouvera dans la forêt sombre* . . .

"This is where Durand wrote *Angelique*," she whispers, and is surprised to have said it out loud.

Her father's arm stiffens. "Yes, certainly it is. This is a beautiful place to write an opera. *Vieni,* it is time to go in."

Sing hesitates, gazing into the dark forest, Durand's dark forest. Angelique's dark forest. She is unable to turn away.

After a moment, her father speaks in a heavy, quiet voice and calls her by a name she hasn't heard in years. *"Farfallina,"* he says, "I leave tonight. But please promise me to stay always on the campus. They say this forest is dangerous."

Sing tilts her head. "That sounds almost superstitious of you, Papà."

He smiles. "I am just being your father, my dear."

If he wanted to, Sing's father could conduct *Angelique* as well as anyone in the world. But Sing couldn't imagine him doing something as impractical as wandering around the very forest that inspired it. Her mother, perhaps. But she didn't attend Dunhammond Conservatory and would never see it now. Who knows if she would have answered the forest's call—or if she would have even heard it.

She shrugs. "I'm not afraid of ghosts."

Her father continues to smile, but his eyes are grave. "That is good to hear."

Three

W HEN THE CONCERT WAS OVER, the crow remained, motionless, its black eyes fixed on the grand piano. It stared until the last rays of the sun were gone, the last light had been extinguished, and the hall had settled into a profound darkness. When it could no longer see the piano, the crow continued to stare through the broken window at the place where it knew the piano was.

And it might have gone on staring forever, if not for a tiny noise—the softest click of something hard and sharp on the tiled roof. Instinctively, the crow took to the air.

But its right leg was entangled in the dense ivy covering the windowsill. The crow fell back, flapping, but couldn't free itself. Its wing became caught as well, as though the tendrils of ivy were reaching and grasping. Still aware of the strange presence on the roof behind it, the crow turned.

It didn't see the long, dark body, precariously, impossibly perched. It didn't see the lashing tail or the yellowing claws. It saw only the eyes, deep and black violet, hungry and pitiless.

The crow had never seen the Felix before, but it knew to be afraid.

Four

Placement auditions. Sing sits on a long maple bench, gazing at the translucent window across the hall. Despite its gloomy exterior, this part of St. Augustine's is sunny. She squints at the stained glass—bright, blocky music notes and swirling staves.

"You're Sing da Navelli." The voice beside her is a vibrant disturbance in the hushed, gaping hallway.

Sing gives a start. Her mind has been drifting. Despite her father's insistence, she did not get a good night's sleep. She was unable to get Durand's aria out of her head—the forest outside her window seemed to be singing it to her all night long.

The copper-haired boy next to her is one of the few teenagers here who isn't clutching an instrument case. Like her, he carries only a black leather portfolio.

"Am I wrong?" the boy asks. "Your name tag says 'Sing.' Or is that just what you do?"

Sing raises an eyebrow. He is probably making fun of her. "Well, wouldn't your name tag say 'Sing,' too, then?"

She flips open her portfolio and studies the introduction to her placement song. *Two measures of four, then one of three, come in on the eighth-note pickup.* She can't mess up the beginning. This audition will establish her place in the soprano hierarchy—and there is room at the top for only one.

"It does."

Sing looks up. "What?"

"Just kidding." The boy points to his name tag: "Ryan," blue to indicate he's a senior. Even without the color code, Sing can tell who the seniors are. Unlike the first-years—panicky, confused—or the second-years—overconfident—the seniors are relaxed. They have done this audition several times already.

Ryan grins, and Sing accidentally grins back. She forgets the eighth-note pickup, and for the slightest of moments she thinks he is good-looking.

Then she notices his eyes searching her face for a response. His good-looking-ness is *calculated.*

Her chest deflates. He must know who she is. As if her parents' shiny fame leaches out of her pores. She gives him a quick, close-lipped smile and goes back to her music. *Remember to breathe before the long phrase here.*

"You're not too friendly, are you?" he says, as though she's a wild animal he's thinking of capturing and putting in a box.

Sing mutters, "I'm friendly with my friends." *Friends?* Could he tell that was a lie? That she doesn't have any friends? She stares at her music but doesn't really see the notes. And she can tell Ryan is still grinning.

"Well, I hope we'll be friends," he says. "I'll take friendly over snippy any day."

She looks up.

Snippy?

She opens her mouth but doesn't say anything. He laughs as though he knows what she's thinking—which can't be true, because even she doesn't know what she's thinking—and says, "Hey, we'll get a coffee later. In the village."

He's so cocky. Sing looks at him, trying to come up with a snippy response. His mischievous gaze is still on her, eyes steady and challenging, smile relaxed . . . shiny hair . . . white teeth . . . He really *is* good-looking. Sing feels herself turn pink and lifts her portfolio to study it more closely, hiding her face.

"I just flew in this morning," Ryan says, as if they are having a conversation. "Haven't even unpacked—had to throw on this stylish uniform and come straight over for placements. What song are you doing?"

From behind her portfolio, Sing says, "I'm not doing a song. I'm doing a twelve-tone vocalise by Janice Bailey."

Did that sound snippy?

"I love Janice Bailey!" Ryan says. "That crazy stuff from the seventies? Rustling paper and shattering glass?"

Sing lowers her portfolio. "I like her new stuff better. More lyrical, more tonal."

"Yeah, I know what you mean." Ryan nods. "She's got less to prove now that she's famous. Maybe she's just enjoying herself."

Sing likes boys who can talk about music.

She scans the corridor, wondering if anyone else is deep in conversation about composers whose only fans are other musicians. But the hallway is subdued. A line of matching slate-blue wool skirts and sweater vests. Knees. Gray trousers and blue neckties. Heads bent over portfolios, mouths sucking on reeds, bows quietly being adjusted or rosined. The atmosphere is thick with musicians trying not to make any music.

"Well, Miss Twelve-Tone Vocalise"—Ryan leans back against the wall—"you must be disappointed we're doing boring old *Angelique* this semester."

Sing's throat freezes. *Angelique?*

Ryan frowns. "You okay?"

"Yes, I—I just didn't . . . It's my favorite opera."

"Lucky you!" he says. "Maybe you'll get a big part!"

An image Sing has tried so long to repress surfaces again—

herself, imagined in the title role. Angelique. The role she has wanted to sing since she was five.

"I'd want to be Prince Elbert." Ryan hums a bit of a melody.

Sing's chest tightens. Prince Elbert, the one who marries Angelique at the end of Act III? The one with whom Angelique sings a passionate love duet?

Ryan strikes a princely pose and begins to sing. *"Tout ce que je vois, tout ce que je veux . . ."*

"Sure." Sing relaxes. She doesn't know which is more awful—his singing or his French. There is no way he will be cast as Prince Elbert.

But he continues. *"Tout est à moi sauf vous!"* Sour, silent faces look at him from all along the resonant corridor. He doesn't seem to mind, however, and pompously puffs out his chest, singing even more loudly. *"Sauf vous! Sauf voooooous!"*

Sing laughs. She can't help it. Everything is so serious here; music is serious. If the conservatory had a motto, that would be it: Be serious. But Ryan doesn't seem to care. He has risen now and is humming the horn part as he marches in place. The scowls along the corridor turn to rodentlike looks of apprehension.

Sing watches Ryan as he sits again, stretching out his legs and putting his arms behind his head. He smells very faintly of cologne. Well, he is definitely *different*. Her pink starts to return. He catches her looking at him and smiles slyly, as though they have been playing a game and he has won.

And maybe he has.

"Well, maybe I'm not cut out for operatic leads," he says. "Don't worry, Sing Twelve-Tone Angelique. I'm sure there are plenty of handsome young men around here who will fight for the honor of singing opposite you. I'll have to stick to being an ass."

Sing laughs again. "I'm sure you have *some* other talents."

"Well," he says, leaning in so that his cologne drifts over her, "I could stand vigilant at your door and protect you from ghosts."

"Are there ghosts at DC?"

Ryan's eyes widen. "Every respectable campus has ghosts. We've got Apprentice Daysmoor, for one. I mean, he's technically still alive, but no one can haunt like that guy."

Sing doesn't want Ryan to move away. "What's he like?"

Ryan lowers his voice. "He's this creepy apprentice who lives in the old tower that sticks out of Archer."

Sing scrunches her eyebrows, intrigued. "Creepy? How? Underground lair? Secret musical genius? Seducer of maidens?"

"Wow, that's where you go first off? Really?" Ryan grins. "That's kind of awesome, actually."

"Thanks," Sing says. "So what's Daysmoor's instrument, then?"

Ryan shrugs. "Piano, I guess, but he's terrible. You know what people call him? 'Plays-poor.' Yeah, it's not great, but it kind of works."

"He's terrible? Really?"

"Oh, yeah!" Ryan raises his eyebrows. "Only ever gave one performance and was booed off the stage. Everybody knows that. But the creepiest part . . . well, you know what they say?"

Sing shakes her head. She feels the chill of the high stone hallway.

Ryan whispers, "They say he's a vampire who was living here when they converted the old church, and he's never left."

They look at each other for a long moment before they both laugh at the absurdity of it.

A jowly apprentice sticks his head out from behind the president's heavy door. "Anita?"

A frizzy-haired girl shuffles over with her nose down, clutching her pristine flute case and portfolio to her chest. Her shiny shoes click and echo in the massive stone hall.

Ryan stands up. "Do they need me yet?"

"No." The apprentice frowns and narrows his small eyes. "Wait your turn."

"I'm Ryan Larkin." Ryan points to his name tag again. Sing thinks he must be very proud of it. But she can't help watching in confusion as the apprentice's expression changes from one of annoyance to one of friendly understanding.

Friendly understanding? An *apprentice*?

"Oh. Right," the apprentice says. "Sorry, man. In there."

Ryan shoots Sing a last smug grin and follows the flute girl into the president's office.

Sorry, man? Sing frowns. Even though she has been on campus only one day, she has become used to being scowled at by apprentices. She definitely hasn't seen one being pleasant to somebody.

Who *is* Ryan?

Five

GEORGE WAS NOT A SUPERSTITIOUS young man, but something about the quad late at night gave him the willies. The lanterns along the road had been snuffed out, and the moon silhouetted the untidy forest behind St. Augustine's. Strange that only an hour before, the concert hall had been stuffed to the gills with musicians and audience members, all there to hear the famous Gloria Stewart.

Now they were gone, the hall quiet and dark. Not that he was *afraid,* he told himself, clutching his notebook to his chest. Back at the Daysmoor School for Boys, he had frequently accompanied his friends on their late-night mischief. And even as a student here at the conservatory, he had always been up for a midnight run to Dunhammond to see what the local boys were up to.

Maybe this strange feeling was the shiny new sense of responsibility that accompanied his shiny new title: Assistant Professor. He no longer felt a watchful presence looming over him; that was now *his* role. Protector, leader, guide.

St. Augustine's heavy door had a habit of sticking, as if it were still a massive living tree outgrowing its stone doorjambs. In the dim light, George heaved it closed. But above the familiar scrape-groan, he thought he heard another type of groan—a human one.

Ears warming even in the chilly air, he froze, his hand still on the black iron ring. Silence.

He told himself to call out, *Hello?* To perform his duty as steward of this venerable school and its people. After all, it could have been the voice of an elderly concertgoer who had stumbled into a ditch. Or a drunken student who had fallen into the bushes. Or . . . or . . . or some other normal thing.

But he did not call out. He listened.

The rustling of trees, the odd snap or scrape from the forest.

The moon illuminated the walkway that ran the length of the building and ended abruptly at the grassy quadrangle, though George knew it in darkness just as well.

Must have been just another creak from the old door.

He moved along the path, trying to focus on the notes he had taken that evening. The Maestro's four-four pattern had seemed to place the downbeat high in the arc—perhaps it allowed for greater intricacy of—

There it was again.

A low, rasping groan coming from the roof. Perhaps not human after all. George stopped and peered up at the imposing old hall, something he normally avoided doing when he was alone at night because of all the gargoyles looking back at him.

Had it been one of *them*?

It had certainly sounded like a stone throat, harsh and deep and grating. But the gargoyles were still, protecting the hall as they had always done.

As *he* should be doing.

George swallowed and called out, "Hello?" His voice was absorbed by the wall and the grass.

He took a step back to better examine the roof. Something white gleamed at the apex at the far end.

What was it?

He squinted hard, then recoiled.

It was a human arm.

It was possibly just thrust over the pitch of the roof, still attached to a person on the other side. Or possibly not.

George knew the conservatory was haunted by both ghosts and stories. The sight of the arm brought some of the grislier rumors to the surface of his consciousness. No one had been killed in the forest for a long time, but legends take longer to die than people. It was said Durand himself had seen the Cat. And a *cat*—well, George didn't know about mythology or anything like that, but even a *regular* cat as big as this one supposedly had been would have no trouble helping itself to whatever bits of people it happened to find appetizing.

As he moved closer, long, slender fingers came into focus, and something else—the arm was entwined with what looked like black ivy. It started at the wrist and curled around nearly all the way up to the shoulder. When George reached the end of the building and could see clearly, he realized it wasn't real ivy at all, but a tattoo.

George peered up at the arm. There was something *wrong* about it. It didn't *look* strange, exactly, except for the tattoo. In fact, it was quite beautiful, as far as arms went, especially the graceful fingers— fingers any pianist would have killed for. But he couldn't quite make himself head back into the hall and climb the rickety stairs to the trapdoor to investigate further; neither could he break away from the vision of it to go alert the president or the police.

So, for a time, George just stared at the arm.

Then one of the pale fingers began to move.

Six

THE AUDITION IS FORMAL. Sing walks slowly to the center of the president's office and stands, shoulders back and feet apart, on a red section of the faded, multicolored carpet. The jowly apprentice who showed her in shuts the door behind him as he leaves.

The president, a tall black man whose neat hair is streaked with gray, is at his desk writing something. Next to him sits the head of the Voice Department, Professor Needleman, a fleshy woman with ruddy cheeks and light hair pulled into a severe bun. Sing hasn't seen them since she auditioned for the conservatory last spring. They were skeptical then—she could see it in their faces even though they tried to hide it. But her father knew she was ready, in a way she hadn't been the year before, and she had proven herself. *Now I just need to do it again,* she thinks.

Maestro Keppler sits next to Professor Needleman, his long hair disgustingly oiled, his bushy gray eyebrows drawn together. He appears unfriendly, or possibly in some kind of gastrointestinal distress, and the lines on his face are so deep and set, Sing wonders if he is even capable of any other expression. This is the man who taught her father conducting during his time at DC? Sing tries to do some quick math in her head—her father is sixty-six, isn't he?

How old must the Maestro be, then? Looking at him, she would swear he is the younger man.

A few other faculty members dot the spacious room, each with a clipboard. All eyes are on Sing. All eyes, she notices, except for two—those belonging to an apprentice seated, or rather sprawled, next to the Maestro.

His head lolls to one side, his eyes are closed, and his jaw hangs limply off his face as though it hasn't been attached correctly. His coal-black hair looks like it hasn't been combed, cut, or washed in some time. Sing wonders briefly if he is dead.

"Miss da Navelli, it's delightful to see you again," the president says. As Sing was expecting, many of the gazes on her suddenly sharpen at the mention of her last name. Even the dead apprentice comes around and peers at her with dull eyes as black as his hair. There is an ugliness about him—not in his features, but in his lackluster gaze. She feels his eyes on her too strongly and wishes he would close them again.

"It's nice to see you, too, President Martin," she says, straightening her spine into an almost military position and raising her chin.

The president goes on, "Did you enjoy your summer? Your father tells me you had quite an education."

Sure, Sing thinks. *Each week a different city and a different opera, with him pointing out everything the sopranos were doing better than me.*

But she says, "Yes, sir. Kapteina's *Butterfly* was particularly inspiring, even though she told us she was recovering from a cold." She can hear her mother's voice: *Never miss an opportunity to name-drop—tactfully, of course, and without effort.* It can't hurt for President Martin to have the impression she is on speaking terms with Ingrid Kapteina, even if it's really her father who knows the famous singer.

"Wonderful. Yes, I heard it was excellent. Now, what are you going to sing for us?"

She can tell he is trying to be friendly, but it is always the same with her principals and conductors and teachers. They know her father is in the background.

"Um, a vocalise—Number Seventeen by Janice Bailey." She opens her portfolio.

"'Um, a vocalise'?" It is the Maestro who speaks now, and his voice is harsh. He twines his fingers together stiffly. "Are you aware that the *placement* auditions are held so that we can *place* you in appropriate groups and roles?"

"Yes, Maestro." Sing feels her face reddening. Is she in trouble?

"And that this is our only chance to consider you for the opera?"

"Yes, Maestro."

The Maestro sighs. "May I ask, then, why you have selected 'um, a vocalise'? Did it occur to you that we might prefer something with *words*? Perhaps *French* words, as we're doing *Angelique*?"

Sing's hands start to shake. She doesn't say, *I can't sing Angelique for real. Not yet.* Admitting that would be sure to squash any chance she has of getting the lead. No, she has to stick with what is safe, for now, and worry about the role of her dreams when she has secured it. There's no need for anyone here to know her secret—that despite her blood and her training, there is still something . . . wrong . . . with her voice.

Instead, she summons her courage and says, "I've studied French at home, sir, and German, and I'm fluent in Italian."

"I can read your form, thank you," the Maestro says.

President Martin smiles. "I'm sure her French is excellent."

The Maestro raises his voice just a little and looks at the president. "You know, my mother was a nurse. Would you come to me if you broke your arm? I mean, what are we trying to do here? I'm sorry the public misses Barbara da Navelli, but it's not our job to bring her back!"

The words take Sing by surprise, and she is silent. Professor Needleman looks uncomfortable. Some of the faculty fidget or clear their throats, glad to be outside the Maestro's notice. Only President

Martin shoots Sing a reassuring glance, a little smirk that says, *Oh, well. He will insist on being that way, won't he?*

No one says, *That's her mother you're talking about.* No one says that.

She unintentionally looks again to the black-haired apprentice, whose hard face is unreadable, his eyes fixed on hers in a dark, burning gaze. For the briefest moment, she is frozen. But then he closes his eyes again, graciously severing the connection.

"Never mind, George, never mind," the president says, patting the desk. "We didn't set any requirements. Goodness, we only officially named the opera this morning; we can't expect all the voice kids to have French arias. She can sing whatever she wants."

"Yes, of course she can, can't she?" The Maestro crosses his arms. "Well, go ahead."

Sing inhales deeply, blinking back the hotness that is beginning behind her eyes, and turns to hand her music to the accompanist. But she stops when she sees a smiling face looking up at her from behind the president's mahogany baby grand piano.

"Don't sweat it," whispers Ryan, taking the music. Sing is too surprised to do anything but give him the nod to begin.

Two measures of four, then one of three . . . She breathes in through her nose and feels her ribs expand, though they are still tight. She wants to roll her shoulders and loosen them but can't seem to find the muscles that are supposed to do it. *Do not fear them! They are lucky to hear you sing!* her father says in her head. *They will soon be lining the streets to hear you sing!*

The first note is flat, but she corrects. She has chosen *Ah,* but regrets it now—*Oo* would have been better. Maybe she will change vowels after the first few phrases. *Breathe.* She shouldn't have had to breathe there. Get a bigger breath next time.

The black-haired apprentice watches her through slitted eyes. She doesn't know why, but she feels him judging her. Was that pointed inhalation a comment on her last high F, not spinning as smoothly as it should?

She forces herself to look away. What does she care what an *apprentice* thinks, anyway?

Most of the faculty look as if they've seen too many auditions today. The president appears to be doing paperwork, and the Maestro is frowning, eyes boring into her. Professor Needleman wears an artificial smile, but at least she's trying.

Smile. Sing has forgotten to smile. Will it look strange if she starts now, halfway through? She does anyway, and her sound brightens. Angelique would have a bright, cheerful sound. She must show them she can do it. *Here's the money note,* as her father likes to say. She sucks in a big breath and dives into the phrase; the note is *good*—very good—but she has wasted too much air on the rising melody and the climax is rushed because she's not sure she can make it through. Then she backs off, worried that if she pushes too hard, the sound will become wobbly or, worse, break altogether. She can't move her jaw. She tries to decrescendo on the last note, but the bottom just drops out and she's left with a weak little whine.

It's an audition, so there is no applause, just silence as the professors make some notes. Sing doesn't look back at Ryan. The president raises his eyes briefly and says, "Thank you," in a final sort of way.

Sing leaves. She doesn't notice the apprentice, eyes fully open, frowning slightly.

Seven

THE FELIX WAS BORN A BALL of light, a soft, twittering, warm thing who saw her own joy reflected in the eyes of her mother. They tumbled and skidded about the sky, and for the briefest of times, all was perfect.

She wasn't to know that her happiness set the universe listing, and something had to be done to put it right again.

So came her brother, mangy and slick, with a film of blood over his eyes. Lashing and snapping, he ripped his way into the universe, took his first fortifying gasp, and set upon their mother like a demon.

The Felix, older and stronger, lashed back as her mother's eyes grew dull and empty. The cubs fought and tore and leapt, their cries audible even at the bottom of the oceans.

Soon the Felix was alone, and might have been happy again even in mourning, with the memories of her mother and the beauty of the stars. But in taking the life of her nameless brother, she had broken her own heart. She was now darkness.

That day, the Felix came to earth, and she has been wandering ever since. Little remains of her now except hunger and ferocity.

Eight

ANGELIQUE WAS THE FIRST OPERA SING ever saw. She remembers it perfectly—how she could have sworn the tall baritone was singing delicately into her ear instead of strutting around on a stage far below. How the chorus was one voice and many voices at the same time, the sound a school of glittering fish who flashed and darted and drifted perfectly together. And how it felt to see her—*her*—take those first graceful steps onto the set.

She doesn't know the soprano's name, and it doesn't matter. She *was* Angelique, her ruffly white dress billowing, golden hair cascading down her back in bouncy ringlets. Sing can still hear her sweet, light voice fluttering over the high notes and gently alighting on the low.

It was one thing to sit in front of the record player and imagine, quite another to experience the tingle from chest to temples as the great singer filled the room with harmonics. Magic.

Afterward, she dug out her father's records and learned Angelique's most famous aria, approximating the sounds of the mysterious foreign words. In response to her debut performance at the dinner table, her parents began to fight—her father saying, *I said all along she was a singer,* and her mother saying, *We discussed this—it's got to be the piano because she has no ear.* Five-year-old Sing put her hands to her head in confusion and found both ears where they belonged.

The piano turned out not to be Sing's instrument after all; her fingers were short and clumsy, and her bad posture—which her mother pointed out with sharp little prods to her lower back—made her wrists and shoulders hurt. When her parents were gone, the nannies couldn't make her practice. Instead, they let her listen to records. The operas were her favorites.

She never sang *Angelique* for her parents again. But she knows the words now. The real words, and the notes and the rhythms, the characters and the story, the emotions and the beauty. She knows them all by heart.

Movement in her peripheral vision brings her back to the present. Her first full day at Dunhammond Conservatory. Her first moments alone on the sunny quad. Is someone already intruding?

She looks back. Yep, that short girl is definitely coming over.

Great, she made eye contact. Now the girl is waving and hurrying across the grass toward the iron bench on which Sing is sitting. Sing checks her watch—forty-five minutes until the official DC Welcome Gathering.

She just wanted a moment alone with her favorite composer. Apparently that was too much to ask. She looks up at the bronze statue, gleaming in the slanted sunlight. Two sizable crows, each perched on a square shoulder, lend an air of menace to the imposing figure. But the subject himself seems benign enough, his left arm cradling a type of small, impractical harp he probably never set eyes on in life, his right hand holding a quill pen. His expression is wistful, eyes heavenward, one foot on an overturned milk pail. FRANÇOIS DURAND, 1811–1877, the plaque reads. FOUNDER, COMPOSER, TEACHER. SURVIVOR OF THE MASSACRE OF DUNHAMMOND, 1862.

This really is his place, Sing thinks. The trees beyond the campus fence beckon her with thousands of leafy hands. *Durand was not afraid of this forest. Why should I be?*

The short girl reaches the bench, a little winded. Her lungs must be no bigger than two large butterfly wings hung side by side. Sing folds her arms and pretends to study the statue's stone base.

"Hi!" The girl sits. "Mind if I interview you?"

Sing raises her eyebrows. "I'm sorry?"

The girl places a black clarinet case on the grass. "Jenny Eisley," she says, rummaging through her backpack. "I've got a notebook in here somewhere. You're Sing da Navelli, right?"

"Yeah. You're pretty direct." Sing isn't sure why she's not walking swiftly away from Jenny Eisley right now. After her mother died, she became very good at ignoring people who wanted something from her.

"I saw you get called for placements," Jenny says. "Was keeping an eye out. I knew you were going to be here—people were like *Ohmygod, famous offspring coming!* Although, frankly, I was kind of hoping you'd be a guy. And hot."

"Sorry to disappoint on both counts," Sing says. "Genetics, I guess."

Jenny laughs. "Oh, I don't know. You're pretty. Like one of those big-eyed, small-nosed cartoons."

"Uh, thanks?"

"Anyway, I couldn't really tell much by your name," Jenny says. "It's kind of a weird name for an Italian kid, to be quite honest. No offense."

"Half Italian." Sing blinks. There is something likable about Jenny, the way she scrunches her nose and moves a little too quickly. The way she thinks "no offense" erases anything that came before it.

Jenny flips open her notebook. "So can I write an article about you?"

"Wait, an article? For what?"

"*The Trumpeter*! DC's student newspaper. I really want to get on

their writing staff. This is my audition. I figured, hey! We've got a
famous person in our class! I should totally talk to him!"

"Her," Sing says.

"I know that *now*. So how about it? Right here, right now? Bask-
ing at the foot of our creator?"

"Look, I'm really not supposed to do interviews without—"

"Oh, give me a *break*." Jenny pops her pen cap.

Sing doesn't know why, but she says, "Okay, I guess."

The questions are innocuous. *Favorite color? Sports team? Blog?
Composer?*

". . . Durand."

Jenny looks up. "Well, that's lucky! Are you totally excited that
we're doing *Angelique*?"

Why is this question so difficult? "Um, sure," Sing croaks.

There is a hesitation in the pen scratching. Another crow alights
on the statue, settling itself on top of the composer's bronze head.
Students cross the grass, alone or in small groups, saying things Sing
can't make out over the distance and the breeze.

"You okay?" Jenny asks. "You seem a little freaked out."

"Oh," Sing says. "Well, it's just that it's my favorite opera and . . .
it kind of ramps up the pressure, you know?" As if her father's ex-
pectations aren't enough stress— Her father! "My father will never
approve of this!" she says, and finds herself surprised to have shared
this with an almost-stranger. Who is taking notes.

"Of *Angelique*?" Jenny furrows her eyebrows.

"It's—it's a long story," Sing says. Which is a lie. It's a very short
story: *My mother died during a performance of* Angelique.

Jenny just shrugs and says, "What's he going to do? Pull you out
of the conservatory?"

Sing blinks. "No," she says. "No, he'd never do that."

"Then forget it," Jenny says. "Who cares what he thinks?"

Sing can think of a lot of people who care about what her father
thinks.

But maybe she doesn't have to be one of them right now. She can feel her heart beating a little faster as the realization sinks in.

"How do you like the dorm?" Jenny asks. This feels like simple curiosity, not an interview question.

"It's nice," Sing says. "How do you like it?"

Jenny purses her lips. "Oh, it'll be fine. All the comforts of prison."

Sing laughs. "I don't think they've renovated in a while."

"At least we don't have to sleep in St. Augustine's." Jenny eyes the old church. "I mean, *gargoyles*? I didn't know we even *had* gargoyles in North America."

"They're fake gargoyles," Sing says. "Well, not *fake,* but, you know, it's not like this place is eight hundred years old. It was built during the Gothic revival, early nineteenth century, by some rich guy. That was before Durand got ahold of it. There was a stone church here before, the real St. Augustine's, which dates back pretty far, though. And some kind of tower that went with it, for protection."

Silence hangs briefly before Jenny says, "Are you, like, an encyclopedia?"

Sing clears her throat. She forgets not everyone has been so thoroughly trained to remember dates and contexts and backstories. "Sorry," she says, "what I meant to say was, 'Gargoyles? Aren't those *old*? Can we please talk about how great that guy's butt looks in those polyester uniform pants instead?'"

Jenny raises her eyebrows, then bursts out laughing. Sing looks to the square dormitory. "Nothing too sinister about Hud, I imagine."

"Nope." Jenny shakes her head as though she is a bit disappointed. "Although that pastel hall carpeting from the eighties is a bit terrifying."

A voice detaches itself from the intermittent rustle of conversation on the edges of the quad. "Hey! Sing!"

Sing and Jenny look up. Two girls and a guy are approaching. The girl in front—long hair, gold hoop earrings—is waving. Sing doesn't recognize her but waves back. As they approach, Sing is startled to see that the guy is Ryan Larkin.

"What's up?" The hoop earring girl arrives at the benches but doesn't sit down. "Hey, guys, look who it is!"

The other girl eyes Sing, while Ryan flashes a brilliant smile that makes Sing tingle. They do not look at Jenny.

"We meet again, Miss da Navelli," Ryan says. "Small campus."

"You remember me, right?" the girl says. "Or was I not important enough to notice?"

Now Sing feels her smile freezing. "I'm sorry," she says, searching her memory.

The girl turns to her friends, theatrically placing a hand to her heart. "I'm sure it's hard to remember the names of *all* the people you screw over."

The breeze is cold on Sing's shoulders. Out of the corner of her eye, she sees Jenny raise pencil to paper, then put it down again without writing.

"Well, Sing," Ryan says, grinning, "it seems you've ruffled some plumage already."

The girl looks at Ryan, then back to Sing. *"Osiris and Seth,"* she says. "As in, the *only* time I haven't made the opera in the *five years* I've done Stone Hill. Because guess what?" The girl crosses her arms. "There was someone new there this year who took my spot. Someone with famous parents."

Now Sing remembers the voice. Hayley somebody. Straight tone, shrill. Convinced that being able to squeak the highest would make up for the problems with the rest of her range. In fact, the only time they've ever spoken before now was the first day at Stone Hill. Hayley worked a brag about her high D into the conversation in under thirty seconds.

Not competition, Barbara da Navelli would say. *Don't worry about her.*

Sing resents the memory of her mother for putting the thought into her head, even if it's true. She swallows. "Well, I'll see you around," she says to Hayley, who blinks, apparently having expected some kind of retaliation. Denied a scene, she and the other girl swagger back across the grass.

"Well played, Miss da Navelli," Ryan says. "Don't let these girls get to you." Then he leans in close and whispers, "You're special."

His words warming her ear, Sing watches Ryan head back across the quad.

"Sheesh," Jenny says. "That girl Hayley used to be tolerable. My sister hung out with her sometimes. And what's-his-name, Ryan. Kinda scummy."

Sing shrugs. "He seemed okay." She can still smell his cologne.

"Hmph," Jenny says. "You don't know boys very well, do you?"

Sing knows boys very well, just not so much in real life. Mostly from opera libretti. Her father doesn't approve of dating when there is so much singing to do. But she pictures Ryan's green eyes and smiles—maybe now that she's here, it doesn't matter what her father would think of *him,* either.

"Seriously," Jenny says, "didn't she bother you?"

Sing shrugs. "I can ignore it." *I've learned to ignore it.*

"Good. Because you haven't even *met* Lori Pinkerton yet." Before Sing can respond, Jenny goes on, "So, how do you like DC so far? You know, other than random girls harassing you about operas."

Sing wants to say, *It's hard enough to start at a new school, but when you're a da Navelli and have to bring your* name *along—I'll be lucky to find anyone who isn't looking to either cut me down or get an autograph. Or both.*

What she says is, "I like it fine."

Nine

GEORGE UNLOCKED THE DOOR and began to ascend.

No one had questioned him, not really. *A new student? Fine, fine. Fill out the paperwork.* George had been stunned. He had expected, *Where did he go to school?* or, *Who did he study with?*

Or at least, *What instrument does he play?*

As he climbed the dusty stairs, George felt the slightest tickle of doubt about his own sanity. Had he invented this young man? But when he reached the room—chilly, sparsely furnished—and saw the breakfast tray he'd brought that morning sitting on the table, he knew it was all real. The bacon and eggs hadn't been touched, but the toast was gone. And so were the clothes.

"Hello?" He crossed to the spiral staircase on the other side of the room. "I'm coming up, all right?"

His shoes clanged on the metal stairs. The small bedroom on the next floor was empty except for the iron bed and an old dresser that had belonged to a former president. George squinted into the dimness above him. "Hello?" he called to the uppermost room, one of its dark windows just visible beyond the top of the staircase.

A gust of fresh air from above was the only response.

The echoey top floor was cold and shadowed, its tall windows hung with dusty curtains. George frowned. The young man wasn't there.

As George crossed the floor to shut the glass doors letting in the breeze, he heard a voice from the balcony.

And there he was. Perched on the ledge, dressed in a nightshirt, the young man had buried his face in his hands, his body shaking with—George watched for the briefest of moments, processing the scene—with sobs.

"Come down from there!" George rushed across the stone balcony, putting an arm around the broad, bony shoulders. "You'll fall off!"

The young man allowed himself to be pulled gently from the ledge before sinking to the cold floor and curling up against the wall.

"What are you doing?" George said. "Why—why—why are you wearing a nightshirt in the middle of the afternoon?" It was a stupid question, but it was the one that escaped his mouth first.

The young man looked down at his attire. "I liked this best. This is wrong?"

George sat next to him. "No. No, it's not *wrong,* it's just . . . Who *are* you?"

The young man was silent for a long moment. Finally, he said, "I am no one."

"You said that earlier. I find it hard to believe."

"No. Before I said I had no name. Now—now I am no one."

It seemed increasingly possible this young man was insane. George put a hand on his shoulder, desperate to make sense of him. "I don't know what you mean. I'm here to help you. It doesn't matter where you came from. I've arranged for you to stay here, if you want to. I've even given you a name. I—"

"If you want to help me," the young man whispered, "help me die . . . I don't know how humans die."

George swallowed. "Here. If you won't come in, at least wrap up." He pulled off his wide woolen scarf and tucked it around the shivering body. "Humans can die of hypothermia, but I'm not going to let it happen right now."

"I don't care," the young man said. "I don't want to live."

"Whatever happened, I will help you." George wasn't really certain why he was making these promises to a stranger. Or why he meant them. For all he knew, he could be dealing with an escaped lunatic. Or, at the very least, a runaway who should be returned to his parents or the government or whoever it was who wanted him.

But he had a strange feeling—a *certainty*—that the person huddled before him now wasn't any of these things. The question was what exactly he *was*.

"Thank you for your kindness," the young man said, his voice hoarse. "But you can't help me. I had only one dream, and it is impossible. So I would rather die."

"Look, you have time for lots more dreams." George smiled. "How old are you?"

"This is my second autumn."

"Your second autumn in Dunhammond?" Silence. George cleared his throat. "Well, you look nineteen or twenty to me. Is that about right?" When there was no response, George rambled on. "I'm twenty-five myself. My dream is to be a famous conductor, but I'm just starting out as an assistant professor here at the conservatory. What is your dream?"

The young man tilted his head back against the wall and closed his eyes. He inhaled deeply. *"Music."*

George put a hand on his shoulder. "Music? But this is one of the best schools in the country! Where have you studied?"

"Studied? I was always surrounded by it. Always. Everywhere. But I could never produce it; it just wasn't my nature. And that was torture enough, but when I came here . . . when I *heard* . . ."

"It's all right," George said. "You're in the right place now. I can help you learn."

"Listen!" the young man snapped, scaring a little bird away

from the balcony. Tears slid down his face again. "Listen. *Listen to my voice.*"

Harsh, George thought. *Savage.* "Oh," he said, realizing. "You—you wanted to be a singer."

The young man's eyes were slits now, looking skyward. "Humans sing so beautifully."

Again ignoring the word *humans,* George said, "Well, yes, some people do. Not everyone, though. Not me, for instance." He laughed.

"Yes. Listen to you." The young man turned his head to George, whose breath caught at the intense gaze. "Your voice is beautiful. Mine—" He raised his hands to his throat. "Mine is ugly. My voice is so ugly, it was the only part of me she couldn't change."

The young man closed his eyes again, and George was suddenly aware of his own ordinariness. Round face, biggish nose, stubby fingers. He stared at the sad, angular face and the long, graceful hands that had captivated him the night before. There was something otherworldly about them—about *him.* Where had he come from? Who was *she,* who had changed him? But George kept his conversation practical; he didn't want this strange spirit to evaporate in the light. "Why do you have to be a singer?" he asked. "If it's music you love, *music,* then why not play another instrument?"

A frown. "I don't understand."

George rose. "Play an instrument. With those hands, I'm sure you'd be a fine pianist. Come here." He opened the glass door to the echoey room. "Come on, let me show you." The young man looked skeptical but held George's eyes. "Look, it's okay. I want to show you the piano. It's okay. Nathan."

"Nathan?" A change came over the young man's face now. He seemed as though he might smile. "Is—is that my name?"

George looked down. "Well, only if you want it. It was my brother's name." He twisted his fingers together. "I had to put something on the paperwork. We can change it if you want to."

"No. No." He spoke softly now, and George wondered if even

this crackling, growling voice might be beautiful to someone. "Thank you," Nathan said, and rose hesitantly. He was tall and moved with a slight, strange awkwardness.

Inside, Nathan's steps grew more uncertain. He kept looking up at the dark ceiling. George pulled up the shades on several of the long windows, and the floating dust motes sparkled and swirled like spirits.

"Here." He gestured as he crossed the room to where a drab sheet covered something large. "Go ahead," he said. "Pull it off."

Tentatively, Nathan reached for the sheet and slid it off the smooth wood. George watched his face, which seemed to brighten at the sight of the baby grand piano. It was just a spare—more trouble to move than let be—but it was a good piano, ornate enough to show its age and dignity, but warm and weathered enough to show its worth as a working instrument.

"There was a piano last night," Nathan said. "At the concert."

"Yes. Gloria Stewart is one of the finest pianists in the world."

Nathan was transfixed by the instrument. He made no move to touch it, but it undeniably held his full attention. George pushed open the cover, revealing the dulled keys. "Try it out," he said. "Make some noise."

Now Nathan looked at George, his dark eyes wide. "*I* could make music with a piano?"

George pulled out the rickety bench.

Nathan carefully sat down. His first note blossomed into the empty room. Then another, and another, and three together, and four. "They are like flowers," he said. "So many of them."

"They are," George said. "And I will teach you how to play."

Nathan turned to him. "I will devote my life to the piano, if you think I can learn."

George smiled. "I think you will be an excellent musician. Especially after we get you some shoes, and you start playing with your hands."

Ten

THE YEAR SHE DIED, in addition to concert appearances and recording sessions, Barbara da Navelli was scheduled to sing three leading roles: Lucia in *Lucia di Lammermoor,* Donna Anna in *Don Giovanni,* and Angelique in *Angelique.* The last was a role written for a lighter voice, a sweeter sound, different from any other she had performed. A role beloved by opera fans. Had it been sheer vanity that compelled her to accept the engagement? Or had she just enjoyed the controversy?

Sing doesn't remember the events immediately following her mother's death in detail—lots of rushing, muttering, lights, hands—but she does remember the nagging, shameful question that pounded her mind: *Why* Angelique?

She was two people that night. She was Barbara da Navelli's daughter, swept away by the current of journalists, doctors, and acquaintances, waiting to be told the worst but already knowing it, cursing her mother for tainting the perfect world of *Angelique* with her last, greatest scandal. But Sing was also an observer, horrified at her own selfishness and by the question *Why* Angelique? *Why did she have to ruin* my *opera?*

Sing sits on a cold stone step of DC's Woolly Theater, her back against a white column. The Woolly is the newest addition to the conservatory, unfinished last time she visited. Now, its gleaming dome dazzles visitors as they arrive.

What shall we call it, carina, *our new theater?* Her father didn't need to ask. He knew the answer even before he wrote the last check to his alma mater under the pretense of the school's one hundred fiftieth birthday.

Sing isn't sure she will prefer this new Woolly Theater to the one at home. At least in the original, a rough little wooden frame and two frayed curtains in her bedroom, she was always the star.

She studies the campus. A few drab, square buildings—the dormitory, the classrooms—lend an air of mundane academia, interspersed with a mishmash of more beautiful structures that illustrate DC's long history. The Woolly's gentle Italian arches and dainty columns evoke aesthetics of centuries past; Hector Hall, the faculty housing, juts a pitched, Victorian silhouette; and St. Augustine's seems to cast its forbidding Gothic shadow over all.

Voices in the evening air tell her the Welcome Gathering, which all students are required to attend, is still going on in the Woolly's spacious lobby. She would rather watch the seniors play Frisbee on the lawn. She's technically at the Woolly—she's on the steps. What does it matter if she goes inside or not?

The slick poster in the glass case next to the door must have just been put up: DUNHAMMOND CONSERVATORY AUTUMN FESTIVAL, NOVEMBER 16–18. CELEBRATING 150 YEARS! It seems as if every group, from a senior string quartet to the symphonic band, has a performance listed that weekend, with *Angelique* looming at the top of the poster and the Gloria Stewart International Piano Competition splashed across the bottom as the grand finale.

It's her first full day at DC; she's gone from orientation to auditions to the Welcome Gathering, and already this poster is shoving the Autumn Festival in her face. Ten weeks until she, her father, and *Angelique* are reunited. Will she be singing the last role her mother ever sang? Or will she be watching from the wings? Which would be worse?

She fights the urge to pull her phone from her pocket to see if Zhin has texted. The handbook was clear: No cell phones. No Wi-Fi. There is no signal here.

"Farfallina, bella e bianca; vola, vola, mai si stanca . . ."

She gets through three verses before she notices herself singing. *It's not a nervous habit,* she tells herself. *I have nothing to be nervous about.*

"Miss da Navelli." The voice is stern and scratchy. Sing looks up into a serious, angular face and the blackest eyes she has ever seen. The apprentice from her audition. As before, his gaze paralyzes her for a moment. She blinks.

"Yes? Sir?" How is she supposed to address apprentices? It feels strange to call someone only slightly older than herself "sir."

"Get up," he says. "This isn't your dorm room."

She scrambles to her feet, surprised by his sharpness, and pats the dust out of her skirt. "I—um—"

"First-years are required to attend the Welcome Gathering."

Sing raises her eyebrows. "I *am,* sir."

"Stop calling me 'sir.' You can go to the Welcome Gathering, or I can write you up."

Does he think she really needs to go to another damn party? Sing crosses her arms. "I am *twenty feet* from—"

"Sprawling out here on the steps like you own the place is not the same as attending," he says.

She sets her jaw. He's not a professor. What right does he have to order her around? "No, you're right," she says. "I don't own this theater." She looks the young man squarely in his arrogant eyes. "That's my father you're thinking of. And I didn't get your name, Apprentice . . . ?"

He steps closer, smelling faintly of pine. "Daysmoor."

Plays-poor. The disgraced vampire. He seems to have the temperament for it. Booed off the stage during his only performance. "I've heard of you," she says.

If he has an opinion about this statement, he doesn't say so. He just says, "And pull your socks up," and lurches into the lobby.

Sing stands with her jaw set for a few moments, then follows.

Inside, the dark red carpeting and gold walls make a vibrant backdrop for the crowd of gray and black robes and slate-blue uniforms. Sing goes to the buffet before attempting to mingle. The idea of not mingling doesn't even cross her mind; she's well trained.

It would be better if Zhin were here, she thinks, *like she is supposed to be.*

She tries not to think about Zhin, who is absorbed in her new professional career now. They were supposed to have three years together, not one summer.

Sing surveys the room. There is no one like Zhin at the Welcome Gathering; she would stand out like a jewel. Sing stands out only when people know who she is—usually because she's among jewels.

The sunlight through the Woolly's tall windows slants with the evening. She spears a chicken cutlet and slides it onto her plate. She must stay in the moment. Barbara da Navelli was always on high diva alert at parties. Who is here? Who's talking? What is everyone wearing?

The wardrobe part is the easiest—teachers in black, apprentices in gray, students in slate blue. The faculty and apprentices converse awkwardly; students cluster in twos and threes and fours. She can tell the second-years—they're the ones who know other people. The first-years huddle with partners, probably roommates, or have been snagged by friendly faculty members. She will have to insinuate herself into a conversation soon. Already she feels the eyes in the room finding her. The only thing worse than being Sing da Navelli is being Sing da Navelli standing by herself.

"Sing!" a shrill voice calls, and she almost drops her plate. It is Jenny, striding across the lush carpet with a lanky, curly-haired girl in tow. Jenny smiles.

Is that smile for Sing?

"This is Marta." Jenny grabs a plate. "Oh, is that chicken? Marta, Sing."

"Hi," Marta says, and looks down.

Sing nods. "Hi . . . I, um, like your necklace."

Marta is wearing a big silver pendant shaped like a dragon, strange and gaudy, which her hand flies to. "Thanks." She grins. "I bought it in town." Sing notices the dark sheen of the metal—it isn't silver at all, probably steel or tin. She herself is wearing a nearly invisible gold chain with a single teardrop pearl, a birthday present from her mother—elegant, expensive, and devoid of sentimental value.

"Some Welcome Gathering this is," Jenny says, skewering cutlets. "'Welcome to DC! Come to our lame buffet or get written up!'"

Marta takes a plate, too, covering it with leaves, dark greens and purples. They make their way to a large window with a polished wooden ledge big enough for three. Uniforms and robes swirl around them; everyone is forcing conversation.

Jenny says, "Marta's a singer, too."

Sing smiles politely. "Great." Marta doesn't look like a singer. She slouches and twiddles her fingers.

"Have you been singing a long time?" Marta asks.

The question takes Sing by surprise. *Two years,* she thinks. *Ever since my father decided I would become the new Barbara da Navelli.*

But that isn't true. She thinks back to all the lovely, solitary afternoons with three closed doors between her and the nearest nanny, a pile of records on her father's desk and the greatest voices on earth pouring from the record player. She sang, then, with effortless joy. Without the wrongness that pervades her sound now. She can almost remember what it felt like.

She says, "I've been singing my whole life."

Marta's eyes widen. "Wow! I just started last year. It's fun, isn't it?"

Before Sing can answer, Jenny says, "You just started last year? And you got into DC?"

Marta looks down. "It wasn't that big a deal. I think I just got in here because of FLAP."

Sing blinks. *FLAP? The Fire Lake Apprentice Program?*

Jenny says what Sing can't. "You did FLAP? You must be awesome! Does that mean you're in line for a contract?"

"No," Sing says sharply. "I mean, it helps, but you never know who's going to get a contract offer. And it depends on the vacancies. It's actually pretty rare for someone our age to get one." She hadn't imagined Zhin would, even though she'd started playing professionally when she was six.

"Did you do FLAP, too?" Marta asks.

"No." Her father thought she would get more attention at Stone Hill. "But my . . . my father is the conductor. At Fire Lake."

There. It's out. Fire Lake, one of the most famous opera houses in the world. Sing searches Marta's face for dawning comprehension, the assumption that Sing doesn't belong here after all, she simply has connections. But Marta grins. "You're Maestro da Navelli's daughter? I got to see him this summer—just from a distance. I took a picture. Wow! I've seen your picture in the newspaper—I didn't recognize you."

The newspaper. "Yes, well, that was two years ago," Sing says, remembering. The stream of reporters, the incessant flash of cameras . . .

Marta flushes a little. "Oh, I'm sorry, I—I—"

"Don't worry about it." A few students holding plates glance in their direction. Conversations ripple through the room.

"That's cool, though, your dad being Maestro da Navelli," Marta says. "Hey, I heard there's a New Artist vacancy coming up at Fire Lake Opera. Wouldn't it be incredible to get it?"

It was how Barbara da Navelli got her start. Nineteen and married to the conductor. But she was an exception. *The* exception.

Sing shrugs. "There's no way Fire Lake would offer a New Artist spot to some teenager, even a DC student. FLAP might be competitive, but it's basically a glorified summer camp, like Stone Hill. Fire Lake New Artists are part of the company itself, and every one has gone on to sing major roles in all the great houses of the world. Most professional singers don't even get to audition. They have to be special."

"It's just a rumor," Marta says. "But I did hear it from Lori Pinkerton."

That name again. "Who's Lori Pinkerton?" Sing asks.

She's met with unbelieving stares from both Marta and Jenny. By now she's getting used to them.

"Oh," Marta says. "She's a—a girl. A senior. Who goes here. I met her at FLAP."

"Resident diva," Jenny says.

Diva: successful, glamorous, talented. Haughty.

Ruthless.

Just like Barbara da Navelli.

"Lori's nice." Marta fidgets as though she's uncomfortable gossiping.

Jenny isn't. "She's not even here yet. They don't make her do placements anymore."

Sing's stomach prickles. The evening chill seeps through the window behind her. Her competition has a name, now.

"She's not here because she still has a couple performances," Marta says. "That's why our rehearsal pianist, Ryan, was late, too. I heard them talking about it at Fire Lake."

Ryan? At FLAP? With Lori Pinkerton?

"You don't even know her," Marta says to Jenny.

"My sister went here; she's an oboe," Jenny says. "She graduated last year—she knows Lori. The darling of the conservatory opera scene."

"Ryan was at FLAP, too?" Sing tries to sound casual.

Jenny narrows her eyes, but Marta buys it. "Yeah. They were excited about doing the opera together."

Jenny frowns. "Oh, jeez, Sing, don't get all freaked out."

Sing blinks. "I'm not freaked out."

"It's okay," Marta says, misreading Sing's paleness. "Jenny's just being dramatic. Lori's nice. I'm sure we'll all get along great."

Sing tries to believe her, but it's hard to ignore her pleasant, open face and kind spirit. Marta wouldn't know a resident diva if one dumped a bottle of purified water over her head.

Eleven

THE FELIX CLENCHED HER FRONT PAWS, pearly claws digging into the bark of the tree limb high above the snow.

Darkness she knew. She remembered it. In the sky, the galaxy glittered, but when she chased the lights, the emptiness between them seemed endless. This never bothered her, when she was all Sky and no Cat. More room to romp and spiral and throw her own sparks into the void.

But this new darkness was different. Close. Trees and little creatures and air pressed in on her, cutting her mind off from the stars. Sometimes she didn't remember the sky at all.

She wasn't sure how the Cat form came into existence. Before she came to earth, there had been something catlike about her. But that vaporous felinity was different from the reality of clinging to this black branch in the freezing night.

And the reality of hunger. She might have retained more of her Sky mind if her Cat hunger hadn't grounded her so solidly in this new, tiny world. She had understood *want,* even *need,* but it was the urgency of physical hunger that first trapped her in this Cat body.

Fortunately, her new form had known what to do. Her first kill was a tom turkey, hurrying through the woods with his family. A few loping pads, a lunge, a snap of the neck, the earthy, sweet scent of feathers, and her teeth clamped down onto satisfying warmth.

The turkey had not expected her to chase him into the air.

She had hunted many times since then. No fear, no hesitation. She had come to look forward to each kill, so tactile and messy. So different from the death of her brother. His blood had splattered the heavens with glitter; his soul had exploded. The creatures of this place died quietly and easily. Even so, the Felix could never quite kill enough of them.

Now, in her old tree, she listened to crunching snow. Her ears twitched. Over the generations, the songbirds and small creatures of this forest had learned they usually weren't enough for her to bother with, and the larger creatures had become timid and scarce. What sort of animal would stagger around so noisily after sunset?

The Felix's tail swished. A dark shape moved beneath her branch, making its way laboriously through the snow. The creature wasn't looking up. She could have dropped onto its shoulders and killed it with her jaws before it knew she was there.

But she was surprised to recognize the creature as *human*. She had watched humans from the sky, she remembered.

They were sometimes . . . interesting. And she had known nothing but waiting and devouring for so long.

The Felix jumped from the branch and landed in front of the man, her massive body crushing the hard crust on the night snow. She watched him gasp, freeze, and turn from her before realizing running was pointless. Then he turned back.

That was slightly interesting. Most creatures ran.

"I have never seen anything like you," the man said, shaking. The Felix took a step toward him, and he covered his face with his forearms. "You look like a cat, but you—you are not a cat."

This was something the Felix had heard from many creatures, in their own languages. The man continued to speak. "I have come here because I am ill." She could smell the decay on him already. "Hunters say a great, terrible beast guards this forest." He lowered his arms. "But I have built a church. I believe we can bring goodness here. And I wanted to tell you before I die."

The man stood, still shaking with cold or fear. The Felix took another step closer and looked into his eyes.

She bristled in surprise. *There* was the brilliant galaxy she had missed for so long. In this man's eyes, she saw the boundless, swirling reaches of his soul. She saw his pain and disease, his hope, his uncertainty. A sleeping part of her mind stirred from where it lay curled around her memories of home. For a moment, she was mesmerized.

Then it passed.

She tore out his throat.

Twelve

BY THE LIGHT OF HER TIFFANY LAMP with the dragonfly motif, Sing reads a sappy novel about orphans. The orphans wear raggy clothes and have open sores and eat rats and never, ever have to go to the opera with their fathers.

When she has inadvertently read the same paragraph three times (the orphans tell one another everything will be okay), she puts the book down and turns over. In the safety of the warm room, she thinks about the audition. She sang the vocalise adequately. She shaped the lines and formed the vowels as best she could. Her father told her that, no matter what, she would be one of the top sopranos at the conservatory, even as a first-year.

She just has to hope that's true. She *did* get accepted after only one audition, quickly—the letter came within three weeks. And she made a splash at her old public school, winning the talent show and the Arts Advancement Scholarship. And hadn't her father been telling her she would be great like her mother? That he could tell? If only she would *learn*?

You hear the breath continue after the vowel, Sing? She does that well.

You see how she moves her hands?

You see the spine there? Even when she is reclining?

You hear the sparkles on that B flat? How it spins?

Yes, she heard. Yes, she saw. And yes, she can do all of it. Why, then, is something always missing?

She buries her face in her pillow, remembering the eyes in the president's office. Daysmoor's unsettling gaze. The Maestro's barely concealed dislike. More than dislike.

Why does he hate her? Sometimes it seems as if the more people loved her mother, the more they hate Sing. They will especially hate it if Sing performs *Angelique.*

But she starts to read over the libretto again, and the familiar, safe feeling returns. The voices and costumes are as clear in her mind as they were when she was five, sitting in that theater yet existing elsewhere. She is alive and protected.

Sing closes her eyes and hums the first aria, starting low and choppy, suddenly soaring up into a heartbreakingly beautiful phrase about how the stars watch over the fields. She shivers as she remembers hearing it for the first time.

Will she ever get to sing it? Will she be cast as Angelique? At Stone Hill, after *Osiris and Seth,* Maestra Collins told her—and her father—she thought Sing could handle a bigger role. Is that true? She knows she has come further in two years than most people do in ten. But does anyone ever go from First Priestess to Angelique in three months?

She pictures herself, as she has done a thousand times, in that white, ruffly dress. Only now, the stage she imagines is a real one—the warm, paint-scented stage in the Woolly Theater, hung with velvet curtains so rich and heavy, they would crush a person if they fell. She imagines staring out, nothing visible except the shimmering spikes of bright light reaching down into the black void of the auditorium. And behind her, the world of *Angelique.* A world of love and honor and courage, held together by beautiful music. She tosses her blond ringlets and smiles, and the music comes, clear and strong and fierce.

Angelique is her secret. It is the hope that has kept her struggling for the last two years, through lessons and repertoire and soirees that were all just a little too difficult for her to do well. The hope that someday, she would sing this role; that she would *be* Angelique. Queen of that perfect world.

If her father knew the conservatory had chosen to stage it this semester, she wouldn't be here. He would have pulled her out of high school next semester instead. But through some whim of fate, she is here.

Voices float in from outside her yellow pine door. Students are heading to the lobby to wait for the lists to be posted by the midnight deadline. Sing closes the score. Maybe she should wait downstairs with the others. Maybe Jenny and Marta will be there.

"Back later, Woolly," she says to the battered gray lamb whose button eyes stare at her from the bed. She puts on her slippers, ties her red silk bathrobe, and tucks the score under one arm.

Downstairs, the moon-faced lobby clock says nine thirty and already the ugly maroon couch and most of the chairs are occupied.

Three girls Sing saw at the Welcome Gathering stop talking as she enters, then begin whispering after she has passed them. She hears, "Sing!" and then stifled giggles. She turns, but as she expected, none of the girls are looking at her. They appear deeply entrenched in their own conversation. "I like to *sing*," one of them says. The other two laugh and snort.

I shouldn't have turned around. They wanted to see if I'd react to the word.

She finds one of the last available stuffed chairs and tries to read. But she hears her name over and over, murmured, whispered, thought. Does everyone here know who she is? Are they all talking about her? That could have been a furtive glance from the stocky boy in the corner, huddled with his friend. That could have been her name coming from a group of heavily made-up girls over by a potted plant. Or it could have been her imagination.

Every few minutes, she looks for a figure crossing the quad from

Hector Hall. But all is dark except for light pooling in front of windows.

In front of her, the windows look out onto the moonlit lawn behind the dormitory. She gazes past the silhouette of an impressive maple tree and into the forest, separated from the conservatory by a tall wooden fence. *When he finds himself in the dark forest . . .* Sing wants to throw open the window, dive through, rush headlong into the cold arms of those shivering black trees.

What about this forest unnerves her father? And what, inexplicably, draws her to it? The spiky pines and jutting cliffs that drift away up the mountainside divulge nothing. But perhaps, she thinks, the woods and mountains north of Dunhammond don't need to flaunt their secrets. Perhaps they—and the conservatory—are so steeped in wild magic that trying to see it out a window is like using a dowsing rod at the bottom of a lake.

Thirteen

Angelique
An Opera in Three Acts
Libretto by Jean-Paul Quinault
Music by François Durand

CHARACTERS

Angelique, *a milkmaid*. . . . . Soprano

M. Boncoeur, *her father*. . . . . .Baritone

Silvain, *a shepherd*. . . . . Baritone

Count Bavarde/Prince Elbert. . . . . .Tenor

Queen of the Tree Maidens. . . . . Soprano

A villager. . . . . .Tenor

The Felix, *a great beast*. . . . . Mute

Villagers, Huntsmen, Tree Maidens

Overture.
ACT I.
A village.

No. 1, Chorus.

The quaint inhabitants of a quaint village describe how much they love farming.

No. 2, Aria & Chorus.

M. Boncoeur, who loves farming more than anyone else, tells about the light of his life—his beautiful daughter, Angelique. The villagers agree that Angelique is kind, innocent, and good.

No. 3, Recitative & Aria.

Enter Angelique, carrying a pail of milk and greeting everyone. She tells of the virtues of hard work.

No. 4, Recitative & Chorus.

Silvain, a shepherd, enters and tells the villagers he has seen the track of the Felix—a fearsome, great beast. The villagers become alarmed and wonder what to do.

No. 5, Trio.

M. Boncoeur says they should go to Prince Elbert for help, but Silvain says he will go and kill the beast himself as soon as he grabs his hunting knife. Angelique begs Silvain not to go.

No. 6, Aria.

Silvain tells Angelique he would die to protect her and runs off into the woods to hunt down the Felix.

No. 7, Finale.

Angelique, M. Boncoeur, and the villagers hope Prince Elbert will be able to help them.

ACT II.

The deep woods.

No. 8, Chorus.

A hunting party has killed a great stag and is bringing it home for a feast. Their leader, Count Bavarde, enjoys hunting quite a lot and everyone agrees he's very good at it.

No. 9, Recitative & Duet.

Silvain enters and is accosted by Count Bavarde. These are Prince Elbert's woods, and poachers are to be hanged. Silvain insists he's hunting the dreaded Felix, but Bavarde and his men don't believe him. Count Bavarde insists Silvain is a poacher and should be hanged. Silvain bemoans his fate.

No. 10, Chorus & Trio.

A bevy of Tree Maidens appears, scolding Count Bavarde. They bring with them Angelique, whom they have found lost in the woods. Angelique says she has come in search of Silvain and now pleads for his life. Count Bavarde comments on how pretty she is. Silvain says the woods are dangerous and that Angelique should go home.

No. 11, Recitative & Aria.

Angelique asks Count Bavarde to let her speak to Prince Elbert. Surely he will understand. Angelique thinks Prince Elbert must be very handsome and noble.

No. 12, Recitative & Aria.

The Queen of the Tree Maidens arrives and chastises Count Bavarde, demanding he release Silvain and reveal his true identity.

No. 13, Finale.

The Count agrees and tells everyone he is really Prince Elbert, enjoying a hunt with his friends without the pressures of his royal title. Everyone thinks it was a clever disguise.

ACT III.
The village—night.

No. 14, Recitative & Aria.

Prince Elbert has come alone to find Angelique. He realizes he has everything he wants in the world except her.

No. 15, Recitative & Duet.

Angelique hears his lament and agrees to marry him if he rids her village of the Felix, which she has just seen prowling near the sheep. Prince Elbert agrees.

No. 16, Chorus.
The villagers hear the cries of the sheep—the Felix is approaching.

No. 17, Duet & Chorus.
Angelique and Prince Elbert bid each other a tearful good-bye. The villagers are heartbroken that Angelique is heartbroken.

No. 18, Aria.
Angelique worries for her love, Prince Elbert.

No. 19, Recitative & Chorus.
A villager returns with news that Prince Elbert has been badly wounded by the Felix and will surely die. Angelique despairs as the villagers grieve for her.

No. 20, Aria, Interlude, & Recitative.
Silvain vows to kill the beast that has caused Angelique sorrow. He and the Felix battle. The Felix defeats Silvain but has looked into his eyes and seen his despair. The beast spares his life and grants him one wish. Silvain chooses to wish Prince Elbert healed for the sake of Angelique.

No. 21, Trio.
The Felix disappears for good, and Prince Elbert miraculously recovers. Angelique thanks Silvain but realizes he is mortally wounded—he has chosen her happiness over his own life. Silvain dies.

No. 22, Finale.
Everyone briefly feels bad about Silvain and then cheers for the happy couple, Angelique and her prince.

Fourteen

T*OUT EST À MOI SAUF VOUS!" Ryan sings. "I have everything but you!"
Angelique hears his lament and agrees to marry him if he rids her village of the Felix. Prince Elbert, handsome in his navy-blue uniform with
gold piping and white buttons, takes Lori's hand. She is dazzling in a
white shepherdess costume, complete with a graceful crook adorned with a
pink bow. Prince Ryan and Lori hope they will be together in some bright
future.*

Sing wakes as the score tips forward onto her face. It is just past
eleven. Students doze on the couch, chairs, and floor. Someone has
turned on the gas flames in the fake fireplace, and a boy and girl
play checkers in its glow.

Marta and Jenny, perched on a coffee table, flip through a magazine whose cover is all hot pink, sun yellow, and bold block let-
tering.

"Oh, you're awake," Jenny says casually. "I was going to poke
you in a minute to stop you snoring."

Sing opens her mouth, but Marta pats her shoulder and laughs.
"Don't listen to her."

Jenny makes loud snoring noises, ignoring the annoyed glances,
and Sing laughs.

The door opens, letting in cold air. Eyes open, spines straighten, checkers and books and magazines are forgotten. A gray robe and faint, piney scent swish past Sing's chair as an apprentice crosses the lobby—Daysmoor. He posts sheets of paper to the bulletin board, long fingers delicately pressing the thumbtacks.

"The lists!" Jenny shakes Sing's leg. Everyone in the lobby hurries to the board. Scowling, the apprentice pushes his way out of the crowd and heads back to the door.

Sing hesitates, but then, inhaling deeply, she rises. It's difficult to see the tiny names beyond everyone's bobbing heads, but she hears Jenny say, "Oh! I got Orchestra Two!"

"See anything?" Sing asks Marta, whose height gives her an advantage.

"Um—looks like I got Concert Choir—and you, too."

"Great." Sing tries to sound enthusiastic. *Everyone makes Concert Choir.* "What about, um, Opera Workshop? See anything there?"

"Let's see." Marta cranes her neck. "Wow! Oh, my God!"

"What? What?" Sing's heart jumps.

Marta turns around. "I got the Queen of the Tree Maidens!"

"Oh!" Sing tries to smile. "Great!"

"You know, that's so weird, because I was just reading about tree maidens—there's different ones, but dryads are the most famous—in *Mythical Beings You Should Know.* It should help me prepare for the role, you think?"

"Um, sure."

Sing notices Daysmoor, arms crossed, leaning against the wall by the door. His face is turned away, and for a moment she studies his dark, angular form. There is something strange about him, something lonely—maybe deeper than loneliness, as though he is a creature from another world. She doesn't realize she is staring until Marta's voice cuts through the chatter.

"Sing, you're Angelique!"

Her heart stops, then kicks on again at twice its normal rate. "Really?" she says quietly. Did everyone hear? What do they think?

The dispersing students don't glance her way. Only Daysmoor has turned his unreadable face in her direction. Can he hear her heart beating all the way over there? He pushes himself off the wall with his shoulders and leaves without a word.

"Oh, wait," Marta goes on, unaware of Sing's heart. "It says 'us' beside it—I think that means 'understudy.'"

"Oh." Sing steps back. The crowd is thin now, and she can see it, too. *S. da Navelli: Angelique, soprano (us)*. And just above it, *L. Pinkerton: Angelique, soprano*. "Oh. Well, that's cool."

Only it isn't cool. It would be better to be in some other group than to have to learn and rehearse the role of her dreams and never get to perform it.

It would be better to just leave.

Fifteen

T HE FELIX, WHEN SHE REMEMBERED space at all, remembered it as unforgiving. Everything about space was relentless—the emptiness, the brightness, the coldness, the silence. But the mountain was different. It could be treacherous one moment and a sanctuary the next.

That rainy summer, the forest was slick and muddy. The Felix spent most of her time in a shallow cave near the summit, staring out at the gray days. Her thoughts, when they came, were simple—noticing the color of a mushroom, smelling new leaves, wondering if the rustle in the bushes below was something big enough to eat. The concepts of *brother, mother,* and *home* were all but lost to her now, but her despair remained, chaining her to the earth.

A pack of wolves adopted most of the mountain as their territory, and the Felix anticipated their infrequent passing with interest. It was a large pack, even after she had eaten two or three of them, and the way they hunted together fascinated her.

One wet morning, she was watching them lying in the shelter of branches below the cave. Large rocks and vegetation hid her bluff, but through the leaves, she could see the long gray bodies among the stones. They had chosen to rest in this rocky depression, comfort outweighing the difficulty their slender legs must have had scrambling down. A cub was playing, climbing over and around the rocks at the bottom of the bluff, snapping at insects. Every now and then, when he scrambled too far, one of the adults would bring him back with a sound or a tug.

At last the cub managed to scale a small boulder under the lip of the ledge where the Felix sat watching. He swatted some glistening grass blades poking up through a crack in the stone, tangling a clump in his paws and rolling onto his back with it. One of the wolves at the base of the cliff called to him, *Too high*. But the cub's nose quivered in the air. He had caught the Felix's scent and didn't know what it was. Eyes bright, he began pawing the loose rock of the cliff, searching for a way up. *Too high,* came the call from below. *Too far. Come back.*

The Felix did not know delight, so she couldn't delight in the prospect of so easy a kill. She didn't know fear or uncertainty, so she felt no relief that her next meal was presenting itself in her own lair. But she disliked padding around the forest when it was wet and gray, and she understood convenience. Her ears twitched and her muscles tensed in anticipation of the cub's final leap onto the ledge.

The wolf cub continued to claw at the cliff face, dislodging stones and rubble. One of the adults began to clamber up the large boulder. The rain intensified, sending the occasional cascade of muddy water down the cliff. The cub pawed and scraped, scrabbling at last onto a high vantage point just below the ledge. With a final push from his short back legs, he propelled himself over the side and tumbled into a furry ball before the jaws of the Felix.

The ground shuddered.

This bought the cub a few more seconds of life as the Felix, puzzled, closed her mouth before her jaws could finish their deadly snap. The shuddering intensified, and she and the cub and the lip of the ledge slid down the face of the cliff in muddy confusion. The slippery, tumbling rocks knocked more of their brothers free; smaller stones easily influenced by shifting mud came loose from their perches, leaving larger stones unsupported and teetering. The Felix heard the cub's frantic yelps as he fell.

They came to rest in a jumble of stone and dead plants and mud at the bottom of the cliff. Instinctively, the Felix leapt to higher ground, settling on the bank overlooking the depression. Here and there a tuft of gray fur poked from between rocks, or a long body splattered with mud and blood lay still.

Then, to her surprise, she saw the cub pulling himself out of the muck. She hesitated, wondering if such a small meal was worth all that filthy fur. With the mud and debris, the depression was now almost level with the ground above it, and the cub began running across it and back again, edge to edge. He stopped at each patch of gray fur and nosed it, twice, three times. But all the wolves were dead.

Finally the cub stopped running and sat down in the middle of the clearing. He raised his nose and started to howl.

The Felix hopped down and loped over to him. A bigger wolf would have been better. But the cub didn't even try to run. He just stopped howling and looked at her.

And in his eyes, she saw whole galaxies, just as she saw in the soul of every creature. But the eyes of this wolf cub were different. *My fault,* the eyes of this tiny creature said. And the rest of that vast inner universe was wordless, soul-rending grief. An entire cosmos of despair looked back at her.

The Cat part of her shrank at this. It shouldn't have been given this insight. It didn't know how to react. But at that moment, the part of the Felix that still clung to a memory of the sky expanded within her earth-body as though she were breathing in lungfuls of it. That part of her felt this cub's despair as acutely as it felt her own. That part of her understood.

Before it curled up and was silent again, the part of her that was Sky wept a single tear for this wolf cub. And the sky noticed. The tear hung suspended in the air, solid and shining, until the wolf cub caught it on his tongue like a snowflake.

That evening, the Felix watched the wolf pack move on, long legs picking their ways over the rocky terrain, gray coats still shedding sparks of sky-magic. The cub stayed close to the adults.

And so the first tear the Felix shed was for the wolf cub.

The last would be for Sing da Navelli.

Sixteen

Sɪɴɢ ɪs ᴍᴜᴛᴇ ɪɴ ʜᴇʀ ᴅʀᴇᴀᴍs. She breathes, opens her mouth, pushes air through, and nothing happens.

Dreams of Lori Pinkerton and Marta singing Baroque duets on the other side of a chasm have put dark circles under her eyes this morning. She follows Marta and Jenny outside, past the tall casement windows of the dining hall. Crows caw unattractively from the tall trees surrounding the campus. The statue of Durand gleams.

"First rehearsal tonight!" Marta chirps.

Sing grunts.

"I've been looking over my aria," Marta says. "Do you know—"

"So do you believe in this deal with the devil stuff?" Sing cuts in. Any topic of conversation other than rehearsal.

"Huh? What deal with the devil?" Marta's eyes widen.

"You know," Sing says, gesturing. "François Durand. That's what they say, anyway. He did some black magic or something, after all those people died."

"Too bad it's old news," Jenny says. "That would be a good headline: 'Civil War Massacre Shrouded in Mystery!'"

Sing's mental clockwork whirs. "Yeah, I've heard it was the

northernmost battle. But it's a bit unclear who was fighting who, or why everyone in the village died. And as far as I know, no one was shot."

"Creepy," Jenny says. "Necromancy. Or aliens. Or plague."

"Oh." Marta snorts. "People mix up their mythology sometimes. Durand didn't make a deal with the devil. His wish was granted by the Felix."

Sing is dubious. "The cat-beast from *Angelique*?"

"Uh-huh." Marta's tone is matter-of-fact. "I read about it in *Monsters of the World*."

"I see," Sing says.

"You don't have to believe," Marta says. "They've found journals in France indicating that Durand's entire body of work was destroyed in a fire in 1860, which is why he got so depressed he left to die abroad. That's a fact. Then—"

"Yeah, yeah," Jenny says. "Then, miraculously, his entire canon reappears, he founds the conservatory in this wilderness and attracts bright students and produces *Angelique* two years later. Hooray."

"It was the Felix," Marta says. "She came down from the heavens and granted his wish. How else would you explain it?"

Well, I wouldn't automatically jump to "magical space cat," Sing thinks.

Jenny leaves them as they pass the building named for Durand, two stories of musty, antiquated classrooms. The handbook says Mr. Bernard's acting class is in the greenhouse at the edge of campus.

Sing and Marta find seats on the stone floor among pots of flowering plants. The greenhouse is old-fashioned, iron and glass. The sound of a forest stream floats through open windows.

Instead of staff robes, Mr. Bernard wears burgundy windpants and a white T-shirt that hugs his jiggly middle.

"Welcome!" he says to the twenty or so students. "I am officially Mr. Bernard, but you may call me Lou. I'd appreciate it if you did so. Just don't let the president hear you!"

Sing sighs. Some teacher always tries to be the cool one, the one to confide in, the one who inspires. She traces the cracks between the floor stones with her fingers.

"Now, you are all singers here," Mr. Bernard goes on. "Tell me, what's the difference between singing and playing an instrument?"

A few hands go up. "Yes?" He points to a boy with glasses.

"Singing has words?"

"Singing has words, most of the time. What do words imply?" No hands.

"Come on, guys," Mr. Bernard says. "Tell me about words!"

Marta says, "They tell a story?" Sing notes her chipper tone. *She* got the Queen of the Tree Maidens. She has nothing to worry about.

Mr. Bernard nods. "Sometimes they tell a story. Sometimes they just tell an emotion. But who produces words? Okay, how about you?"

Silence . . . until Sing realizes he's pointing at her. She shrugs. "People?"

"Bingo!" Mr. Bernard claps. "People!"

Sing rolls her eyes behind closed lids.

"Sometimes animals, if it's an animal character," says the boy with glasses.

"I'm glad you brought that up," Mr. Bernard says. "You said the magic word: *character*. When we sing, and by 'we' I mean 'you,' because I sing like cats in a bathtub, we are becoming a character. Now, that's not to say that other instruments can't represent characters or tell stories, but it isn't the instrument itself that's doing it, it's the sound. When we sing, we *become* someone else. We express ourselves with sound, and with our faces and our bodies. That's acting!" Some of the students smile or nod, some look skeptical.

Sing has taken acting classes before. Her father insisted. She's never been good at it. Mr. Bernard talks about emotions, asking the students first to feel anger—"It's the easiest," he says—then sadness, and finally joy. "These things live inside you. You need to recognize them for what they are before you can hope to inhabit someone else's body. You need to separate them."

A few minutes go by. The other students concentrate. Some breathe heavily, some smile. One or two have tears running down their cheeks. Sing watches with interest. She tries to call up anger, then sadness. But nothing comes. Inside, she is as hard and smooth and dark as obsidian.

Marta's eyes are closed, her face twisting with rage, then sorrow, then happiness. *Good actress,* Sing adds to her list of Marta's strengths.

Mr. Bernard goes on after a while. "Hundreds of emotions live inside you—they are what make you yourself. Fear, envy, pity, resentment, love, lust." That elicits a few giggles. "What are you feeling today? Can you name it?"

Sing glares at Mr. Bernard as if daring him to expose her. *Go ahead,* she thinks, *tell me I'm a jealous little witch.*

He hands out index cards. "I want you to write 'I am' on your index card. Follow it with whatever you like. Okay? Go!"

Sing stares at her index card. Some of the other students are staring, too.

This is stupid, she thinks. How good an actor does an understudy have to be? It's not like she's ever going to be an opera superstar. It's not like she's her mother.

Sing picks up her pencil and writes "I am not my mother" on the index card.

Seventeen

T HE FELIX WAS BORN A THING of beauty, and despair, as is its nature, only made her more beautiful. She resembled a great cat, yes, but in the way the sky resembles its reflection in a still lake. Even after her fall, she kept the color of the sunset, her favorite time—the beginning of a starry night—and the stars themselves she kept dotted throughout her sleek fur. Her eyes were nearly black nebulae; creatures unlucky enough to be mesmerized by their violet tinge would live to see nothing else ever again. But her teeth and claws, once pale and lustrous as the moon, became a crimson-edged yellow under the dark, bristling trees.

Nevertheless, something continued to shine out of her, a soft, white star-light, now laced with blood, but still bright. Animals ran from the strange shadows it cast.

One century, it caught the massive, rolling eye of the spirit of the Forest himself. He was so taken with this lovely, sad light that he left his sleeping bear caves and diligent worms and shivering nests and, for a time, thought of himself as a great cat instead.

Eighteen

Sɪɴɢ ꜱᴛᴇᴘꜱ ᴛʜʀᴏᴜɢʜ ᴛʜᴇ ᴏʀᴀɴɢᴇ door with the chipped paint into a cold, damp classroom filled with old chair-desk hybrids.

This is a mistake.

She should have listened to her father when he suggested she take The Artist's Life as her arts elective. It is common knowledge that Anybody Who is Anybody takes The Artist's Life. But she couldn't stand a semester learning the elusive rules of making it in the professional world. She's already had seventeen years of that.

So she chose The Nature of Music. An easy A, right?

But she is shocked to find strange, ten-lined staves covered with spiky, shaky notes on the whiteboard. The walls are hung with scientific-looking diagrams of what appear to be upside-down larynxes and tracheas and lungs. Has she stumbled into a science-fiction movie?

The teacher looks like someone's cookie-distributing grandma. Her white hair puffs as she takes papers and books from her tote bag and arranges them on the desk at the front of the classroom. The lenses in her silver glasses look like bubbles.

Sing, not fooled by the teacher's benign appearance, scowls at the strange staves—this class is going to be weird and technical, not philosophical. Something else for her to fail at.

She finds a seat by herself, which isn't difficult; there are only four other students in the room. She sits two chair-desks behind a small boy with curly brown hair and three chair-desks over from a pair of older girls—one large and dark, one small and fair—who seem to be best friends. The only other student is an athletic-looking guy with a goatee. As Sing grudgingly gets out her notebook, he is joined by another athletic guy with unappealing sideburns.

"All here, I think?" the teacher says. "Great! Welcome to The Nature of Music. I'm Mrs. Bigelow." Sing flips open her notebook and starts to doodle.

Mrs. Bigelow begins with, "What is music?" and Sing begins to drift. She knows the discussion will turn to alternative instruments, unfettered dissonance, string quartets in helicopters—all the crazy stuff students are supposed to be impressed by. She's never been able to get her head around most of it. It feels like pretend.

But a few minutes into the lecture, Mrs. Bigelow hefts an ancient tape player onto her desk and presses "play." Sing hears the rustle of a breeze through leaves, then a birdcall. It starts as a little growl, then shoots up high and back down. *Grrrrrlll, grrEEEEEEooo. Grrrllll, grrEEEEEEooo.*

Mrs. Bigelow lets the call play five or six times. "I'll be impressed if any of you can identify that bird."

The large girl says, "Sparrow?"

"Nope."

The curly-haired boy says, "Grosbeak?"

Mrs. Bigelow smiles. "Nope. It's a little bird from Southeast Asia called the silver-eared laughingthrush. Here's a picture." She holds up a large book, open to a page with a color photograph of a grayish bird. The bird has dull yellow patches on its wings and a funny red pattern on its head that looks like a hat. Sing's gaze lingers on the picture for a moment before she goes back to doodling.

"Did you catch the song?" Mrs. Bigelow asks. "It's a fairly simple one. Can anyone sing it back to me? Sing?"

Sing looks up. Why are all the teachers calling on her today? She keeps her expression neutral: not hostile enough to be considered insolent, but definitely not engaged.

"No?" Mrs. Bigelow says. "Laura?"

The pale girl looks around nervously, then tries, "Um, grrrrll, cheeEEE!"

The other students laugh, not unkindly, and the girl looks at her best friend and giggles. Mrs. Bigelow says, "That was pretty good. Tom? How about you? Want to try?"

Sideburns exchanges a look with Goatee and says, "Bck, bck, bck-AWW!"

The teacher laughs with the students. "While that wasn't quite a silver-eared laughingthrush, it was brave of you to try. You are definitely not a chicken." The other students chuckle. They're warming up to Mrs. Bigelow, even as Sing's heart grows colder.

"So imagine you are a juvenile silver-eared laughingthrush, instead of a juvenile human being." Mrs. Bigelow shoots Sideburns a lighthearted glance. "You need to communicate with others of your species. You need to be able to say things like 'I'm in danger!' or 'I'm looking for a mate!' or just 'I'm here!' How do you learn to do it?"

The pale girl raises her hand. "Instinct?"

"Not as much as you may think," Mrs. Bigelow says. "Anyone else?"

"Listen to your parents?" Goatee says.

"Exactly! Most songbirds learn their songs from their parents, the way you and I learn language—and, for many of us here, music."

Was that a glance in Sing's direction? It better not have been.

Mrs. Bigelow presses "play" again, and more birdsong hisses

through. It is the same song . . . *almost,* Sing thinks. *Something's not right.*

She realizes what the strange, many-lined staves are just before Mrs. Bigelow says, "Here are sonograms of the two different songs I just played you. Left to right represents time, and low to high is frequency. The smudgy lines that look like notes are the sounds the birds are making. As you can see, the second song—which is the juvenile—is just slightly different from the first. He hasn't quite learned it yet."

Pencils scribble things in notebooks. Sing wonders what everyone's writing. She looks at her doodle. A shepherdess in a flouncy dress.

"We don't have any silver-eared laughingthrushes here," the teacher says. "But I brought a couple of field guides to help you. You're each going to choose a common local bird—nothing too hard to find, please, since you'll have to study it—and learn its songs. Birdsongs can be quite lovely and inspiring; several famous composers, like Olivier Messiaen, have even tried to imitate them in their works. I'll give you until the end of class to choose your species."

Mrs. Bigelow hands a book to the best friends and another to the athletes. The curly-haired boy moves over to the best friends, but Sing stays put, adding a crook and bow to her shepherdess. Mrs. Bigelow doesn't say anything.

What am I doing? Sing thinks. *Do I think my life will be better if I get bad grades? If I get kicked out of the conservatory?* She imagines telling her father she's coming home, going back to her old school. That she couldn't cut it here. She can see his placid face, hear his disappointment.

Yet she continues to doodle. She draws the Felix now, Durand's "great beast." A big cat with oversize teeth and small, mean eyes. She has never understood why the beast is always portrayed as a cat—doesn't *felix* mean "happy," not "cat"? She has a feeling Marta would know.

Marta.

Sing draws the Queen of the Tree Maidens, tall and skinny and knobby, with lots of freckles, tangled hair, and enormous, vapid eyes. She's just putting leaves around her face like a foliage beard when Mrs. Bigelow says, "Okay, we just have a few moments left, and I'd like to hear from each of you which species you chose." She writes the students' choices: grosbeaks, mourning doves, tufted titmice (Goatee and Sideburns snicker), chickadees.

"Cardinals," Laura says, and Mrs. Bigelow looks up.

"Hmm . . . I think I have seen some this year, yes?"

"I saw one on the way over." Laura points to the small, open windows. Mrs. Bigelow nods and writes it down. Sing looks; she can see the fading green of the quad, the turning leaves. A lone, massive tree sits across the way, bulbous and smooth, like molasses that's oozing from the ground into the sky. A pair of crows sit on one of the middle branches.

"Sing? What species did you choose?"

"Crows." The other students snort and murmur.

Mrs. Bigelow frowns. "Crows aren't exactly songbirds."

"Awwww! Rrraaaaw!" the crows outside hiss. Sing answered impulsively, to get a rise out of Mrs. Bigelow, but now she wonders, *What are they saying? "I'd like a mate"? "I'm in danger"? Or just, "I'm here"?* She says, "I'd like crows, if it's all right with you."

Mrs. Bigelow keeps frowning but says, "Okay. *Crows* it is."

She says the word *crows* as if it is strange, out of place. As if it doesn't belong. As if it isn't worthy of belonging.

Nineteen

BEETHOVEN'S *PATHÉTIQUE* SONATA IS ONE of the most popular pieces in the world. George didn't know how many times he had heard it. Hundreds? Thousands? He played it and taught it and studied it. And while the *Pathétique* would always be exquisite, there were other pieces, other composers, other sounds. George moved on, as one does.

I've learned some Beethoven, Nathan said. Now, in St. Augustine's bright hall at this ungodly hour on a Saturday, George sat and listened to the *Pathétique* again.

During lessons, Nathan was attentive and quiet, absorbing theory and history as quickly as his muscles learned to meet the strange new demands he was making of them. And when George played, Nathan watched his fingers with a savage hunger.

George knew his student's ear was extraordinary and that his technical precision was already becoming masterful.

But now, as Nathan played the first movement of the *Pathétique,* the ebb and flow of his raw being lent a sweetness and urgency to the music that stirred something in George he had forgotten was there.

He could not imagine Beethoven himself playing it better.

From his usual place next to him on the bench, George watched the young man's long fingers, the curve of his wide shoulders, the exhilaration on his handsome face.

George's face, next to Nathan's in the reflection on the shiny music rack, looked almost like a poor copy, a homely older brother. Droopy curves instead of delicate lines, pockmarks instead of liquid smoothness. But when Nathan's reflected eyes caught George's, their gaze was nothing but warmth. George allowed himself to indulge in those eyes for just a moment as the last chord rang.

"Wonderful!" A shrill voice cut through the piano's reverberations.

George leapt to his feet. "Betty! I didn't hear you come in."

Nathan stood, smiling politely. "Professor Hardy, what a pleasant surprise."

The professor leaned against the doorway, hip cocked. "The pleasant surprise was all mine, my dear. George, I was beginning to think your protégé was just a pretty face. But it seems he plays after all, and damn well. Isn't that something?" She flashed a red-lipsticked smile. Nathan blushed.

"Of course Nathan plays well." George pulled the fallboard over the keys with a thunk.

"But you're not a pianist, George, not really," Professor Hardy said. "Nathan is beyond you. He needs a new teacher. New opportunities." She approached, the click of her heels echoing. "I wouldn't mind taking him on myself."

"That's very nice of you," Nathan said.

"Come see me if you're interested." The professor smiled, and George watched Nathan's eyes following her as she walked away.

"I don't think that's a good idea," George said.

Nathan's eyes crinkled in a smile. "Why not?"

"Have I ever steered you wrong?" George's voice now held a strange roughness. "Don't you trust me?"

Nathan patted George's shoulder and laughed. "Don't worry, George, for goodness' sake! I'm not going to leave you for Professor Hardy. Forget it, all right? You know best, I'm sure. Shall we have lunch?"

George exhaled. "Yes. That's an excellent idea."

Twenty

SING, MARTA, AND JENNY eat lunch at a picnic table next to the wooden fence separating the campus from the piney woods behind it. The fence is made of vertical logs lashed together and whittled to sharp points, and over the top rises a ledgy, snowcapped mountain. Yellow signs reading DANGER and sporting skulls and crossbones are posted every thirty feet or so.

Sing pokes at her potato salad, disengaged. Jenny's brash tone carries over the other conversations at other tables while Marta fiddles with a silver unicorn hanging from her neck.

Jenny is saying, "You should totally take it next time. We're building our own violas from scratch! Mine's going to be complete garbage, but still. Take it if you get a chance."

Marta says, "Yeah, I have to take Functional Piano this semester since I didn't test out of it. I wanted to take Nature of Music. It sounds really cool."

Sing snorts, eyes on her lunch. Marta continues, "Sing, aren't you taking that? I thought I saw you head over to Durand after drama."

Sing shrugs. Was that a dig, because she's not taking The Artist's Life? At least she doesn't have to take Functional Piano!

Jenny says, "What's up with you, Sing?"

Marta shushes her, but Sing looks up coolly. "What do you mean?"

Jenny looks right at her. "What's the matter?"

"Nothing."

"Leave her alone, Jenny," Marta says, cutting steamed carrots.

"No! She's been acting rotten all lunch. I'm sick of it."

Sing is silent, in no mood for Jenny's frankness. Her hackles rise. *Go ahead,* she thinks. *Tell me I don't belong here. Tell me my father is buying my career. Tell me I'll never sing Angelique for real.*

She is completely surprised when Jenny stretches out a hand and says, "It sucks that you didn't get the part you wanted. I think maybe it sucks more than Marta and I know. But look, we're on your side, okay?" She looks into Sing's eyes, and Sing feels real in a way she hasn't for a long time.

Sing exhales quietly and, somehow, it's more than air that leaves her lungs. She looks at Jenny's hand resting on her own, and a burning tightness that has been rising since her first moment at the conservatory subsides a little.

And they are friends.

As reality bubbles back around her, Sing's brain fully registers the strange wooden fence for the first time. Partly for something to say, partly because she wants to know, she gestures and asks, "What's in the woods? Why this crazy fence?"

"Keeping out the barbarian hordes?" Jenny says, and Sing and Marta snort.

"My dad says it's dangerous out there," Sing says.

"Probably nuclear waste," Jenny says. "That's why all the apprentices are mutants."

"That's not what I heard," Marta says, and her voice is so uncharacteristically smug that Sing and Jenny turn in surprise. Marta's eyes are wide and her pleasant face radiates excitement. "I heard *the Felix* still lives out there." Jenny looks like she's trying not to laugh.

But part of Sing can't help prodding. "The Felix is a myth," she says.

"It's not a myth," Marta says. "It's known as a myth because of Durand's opera, but I think he was writing from experience. He *saw* the Felix and it granted him a wish."

"Maybe it wrote *Angelique* for him," Jenny says. "That's the only thing he ever wrote that's any good."

"If *Angelique* was written by a cat, there would be more mice in it," Sing says.

Jenny nods. "And laser pointers."

"He's got some very nice chamber music," Marta says.

"Myth or not"—Jenny puts her fork onto the table with a clatter—"there are tons of stories about a huge, scary cat being seen around here, and it certainly doesn't go around granting wishes. It goes around eating people. They say that's what happened to Brother Bessette, who built the original church. He wasn't inspired. He was breakfast. Look it up."

Sing can see the tops of the pine trees beyond the fence. The sun still warms like summer, but a chill sweeps down from the mountain.

"It does eat people," Marta says. "Remember those hikers about ten years ago?"

Sing doesn't, but Jenny says, "Well, you're not supposed to hike the mountain."

"What happened to the hikers?" Sing asks.

"We don't know," Jenny says. "Probably wolves. Or a bear."

"Wolves and black bears tend to stay away from people," Marta says. "And most animals eat their kills."

Sing is curious. "The hikers weren't . . . eaten?"

Marta shakes her head. "Only their throats."

Jenny tosses her napkin onto the table. "And I'm done with lunch."

"The Felix will kill anything it catches," Marta says. "Except if it looks into the eyes of its prey and sees there a deeper sadness than its own. Then, instead of killing, it will shed one tear and grant a wish. Read *Angelique*. It grants Silvain's wish at the end."

"That's just a story," Jenny says, agitated. "The r—" She stops herself.

Sing raises an eyebrow. "You were just about to say, 'The *real* Felix . . .'"

Jenny reddens but laughs. "All the creature books Marta's got living in our room are getting to me, I guess. But Felix or no, the important question is what is everyone wearing to the party tonight? We have to represent the incredibly stylish first-years since we're the only three invited."

Marta's jaw drops. "You got us invited? To Carrie Stewart's party?"

Jenny efficiently wraps spaghetti around her fork, lunch apparently being on again. "If you think *I'm* cool, you should meet my sister. Her coolness remains even after she graduates. Of course I got us invited."

Sing laughs. It feels good. She says, "Marta and I have rehearsal tonight. We'll have to meet you there."

"Hell, no!" Jenny says. "Meet me in our room. I'm not going up to senior floor alone!"

"Okay." Sing's smile fades as she thinks of the coming rehearsal. "Hey, do you know if Lori Pinkerton is here yet?"

"Not yet," Jenny says. "She's supposed to be in my analysis class, but she wasn't there this morning."

"So you might get to sing Angelique tonight at rehearsal!" Marta says.

Sing traces a knothole with her fork. "Yeah."

Jenny is silent, but Marta says, "You don't seem too happy about it."

Years of being told not to whine clamp Sing's mouth shut. But she meets Marta's gaze, and before she can stop herself, she says, "I guess . . . I was so disappointed I didn't get the part, because . . . well, lots of reasons. But it would be so much easier just to move on, you know? I mean, the thought of having to sing it now, in front of everyone, and then Lori Pinkerton singing it better, and everyone knowing she's better because the Maestro said so . . ."

Marta starts to say something, but Jenny cuts her off. "Look, Lori's a total diva. We know this. But you are, too—in a good way, I mean. Jeez, you're a first-year and you're understudying the lead?"

"I'm seventeen," Sing says. "I'm a year older than most first-years."

Jenny slaps the table. "Who cares? It's amazing! You must be freaking unbelievable! You're going to kick total butt when you're a senior, right?"

"I have no idea."

Marta laughs. "You'll both be sorry when you meet Lori and she's nice. You're getting all worked up over nothing."

"What you need to do," Jenny goes on, "is iron that shirt, fix your hair, get your attitude on, and *own* that rehearsal tonight! Am I right?"

Sing smooths her shirt. These uniforms wrinkle so easily.

Twenty-one

Tʜᴇ ᴡɪɴᴅᴏᴡ ᴏᴠᴇʀʟᴏᴏᴋɪɴɢ ᴛʜᴇ ʀᴜᴇ du Faubourg Saint-Honoré was as grand as the hotel room it adorned. Its green-striped silk valance matched the chaise longue; the gilt accents in the molding set off the roses on the wallpaper. George sipped a brandy. Through the glass, he could see twenty or so *patrons des arts* still gathered by the stage door across the street, their hats and coats darkly speckled by the rain.

His pale reflection quivered with the raindrops that slithered down the glass. He was a distinguished man, experienced and competent, with years of conducting behind him. But the face that looked uncertainly back at him could have belonged to a young apprentice.

George looked exceptionally good for his age, and that wasn't just the magic of Paris talking.

He wasn't a superstitious man. But he knew, in his deepest heart, that everything had changed the night of Gloria Stewart's benefit concert at St. Augustine's. He barely remembered the concert now, though the events afterward were still perfectly clear—standing transfixed by the tattooed arm, finally gathering his courage to ascend the rickety stairs to the roof, hesitantly approaching the still body of the young man. *Nathan.*

He hadn't meant to steal. He wasn't a thief. Those beautiful hands were just so spellbinding, he had to touch one. He had to turn the delicate fingers over. It wasn't his fault that what the hand had been holding came loose and clattered onto the roof tiles. It wasn't his fault that he put the small, brilliant object into his pocket and forgot about it until days afterward. If Nathan, when he finally came around, had asked for it back, George certainly would have given it. But he didn't ask; it was as if he didn't even know about it.

The crystal was in George's pocket, as it always was. He reached for it, slid his fingers over the cold surface. He brought it close to his face, its reflection making the streaks of rain on the dark window glint like veins of silver. This beautiful little thing seemed to shimmer from the inside, an entire sparkling, ice-covered forest condensed into a single teardrop. It seemed to radiate sadness.

Ever since Nathan's crystal had come into his life, George had sensed time slowing down for him. He had tried to ignore it, focusing on his work. No one at Dunhammond Conservatory seemed to notice. But lately, with these European tours, outside the safety of his small, lonely school at the base of the big, lonely mountain, it was becoming clearer that the years were actually passing him by. Time had almost forgotten him.

But what good was it? If only he could leave Nathan at the conservatory where no one would see him, *then* George could have a career of his own without fear of unscrupulous people swooping in to take Nathan away.

He had tried, once. Just a weekend at a conference, in a city a mere hundred miles south of Dunhammond. Nathan had vomited for three days and was bedridden for two weeks afterward. It wasn't a stomach flu, as the doctor had said. George had felt the crystal in his pocket yearning for its master the whole time he was away.

The door to the hotel room opened and Nathan burst in, stamping his feet and shaking the raindrops out of the flaps of his black trench coat. "George! Here you are."

A man stepped in behind him, neatly dressed, with thinning blond hair and clear eyes. "Maestro, Paris adores you!"

George smiled, sliding the crystal back into his pocket. "I highly doubt that. But it was a good performance." He allowed himself this small boast. It had been an exquisite performance.

"They waited for you, you know, by the stage door," Nathan said, pouring himself a glass from a decanter. "I thought you had just run up here to change." He put a hand on his hip. "You *are* coming for drinks, aren't you?"

"Of course he is. You must, my friend!" the man said. George had been introduced to him before the concert—Henri Maneval, managing director of the prestigious Parisian *orchestre* that had lost its elderly conductor in 1961. George had been courting the orchestra for the better part of the five years since. Postperformance drinks were a very good sign.

But there was something else. A creeping discomfort that had started scratching at him as he watched Nathan taking in this city for the first time. The young man seemed to absorb its vibrancy, brought to new life by the smells of the patisseries, the colors of the street vendors' bright artwork, the fresh flowers from Holland. Nathan was so much more noticeable here.

George set his empty snifter on an end table and turned back to the window.

"Henri has been paying you the most embarrassing compliments behind your back," Nathan said. George could hear his disarming smile, even though he couldn't see it in the window's reflection.

"If you'll indulge me," the director said, "I'd like to pay those compliments to your face, Maestro. Do come out with us—a quaint piano bar down the street. And your friend has promised to provide some entertainment!" He laughed, and Nathan joined him.

George turned sharply. "Entertainment?"

Henri Maneval put a hand on Nathan's back. "If your protégé

plays half as well as you conduct, monsieur, we shall have a very good time!" He glanced at his watch. "It will not do for me to be too late, my friends. You know how these musicians are. *A bientôt, mes amis*." And he gave a nod and slipped away into the softly lit hallway.

George sank onto a velvet settee and put a hand to his forehead. *Five years* he'd worked for this. More than five years. He'd dreamed of taking the helm of a major orchestra since his days as a student at Dunhammond Conservatory, more than forty years ago.

Nathan closed the door. "Well? Aren't you going to change?"

George shook his head. The rain was falling heavily now, pattering at the window like a muted snare drum.

"Are you all right?" Nathan crossed the room and sat lightly on the settee, opposite the venerable maestro. "George, what's wrong?"

"What's wrong?" George's voice was harsh. "You would *embarrass* me?"

Nathan's mouth opened slightly. "Never! What did I do?"

George ran a finger along the back of the settee. "Entertainment? Did you give M. Maneval the impression you would *play* for him?"

Nathan lowered his gaze. "I . . . thought tonight we could celebrate."

Now George's voice softened. "I understand, my friend. But you know you aren't ready. You can't play for someone as refined as M. Maneval—the *managing director* of one of the most influential symphonies in the world—before you're ready! Especially when he is considering *me*."

"I thought I was ready," Nathan said. "I feel ready."

George forced a sad smile. The plan that had been forming in his mind ever since they landed in France was finally solidifying. Of course, it would involve abandoning Paris—abandoning everywhere. But he saw no alternative. "My dear boy, if you think you're ready, why not start with a competition? Why force yourself and your talents on two of the best ears on the planet?"

Nathan nodded. "You're right. I'm sorry. I got ahead of myself. . . . This is such an exciting city."

"Here," George said. "They are having a new competition in New York in just a few months. Named after the great Gloria Stewart, whose playing you admire so much. Why not compete? Then, if you are successful, it would be acceptable to start performing for larger and more sophisticated audiences."

I'll miss Paris, George thought. It was clear that, were he to meet Henri Maneval and a few choice orchestra members for drinks, his position would be assured. But at what cost? How could he keep Nathan hidden *here*?

Safe, he meant. Safe, not hidden.

"You always know what to do, George," Nathan said, leaning back against green velvet. "Thank you."

The conservatory really was the best place for them.

"I wish you'd cut your hair," George said, winding a black lock around his forefinger.

Nathan smiled. "No, you don't."

Then he rose to hang his wet trench coat on the rack by the door.

Twenty-two

Sing walks into rehearsal exactly on time, hair brushed and shiny, white shirt ironed, sweater vest and skirt de-linted, kneesocks pulled all the way up to her knees. St. Augustine's concert hall smells like varnish and cool stone.

A few students flip through their new *Angelique* scores. Sing carries an older edition, with FIRE LAKE OPERA stamped on the cover and "Ernesto da Navelli" written in the upper right-hand corner of the first page. Her father has never conducted *Angelique*, and never will, but the music is covered with faded pencil markings—he has thought about how he would do it.

The soft, echoey thud of the door announces the Maestro.

The Maestro isn't particularly tall. His nose isn't particularly hooked, though it is a little big for his face. He doesn't stride into the room or march up the aisle with sweeping gestures. He simply is not there, and then he is, and then everything becomes more nervous, as though even the masonry itself is worried it's out of tune.

Sing's mouth is dry. She nibbles the edges of her tongue to get her saliva glands working.

"Welcome to Opera Workshop." The Maestro places his score

onto a music stand, *clink*. "Our first production, for the Autumn Festival, will be Durand's *Angelique,* which, of course, was written here at the conservatory. I am also pleased to announce"—he couldn't look less pleased—"that this year, thanks to our new theater, the festival will also be hosting the Gloria Stewart International Piano Competition for the first time since its inception in 1967."

The assembly murmurs excitedly at the news. Sing, not being a pianist, hadn't given the prestigious competition a thought since she arrived. But her father is to be one of the judges—and she realizes with a sickening feeling that this means he will definitely be here for the performance of *Angelique*. No chance of his schedule interfering or of his being fooled should she "accidentally" tell him the wrong dates.

"Maestro," a scratchy voice says. Apprentice Daysmoor sits behind Ryan at the piano—the page-turner position—looking bored and slightly menacing, though at least he is managing to appear awake. "I'm curious—where did the conservatory ever find the money for such a beautiful, spacious new theater? To whom do we owe this *enormous* debt of gratitude?"

He looks at Sing. Her body jolts.

The Maestro, mercifully, responds with, "A generous benefactor."

What was *that*? What is Daysmoor's problem? She shoots him a look, but he has crossed his arms and closed his eyes.

The Maestro frowns. "I don't have to remind you that rehearsals, whether with myself or Mr. Bernard, are mandatory. Principals, your coach is Apprentice Daysmoor. Please bother him, rather than me, with your questions and concerns."

Sing makes a mental note not to have any questions or concerns.

"We will begin with act three, since everyone is in it," the Maestro says, flipping open his score. "Principals to the stage."

As she makes her way to the raised platform at the end of the room, Sing sees Hayley's face in the chorus. Great. One more person who'd love to see her fail. Maybe it would be better if Lori Pinkerton arrived right now.

She finds a seat next to a boy with a thick neck.

"Are you Angelique?" he asks.

"Yes. Well, no. I'm the understudy."

"Oh!" His face brightens. "I'm Prince Elbert." Now he has the audacity to blush a little. Sing smiles without her eyes.

"Top of page 213," the Maestro says, and Sing realizes her score has different page numbers from everyone else's. She looks over at Prince Elbert's, but Ryan has already started playing, and she recognizes the introduction to the second recitative, which means she has to start singing right—

"Stop." The Maestro—everyone—is looking at her. She is still finding the page . . . there. Maybe he won't say anything else.

He does. "Miss da Navelli, are you ready to begin?"

"Yes, Maestro." *Miss da Navelli.* There they are again, those wondering stares. Almost everyone in the hall wears one now. Her face is hot with embarrassment, but she pushes her shoulders back and glares. Once again the Maestro cues Ryan, who looks over at her and winks.

Winks.

What is that? Is he making fun of her? Telling her not to worry? Flirting?

Could he be flirting?

She stares at him, but his focus is now on the music, which she should be paying attention to. Prince Elbert looks pinkly at her and she doesn't mean to look pinkly back at him, but she does, and then they have to sing about falling in love with each other.

She manages to croak her way through the little recit, and then the duet begins. Prince Elbert's part is first. His voice is rich and strong, yet another reminder she's no longer a big fish in a small pond. He sounds like the tenors at Stone Hill, a little pressed but confident, not like the cocky, straining, Music Club boys at her old school.

No one else seems that interested in the polished sound coming out of this dumpy-looking prince. They follow along in their music or sip from their water bottles. Even Ryan is intent on his score, his body rocking back and forth as he plays.

Her turn. Her voice echoes in the grand hall, and it takes her a few beats to find some good harmonics. She focuses on breathing, but the harder she tries, the tighter her chest feels. Some of the words escape her, and twice she comes in early. At least when Prince Elbert comes back in, she can blend with him.

The duet ends. Rehearsal goes on. The Maestro's attention stays focused on the score and whoever is singing it. Sing sits back and looks at the ceiling, wishing she were nestled safely among the chorus members clustered in the house.

What is happening to her? She knows her voice inside and out. She knows resonance. She knows air.

Why can't she *do* it?

Halfway through the men's chorus, the big doors open and Lori Pinkerton strides in, a brown leather messenger bag slung over her shoulder.

Sing knows it is Lori Pinkerton, because she is everything Sing imagined her to be. Her long blond hair sways as she walks, her graceful neck holds her porcelain face high, and her pink-glossed lips curve downward in a disapproving pout. Her uniform *must* be the same as everyone else's, yet it clings and flows in all the right places, making men in the chorus turn slowly to follow her progress up the aisle.

Well, at least it's over now.

Lori sits on the other side of the stage, back straight and ankles crossed, as Monsieur Boncoeur, a middle-aged man brought in for the role, sings his recitative.

Sing watches Ryan's eyes stray in Lori's direction while he plays.

They were at FLAP together. Who knows what happened there, on the shores of beautiful Fire Lake? Sing pictures the still waters touching the perennially ice-sheathed mountains to the east, the red glow of sunset causing both to gleam like flames. She has seen the fire of Fire Lake many times, but always alone, as her father conducted or her mother sang. Did Lori and Ryan watch the blaze together?

It would take something phenomenal to pry Sing's jealous gaze from Ryan's face, but something phenomenal happens.

Marta begins to sing.

Everyone in the hall turns to her, Ryan and Lori included. Her sound is sweet and resonant, and she sings with such honesty and joy that the hairs on the backs of Sing's arms stand up. Marta closes her eyes as she navigates the acrobatic lines. Sing watches her jaw, spine, fingers, all moving fluidly with the notes. She'll have to work on her French, though. With decent French, she would be amazing.

Sing blinks. *Am I feeling a desire to see a fellow soprano—a rival—succeed?*

I've only been away from my father for two days.

A distinct type of silence follows Marta's aria. There would never be anything as vulgar as *applause* at a rehearsal, but from time to time, a special silence comes from everyone thinking the same thing: *That was great.* Sing catches Marta's eye and smiles, and Marta grins back, silver unicorn pendant glinting.

The Maestro cues Ryan to begin Angelique's most famous aria, *"Quand il se trouvera dans la forêt sombre,"* and Lori stands. Sing prepares for the worst.

It is worse than she fears.

It's actually really good.

Lori fixes a tiger's gaze on the high windows at the other end of the hall; she looks as though she is shooting lasers from her eyes. Her glossy lips protrude in exaggerated vowel shapes, and her white teeth gleam. The sound is loud and fat and confident, though not as pleasant as Marta's. Lori doesn't look at her score. She gestures and moves as Angelique would, hair shining, shoulders back.

Prince Elbert can barely contain himself.

Afterward, the Maestro calls Sing over. She's not sure how he does this. He doesn't say anything or gesture, but she knows she is being summoned. She hopes Ryan will linger, but he is already heading for the door, talking to Lori.

No, her only potential ally is Apprentice Daysmoor, standing crookedly behind the Maestro with a look of complete indifference. So much for that.

The Maestro clicks his tongue. "Miss da Navelli"—there's her name again—"I hope you will pay closer attention at future rehearsals. You are not in the chorus anymore. Set an example."

"Yes, Maestro."

"And you need to get in the gym. You heard how polished Lori sounded today—she was at FLAP over break, doing *work*. You sound as though you didn't croak out a note all summer."

"Yes, Maestro." *He knows I was at Stone Hill. He knows I've been working hard.*

"Your first rehearsal with Apprentice Daysmoor is tomorrow. Please take advantage of his guidance."

Sing notices the apprentice's dull eyes on her face now, arrogance radiating from him like chill off a cadaver. *His* guidance? She glares back; she will *never* take advantage of his guidance. "I'll be fine, sir," she says, and, searching for strength, finds the memory of Ryan winking at her. "With the rehearsal pianist."

Is it her imagination, or has Daysmoor's expression changed from indifference to disgust? She inhales broadly.

The Maestro lowers his voice. "I will be frank with you. I didn't choose this opera. It is famous, beloved, and inextricably tied to this school, and the administration would have no other piece open our new theater. But Angelique is a difficult and inappropriate role for someone your age. Considering how badly you butchered your audition, I should have cast you as the mute. But the plain fact is we need an understudy, and you were the only decent soprano available."

Decent. Well, that was nearly positive.

It doesn't last, however. The Maestro says, "If it were up to me, Lori Pinkerton wouldn't even have an understudy."

"Yes, sir." Sing's face is red again as the Maestro stalks away.

Apprentice Daysmoor starts to follow, but she calls out, "Hey!"

The apprentice turns, raising his eyebrows.

She is still stinging from the Maestro's words but can't put her frustration where it belongs. "I don't appreciate being stared at. Just so you know."

He stares a moment longer. Then he leans in. His voice is low and ravaged, almost a whisper. "Well, just so you know, my name is not 'Hey.' It's Apprentice Daysmoor, to you. And just so you know, coaching Opera Workshop is not number one on my list of things I like to do. In fact, it's not on there at all. And I like it even *less* when I have to put up with stuck-up little divas."

Fighting tears for the second time in a week, Sing says, "Well, if nobody wants me here, why did he cast me?" She didn't mean to sound so young and pounds her fist against her leg.

A flicker of something approaching emotion crosses Daysmoor's face. After a long moment, he says in a softer voice, "Because someone he respects assured him you could do it. Someone . . . must have seen something he didn't."

He looks at her, frowning, for a second more before the harsh call of "Daysmoor!" echoes across the room. The apprentice turns, obediently following the Maestro through the double doors.

As Sing's anger dissipates, she stares at the shiny floor. Who could have convinced the Maestro she is worth something?

Is she worth something?

When she looks up, Ryan is standing there. "I thought you

might need to get that coffee," he says, catching her with his sparkling, steady gaze. "Want to walk down to the village?"

"Really?" she says. *Stupid thing to say.* But he smiles at her anyway, just at her. Warm shivers course outward from her diaphragm; she doesn't dare move in case she falls over.

Ryan laughs. "Come on. Aaron and Lori are waiting."

Now Sing freezes for a different reason. Ryan has gestured to the big doors, where a skinny, swarthy boy stands with Lori Pinkerton. Are Aaron and Lori together? It doesn't seem that way; he isn't trying to disguise his adoration, and she isn't trying to hide her disdain. In fact, it seems like the more Lori pulls away, the more sappy Aaron's eyes get. So are Lori and Ryan together? Or are they all friends? And where does Sing fit in?

Ryan pulls her focus back by taking her hand, which she is certain is disgusting and sweaty. "Hey, take it easy. You look like you're afraid or something."

She tries to smile, but it probably looks weird and uncomfortable. "No! No, not at all. Coffee sounds great."

"Good. I'm glad to hear it." He is still holding her hand. Is that presumptuous or exciting? Her fluttering lungs tell her it's exciting. She pictures the trip down the mountain to Dunhammond, dusky and quiet, the pine forest becoming leafy below the conservatory, the gravel way enfolded by foliage until it reaches the village. Tonight, the road will be warm, hidden, and lit by a thousand stars.

Ryan squeezes her hand. "Let's go."

She smiles. Who cares if Lori Pinkerton is there? Ryan isn't holding Lori Pinkerton's hand right now. Ryan isn't putting his arm around—

Putting his arm around!

—Lori Pinkerton right now. Wait until Jenny and Marta—

She stops. Carrie Stewart's party!

A cursory scan of the hall tells her Marta is gone. They are probably both in their room already, waiting for her. Brushing their hair. Excited.

Ryan sighs and turns to her. "What's the matter?"

"I'm sorry—I can't get coffee now. I'm sorry. I forgot. I have to go to Carrie Stewart's party." Her shoulders slump.

"Yeah, we're going, too. Later. It's fine."

"No," she says, "I've got friends waiting for me. I—I'm sorry."

He looks at her, eyebrows drawn slightly. Does he think she's lying?

"Oh," he says. "Well, whatever. Have fun." Then he smiles that easy smile, shrugs, and walks away.

Sing knows what that means. It means there are plenty of girls who *are* available for coffee. She sees many pairs of mascaraed eyes discreetly following Ryan as he crosses the hall.

Lori puts her arm through his as they leave.

Twenty-three

FOR CREATURES SO NATURALLY FEARFUL, humans had a knack for wandering into danger. This occurred to the Felix one evening when the aurora borealis was so bright that her mind became clear again. By the next day, her thoughts had become simpler, but she still observed the humans and their horses and stones and noise from her perch overlooking the abandoned church.

She rarely came to this place. It was too low and exposed. Being chained to the earth was like drowning, but coming down off the mountain was like being buried alive. The last time she ventured down, she was called by the scent of humans. They had built the church and the tower. She ripped their lungs out.

Now there were more of them. A settlement below the church, more horses, more noise, more plowed earth and wood shavings, metal and smoke. They had been gathering for months, or years. She didn't know. She only knew they meant to stay on her mountain forever. She had to kill them all.

It was easy. Down here, there was no connection to the sky. The only memory the Cat grasped was rage, eating her guts, shooting outward. Each human that fell was her brother, screeching and bleeding and dying over and over again.

When the moon rose that night, all the humans were silent. The flies would arrive in the morning with the sun—she had never figured out how to kill flies efficiently—but for now, the Felix padded softly back toward the mountain in peaceful stillness.

When she arrived at the clearing, she was surprised to see a man standing near the stone tower. Just standing there, arms at his sides, looking at her. Growling, she bounded over.

"You should have taken me first, madame," the man said. "For I was the only one here who came seeking death."

The Felix exhaled rotten breath, her eyes level with the man's own.

"I know who you are," he said. "I dreamt of you. You were born in the light, but you cannot find your way back."

The Cat didn't understand him, but hesitated.

"Do you want to hear my story?" he asked. "I will tell it, and if it displeases you, you will rend my guts. That is not my rule—it is yours." Now he studied the black-violet eyes of the beast. "But maybe you know my story already?"

And looking into his eyes, she did. The Sky part of her mind awakened in the gathering darkness. In the eyes of this man, she saw loss and despair, as she saw in all creatures. But this loss was different. It wasn't the loss of a beloved, it was the loss of *being*. Annihilation.

"Ah, you understand, I think," the man said. "I foolishly transferred my soul to paper, and it burned to ashes. So you see, I am ready for death, for I am already dead."

The Cat's teeth tingled, but, as it did on rare occasions, the power of the sky flowed through the Felix's heart and trickled down her blood-soaked face, solidifying into a single tear, this time stained red.

The man caught the tear in his hand and blinked. "You have given me a gift. I . . . did not expect that. I would use it to bring back those whose lives were lost today, if it has that power."

But the eyes of the heavens, who weep through their despairing sister on earth, see only the depths of the soul. And what François Durand really wanted was his life's work restored to him, and a sanctuary of learning where music could be protected from the horrors of the outside world.

Twenty-four

SENIOR FLOOR SMELLS LIKE SANDALWOOD incense, fifteen different perfumes, sweat, and beer. Sing sits on Carrie Stewart's bed next to a lamp that has been covered with a red scarf and now casts dim, bloody light. Marta and Jenny giggle nearby.

It was as she predicted: There they were in their room, giddily spraying hair spray and applying makeup, giving each other fashion tips. She tried to seem excited, too, but couldn't help dwelling on the fact that she was going to yet another party instead of on a moonlit walk with a boy. A real boy, who actually seemed to like her. And who, she might as well admit, she likes back just a little bit. But she ruined it.

The party spills out into the hallway, more open doors. Someone has turned off the hall light and brought out a lamp with a spinning shade that throws blue star and moon shapes onto the walls. Music blares from one of the rooms, Eastern European techno that shakes the floors, and the dancing is energetic.

Sing sips at a wine cooler in a red plastic cup and rests her head back against the wall. It doesn't matter where the party is. Senior floor, Fire Lake, the mansion of a dignitary—she pretends to be having a good time until the important people are ready to leave.

Right now, Marta and Jenny are the important people, enjoying the inane conversations, the thrill of a usually forbidden location, and the exhilaration that accompanies thunderous music. Even if it is only four chords.

She has to admit, though, this is better than a soiree or, shudder, a *gala*. At least she's wearing jeans and a sweater, not silk and nylon and double-sided tape. No makeup is nice, too; makeup always feels like something to be worn in performance, not real life. Parties are always performances.

Two guys sit down next to her. One wears an old-fashioned brimmed hat in dark plaid; the other seems dressed for some kind of sporting event, lots of cotton in primary colors with big numbers.

Sports Guy cozies up. "Hey."

Sing sips her drink. *Am I a mark or a sideshow?* She glances at the tanned, tank-top-covered torsos moving confidently around the room, the long hair swishing. *Sideshow.*

Sure enough, Plaid Hat says, "Hey, are you related to Barbara da Navelli?"

Impressive. They're not usually this straightforward. "Why, are you?" she asks.

They laugh. Sports Guy smells like beer and the type of cologne adolescent boys wear by the gallon. "Teddy," he says, and when she looks confused, he adds, "My name. Teddy Lund. This is Connor."

Teddy waits expectantly, because apparently now that he has given her this crucial information, he deserves her life story.

Connor stares, nervous, leaning in and smiling. "So? You gonna tell us?"

Sing sets her jaw but sees no reason to lie. Keeping her face blank, she says, "Yes. Barbara da Navelli was my mother." Where have Marta and Jenny gone? What time is it?

Both guys laugh nervously. "That is so crazy," Teddy says.

What is it about freaks that attracts guys? Connor snakes an arm around her shoulders, and Teddy watches.

She shifts a bit, which Connor apparently takes as a good sign, squeezing in closer. Marta and Jenny are nowhere in sight. Some friends. She tries not to think about what Ryan might be doing right now.

Connor says, "So . . . were you, you know, *there*?"

She freezes.

"Hey, man, that's not cool." Teddy shoves Connor, who relinquishes her.

"I'm just asking!"

"Idiot!"

Were you there?

She's gotten that one before, of course. Everyone wants to know about Barbara da Navelli's famous farewell performance. And she can't help saying the answer, *seeing* the answer, in her head. *Yes. I was there.*

Connor leans in too close. "What happened? Come on!"

Angelique's most famous aria . . . She closes her eyes, afraid that if he looks into them too deeply, he'll see everything. *Barbara da Navelli in shimmering white—she wasn't Angelique, she could never be Angelique, not like that mystery soprano Sing saw when she was five. But she was beautiful. The audience, rapt, made no sound; no one breathed, no one blinked. It was to be a night for the history books—the union of That Voice and That Role. Sing watched Barbara da Navelli's graceful hands tell her story, heard the voice that never quite sounded like "mother" scattering glittering diamonds of music across the theater, lingering over notes like pearls, round and smooth and expensive. Then, suddenly, the voice was gone. Sing remembers the brief look of quiet puzzlement on her mother's face before she sank silently to the floor, the white dress deflating as though the woman inside had been nothing but air.*

"Hey. Neanderthals," a clear voice says. A pixie-faced girl with her hands on her hips looks down. "Why don't you go bother somebody else?"

The two guys protest, but the girl bats at them until they shuffle away in search of something to drink.

"Sorry about them," she says. "I'm Carrie. Senior violin. Having a good time?"

Sing nods. "I'm Sing. Um, first-year singer."

"I know."

Sing feels her face fall just a bit and hopes Carrie doesn't notice. But she does. "Sorry. Everyone knows who you are."

"Yeah, I'm used to it."

Carrie sits next to her on the bed. "I'm sure you are. But that doesn't mean it doesn't suck sometimes." She sips from her own red plastic cup.

No one has ever said this to Sing before. "Yeah." Then her brain kicks in. *Carrie Stewart. As in the legendary pianist Gloria Stewart?*

"I had a famous great-grandmother," Carrie says. "But you probably knew that."

"I figured maybe." Sing holds her cup out. "To famous relatives."

Carrie laughs, and they toast.

Carrie turns out to be popular, and soon a variety of seniors have settled around them on the bed, including Anita the flute and a chinless young man Sing recognizes as Silvain from *Angelique;* his real name is Charles.

She relaxes, letting Carrie refill her red cup, interacting with other humans in a comfortable way that would make Zhin proud. It's only after Prince Elbert—Tanner Something-or-other—arrives that the conversation turns awkward.

He apparently doesn't remember her, which is surprising after all the pinkness they accidentally shared, and says to Charles, "Didn't Lori sound incredible? Too bad we didn't get to do the duet. Man, I thought she'd never get there."

Uncomfortable silence. Then dawning recognition on his wobbly face as he meets Sing's eyes. She almost enjoys watching him stutter but mercifully cuts him off and puts on her schmooziest professional voice, the mask her family wears so well. "Well, we all get nervous, don't we?" She is glass inside, smooth and hard, brilliant. "Lori sounded fantastic. She'll do a great job."

Tanner looks relieved. And Sing almost pulls it off, face placid, hands steady, eyes calm. The magic party mask.

But then Lori appears, accompanied by the smell of roses—*roses!* Aaron hangs in the doorway as though he's deciding whether or not coming in is really worth his time, but Lori strides right over to where Carrie is seated and smiles warmly. "Hey!"

Carrie hugs her. "Lori! Glad you made it."

"Yeah, Ryan and I had some catching up to do." She giggles.

Catching up? After less than a week?

Sing hates her.

She tries to shrink, but it doesn't matter. By all appearances, Lori doesn't even notice she's there.

Ryan drifts in, fingers in his hair. "What's shaking? Hey, Sing."

Sing watches Lori's eyes flick in her direction, sees her smile quiver for just a second. *So! Lori has a party mask, too.*

As if she is aware Sing is on to her, Lori draws herself up, face serene. She sits on the bed next to Tanner, who looks as though he may faint, and then pats the space on her other side. When nothing happens, Lori looks at Ryan, patting the space again. He obeys, lowering himself onto the bed as Lori ruffles his hair.

And there they all are. How cozy.

Sing can't take it. She rises clumsily, putting her knee down on Tanner's hand.

"Ow!"

"Sorry," she says. "I have to go to the bathroom." Not the suavest of excuses.

To her surprise, Carrie says, "Me too."

The bathroom is old, with flickering fluorescent lights. When they are both washing their hands at the row of cold sinks, Carrie says, "I guess Lori's found her mark for this semester. Sickening, isn't it? She always gets the best ones."

Sing focuses on rinsing. "You mean Ryan?"

"Yeah." Carrie rips a paper towel. "You know him, huh?"

"No. Not really."

Carrie leans against the tiled wall. "You like him?" Sing is silent, and Carrie says, "Sorry. None of my business."

Sing shrugs. "No, that's okay. I just . . . I thought Lori would set her sights a little higher. I mean, she seems like the big fish around here."

"Are you kidding? What's better than a gorgeous rehearsal pianist?" Carrie pushes the door and they step into the hall. The harsh light from the bathroom briefly illuminates knots of people, dancing, speaking, watching.

Sing stays close to Carrie. "I don't know. I thought she'd be the type to date an apprentice." *Or a professor,* she thinks.

Carrie snorts. "Have you *seen* our apprentices this year?"

"There must be a few decent ones," Sing says. "And I don't think Lori would be picky as long as she got to wear someone with power." *Do I mean Lori?* she thinks. *Or my mother?*

"Students and apprentices don't mix," Carrie says. "Not ever. School policy. Got to keep things in their proper place, right?"

"Well, I don't know," Sing says. "That charming Apprentice Daysmoor—I'm sure the ladies have to try extra hard to keep away from him."

Carrie laughs now, and Sing likes the sound. She says, "What's the deal with him, anyway? Why is everyone so creeped out by him?"

"You don't think he's weird?"

"I don't know what to think. Is he an egomaniac or what?"

Carrie crosses the hall, three steps, and gazes out a black window. "Come here," she says. "Look at this."

Sing peers across the dark quad. Carrie points. "You see Archer?"

Archer sits opposite Hud, the dormitory in which they are standing, and like Hud, it is as square and drab as it can be—except for a strange round tower that rises inexplicably from one end. Sing looks at Carrie. "That must be the original tower. From when the first St. Augustine's was built."

"It's old as hell, yeah," Carrie says. "So besides the practice rooms, Archer's got the apprentice quarters. That tower is where Daysmoor lives."

Sing frowns, squinting at the shadowy shape; it looks like a huge, crusty barnacle latched on to the hull of a ship. "Now *that* is creepy."

"Put that crumbling old thing together with Daysmoor's perpetual scowl and murky past, and you've got the stuff of legend." Carrie leans against the wall.

"Murky past?" Sing isn't ready to go back into the room across the hall. "What, like a criminal record?"

Carrie laughs. "Not exactly. But how old would you say he was?"

Sing shrugs. "The same as the other apprentices. A bit older than you, maybe. Twenty? Twenty-one?"

"Yes. Well, that's the other fun thing about him. He's been an apprentice here for three years. It's true, you can look it up in the administration office."

Sing leans against the window. The glass is cold on her forehead. "Okay, so that works out."

"Yes, it does." Carrie smiles. "And it worked out three years ago, too, when my brother was a senior here, and Daysmoor had been here for three years."

"What?"

Carrie glances out the window and shrugs, putting her hands in her pockets. "Oh, you can't prove it. Most of the students don't seem to notice, somehow. The faculty look at you as though you're crazy if you suggest it. And sometimes I think we are crazy, those of us who know about him, like maybe my brother and I are closet conspiracy theorist crackpots and we're not even aware of it. Who knows? Maybe there's been a whole series of Apprentice Daysmoors, each as unpleasant as the last. I enjoy him, honestly. Apprentice Plays-poor—our eccentric little oddity."

Something in Sing twinges. "You talk like he's a novelty," she says. "I imagine there's *something* special about him, or he wouldn't be here."

Carrie turns back to her room. "You can imagine anything you want. And that's all you'll do, because no one ever hears him play. Come on." And she is through the doorway.

Sing hesitates, glancing at the cluster of bodies on the bed, red light shining on long blond hair next to copper. Lori leans close to Ryan and says something. He turns his head to speak to her, and their glowing faces are suddenly so close together; his eyes dart to her lips as she speaks again. Sing remembers those pink-glossed lips protruding with Lori's exaggerated vowels in St. Augustine's hall. She isn't particularly religious, but there was something *wrong* with those lips in what used to be a church. In what is still, for some, a holy place.

Sing doesn't go back into Carrie's room. She surveys the crowded hallway with little interest before making her way back to the stairs.

If I sang like Lori, maybe Ryan would be whispering to me on Carrie's bed right now. It's childish. But now, for the first time in her life, she wonders whether she will ever *really* sing. For the past two years, she has felt on the cusp of greatness—just one more lesson, one more soiree, one more vocalise, and she would be there. She has felt it bubbling, one note away from breaking through. One intangible element lacking.

But she doesn't feel like that now. Not with *Angelique* and Ryan and her small, past successes slipping away from her. Maybe it was her mother's greatness she felt, not her own, and now it is fading. New, vibrant stars are skyrocketing, old ones growing still and silent, a lovely, painted backdrop.

She pauses at the top of the landing and turns her face to a window. The great, black forest betrays no sign of life, no indication of a magical, wish-granting beast. Sing wonders what she would wish for given the opportunity.

Twenty-five

THERE HAD BEEN ANOTHER CAT, for a short time. The Cat could still sense him—*cat*—but the Sky, when it remembered, recalled him as a kindred spirit of the cosmos, tied to earth rather than space, but as its master, not its prisoner.

Still, most of the time, it was the Cat who was most awake. The Felix rubbed her neck against a tree, sniffed a patch of leaves, swiveled her ears toward the forest. That he was gone was certain, but that he had been *here* was just as certain, but fuzzy in her memory.

And now, in her cave on the summit, there was yet another cat. Like herself, but small. Easily torn apart, easily digested. But for some reason, she hadn't done this yet.

She had been bringing it food.

She had been curling her body around it at night to keep it warm.

She had been licking the soft fur between its ears.

Sometimes, something pricked her mind. Others like her, elsewhere. A time before rage and guilt and despair. But this feeling was always fleeting.

Twenty-six

WHAT DOES MUTATION FEEL LIKE? Sing climbs onto a picnic table and swings her leg over the moonlit wooden fence. Is it a tingle? A burn? A sickness? Or just silence? This lonely peak would be just the place to hide a secret toxic waste dump. Or a mad scientist's lair. What would her father say if she came home contaminated? *I know you are trying,* carina, *but the great sopranos—none of them are glowing green, eh? Do you think the major opera houses want green sopranos? And now you have developed a third eye, of all things! It will not do. Go practice your scales.*

But a wooden fence wouldn't be any sort of protection against toxic waste. It's probably the bright, mysterious DANGER signs, straight out of a sci-fi B movie, that are making her think these crazy thoughts.

The muffled noise of the party carries across the lawn and over the fence, punctuated by sharper, closer sounds—squeaking branches, crackling leaves, the hissing of the wind. Her father's warning, coupled with Marta's declaration that the Felix is real, bothers her. Even though the idea of a giant, mythical cat is ridiculous, something itches in her mind. Something that says, *This forest is real. The Felix is real.* She tries to toss the thought aside.

Perhaps the danger the signs warn of is simply that the land beyond the fence is wild and cold and tangled, no place for a wayward conservatory student. Sing drops to the crunchy ground, washed in gray light.

If Lori hadn't started singing, maybe Sing could have gone back into Carrie's room. But when she heard those bold, playful snatches of song, the familiar, knotted bitterness came creeping back, and she knew she had to go. Maybe for the night, maybe for just an hour, but she had to get away. No, not away—

To.

She had to come to the forest. It has been watching her, waiting for her, since her arrival on campus. Dark, lonely, and quiet. The forest is everything Sing hasn't known for two years.

Is she jealous of Lori Pinkerton? Of Ryan's attraction to her? Of her long blond hair? Her confidence? Her voice? Lori is so much like Barbara da Navelli, and Sing has spent the last two years trying to be like Barbara da Navelli. Could she be jealous of her own mother—her own *dead* mother?

Marta and Jenny didn't even notice her leave the party, and that's all right with her. She doesn't want them to see her now, not when she doesn't know who she is anymore.

The woods smell of winter, and she is glad she brought her thick school jacket. She starts walking along the fence but gradually moves away from it, keeping it on the edge of her vision. The forest floor crackles like flames even as she shivers. The pine trees cast straight, crisscrossing moon-shadows.

Quand il se trouvera . . . She begins to hum Angelique's most famous aria. At first, she isn't sure if she is humming only in her head or into the forest air as well. But the hum grows, and eventually the words come with it. Her voice spirals upward and entwines itself around the jagged branches, slipping over and under them and up into the sparkling sky.

It is the first time she has really sung in years.

Singing is so *effortless* here. She calls on the notes and they are there. She calls on the air, and its gentle pressure carries her voice and her whole body through the woods in every direction; the sound is a soft golden bubble.

Suddenly, the faintest of noises stops her. Her body is jolted back to earth, lungs first. Cold air burns her throat.

A rustling in the bushes.

Probably a raccoon or a fox. Or some kind of night bird.

The bushes are silent now. The sky has darkened with clouds. Sing tries to sense where the fence has gotten to without taking her eyes off the place where the noise came from.

Was that another rustle, or just the breeze through the leaves?

She sees again the image of the yellow DANGER signs. What dangers could possibly be out here? Bears? There are probably bears. But shouldn't they be hibernating?

She crouches, eyes straining at the dark underbrush. Another rustle, and two blue eyes appear, level with her waist. Frozen, Sing looks into the blue eyes and sees her fear reflected. Yet the eyes keep her in their gaze, wide and terrified but steady.

Despite her own prickling nerves and thudding heart, her instinct is to comfort this frightened creature. "Hello," she says softly, a coo, three legato notes. The eyes creep closer. "Who are you?" She keeps her voice clear and gentle. The eyes creep closer still, and the moonlight falls on soft fur, oversize triangular ears, and paws too big for the legs they are attached to.

Sing feels warm blood running through her body again as her own fear vanishes. "You're a kitten!" she says. "You're a big kitten, my love."

The big kitten studies her, eyes wide, ears swiveled in her direction. She feels him trying to connect, to ask, to communicate, but all he can do is look. And listen.

"Did you . . . did you hear me singing?" she asks, and his ears twitch. *I'm talking to a wild animal,* she thinks. *A big wild animal. With big teeth.*

But he's so adorable.

The big kitten blinks. Sing begins to hum again, and he closes his eyes—once, twice—in a cat-smile. She can't help a laugh that briefly interrupts the song.

The ashy smell of winter is weaker here by the shivering brush, and she is soothed by the black, silent trees that surround her. The conservatory's lights and movement are a thousand miles away; she is at the bottom of a giant lake of calm shadows and rippling starlight.

But something prickles her mind. Here next to her, in the legendary haunting grounds of Durand's great beast itself, is a cat. A big cat.

All around her is shadow and silver moonlight, vague shapes and colorless night. But the cat is vivid. He is solid, of that she is certain, but he seems to exist both here in the forest and elsewhere: a different space, a different part of her mind. She can see him so clearly.

But for his coloring, she would swear he is a large mountain lion cub. His clean, soft fur is an unusual light orange at his head and over his front legs, which deepens to downright unnatural shades of lavender and then deep purple around his midsection, continuing over his back legs. Tiny, silvery tufts are dotted here and there, particularly around his hindquarters and along his tail, which is nearly black at the very tip. He looks like dusk.

She allows herself to think the word, for the first time entertaining it as something true. Something real. *Felix.*

Could this be a—a baby Felix, then? She stops humming, and the big kitten opens his large, questioning eyes. She can't imagine being held by the malevolence of his gaze the way the Felix's victims surely would be. But there is something supernatural about him, a faint blurriness around his edges, the smallest suggestion of a glow from within the glistening blue.

"Felix?" she whispers.

He doesn't indicate the word means anything to him, and she

feels a relief she knows is unjustified. After all, why should a myth-ical creature know or care what humans call it?

But as the light breeze surrounds her with the comfortable fra-grance of dead leaves, she knows she doesn't want him to be Felix. "I'll call you Tamino," she says, "after Mozart's hero of *The Magic Flute,* who had to pass many tests to win the princess Pamina. I see from the ice in your eyes that you've been through the trial of water, and from the flames in your fur that you've done the trial of fire."

This suggestion seems to agree with Tamino; he sits, awkwardly lowering his back end and wrapping his long tail lightly around his legs. Sing exhales.

Tamino is waiting for something. A song.

Twenty-seven

WHEN THE BREEZE TURNS from fresh to chilly, when her body and voice begin to complain subtly of the lateness of the hour, Sing leaves Tamino and makes her way back to the fence. He does not follow, at least not where she can see him, although she thinks she feels his presence as she moves through the bony, clattery brush.

She finds a dead tree lying next to the fence and gets herself up; it will be enough to allow her to clamber back over. As she stands on the tree trunk, grasping the fence posts, it takes her a moment to get oriented. The strange stone tower sits enigmatically at the other end of a neat lawn, and she realizes she's all the way across campus, behind Archer.

Just as she shifts her weight to throw a leg over the fence, a voice crackles through the still darkness, causing her to gasp. "Playing in the woods, are we?"

She peers back into the forest. There is no one around. Her body tingles. She tries to remain completely still, but the cold and her nerves are making her hands shake.

The voice says, "Singing to the trees? Do you work in the choreography, too?"

Now she knows that grating, ugly sound. "Apprentice Day-smoor?" Her ears ring with their straining into the silence.

"Up here," is the response, and she raises her eyes to find the pale face of a ghost staring back at her from a high branch. She covers her mouth.

"Oh, for goodness' sake." Daysmoor hops down to another thick branch and starts to lower himself to the ground. "I'm not going to eat you, you know. Although I can't speak for everything that lives in this forest. Crossing that fence was profoundly stupid of you."

She finds her voice. "What are you doing out here?"

"None of your business," he says, jumping down. "What are *you* doing out here, besides trying to get yourself killed? Communing with . . . nature?"

What does he mean by that? Did he see the big kitten? He is close to her now, the warmth from his body making her realize just how cold she is.

"Just sprawling around the forest like I own the place," she says. That clearly catches him off guard. He tilts his head, his dark eyes fixed on her, and for a few long seconds, she isn't sure if he's going to scold or laugh.

But he does neither. Instead, he hops onto the dead tree and vaults a little awkwardly over the fence. "Don't come into this forest again. You should be in bed. Or at Carrie Stewart's party, hoping no one finds out you've got wine coolers."

"How did you—"

But he cuts her off with a violent gesture. "Get down."

"What?"

"Get down!" he hisses. "Behind the fence!"

A robed figure is striding across the lawn toward the fence. She can't be sure, but it looks as though he is wearing black faculty robes. Daysmoor goes to meet him, a distance from Sing's hiding place.

The black-robed figure says something Sing can't make out; his tone is low and calm. Daysmoor answers. They continue like this for a few minutes, voices getting louder as the conversation progresses. Finally, Sing hears Daysmoor shout, "What are you going to do? Lock me up? You can't stop me."

The black-robed figure continues speaking. He puts an arm around the apprentice, who throws it off violently. Then the figure raises his voice, and Daysmoor is silent. He allows himself to be led back toward Archer, and their path takes them closer to where Sing is hiding. As they pass through a pool of moonlight, she sees the face of the black-robed figure—the Maestro.

When they have gone a safe distance, Sing scrambles over the fence to head for the quad and her bed. But something catches her eye—a flicker by the fence where the two men stood. There in the cold, dark grass, her fingers find a small stone. It rests on the leaves as though it has been dropped, and when she holds it up to the moon, it glitters. She puts it in her pocket, and its strangely cold surface makes her leg tingle.

Sing turns again to the two men and watches them recede into the shadows. The Maestro's arm never leaves Daysmoor's hunched shoulders.

Twenty-eight

GLORIA STEWART WOULD HAVE APPROVED of the venue for the first competition in her name. Carnegie Hall was one of her favorite places to perform.

"I'm very proud of you, Nathan," George said, brushing a speck of lint off the young man's deep black tuxedo. The garish lighting in the small, decrepit room in which they waited deepened the shadows on Nathan's face.

The other pianists in the room chatted nervously and drank glasses of water. George watched them out of the corner of his eye. "Well, my friend," he said, "it's time for me to go."

Nathan looked at his watch. "Now? You're sure you can't take a later flight?"

"I'd stay the night if I could," George said. "You know that. But I've got exams to give in the morning." It used to be hard to lie to such a beautiful face. It was getting easier.

"I'm so grateful to you, George," Nathan said, embracing him. "For everything."

"Yes, yes." George pulled away. "Just remember—whatever happens, it's for the best." He adjusted Nathan's boutonniere, a white rose.

"Of course," Nathan said.

There were no real elevators, designed for people rather than pianos, in the recesses of Carnegie Hall, so by the time George had hurried down six flights of echoey stairs, he was a little out of breath. Even so, when he saw the taxi across the street, he ran.

He checked his watch six times on the way to the airport. It would be fine. Last minute, but fine. The important thing was that he be as far away as possible when Nathan began to play.

He did feel a pang when he pictured Nathan striding onto the stage, gilt behind him and polished wood beneath him. For a moment, everyone in the hall would know in their hearts he belonged there. If only George could see it just once.

He patted his pocket. The crystal was ice and getting colder as the taxi sped away.

It was for the best.

Twenty-nine

S ING IS ALWAYS MUTE in her dreams.

Except tonight.

Tonight, she awakens euphoric. She *sang* in her dream. It was so easy. The missing piece was there—if only she could remember how to do it.

A tingling feeling spreads across her body. She puts a hand to her chest and finds the little crystal that was lying in the dark grass. It hangs around her neck now in place of the teardrop pearl, fitted into the same grasping, gold tentacles. Why did she replace her mother's pearl with this strange little object?

And who does it belong to?

Be professional. Ryan is just another accompanist.

Archer's glossy white walls and square windows make Sing think of an elementary school, but Apprentice Daysmoor's strange stone tower rising from one side looks more like some kind of mountain stronghold. She tries not to look at it as she crosses the quad.

The campus seems so small this morning. Sing feels the sprawling forest pushing up against the fence on all sides. But what did she find there? Escape? Yes, but only temporarily. The forest is not a refuge. She thinks of the big kitten, standing as tall as her waist. She must have imagined his weighty expressions, his attention to her singing. He must have been a curious mountain lion, and she's lucky he didn't bite her. She thinks for the first time of the wayward hikers with their throats torn out, and she shivers.

She pushes open one of Archer's metal doors, set with windows whose glass is crisscrossed with wire. To her left are the student practice rooms; to her right, a hallway with two doors marked REHEARSAL ROOM 1: INDIVIDUALS and REHEARSAL ROOM 2: SMALL GROUPS. She takes a deep breath, adjusts the bag over her shoulder, and knocks on the first door.

"Come in." It is Ryan's voice, much more chipper than Sing feels.

He sits on a folding chair, looking at the brand-new issue of *The Trumpeter*. His uniform is crisp and clean; she detects the pleasant scent of laundry detergent. Without looking up, he says, "Sunshine isn't here yet."

Her eyebrows gather in confusion, but then she realizes he must be referring to Apprentice Daysmoor. His impertinence shocks her just a bit.

"I'm surprised they've cranked one of these out already." He rustles the student newspaper, then reads aloud, "'Sing da Navelli: Second-Generation Superstar?'"

Sing turns red. "Oh, no!"

Ryan peers theatrically at the article. "A-*ha*! Look at all these secrets! Oh, you're going to have a hard time living this down!"

"Let me see it!" Sing says.

He laughs and hands over the paper. She reads and exhales. It isn't a big deal, really. Just a little paragraph nestled amid a few other student profiles. Jenny's first article.

"You're quite the celebrity!" Ryan says.

She pulls out her score and places it on a music stand. "Hey, I'm sorry I couldn't go with you guys last night." She hopes her voice sounds normal and not as nervous as she feels around him.

"Don't you worry about it," he says. "The place closed early, anyway. Some other time, huh? You and me." He sits at the piano and flips open a score.

"Okay." *You and me.* Did he just ask her out? Sing rolls her shoulders and pretends to be interested in the wall. Ryan begins to play something fast and flashy, and when she glances at him, he makes a face. She laughs. He is fooling around, but he's also showing off—and she realizes just how highly skilled a musician he is.

"Nine oh two," he says after a moment. "Shall we start without him?" It's a challenge—no, not a challenge: a dare. Now she catches his eye, and he smiles, shoulders relaxed. He is not angry with her after all.

"I don't care," she says. "I don't care what he thinks, anyway." She is immediately embarrassed, but exhilarated, too. Why did she say that?

Ryan laughs in a high voice, a real laugh, and keeps playing the fast, flashy music. "Well, good for you. I don't either. I'm only interested in the Gloria Stewart competition, to be honest. Opera Workshop is such a pain in the ass—except for the lovely company, of *course*." Sing blushes. "And I don't much care for apprentices, anyway. They're just mistakes the administration wants to keep close to home. Keep them from spoiling DC's reputation in the real world."

Sing frowns. "What do you mean?"

"Oh, everybody knows," Ryan says, still playing. "If a student is less than competent, they don't want him out playing for other people, do they? Other people who'll say, 'Sheesh, DC gave *that* guy a certificate? Looks like things are going downhill.' So they let 'em cook a little longer if they're not quite done yet. That's all."

"Like Daysmoor," Sing says, tingling from the gossip.

Ryan's eyes sparkle. "Oh, I bet *he's* got a real good story. You're friends with that *Trumpeter* girl, right? You guys should do some digging on Apprentice Plays-poor!"

Sing tries to swallow the jealousy that crept up her throat when Ryan mentioned Jenny, whose name he didn't even know. On cue, the door opens and Daysmoor slouches in. Did he hear their conversation? If so, he makes no indication of it; he just drips into a chair and says, "That doesn't sound like *Angelique*."

Ryan finishes with a flourish. "Liszt," he says. "The handsomest composer who ever lived." He winks at Sing, whose heart jumps. "It's my piece for Gloria Stewart International."

Daysmoor stretches his legs out onto another chair. "I'm sure the judges will be very impressed with all your fast little notes."

"I'm sure they will be." Ryan smirks. "I suppose *you're* playing something terribly serious and meaningful and tortured."

"I'm not playing anything," Daysmoor says flatly. "You don't need to worry. Competitions aren't my thing."

Ryan raises his eyebrows and glances furtively at Sing. "Do tell."

But Daysmoor simply looks at his watch and says, "Why haven't you started rehearsal?"

"We were waiting for your blessing, sir," Ryan says, and Sing nearly laughs.

The apprentice betrays no emotion. "What is it to me? I'm not going to be out on that stage underrehearsed."

Now Sing doesn't feel like laughing anymore. *I'm not going to be out on that stage, either.*

"Oh, by the way . . ." Daysmoor reaches into a pocket, finds a blue piece of paper, and holds it out in Sing's direction. She hesitates. "It won't bite," he says. "That much."

Ryan clucks. "Uh-oh, what did you do?" His tone is somber, but Sing notices a sly smile.

"What do you mean?" she asks, suddenly shaky. What is that blue paper? Is she in trouble?

Daysmoor shakes the paper. "I suggest we start this rehearsal. Please take your censure and we can get on with it."

"Censure?" A dull horror creeps up from Sing's stomach into her chest. She gingerly takes the blue paper from Daysmoor's outstretched hand. "What—" She unfolds the paper and stares down at it. Below the embossed letterhead, her name, and the date is the word INFRACTION, followed by the words *Trespassing, reckless endangerment* and three check boxes. The two boxes by NOTIFICATION and WARNING are unchecked, but the one next to CENSURE has a thick black mark in it, presumably made with the same pen used for the elegant signature at the bottom—President Martin.

Daysmoor lets out a frustrated sigh. "Someone shouldn't have taken a little field trip into the woods last night. The president frowns on that sort of thing. Three of these and the trustees are notified. Meaning you're expelled. Okay? Now can we start?"

Sing gapes at him.

Ryan whistles. "Running around in the woods, huh?"

"Mr. Larkin," Daysmoor says, a little less evenly than usual, "if you would be so kind as to open your score and focus on music instead of gossip." Ryan obediently takes his score but wags an admonishing finger at Sing.

The lightness with which Ryan seems to be treating the situation makes her feel a little better. Just a little. How easy is it to get a censure? Will she get three without even knowing it, just as she never suspected she'd get in trouble for visiting the forest? Correction—she never suspected she'd get *caught* visiting the forest.

And Daysmoor *ratted her out,* as her father would say.

Traitor! How could he pretend to be hiding her from the Maestro, only to go blabbing to the president that she was there? She studies his face, but he is impossible to read. She folds the censure and puts it in her pocket, seething.

"Page 324," Daysmoor says, businesslike. Sing sees Ryan arch an eyebrow, though he doesn't say anything as he flips through his score. She looks at the page over his shoulder and finds the place in her own score—*"Quand il se trouvera dans la forêt sombre,"* Angelique worrying about the fate of her love, Prince Elbert. The most difficult aria in the opera. Sing inhales, unsure—she is comfortable with her French, but in truth she has never sung this aria in front of anyone else. *He chose this one on purpose,* she thinks, anger at the apprentice starting to thicken. *He wants to see me fail.*

"Let's see how it goes," Daysmoor goes on. "You need to pay attention to the lines, Miss da Navelli. Your phrasing in the duet yesterday was lousy. Please observe the composer's markings."

"I always observe the composers' markings," Sing says.

"Then we'll have no problems." Daysmoor closes his eyes. "When you're ready, Mr. Larkin."

Ryan begins with the famous five-beat introduction. The thick chords have always made Sing think of heavy footsteps, perhaps Prince Elbert going to his grave, or perhaps Death himself approaching. Ryan leans into the keys, face solemn.

Sing breathes. *"Quand il se trouvera . . ."*

Sad and light, she thinks. *Innocent.*

" *. . . dans la forêt som*— Sorry, wait. That rhythm was wrong."

"I know," Daysmoor says.

"Can we go back?"

The apprentice sighs. "Beginning again, Mr. Larkin."

"We don't have to go all the way back—I just—"

"Beginning."

Sing rolls her shoulders as Ryan begins again. *Stupid! You* know *this music!*

"Quand il se trouvera dans la forêt sombre, il se comprendra . . ."

Why does her voice sound so strange? Harsh? *If only he'd heard me last night, in the woods,* she thinks. *If only I could sing like that here.* She backs off.

Daysmoor barks, "Don't try to disguise inadequacy as emotion."

She falters a little. *What did he mean by that?* Should she sing louder? She tries, but her sound goes all wobbly. She retreats again.

"Stop." Daysmoor frowns at her. "What are you doing?"

She stares at him, mouth open. "I . . ."

"Relax, breathe, support. Okay?"

"Okay."

Relax. With his scowling face looking at her the whole time? *Sure.*

They begin again. She tries to breathe. Why are her lungs so small all of a sudden? *"Quand il se trouvera—"*

"Stop." This time, Daysmoor rises and crosses to her. "What is the problem?"

Her body is frozen. "I don't understand."

"Where is the rest of your voice?"

"I . . . my voice?"

He fixes her with that black gaze. "When you concentrate, you have notes. You have rhythms. You have air and tone and line. But there's a hole in your voice so big I could roll a bass drum through it."

"What . . . do you mean?"

"*When* you concentrate," he says. "And when you don't, your nerves take over. This is not the place for nerves, Miss da Navelli. I don't care how terrible you think you are, or what type of weird psychological baggage you're carrying around. You're letting your anxiety ruin your singing. Get it together or get out."

Sing is stunned. No one has ever spoken to her like this. She is paralyzed, her whole body sparking. Ryan peers silently at the score.

The apprentice retreats and pours himself over two chairs, tilting his head back and closing his eyes in a final sort of way. "Angelique's *first* aria, then," he says. "The easy one. And continue from there, please. I might close my eyes in order to listen better. If I start to snore, it means I'm listening especially closely."

Thirty

G EORGE KEPPLER SAT AT HIS desk, making notes in the enormous, yellowed score of Mahler's Second Symphony. The radio behind him spilled a live broadcast from the Metropolitan Opera into the dark little office, a performance of *Romeo and Juliet* starring the famous young soprano Barbara da Navelli. Outside, just visible beyond the small window, the trees glittered from top to bottom—living ice sculptures, rattling and creaking in the snowy gusts.

Looking at the score again made George almost giddy, brought him back to his ambitious days as a young conductor. Was it during only his second year as maestro of the conservatory that he had last performed Mahler 2? He smiled. What nerve, choosing such a monumental piece! It hadn't been half bad, either.

His smile faded as he tried to calculate the year. Could it really have been fifty-five—no, *sixty-five*—years ago? Yes. That would make him how old now? Ninety-seven.

Slowly, unconsciously, George slid open his upper right desk drawer and pulled out a small mirror. He inspected his face. The lines on his forehead and around his mouth and eyes were a little more pronounced than the last time he'd looked. Just a little. *Ninety-*

seven? It wasn't possible. No one would think him a day over fifty. He could pass for forty-five. His hair wasn't even gray.

The crystal was in his pocket, as always. He slid it out and put it to his face, his fingers running over the lines around his mouth. Time would not forget him forever.

A knock at the door startled him; he closed his fingers around the crystal and let his hand fall to his lap. "Come in!"

A young man wearing apprentice robes poked his head in. Strikingly handsome, with blue-black hair and eyes like soft coal.

Nathan.

"Are you busy?"

George shook his head. "Not at all. Just marking up the Mahler. Have a seat."

"Thanks." The apprentice pulled up a leather chair. George noticed an unusual lightness about him this morning; he was known for his easy manner, but today he seemed especially cheerful—excited, even.

"Look at this." He slid an opened letter onto George's desk.

The letter was short and official. George read it through twice, examined the signature at the bottom, and laid his hands flat on the desk. The two men sat in silence.

Finally, Nathan said, "Europe and the Far East, then back here—a full two years! Pending the live audition, which I'm not afraid of. I know you're nervous about things like this—and they do suggest I get representation, of course—but don't you see? This proves I'm good enough! I can have a career! All my years of studying and practicing and teaching—"

"Where did this come from?" George couldn't keep the irritation from his voice. What he meant was, *How did someone else hear you play? Someone who mattered?*

Nathan's smile faded. He folded his hands. "My students wonder why I'm not established, you know. It's harder and harder to make them think it's just my—age."

"What do you care if your students wonder about you?" George said. "What does that have to do with anything?"

"Apparently one of them recorded me and sent it—"

"What! I told you—"

"I didn't know he'd done it!" Nathan sighed forcefully. "They often record their lessons—why would I be suspicious? Why don't you want anyone to hear me? Why do you want to keep me here?"

George tapped his desk. "Don't you remember what happened?"

Nathan's gaze fell. "That was years ago," he said, but there was a note of defeat in his voice. George had become used to this note, always clear, always in tune, just as he had taught Nathan to feel it that horrible night in New York. But it had been so long since the Gloria Stewart competition. George feared more and more that some of his protégé's old swagger would return.

He studied Nathan's face, exactly as he remembered it from all those years ago. Whatever time-slowing magic the crystal held, it was meant for him. George—somehow—was just managing to absorb a little bit of it. A familiar pang of panic stabbed him. What would happen to the crystal if its true master left? Would it still radiate its magic, or would it crumble to dust?

Would Nathan *die* if he were separated too long from the crystal that kept him young?

Would George?

He took a deep breath. "Look, Nathan . . ." But he couldn't find the right words.

Nathan leaned forward. "It's *me*, George. I can handle the world outside Dunhammond. You had no problem with me coming along to all your international engagements. Prague, Moscow, Vienna, Paris—you certainly had no problem *then*. My God, what happened to the old days?"

"Those days are gone." Maestro Keppler was surprised to feel a lurch in his chest as he said it. "They're gone. The conservatory is a safe place for you. People forget you here. I believe it is the forest that protects you from their questions." He did believe that.

The young man said quietly, "My students are going to keep asking questions."

"Well, perhaps it is no longer safe for you to teach private lessons." The Maestro hadn't meant to say it. But now that he had, he was resolute. It was the best solution. "You can still practice, of course, and help with the voice students occasionally—you do have enormous talent there. But this is really the best way."

"You can't take my students!" Nathan cried, growing pale.

The Maestro threw up his hands. "Your students don't even *remember* you! Three years you taught Molly Stewart, and she *introduced* herself to you at the alumni banquet last week!"

"They may not remember me, but I remember them," Nathan said quietly.

The Maestro's face became hard. "I'll recommend to the president that your talents would be put to better use elsewhere."

Nathan's mouth was set, his eyes dark. "It doesn't matter, anyway," he said. "Tell the president whatever you want. I'm going on that tour. You can't stop me."

He was serious. He was going to leave. *Leave.*

George looked back at that youthful, defiant face and struggled to keep his own face placid as the anger welled inside him.

"I've given up a lot for you, Nathan, so we could be here. A real career."

"I never asked you to."

"Damn it, I've given you *everything*. Even your damn name!" George's heart felt hot, pounding against his ribs. His fingers clutched the crystal as he seethed, face reddening, breath becoming blustery. Nathan said nothing.

From the desk, a boy looked happily out of an old photograph. Crooked teeth, muddy clothes. George felt his brother's faded stare, the real Nathan, the Nathan who should have survived that plunge into the river. Who was this ungrateful young man who stared at him now with such ferocity, jaw set, from the other side of the desk? He clenched the crystal hidden in his hand so hard, he thought his bones might break.

And as he did so, a strange thing happened—Nathan's breathing became more rapid, his shoulders stiffened, and he doubled over in his chair. Fascinated, George squeezed the crystal more tightly, using both hands now, hidden under the desk where the apprentice could not see them. He channeled his rage through his fingers; he could almost feel it sparking. Nathan began gasping violently and slid out of his chair altogether.

George was exhilarated. He knew he was doing it, through the crystal, with his strength or his anger or the sheer force of his will. He released his grip and tried to force a neutral expression, though he could barely keep from grinning. Adrenaline shot through his chest and arms and legs. Nathan looked up, eyebrows drawn, eyes wide, as though he had seen a monster.

The Maestro leaned forward. "I *can* stop you, my boy. I can."

Something about Nathan changed in that moment. The lightness around him dissolved, his handsome face fell into an ugly, droopy mask, and his eyes dried into hard, dull stones. He left without another word.

The Maestro tossed the crystal onto his desk. He put his hands to his face and laughed, then sighed, stopping himself before the sigh became a sob.

And so I have robbed the world of one of its great artists. It was unconscionable. But it was for the boy's protection, wasn't it? George couldn't just pick up and leave the conservatory, follow Nathan across continents, watch from the shadows as the world fell in love with him. No, Nathan must stay here. With the crystal. With George.

And now, George knew how to make him stay.

The Maestro laid his head on his vast desk.

After seventy-two years, it was the first time Nathan Daysmoor had asked to leave.

Thirty-one

SING IS SO MAD, SHE COULD STOMP. She could stomp right on Apprentice Daysmoor's smug face. How dare he? How *dare* he say those terrible things to her? How *dare* he sleep through the rest of her coaching session? Maybe if he weren't up all hours sitting in trees, he'd be able to stay awake.

And how *dare* he report her to the president and get her a censure? She should report *him*. She should go straight to the Maestro, request a new coach, turn Daysmoor in for being the useless, self-absorbed lump he is.

She storms into the lobby of Hud, wishing the doors weren't so frustratingly civilized and would allow themselves to be slammed. But no, despite her best effort, they gently hiss closed as she clomps across the lobby to the stairwell.

Jenny answers the door after three sharp knocks. "Sing, what's up? I was just about to go to quartet practice."

"I need your help." Sing brushes past her and plops onto the closest bed. Jenny and Marta's room looks like it was decorated by a monster that vomits dirty laundry, hair care products, New Age boutiquery, and sheet music.

"Um, okay," Jenny says.

"I need dirt on Apprentice Daysmoor. Something really embarrassing. Or awful. Ryan says all apprentices have stories."

Jenny cocks her head. "Wow. I know he's a wet blanket, but why the venom?"

"It doesn't matter," Sing says, trying not to think about the question. "Do you have any info on him? Can you get some from your newspaper or something?"

"Generally, if the newspaper has interesting info, they print it," Jenny says. "But I can maybe dig through the archives. There isn't much digital right now, and I'm sure as hell not going to read three years' worth of papers just to help you satisfy your weird rage, but we are developing a computer directory that might be useful."

"Thanks." Sing strides out of the room and down the stairs to the lobby. She sinks into an ugly maroon chair and tosses her *Angelique* score onto a battered coffee table. With sharp, jerky motions, she pulls a notebook and pencil from her backpack and begins writing.

> *Dear Papà,*
>   *How are rehearsals for the new season going?* [Interest in what he's doing, a good way to start.] *School is fine. My classes are fairly decent so far, except trigonometry, which is hard, and Nature of Music, where we just listen to birds all day. I'm understudying the lead in the opera.* [This revelation might elicit a curt note to the Maestro or President Martin, but she doesn't hold out much hope it would change anything.] *Rehearsals are fine, except for my coaching, which is useless. I don't even have a real coach, just some Apprentice—Daysmoor—who sleeps all the time and doesn't know anything about singing.* [Offhand enough not to seem like whining.] *Anyway, the scenery is very nice, and I can't wait to visit the village. Say hi to Zhin for me. I hope she is making you proud!*
>   *Baci,*
>   *Sing*

She frowns at the last two sentences, then erases them.

She can still hear Daysmoor's horrible, raspy voice. *Breathe. Support.* No kidding. Did he think that was helpful advice, that she didn't know singing requires *air*? *Stuck-up little diva,* he called her. Since when is "diva" a bad word? A diva is a queen, just like Barbara da Navelli was—queen of the stage, queen of the business.

Sing knows she struggles with her own diva-ness; her mother was always telling her to act the part more. *If you play a thing strongly enough,* she used to say, *you make it true.*

Yes. Yes. Make it true.

Writing the letter has helped her anger to subside. She lets her shoulders fall and sinks into the chair. Then she reads it over one more time. It's very *diva,* she realizes. Her mother would be proud.

She tears it out of her notebook and rips it up, clutching the pieces in her fist.

Thirty-two

I N THE PARKING LOT, swirls of bodies huddle in groups, duck into cars, shake umbrellas. Gray clouds spit out masses of rain in bad-tempered torrents. Sing and Marta stand awkwardly in the main doorway to Hector Hall, rain pattering in a steady hum punctuated by short, blustery bursts.

Sing hasn't worn her regulation raincoat before; it looks more like a black garbage bag tied in the middle. "We don't have a car," she says, making an indeterminate gesture at the weather. "You want to walk all the way in this?"

Marta peers through the rain. "Mr. Bernard said he could take a few people." Her raincoat, though still garbage bag–esque, looks slightly better than Sing's because she's taller and thinner.

Hopping a ride with the teacher. Great. Sing pulls her regulation rain hat down over her eyes.

"Don't you want to go?" Marta says. "It's supposed to be a blast."

Mr. Bernard's famous getting-to-know-you excursions are sup-posedly one of the highlights of making Opera Workshop. But Sing doesn't feel up to a rollicking night on the town.

Still, it is an opportunity to make connections. "Yeah," she says,

pushing her hands into her garbage bag pockets. "We should probably schmooze, right?"

"I've heard it's the thing to do," Marta says, laughing a little.

Sing can't picture Marta schmoozing. She realizes with a pang
of pity that Marta will never have a career without this essential
skill. "It's how the business works," she says. "It's how my mother
got her career, really."

Marta seems taken aback. "Your mother was *wonderful,* Sing.
She was *amazing.*"

Sing feels her cheeks reddening. "Well, yeah, she was." *Was she?*
"But she wouldn't have been anything without my father. He already had a name, you know. He was already world-famous. She
used that." Marta's gaze snaps away. Sing doesn't know why, but
she continues, speaking softly to the back of Marta's shiny, plastic
shoulders. "She would have used anyone, I think, who could have
helped her. I'm not sure she even loved him."

Marta turns back but doesn't acknowledge Sing's words, which
is just as well. "Thought I saw Mr. Bernard."

Sing squints through the rain, half hoping their teacher has already gone. Her eyes are drawn to a cozy scene over by a little alcove,
and after a moment she realizes she is staring.

You're obsessing. She hears Jenny's voice even though she's not
there. *That's not true,* she tells herself, turning away. She isn't even
remotely interested in what Ryan and Lori Pinkerton are doing
over there under that umbrella. Not even remotely.

"I like your necklace," Marta says, studying the strange crystal
Sing now wears every day.

Sing says, "Thanks," but tucks the necklace into her shirt, where
it chills her skin.

Marta shouts, "Hey! Mr. Bernard! You have room for us?"

Please, no, Sing thinks. But Marta grabs her elbow and leads her
across the lot to where Mr. Bernard is standing next to a decrepit
old coupe. "But of course!" he says. "There's always room for a
couple of sophisticated ladies!"

Sing insists Marta take the front and clambers into the cramped, muggy backseat. Her knees press into the back of Marta's seat as the coupe wheezes itself to life.

"I can't wait to start blocking *Angelique*," Mr. Bernard says, the car still in park. "We're going ultratrad on this one—none of that 'setting it in an office building with everyone in business suits' crap. We are talking *wigs*! Period costumes! Backdrops with trees, not triangles and splotches or whatever the hell else is *arteestic* lately." Marta laughs, and Sing can't help but join her. Mr. Bernard taps the steering wheel. "Sorry, girls, we're waiting for one more. Sheesh, I'm going to be late to my own party. Oh, here's Cinderella now!" He waves. The rain on the window obscures the figure crossing the lot toward them.

"Is that Apprentice Daysmoor?" Marta asks. "Is he coming?"

"Sure." Mr. Bernard creaks the car into gear as the figure approaches. "Wouldn't miss it!"

Sing says, "*The* Apprentice Daysmoor? The one who looks like a corpse?"

"Only less charismatic?" Mr. Bernard adds, then says, "Sorry! Sorry, forget I said that."

Marta giggles. "Oh, he's not that bad."

The door creaks open and Daysmoor folds himself up in the seat next to Sing, knees up to his chest. She turns to the window as the car lurches into gear.

"Glad to have you with us, Nathan," Mr. Bernard says as they rattle along in the rain.

"One of us has to make an appearance, and George sure as hell wasn't going to come," Daysmoor says.

"Delightful. Well, I hope you'll grace us with a performance later. There's a first time for everything, right?"

Sing frowns. Performance? What kind of dinner is this?

Daysmoor doesn't answer, and Sing glances at him. He is staring out the window. Thinking about his last "performance"?

Marta's hair bobs. "I've been thinking, Mr. Bernard, about my character. You know, in Greek mythology . . ."

And she's off. Sing likes Marta, but it just seems like her ears turn off when Marta starts in about mythology.

Daysmoor is absorbed in the misty trees ambling past. Sing asks, "So what's this performance?"

He doesn't turn to her. "You'll see." He doesn't say it in a way that invites her to investigate further.

Sing huffs, not caring if he hears. *Fine.*

The car crackles through some sizable puddles as the raindrops rattle the windows. Mr. Bernard and Marta chatter away in the front seat.

"It's just a stupid party game," Daysmoor says after a moment.

"Fine," Sing says, more rudely than she meant to.

Now Daysmoor turns to her, fixing his shadowed eyes on her face, and she gets a strange sensation in her stomach. Quietly, almost as though he doesn't want the front seat to hear, he says, "That—that song you were singing in front of the Woolly, the night of the Welcome Gathering. Just sing that."

She feels her mouth open. "The *farfallina* song? It's just a kids' song. It's silly."

He turns away again. "Or don't," he snaps. "I don't really care."

Thirty-three

IT IS THE DAY THE FELIX'S CHILD goes missing.

No longer content with the songs of birds and streams, he has been tempted by *other* sounds: the pining of violins, the airy babble of flutes, and above all, the enchanting, mysterious wails and growls of human voices. And the girl, who made the sounds he prefers over all others.

The clouds have been gathering worriedly for days, finding and clinging to one another; some ripple and billow, some drift quietly in a morose calm. The Felix's child pads hesitantly away from the dark softness of the den and into the gray afternoon light.

He must find the sounds again.

Thirty-four

THE VILLAGE OF DUNHAMMOND huddles quietly at the base of the mountain whose snowcapped summit watches over the conservatory. Main Street is home to most of the local businesses, while a few small farms nestle along the smaller dirt roads. Low stone walls trail out from the center of town in all directions like a spiderweb.

The Mountain Grill is not entirely equipped to handle the bubbly, wriggly, forte group of students who follow Mr. Bernard through the low, dark front door into the low, dark dining room. Tables are hurriedly pushed together in a row; the lone waitress scurries back to the kitchen and appears again a moment later, looking frazzled.

Sing and Marta sit next to each other at the end of the row of tables. Mr. Bernard is in his element, patting students on the back and remembering everyone's names even though it's still the first week of school and all the students are wearing identical clothing. Daysmoor acquires some kind of beverage nearly instantly and slouches into a chair at the corner of the table, not speaking to anyone. The empty chairs gradually fill with bodies until there are only two remaining seats, the ones directly across from Sing and

Marta. And it appears they will remain empty until the low door creaks open once more and Lori and Ryan stumble in, laughing.

Sing stiffens. Lori and Ryan sit down, Lori greeting Marta like an old friend while retaining one hundred percent of Ryan's focus.

"I don't think we've really met," Sing says as Lori is turning back to Ryan. "I'm Sing."

"Oh," Lori says. "Hi, Sing. Nice to meet you."

She hasn't told me her name, Sing thinks. *She assumes I know it.*

Lori snakes her left arm around Ryan's right. "And you know Ryan Larkin, of course."

"Yes," Sing says, not meeting Ryan's gaze, which she thinks is probably on Lori in any case.

"Sing is a singer, too," Marta says.

"Lucky, with that name!" Lori laughs. "Anyway, of course I know all about Sing. She's my understudy." She leans in, and rose fragrance prickles Sing's nose. "You must be very talented!"

Sing shrugs. "It's just an understudy."

"She *is* talented," Ryan says. "She sang a Janice Bailey vocalise for her placement." Sing's heart gives a hopeful flutter.

Lori raises her eyebrows. "Wow! How did George like that?"

She means the Maestro, Sing realizes, and wonders if she calls him George to his face. "Not very much."

Lori frowns, jutting her lip out in a mock pout. "He is *so* old-fashioned sometimes. Don't worry. I'm sure you sounded *great*."

Sing stares, glassy-eyed, at the remains of her cheeseburger. Lori is telling a story about losing the heel of one of her designer shoes just before she had to go onstage for a recital.

"So I just kicked off the other one! I mean, the dress was right to the floor, right? Who was going to know? But when I did my bows, one of my *naked feet* poked out. Oh, my God, I thought Benny was going to *die*."

"Benny" would be legendary composer Benjamin Stanhope,

who gives master classes at Fire Lake during the summers, and Lori clearly enjoys the admiring gasps her clumsy name-drop prompts. Sing purses her lips. None of these people know that "Benny" is famously outgoing and is on a first-name basis with legions of students.

Lori barrels on. "It's so lucky Hayley had convinced me to get a pedi the day before! At least my toes were presentable!"

Everyone laughs except Sing. Even Marta, whose smile hasn't faded all evening, chuckles a little.

"Hayley can always be counted on to peer pressure you into a spa," says Ryan, and Lori punches his arm playfully.

"You know you love the spa!" she says. "Let's see your pedi! Come on, I know your tootsies are all pretty!"

Sing wonders if she could possibly fake food poisoning to get out of the rest of dinner. It wouldn't be that hard to make herself vomit.

At least Apprentice Daysmoor, when he glances their way, seems even more nauseated with Lori than Sing is. He has spent most of the evening blearily contemplating his salad, as though it's trying to communicate with him and he isn't impressed with what it has to say.

Mr. Bernard rises and taps his water glass with his fork. "Ladies and gentlemen!" The chatter dies down. Even Lori composes herself and turns politely toward the head of the table. "It is time for the Noble Call!"

Sing looks at Marta, who shrugs. Some of the students look confused, but others laugh or cover their faces. An older boy conspicuously makes to leave, but Mr. Bernard pushes him down, laughing, and says, "Just for that, Derek, you're first!"

Derek, whom Sing recognizes as one of the chorus members, protests, but Mr. Bernard shakes his head. "I am lord of these lands, and I decree that you shall be first! Noble Call!"

"What's a Noble Call?" Marta whispers.

"Some kind of tradition," Ryan says. "Irish or English or

something. The Noble—that's the person throwing the party—has the right to make everyone else perform."

Sing groans. So this is what Mr. Bernard was talking about in the car. Why is her life nothing but performances?

Ryan laughs, reaches across the table to pat her hand—thank goodness she had her hand resting there!—and says, "It's not bad, really. You don't have to do anything if you don't want to. You could just say, 'My cheeseburger was really good,' or something. He won't pick you early, since you're new, so just watch everyone else and decide."

Derek has chosen to recite a poem, something about a man who gets drunk and wakes up in a ditch next to a pig. Mr. Bernard looks scandalized, in a theatrical sort of way, and hoots along with everyone else at the punch line.

Several students recite poems, a few sing, and one girl even does an Irish step dance in honor of the tradition's heritage. Marta, surprisingly, does a magic trick involving a napkin and a disappearing butter knife and earns hearty applause. Ryan regales them all with a dreadful yet enthusiastic version of the famous aria *"Nessun dorma"* and earns equally enthusiastic boos as well as two dinner rolls to the head.

"Princess Pinkerton," Mr. Bernard booms, pointing, and Lori stands to scattered claps and whistles.

Sing expects her to play the insincerely modest "Oh, gosh, whatever shall I do?" card, but Lori is a true performer. There is no hesitation in her expression or her voice—her fierce gaze and confident body language instantly command attention. Sing notices with a sickening feeling that Ryan's eyes seem to sparkle as he watches the resident diva.

Lori sings a musical theater song—bouncy, funny, animated, and with the obligatory money note at the end. Sing estimates it's a high C and that it can be heard all the way to the conservatory. The Grill bursts into ecstatic applause, and Mr. Bernard makes a big show of cleaning out his ears with his fingers.

Lori nods and sits gracefully, and as the applause dies, Sing realizes with horror that Mr. Bernard is now pointing at her. "Duchess da Navelli!"

Follow Lori? Is he crazy? How can she out-diva the resident diva?

She stands, trying to keep the motion smooth and confident, and looks out over the crowd of students. They are quiet, expectant. What can she do? It would be pointless to do an aria; even if she sang flawlessly, no one here would appreciate it—they're all still under the spell of Princess Pinkerton. Going for another money note would just seem like copying, and frankly, she realizes with a sinking feeling, she's not sure she could outdo Lori's high C. It was good.

But she is standing, and everyone is looking at her. She scans the room, buying time, trying not to make eye contact.

She sees Daysmoor watching her. Of all the faces in that room, why has she found his? No smile of support, no thumbs-up. Nothing to indicate he gives a damn whether she triumphs or fails in front of all these people. Just that inscrutable stare from those eyes that unnerve her.

He wanted her to sing the *farfallina* song, a silly kids' song! But somehow, frozen, she can't think of anything else.

So she starts in, remembering how her father sang it when she was little. Her father, whose voice is as ratty as old burlap.

"Farfallina, bella e bianca; vola, vola, mai si stanca . . ."

She sings it the way he used to, letting his voice laugh a bit at the funny lines and cry a bit at the sad ones. *Little butterfly, beautiful and white; fly, fly, never get tired . . .*

It occurs to her as the swelling applause starts that it is probable no one else fully understood the words; maybe a few other singers, since they've studied Italian. The audience's warm reaction, therefore, surprises her even more. Everyone applauds heartily—even, she notices, Lori.

But above her broad, fake smile, Lori's pretty eyes convey

nothing but a new dislike. Despite herself, Sing can't help but stare back, fascinated and triumphant. She has seen Lori's expression before, on the face of each city's most popular soprano when Barbara da Navelli came to town. It is the look of a resident diva who fears for her throne.

As the applause increases, she notices Daysmoor isn't clapping. But he gives a curt nod when she meets his eye, and it makes her stomach buzz.

Sing pries her gaze from the apprentice and smiles genuinely at the crowd. And when Ryan whistles appreciatively, she can't help but beam.

Thirty-five

AT THE EDGE OF THE FOREST, the Felix watches the tower. She stares wide-eyed into the yellow windows, ears pricked to capture what they can. She still does not understand the patterns of sound that captivated the crow those years ago. All she understood then was his despair, his longing. That she understood well.

But ever since, she has wondered. For the first time since her fall, she has wondered about the world outside despair. And somehow, watching the tower makes her feel closer to that world, watching the man-crow play his instrument. Every night he plays, and every night she watches.

Recently, she has begun to feel that the child should be with her. That perhaps he too is a link to this other world and not just a thing she must feed rather than kill for reasons she can't quite grasp. This evening, under the gray sky with the gentle but chilly breeze riffling her fur, she feels it especially. Enough to pull herself away, back through the crunch and scrape of the piney woods, through the icy streams and into the safe, tamped-down place where he will be waiting.

But she returns to find only marks in the earth and his scent. He is gone.

The rain starts.

Thirty-six

THE STEEP ROAD FROM DUNHAMMOND to the conservatory is less appealing after dinner. Skipping down the hill and playing in the puddles along the way was fun, but now most of the students are hitting up those with cars for rides rather than walking home, tired, in the rain.

Marta has again chosen Mr. Bernard's old coupe, but now Lori squeezes into the backseat as well. Sing decides to walk.

She pulls up the collar of her garbage bag raincoat and starts up the hill. *It's only a mile,* she tells herself as her right boot squishes down into a cold mud puddle. Chilly raindrops slide down her face and under her collar, but they don't bother her. Though it will be dark soon, she is still full of light and warmth from the Noble Call.

After a moment, she hears the splash of someone running up behind her. Before she can turn around, an arm is around her waist and a friendly voice breathes into her ear, "A little damp?"

Ryan slides his umbrella open and holds it up. Sing is grateful for the shelter, but she's also afraid she is going to collapse—it can't be healthy for someone's heart to be beating as forcefully as hers is now. She turns to him and says, "Thanks," in a completely professional voice, but she makes the mistake of looking into those mischievous green eyes and nearly falls over.

"Easy, there!" He catches her elbow. "We've still got almost a mile to go."

Remain calm, Sing thinks. *A gorgeous rehearsal pianist has his arm around you and is protecting you from the weather with his own umbrella. Don't screw this up!*

Indifference—that's always a good tactic. She remembers Lori's indifference toward Aaron and how it seemed to make him even crazier about her.

Sing smiles. "You should have gotten a ride. It's going to be a pretty soggy walk." Was that indifferent enough?

Ryan feigns indignation. "And leave a damsel in distress to slog back to the castle alone? What kind of knight in shining armor would I be then?"

"Oh, is that what you are?" Sing raises her voice above the wind, the swishing trees, and the clatter of the rain on the pavement. It is difficult to flirt when it's cold and noisy out.

But Ryan doesn't seem to notice. "Did I not win your heart with my love ballad back at ye tavern?"

"You're lucky I didn't have you thrown in the moat!"

He laughs and squeezes her. "You sounded amazing, by the way. But I'm sure you know that."

Sing hopes he won't notice her pink cheeks. Does he really think she sounded amazing?

Ryan stops abruptly. "Hey, can I show you something?" He gestures to a heap of large rocks at the side of the road where an old stone wall must once have been.

Sing looks dubiously at the rocks, which seem to her as ordinary as the dripping pines behind them. But she notices the adorable way his copper hair is just a little damp and disheveled and says, "Okay."

He takes her hand and pulls her to the tree-lined roadside, around behind the rocks, which hide a biggish boulder. In this shelter, he perches the umbrella between the boulder and the top of the rock pile.

Whatever fascinating thing is back here, Sing is relieved to get a bit of respite from the weather. This little protected area is fairly dry and beautifully quiet. "Okay," she says. "What did you want to show me?"

He smiles and throws up his hands. "Nothing. I'm so sorry. I'm nothing but a dirty liar."

Sing laughs.

"Really," he says, moving closer, "I just wanted to get out of the rain and ditch that umbrella for a minute. I needed both my arms, you see."

And before she knows what is happening, both his arms are around her, and he is kissing her. He smells of aftershave and skin, he is warm and enveloping, and he is kissing her, not Lori Pinkerton, at least right now. She slides her fingers up into his copper hair and he holds her more tightly, and she is absolutely certain her heart is going to thump its way right out of her chest and fall with a splat onto the wet ground.

Thirty-seven

THE FELIX PACES THE TAMPED-DOWN place. She cannot smell the child anywhere in the forest. She cannot see him in the sky. But she knows, now, that she wants him back. She wants to run her tongue over his soft face, to nuzzle his pine-scented fur, to curl around him in the tamped-down place and shield him from the cold. She feels these wants more deeply than any she has felt before.

She calls on the power of the sky and the stars, of her mother and the spirit of the Forest. The power dissipates like mist. The part of herself that is Sky is weak. But the part of herself that is Cat grows stronger. The Cat wants her child back, too, and knows what to do.

She sniffs the wet air. She cocks her ears.

The Felix bounds through the forest, sometimes forgetting to put her paws to the earth. His scent is more powerful *here,* now *here* . . . She skids and floats down the mountains; pine trees give way to beech and maple; the ground is more slippery here, covered with wet leaves.

Voices slow her pace. She has come to the road. Her child is very near. . . .

There. Across the road, creeping along just behind the trees—a shadowy, familiar shape; large, triangular ears followed by the slinky curve of a little back and long tail. The Felix gives a soft *chrrrp* and rises.

But she cannot summon the child or call to him. He has surrounded himself with his own magic, and it is all focused on—

On *that human*. The girl plodding up the hill in the rain with another human. The Felix's tail begins to lash. The child's adoration of this girl is a glittering blue fog that envelops them—he does not even know he is doing it.

The Sky part of the Felix's spirit, fallen and separate from its place, wants to lunge at them and tear them to pieces.

But the Cat wants to wait at the edge of the woods. And so the Felix, crouched, watches with narrow, violet-black eyes as the humans pass.

Thirty-eight

THE RAIN HAS LET UP, but it is dark and cold when Sing and Ryan get back to campus. Sing doesn't feel the chill. His arm is around her waist, and she is snuggled against his shoulder in a way that makes walking a little awkward. It is quiet inside the grounds; Mr. Bernard's other students have long since returned from dinner, and now the sparse pools of light from various windows are the only indication anyone is awake.

The wet gravel crunches under their feet as they make their way toward Archer. Sing finds herself wishing the walk home were twice as long.

"Home, sweet home." He releases her in the square patch of doorway light. Sing studies his face, partially shadowed, and it strikes her how much of his attractiveness he owes to his easy smile. Right now, she would follow that smile anywhere.

His gaze flits over her shoulder. "I'd ask you up for a nightcap, but I think the warden's watching."

She turns around, looking up to see the silhouette of someone standing in one of the tall windows of Apprentice Daysmoor's tower. Watching them.

"Creepy," she says.

Ryan laughs. "Probably just jealous." And he kisses her again, and she feels the familiar flutter in her chest, but a small part of her hopes he isn't doing it just for Daysmoor's benefit. When Ryan steps back after a few moments, Sing glances behind her, up at the tall window. There is no one there now.

"Good night, pretty girl," Ryan says. "Thanks for walking me home." He flashes that bright smile before pushing open the door and going inside.

Sing leans against the wall, trying to keep the memory of him fresh. A minute passes, and she starts to feel the night air; her regulation raincoat doesn't offer much protection from the cold.

She leaves the doorway and continues on the gravel footpath. Hud sits across the quad, barely visible. Unsettled by the shadows, she wishes Ryan had walked her all the way back, then scolds herself for being silly. Archer is closer to the road; it's only natural he left her first. It's not his fault the rehearsal pianist is housed with the apprentices. If he were in Hud with the other students, he probably would have walked her all the way to her room. It doesn't matter that Lori might have seen them. He definitely wasn't trying to hide their new relationship from Lori.

Definitely.

Sing suddenly remembers seeing Ryan and Lori under his navy-blue umbrella only that afternoon. She remembers his hands running over that long blond hair.

That doesn't mean they're together. And even if they were, they probably broke up.

. . . Over dinner.

As she plods down the footpath, her mind is a swirl of fairy-tale euphoria overwhelming something deeper and sharper. Fresh memories jockey for attention—the feel of Ryan's arms around her, the swelling applause at the Mountain Grill, the fierce dislike in Lori's pretty eyes, Apprentice Daysmoor's dark stare.

"Who cares about Lori Pinkerton, or any of them?" her father would

say. She doesn't want to hear that now. She cares about Lori Pinkerton. Power was something her mother always understood better.

"You have shown up the resident diva," her mother would say now, granting Sing a rare moment of undivided attention. *"You have beaten her at the Noble Call, in front of everyone."*

Sing inhales cold dampness, but her body feels warm and strong. *It's true. It's true, isn't it?* She clearly bested Lori at the Noble Call—that much was obvious from Lori's icy stare. And it feels *good.*

No.

No. Singing feels good. Singing *well* feels good. Showing up someone else should not feel good. Lori Pinkerton doesn't matter—that's what her father would say.

"And you have stolen her boyfriend," Barbara da Navelli would say.

Ryan felt good; everything about him. His voice, his skin, his hair, his warmth, the fact that he should have been unattainable. The fact that he was the one prize Lori Pinkerton clearly stamped the word *MINE* all over from day one.

Well, no, she realizes. *The conservatory holds* two *prizes stamped with Lori's pink, glossy MINE.*

The other is Angelique.

Beginning to shiver, Sing quickens her pace across the dark quad. *Barbara da Navelli would have known how to take Angelique away from Lori, too.*

No. Barbara da Navelli would have been cast in the first place.

When she has just about reached Hud, her eyes stray to the glistening black pines beyond the campus. Something stays her gaze—something big and still and quietly luminescent, just at the edge of her vision on the other side of the fence. *Tamino?*

The stone hanging around her neck, the glittering, glassy crystal she found the night she went into the forest, feels heavier, cold against her skin, and she pulls it out from her shirt.

Hud's double doors glow yellow, but Sing moves away from

them now, across the lawn, past the big maple tree to the picnic tables, and peers through a gap in the rough wooden fencing.

The big shape is hard to focus on; it feels like a trick of the moon and shadows. But there is a solidness to it she can't dismiss.

She promised her father not to go into the woods. She has already broken that promise once and gotten a censure because of it.

The shape, still shining faintly, recedes, and she feels it pulling her.

Up onto the slick picnic table, hoisting herself over the damp fence, and she is in the forest again. The crystal feels cold even through her raincoat, sweater vest, and shirt. She picks her way toward the dull, pearly glow of the distant shape, which seems to keep moving away. Wet leaves slide under her feet, trees shiver clatters of raindrops onto her as she brushes past, and something deep inside her says, *Go back.*

But she doesn't go back. Her mind is tingling, fluctuating between the chilly forest and the new, exultant feelings bubbling up inside her—Ryan, Lori, the Noble Call. Will her small triumph at the Mountain Grill simply become smaller and more distant as time moves on? None of her past successes have solidified themselves into stepping-stones along some kind of great journey; they have all vanished like pebbles into a vast lake.

She pulls her raincoat tighter around her neck, and her ears buzz not with the eerie silence of the still night, but with the memory of applause—the applause, at last, of her true peers, not just the mediocre musicians from her old school. And her chest tingles with a strange new sensation: *triumph.*

The forest is darker tonight, the tree trunks circling her have the sheen of liquid tar, and she knows if she looks back now, the conservatory will have vanished completely. The glowing shape is gone, too, but she keeps moving forward. Forward, and up.

After a while, amid the noises of the dripping forest, she senses other, closer noises—rustles and swishes. She pauses, squinting into the inky background. It occurs to her for the first time that she is lost in the woods.

"*Chrrp?*"

The sound startles her, but she laughs with relief as Tamino emerges. His eyes are larger than she remembers, and his orange fur inexplicably seems to give off a blue, misty glow—different from the pearly shimmer she followed into the forest.

"What are you doing up so late, little guy?" She runs her hand over one side of his head; his ear flattens under her palm and then pops up again. "I don't suppose you know the way back to campus, do you?"

"*Rrrp? Hrrrrawl?*"

Sing laughs again and shivers at the same time. "Maybe for a song? How about, *Farfallina, bella e bianca; vola, vola—*"

But even if she had been paying attention, she wouldn't have heard the Felix coming for her.

Thirty-nine

THE FELIX SPRINGS. The girl is light and brittle and falls without a sound, like a feather. The Felix's child cries and leaps, but he is too late; the great cat extends her lustrous claws.

But something gives her pause. She looks up.

It is the crow. The man-crow she made that night, the last night she was drawn too close to human sounds. Those eyes stayed her claws then, and they do so again. The crow, transformed now for nearly a century, reaches the Felix's vaporous heart with their shared history. She asks him a question with her own eyes.

"Please," he says, placing a hand on one of her great paws.

The child rubs his head against her. Already the glittering blue mist, the magic he used to hide himself, has faded away. Rage churns inside the Felix, and she bares her teeth at the girl, who lies motionless on the damp ground. But the man-crow places his other hand on her other paw and looks into her eyes. "Please," he says again. The child gurgles, *chrrrrrp,* and she inhales his sweet, piney scent. He has missed her.

The Felix turns away from the man-crow and snarls at the girl, tensing her jaws for the final snap.

And then she hesitates. She stares at the girl, at the gleaming object around her neck, and then at the man-crow.

The Felix's low, warning growl shudders the pine needles, and she lopes back into the woods with her child.

The man-crow takes the girl in his arms.

Forty

Before Sing remembers she doesn't have a phone in her dorm room, she has awoken and answered the ring. Pain ripples down from the top of her head.

"Sing?" Her father's voice is distant and strained.

"*Sì, Papà.*" She blinks to clear up the blurry room. "How are you?"

"How am I? *Ma carina,* how are you? Are they taking care of you? Do you want me to come?"

This is not her room. The wallpaper is cream-colored, and a vase of white flowers sits on the dark wood dresser on the opposite wall. Sunlight shines through the lace curtains of wide French doors to the left. "Where am I?"

A sudden pressure, weightlessness, falling . . . Images begin sparking in her mind. *Teeth. Eyes . . . black eyes tinged with purple . . . inhuman eyes . . .*

A door to the right opens. A stout woman dressed in printed cotton steps through and frowns.

"You don't know where you are?" Sing's father sounds ruffled. "You are in the infirmary, my dear. Is someone there with you? Call for a nurse."

"Oh, yeah," Sing says. "I think the nurse just came in."

"Hm," the nurse says, putting a hand to Sing's forehead.

"Are you all right?" Sing's father asks. "They said I do not need to come. But I can postpone—"

"No, Papà. I'm fine."

Is she fine? The nurse looks into her eyes and is apparently satisfied with whatever she has found there. She turns to the French doors and opens the curtains. Sing shifts the phone to her other ear. "Papà, I should go. I'm okay, all right?"

"Good, good. Listen, my dear, I want you to know—Harland will be at your Autumn Festival."

Harland Griss, managing director of Fire Lake Opera. Why is he telling her this? "Oh. It will be nice to see him."

Her father laughs. "So polite. This you get from me, eh? He will be there on business. I want you to know. Don't let it get out, all right?"

"All right." Business? What business? "I'll see you later, Papà. At the Autumn Festival."

"Okay, *carina*. I may see you before then, eh? And Sing—we will talk later about your censure."

They told her *father*? Sing's chest judders. What is he going to do?

Wait a minute—*she was in the woods again!* Wasn't she? Her mind is fuzzy, but she is fairly certain. Will she get another censure for being in the woods? And how did she get there?

How did she get *here*?

"Call me if you have need of anything," he says. *"Ti amo."*

"Ti amo, Papà. Ciao."

The nurse takes the phone from her and replaces it.

"Your dad? He's been worried. I'm glad he got through to you. I'm Mrs. Foster." The woman's voice is comfortable, and her face, though serious, is pleasant. She smells like plastic. "How are we feeling?"

"Okay."

Mrs. Foster takes Sing's wrist and presses. "Any pain?"

"Not much. A bit of a headache, I guess." She almost doesn't ask but can't help it. "What happened?"

The nurse puts on a bland smile. "You don't remember anything?"

Again, Sing pictures those black-violet eyes. But for some reason, she says, "No." She *doesn't* remember what happened, she assures herself. Not really. She doesn't want to acknowledge the idea floating and buzzing at the back of her mind. *Something dangerous in the forest . . . Durand's great beast . . .*

No. The Felix is a myth, that's all. Sure, Marta believes, but she probably also thinks rainbows are made of flying unicorns.

Mrs. Foster sighs. "You fainted out on the quad last night. Someone saw you and brought you in. Good thing, too, with the cold."

Sing blinks. "I—fainted? On the quad?"

"Probably exhaustion. Or stress. You needed the sleep, my dear. Goodness knows how they run you kids into the ground. It's a wonder you're not all dropping like flies." Mrs. Foster clicks her tongue in disapproval.

Exhaustion. Was it exhaustion? Could those eyes have been just a hallucination? Yes. Yes, she was on the footpath. She had just left Ryan—

Ryan.

The nurse has turned to the door, but Sing says, "Mrs. Foster, have I gotten any visitors?"

"No," she says. Sing's face falls a little, and Mrs. Foster adds, "I'm sure your friends are very worried about you. But they wouldn't have been allowed in while you were still resting. You've been awfully groggy and difficult to rouse for the last twenty hours." And she leaves, moving with the purpose of someone who has somewhere else to be.

Sing lets her head slump to the side. After all that sleep, she feels like getting up. Especially since she knows if she closes her eyes, that terrible, snarling face will be there. Or maybe Ryan's face will appear. Would that be worse?

Maybe he will come soon. Maybe he will assure her of what she can't believe right now, that he really did kiss her. He really does like her. Her, not Lori.

She sits up, and though her head complains a little, the rest of her feels decent. The light coming from the French doors draws her. She finds a thick bathrobe draped across a chair and pulls it on.

Opening the doors reveals a ground-level private terrace and Hector Hall's impressive back garden. The sky is gray but bright, and the air is warmer than Sing expects. She lowers herself slowly onto a curvy stone bench. The damp breeze feels good on her face as she gazes at the dying garden.

The pain in her head is dull and not overly terrible, but each throb seems to murmur another question. *What happened? Who brought me here?*

The garden is a small, meandering landscape of stone fairies, gravel, dry grass, and wide beds of drooping brown flowers. Crows disagree with one another from the trees.

Suddenly, a sound comes from just over her shoulder, almost as soft as the breeze itself, but so close it makes her heart jump.

"Chrrrrp?"

She has the presence of mind to turn slowly, and when she does so, she is met by a pair of ice-blue eyes with big, black cat-pupils.

Tamino stands calmly on the other side of the stone railing, his large head level with Sing's own. In the even, gray wash of the afternoon, he stands out like a sunset jewel. She looks around furtively. No one.

"Chrrrp?" It is decidedly a question, but which question, Sing has no idea.

"I don't think you're supposed to be here," she says. Tamino leaps easily onto the stone railing that separates the terrace from the garden and begins to purr.

"Big cats are unable to purr," she says, but he continues anyway, pushing the top of his fuzzy head into her shoulder, which nearly knocks her off the bench. She scratches between his ears and he closes his eyes.

"Were you in the woods last night, little guy?" she asks. "I feel like you were—like we both were." She realizes that if she was attacked—and she is more and more certain she was—this big kitten might be her attacker.

Ridiculous. She smiles to think of it. But her smile fades. *Of course, if there is a kitten, there must be a cat.*

The owner of those death-violet eyes in her memory must be connected to this strange kitten, perhaps even its mother or father. How could she not have thought of it before? Or has she?

Tamino only closes his eyes in a cat-smile.

"Do you know about Prince Tamino, your namesake?" she asks. "He loves the princess Pamina. He fell in love with her picture before he even met her. But they have problems. The princess sings a sad song to Tamino about her tears." She keeps scratching his head and sings, *"Sieh', Tamino, diese Tränen fließen, Trauter, dir allein."* It seems as if princesses and shepherdesses and servant girls in operas are always singing sad songs about their beloveds. Is love always sad? Is it always difficult? She thinks of Ryan's relaxed smile. Is anything difficult for him?

"Miss da Navelli?" Mrs. Foster calls from behind the French doors. Tamino tenses and is gone.

"I'm out here on the terrace."

The doors open as the nurse says, "You have a visitor."

Sing's heart tickles and she sits up straight. Could Ryan be here, now, just as she was thinking about him?

A stooping, dark form emerges from the doorway. It isn't Ryan after all.

It definitely isn't Ryan.

"Don't stay outside too long," Mrs. Foster tells her. "A little fresh air is fine, but don't get cold."

"Okay."

Mrs. Foster is gone again. Sing's eyes flit to Apprentice Days-moor, who stands still in the doorway, perhaps a little awkwardly. He is the last person she wants to see right now. She doesn't know what to say to him.

He clears his throat. "I'm sorry to have surprised you, Miss da Navelli. I can see you were hoping I'd be someone else."

Did her disappointment show that clearly on her face? She feels a pang of embarrassment; she was rude.

"No, I was just . . . *expecting* someone else. That's all."

He nods but doesn't approach. "How are you feeling?"

"Fine," she says, and adds, "Thanks for coming." A hint to leave.

But he crosses the terrace and puts his hands on the stone rail-ing. "How are your spirits?"

His grave tone surprises her. "Fine," she says lightly. "I'm a little rattled, I guess, but that's probably normal. Well, you know, if there is a 'normal' for this type of thing."

He looks at her now, and she thinks his dull black eyes are a little less dull. She feels the weight of her secrets, as though he is searching for something behind her own eyes.

"I overheard you just now," he says. "You were singing a very sad song."

"Oh," she says. "That was just Pamina's aria from *The Magic Flute*." *Does he think I'm crazy?*

"I know what it was." The familiar, arrogant edge returns to his voice, and he turns his face to the garden.

"Well, thanks for your concern"—Sing hears an edge in her own voice now—"but I was just singing. I'm not lamenting my lost love out here or anything."

"No, I suppose not."

He says it in a way that just *invites* her to snap, *And what does that mean?* But she doesn't. She remembers his silhouette in the window just before she and Ryan said good-bye. *Jealous,* Ryan had said. Yes, he's probably jealous of Ryan's talent, his good looks, his charm. And he should be.

She sets her mouth, crosses her arms, and leans against the bench. They are silent for a few moments.

"Tamino's not lost," Daysmoor says.

Her head jerks in surprise. "What?" How much did he overhear just now, exactly? What does he know about Tamino?

"When Pamina sings that aria," he says. "Tamino isn't her 'lost love,' he's undergoing the test of silence. When he won't speak to her, she thinks he doesn't care about her anymore."

"I know *that*," Sing says. Everybody knows the story of *The Magic Flute*. Daysmoor doesn't know about the big kitten after all.

He seems to study something in the distance. "That's such a tragic scene. Having no voice."

Watching him, Sing is reminded of the night he found her beyond the fence. What does he know about this forest, and the creatures who live there?

She says, "Marta says the Felix really exists."

Daysmoor doesn't move, but Sing feels a decided stiffness pervade the atmosphere. She can swear his fingers, which had been lightly touching the railing, tense just for a moment into claws. The garden is quiet except for the rustling of dry leaves and the intermittent cawing of crows. Did she cross some kind of line?

"Does she?" he says without emotion. "And what do you think?"

Before she can think, the truthful answer escapes. "I don't know."

"Is that why you were running around in the woods that night?" he asks. "What did you find there, I wonder?"

"What did *you* find there?"

He shrugs. "It's no secret that I go to the forest sometimes. Most people just don't notice. And *I'm* not going to get a censure out of it."

What does *that* mean? Her head aches. "Maybe you should," she says without meaning to. "Since you love giving them to other people so much."

Okay, that was rude. She almost claps a hand over her mouth but instead turns her head toward the dying garden, hoping he will evaporate.

"What?"

She lets her eyes flick to his face. For the first time, she can read his expression clearly. He is confused.

She doesn't say anything. Her sockless feet, tucked up under her, are cold.

His confusion seems to resolve itself to amusement. "You think *I* turned you in after your little escapade in the forest?"

Does he seriously want to feign innocence here? "I don't know," she says. "I'm a little groggy."

Cautiously, he moves a step closer to the bench. "Do you . . ." An uncertain pause. She frowns at him. He begins again. "Do you think it was the Felix who attacked you last night?"

She looks away, voice hard. "I wasn't attacked by anything. I fainted out on the quad."

He stiffens. "Of course. Why would I think that?"

"I don't know. Why would you?"

Now he leans in uncomfortably close and lowers his voice. "Somehow, I got it into my head you were attacked by an animal in the middle of the woods, where you shouldn't have been. Isn't that strange? I got it into my head you collapsed in the dark, cold, wet middle of nowhere, and that someone had to haul your carcass back to campus and then lie about it in order to avoid your getting another censure."

She opens her mouth, but no words come out.

He straightens up. "I know, it would have been so much more romantic if it had been your handsome boyfriend. Oh, well."

"That's not what I—" She brushes aside the image of Ryan using Excalibur to hack his way to her through nettly underbrush. "It's just—*why?*"

"Why not leave an unconscious soprano to freeze to death in the woods?" He taps his fingers on the stone railing. "That's actually a very good question. I have no idea."

Sing almost laughs. "I mean, why would you care about my getting another censure? Why lie for me?"

He sighs theatrically. "Look, I know it may create an imbalance in the world you're choosing to live in, but I am not, in fact, out to get you. And by the way, a student reported you going into the woods after the party that night, not me."

She raises her eyebrows. "Really?"

All he does is blink.

It is a long shot, but she has to try. "Who?"

His eyes crinkle just slightly. "You know I can't tell you that."

"Okay."

"But her initials are Lori Pinkerton." Now Sing does laugh, and Daysmoor says, "Aha, has the egg finally cracked? Is that what you asked the Felix for—the ability to smile?"

"Why? Is that what *you* would ask for?"

He is silent for so long, she feels she must have overstepped her boundaries. But eventually, he inhales broadly and says in a light tone, "What makes you think the Felix would even grant me a wish? She must find utter despair in your eyes before she'll do it, or she'll just eat you. Do I really seem that miserable?"

Yes, she thinks. But, studying his face, she realizes it isn't true. He doesn't look hopeless or despairing—a little sad, yes. Tired, yes, and too guarded for someone so young. "Not right now," she says. He catches her eye, and for just a moment she thinks his face lightens; his features come together somehow, the straight nose, the smooth jaw, and those tired, sad eyes, almost lovely in the gray light.

Sing's head throbs and she blinks. *What is the matter with me?* "Anyway," she says, "it's despair greater than hers she has to find. I wonder what she's so sad about? You know, I've listened to *Angelique* hundreds of times, and I've never wondered that before."

Daysmoor smirks. "That's step one to becoming a diva I can tolerate."

Sing draws herself up. "Oh, thanks."

He puts up his hands, mockingly protective. "Sorry, sorry. Well, Miss da Navelli, what would *you* wish for? Fame and glory?"

She doesn't know right away why the remark wounds her. Then it strikes her—that's the goal, isn't it, the legacy of the da Navellis? *Fame and glory.* "No," she says, running her hand along the curve of the stone bench. She sees him turn to look at her out of the corner of her eye. "I mean, fame and glory would be . . . would be . . ." *Nice?* As nice as they were for her mother, dead at thirty-eight from heart failure due to some outrageous combination of drugs and stress? As nice as they are for her father, gray-haired, never home, hounded by the press? "It would be nice to get to sing the roles I want, yes. But I'd rather get there on my own."

"I wonder if you mean that," he says, his raspy voice crackling like the dry brush around them.

"I don't know what I'd wish for," she says, truly imagining for the first time the weight of such a choice. "I suppose if the Felix ever caught me, and saw despair enough to want to grant me a wish, I'd already have something to wish for then."

He is studying her. "Yes, I suppose you would," he says quietly. "But what would the Felix want with you? Why would she seek you out, if not to grant you a wish?"

She watches his fingers, which are remarkably long and somehow entrancing. All of a sudden, he reaches for her crystal pendant. "What is this?" His eyes are fixated, his voice sharper.

She pulls it away, wrapping her fingers around it. "It's my necklace."

"Where did you get it? What is it?"

His tone disturbs her, and his sudden intensity. "I found it," she says. "I found the stone. On campus, in the grass." Then, without knowing why, she asks, "Is it yours?"

He frowns and takes a step back. "No. I . . . don't think I've ever seen it before. I just—I probably just noticed it because it sparkled. I—like shiny things. But it . . . *feels* like it's mine."

"Oh." The glassy object is cold in her hand. It glimmers unnaturally in the gray light, as though it is lit from within. "Here, then," she says, unclasping the necklace. "You can have it."

Daysmoor looks at her for a long moment as crows caw in the distance. Then he reaches out, but doesn't take the necklace; he curls his fingers around hers and gently closes them over the stone. "No," he says. "I think you should keep it. And keep it hidden."

Forty-one

Sing clasps and unclasps her *Angelique* score as she walks across the dewy grass, the cold morning sun making her squint. Marta plods beside her, smelling of cinnamon. Her curly hair bobs in the restless air.

In truth, Sing hoped to get Marta alone this morning, but now that they have these few minutes crossing the quad, she's not sure exactly what she wants to ask or how to begin. *I found this perpetually cold crystal on the lawn, and I've been singing to this wild orange cat, and then Daysmoor said all this weird stuff, and now I think the Felix might be real.* No. Definitely not.

"*Les oiseaux chantent dans mes bras . . . ,*" Marta sings lightly as they walk, the harmonics of her voice almost completely dissipated by the outdoors.

"You've got to connect *les* and *oiseaux,*" Sing says automatically. "*Lay-zwa-zoh,* not *lay-wah-zoh.*"

"Oh, I knew that!" Marta wrings her hands. "I have so much trouble remembering when they connect and when they don't."

"It's okay," Sing says. They are already halfway across the quad. "I make those mistakes all the time. Just listen to a recording."

Marta adjusts her books. "I know. I just don't like listening to recordings. I want to sing my own way." She laughs. "I guess that's not such a good idea if I get the words wrong."

"I know what you mean about singing your own way," Sing says. "But sometimes listening to a great singer will help you figure out the song a little better. The parts she chooses to make important, you know?"

"Yeah. You're right," Marta says. "You know a lot about singing, don't you?"

"I don't know." Sing feels the heat creeping up her face and curses her mother's fair skin.

"And you speak all these languages. I'd *love* to speak another language."

Sing focuses on the grass in front of her. "I only speak English and Italian, and that's just because of my parents. I can just pronounce the others. I couldn't make sentences by myself or anything."

"Still."

Sing finds an inroad. "But *you* know all this stuff about . . . about magical creatures and stuff, right?"

"Yeah, that's so useful, isn't it?" Marta laughs. "I'd rather be able to speak Italian."

"But, like, you know all about the Felix, right?"

Marta's pace slows just a bit. "Did you want to ask me something?"

"Well . . . I don't know." Sing takes a deep breath. "Do you really think it's real?"

Marta surprises Sing by coming to a full stop. ". . . I do. I think I do. I *want* to." She looks into Sing's eyes. "Sometimes I worry that belief and hope are the same thing, and that truth is something else entirely."

"I understand," Sing says, trying to. "Can I ask you something?"

"Of course you can."

Sing tries to get her mind around a single question. She decides to start with, "How many Felixes are there?"

They start walking again. "Just the one, as far as I know," Marta says. "Why? Have you been seeing them?" She laughs.

Sing forces a laugh. "Oh, *Angelique*'s got me thinking, I guess. And being here, you know? Where Durand was."

"Oh, I know," Marta says, a new excitement in her voice. "It's this exact forest that inspired him. I mean, the librettist *wrote* it, and added the villagers and the royalty and blah blah blah, but Durand was *mesmerized* by this forest. It's where he—it's where they say he actually met the Felix. It's why this place is so—magical."

"So if the Felix gives you a wish," Sing says, trying to steer the conversation back on course, "what happens? Do you get a—a magic stone or something?" She has an image forming in her mind, amorphous and dim right now but amassing itself around a few scattered seeds.

"A magic stone?" Marta looks at her sideways. "I've never heard that. It just grants your wish and goes away. That's it. Well, actually, it cries you a tear—the tear is the wish. That's kind of like a magic stone, I guess, now that you mention it. Except I don't think the Felix grants many wishes. Mostly it eats you."

The tear is the wish. Could this strange, cold crystal be a tear? Sing looks down, afraid Marta will see her thoughts.

Marta stops and turns to her, eyes serious. "Sing, what are you getting at?"

Taking a deep breath, Sing pulls the gold chain from inside her shirt. "Well, what do *you* think it is?" She holds the crystal up. Marta takes it between her thumb and forefinger, peering.

On first glance, it is just pretty. Sparkly. Sing knows this. But she lets Marta study it, and after a moment, Marta's eyes start to take on their own otherworldly shimmer. "Where did you get this?"

"I found it on the quad, near the woods. Is it . . . do you think it's . . . ?" Sing can't say *magical*. What does that word mean, anyway?

"It feels cold," Marta says. "And—sad, somehow."

"I know."

Marta folds her fingers around the crystal and closes her eyes. Then she opens them again and opens her hand, letting the chain fall back into place around Sing's neck. "This little thing . . . it's shaped like a tear, right?"

"Right," Sing says.

"And it clearly has some kind of power. You can feel it, can't you?"

Sing feels her body cringing at this line of inquiry, but she thinks of Tamino, of the glowing shape she followed into the woods. She looks at the crystal. And she knows what it is.

"I think," Marta says, "I think it must be a Felix tear. Someone's wish, Sing. Is it yours?"

Sing stares at the tiny, shimmering shape. "No," she says. "It's not mine."

"Hey!" an unmistakable voice calls across the campus. Sing tucks the crystal back into her shirt.

Jenny is half walking, half jogging across the grass. "Dirt!" she yells.

"Dirt?" Marta says.

"Plays-poor!" Jenny is rummaging in her backpack as she reaches them. "Purely by accident, I might add," she says, "since I'm not in the business of drama for drama's sake."

"What does *that* mean?" Sing crosses her arms. "I have a legitimate—"

"Yeah, yeah." Jenny's face is flushed with exertion. "I'm doing an article on the Gloria Stewart competition. It's kind of a huge deal that it's here this year for the first time. 'Thank you' to your dad, by the way. Mr. Hey-Howzabout-A-Brand-Spanky-New-Theater."

Sing isn't sure how to respond. "Yeah, I'll—tell him."

"Your dad must be really nice," Marta says.

Jenny pulls out a piece of paper. "So I went through the *Trumpeter* database for the heck of it, and our favorite apprentice comes up in this article about a different Gloria Stewart competition, at Carnegie Hall." She hands the paper to Sing. "Kinda horrifying."

DC PRODIGY DISAPPOINTS IN NYC

Nathan Daysmoor, a favorite to win this year's inaugural Gloria Stewart International Piano Competition, failed even to complete his performance last night at Carnegie Hall. Despite the hype leading up to the competition, Daysmoor, a protégé of DC's illustrious Maestro George Keppler, had never given a public performance. It is easy to see why. He fumbled his way through thirty seconds of barely recognizable Rachmaninov before being booed off the stage by an unappreciative crowd. Perhaps next year, DC will send a competitor based on talent rather than looks and charisma.

"Yes, folks, you heard it here," Jenny says. " 'Looks and charisma.' "

Sing's mouth hangs open. "When did this happen?"

"That I don't know." Jenny folds the paper again. "The database is so incomplete and screwed up."

"Nineteen sixty-seven," Marta says. The other two look at her. She shrugs. "It says 'inaugural.' That means the first one. Which was in 1967."

Jenny puts her hands on her hips. "Marta Kost, I love you dearly, but which do you think is more likely? That Daysmoor is some kind of immortal, talentless Phantom of the Opera with a slightly better complexion, or that some first-year *Trumpeter* journalist didn't know what 'inaugural' meant?"

"I know what's more likely," Marta says. "I just don't know what's true."

Forty-two

MAESTRO KEPPLER GAZES OUT at the dark, empty theater. It's a strange vantage point. He is used to focusing on the orchestra, not the audience. Sitting alone here, center stage, feels alien. Or is it the absence of the crystal?

How could he have been so careless as to let it slip from his pocket? How could he have done that?

His only consolation is that Nathan doesn't know it exists.

But thanks to that idiot da Navelli trying to buy his daughter's career with this new theater, the damn *Gloria Stewart competition* is coming up! Here! With Nathan getting it into his head to enter!

Luckily, George is confident he has killed that idea, for now. Nathan has been so much more reasonable these last ten years or so, since George learned how to use the crystal. He just has to hope Nathan doesn't decide to test the limits again.

He has to find the crystal, before it's too late.

Forty-three

THE RAIN CAME DOWN in buckets all night. The gray sky and chilly, damp grass are keeping Mrs. Bigelow's other students off the lawn this morning, which suits Sing fine. Let them do their research in the library. It will be easier to listen to the crows out here.

She has set up under the large maple tree behind Hud, near the barbarian fence, and sits cross-legged on an old blanket, notebook in hand.

"*Caaaaw,*" the crows say.

Maybe Mrs. Bigelow was right. Crows are certainly not songbirds. In fact, the only song Sing has written out in the notebook over the past month of observation is, "*Caw* (crackly)."

Yet she feels she is getting to know them just a bit. Unlike their more musical neighbors, the crows radiate an intelligence that Sing finds fascinating. They have strong opinions about people—not people in general, but individual people. From her first day studying the crows, Sing has taken pride in the fact that they don't fly off when she approaches their big tree. Lately, they've even stopped making an irritated fuss when she arrives, ruffling their shiny feathers and shifting their weights from one clawed foot to the other and back again. Being accepted by the crows—even grudg-ingly so—has to count for something, she thinks. There must be something fundamental about her that is good, or pleasant, or kind. Something utterly un-diva.

She has not felt good, or pleasant, or kind, since the night of the Noble Call. She can't shake the memory of the exhilaration of beat-ing Lori Pinkerton. It makes her feel powerful. But it also makes her sick to her stomach.

"*Caaaw,*" the nearest crow says from its perch on a springy branch that still sports a few brilliantly red leaves.

"*Caaaw* yourself," she answers, and the crow cocks its head sus-piciously, which makes her laugh.

Suddenly, silently, the crows leave. A few leaves drifting down and some bobbing branches are all that indicate the presence of these big black birds only seconds before. Sing frowns and looks around. She listens but hears nothing. Still, *something* disturbed them.

Without the crows to occupy her, she begins to feel the sting of the damp air. What did they see, or hear, that threatened them?

There's no reason to sit here all nerves. She closes her notebook.

The slightest rustling from the unruly bushes next to the fence catches her ear.

She smiles. Then, mind empty except for a warm peace, she sings, "*Farfallina, bella e bianca . . .*"

Was that the glint of a wide blue eye, half hidden by the dark leaves?

"*Vola, vola, mai si stanca . . .*"

Tamino emerges hesitantly, soft ears swiveled in Sing's direc-tion.

"So *you* scared my crows away," she says. "You shouldn't be out here during the day, my love." The last three weeks have gushed by in a wash of wet gray skies and brown leaves. She has taken to getting up early to meet Tamino near the picnic tables at the edge of campus. He doesn't always come, and their time together is cold and dark, but she gets to do her warm-up exercises early and he gets to listen.

"You are easy to please," she says as he butts her shoulder with his big head. "I don't think the Maestro would be moved by children's songs."

The large, ice-blue eyes watch her expectantly.

"Gira qua, gira là." *She turns here, she turns there.* Sing flutters her fingers, stretching her arm and moving her hand in a jerky, irregular figure eight. *"Poi si resta sopra un fiore."* *Then she rests on a flower.* Sing swoops her hand down to gently grasp Tamino's nose. He follows the motion with his eyes, and she laughs. "I can remember three more verses. Would you like to hear them?"

He would. She sings, and Tamino listens.

"If only it were that simple," she says after all the verses are done, as she scratches the fuzzy orange fur between his ears. "If only we *could* just sing."

If he has an opinion, he doesn't voice it. After a few minutes, a subtle, humming change in the atmosphere quickly becomes a swelling, chattering, rattling cacophony that signals the change of classes. Tamino disappears into the bushes.

Sing gathers her things and rises, her mind returning to the conservatory, her classes, her music. As she leaves the shadow of the maple tree and joins the crowd of students, an arm snakes around her waist. "And how were your little crow friends today?"

"Just the same."

Ryan pulls her close as they walk, and she enjoys the envious stares. As usual, though, she dreads meeting Lori. What will she say? Sing knows it's too much to hope the three of them will never meet by chance on such a small campus. Lori has been as distant as ever at rehearsals, but she must *know*, right? She must know about Sing and Ryan and their . . . whatever it is they're doing.

"How's the Liszt going?" she asks.

"Funny you should ask." He pulls an envelope out of his pocket. Sing reads the letter inside.

"Wow! Congratulations!"

"Yup," he says, folding the letter again. "Passed the recorded audition. They're only going to hear twenty-five in the Amateur Over Sixteen category, and one of those twenty-five is going to be me. And none of the other DC students, I might add. So, to answer your question, the Liszt is going well."

Sing smiles, catching the eyes of two snobby-looking girls. "How'd the faculty do?"

"Very well. Both Hawkins and Dunlop made it to round two in the Professional category, and we've only got four piano faculty as it is. Oh, and Plays-poor? He was telling the truth, you know; he didn't even submit a recording."

"Figures."

"So now I've got two weeks to practice my little fingies off." He tickles the back of her neck and she laughs.

Then it dawns on her—*two weeks!* The Autumn Festival is only two weeks away! She had the date in her head, of course, but hadn't really thought about it in terms of weeks. It seems so much closer now.

Two weeks until her father finds out about *Angelique*.

"Hey, what's the matter? You okay?" Ryan slows his pace.

"Yeah, it's just . . . my dad. He doesn't know we're doing *Angelique*." She knows she doesn't need to explain, but part of her wants him to ask.

"Oh. He'll still judge Gloria Stewart, right?" he asks. "You don't think he'll have a fit or something?"

"No. He'll be there." She wonders again why her father told her about Harland Griss coming to the competition. She has met Griss several times; another schmoozing opportunity isn't really that noteworthy. So what was her father getting at?

"Well. Aren't you sweet." The cold voice catches Sing off guard. She stops abruptly. Lori Pinkerton takes a sip of coffee from a cardboard cup while two other girls—Hayley and someone Sing doesn't recognize—stand behind her, watching, shoulders and hips skewed fashionably.

"Thanks," Ryan says. He smiles as easily as if he were talking to a cute stranger instead of a clearly hostile ex-girlfriend.

Sing is frozen with the heightened awareness of the other students swirling around them, and the vast gray sky overhead.

"Haven't seen much of you lately, Ryan." Lori says his name confidently, with ownership. "Too busy with your famous girlfriend, huh? Too bad. She was an innocent little thing, wasn't she? You must have had to teach her a lot." The other girls giggle.

"Jealousy doesn't become you, Princess Pinkerton," Ryan says, winking at Lori's friends, who giggle more. Sing feels her face reddening.

"And lying doesn't become you," Lori says, smiling at Ryan. Then she fixes Sing with her dazzling eyes. "Aw, don't mind me, Miss da Navelli. I'm just looking out for you. He isn't what he seems."

"Gorgeous and charming?" Ryan says, eliciting more giggles.

Lori steps closer, her pink lips close to Sing's ear. "I'm not worried. I'll have him back as soon as Gloria Stewart is over with. Don't you know? If your father wasn't judging, Ryan would still be with me." She shrugs. "Hey, I'm not mad. I'd do the same thing."

The shine of Lori's blond hair, so close to Sing's face, and the maddening smell of roses, make something in Sing's mind snap. She steps between Lori and Ryan, her face smoothing into the most perfect, porcelain party mask she has ever worn. "Ryan doesn't need anyone's help to win Gloria Stewart," she says. "But thanks for the confession. I guess some people have to use people to get ahead, instead of having talent. I don't really know what that's like."

The girls behind Lori suck in their breath simultaneously. Lori juts her jaw. "Your talent wasn't enough to get you the lead, was it?" And she swishes off, hair and messenger bag swinging, followed by her two not-quite-as-beautiful friends.

Ryan smiles at her, but she pulls away from him a little. They reach the door to Durand, and he kisses her on the cheek as the other students flow by. She senses their glances, and the pride that has churned her stomach since the night of the Noble Call gives a lurch. But she feels it suppressing something else. Is it the uncertainty, the half arrogance, half terror that used to be there? That is there still, chipping away at this new pride?

There is still something missing from your voice, she tells herself. *You will never be great without it.* She almost drowns out the words with the noise of her own confidence. But not quite.

She has heard her name in the crowd again and again these last few weeks. Her mother's name. Being with Ryan has done nothing to stave off the whispers; he is not protecting her, only bringing her into greater prominence. She feels like she is being dragged head-first up a hill.

Forty-four

IT HAS BEEN A DELICATE OPERATION these last few weeks, arriving *just* as her voice lesson is set to begin. Sing knows she is being cowardly, but she doesn't want to risk meeting Lori, whose lesson ends fifteen minutes before hers starts. Today, however, Lori has apparently lingered to talk to Professor Needleman. Sing sees her long hair through the narrow window in the door.

She leans against the wall and looks at her watch. Five minutes pass. Ten. Sing knocks tentatively on the door.

Lori's eyes meet Sing's. Professor Needleman calls, "Come in," and looks at the clock on the wall.

"Sorry, Professor," Lori says. "I'll get going."

"That's quite all right, Lori." Professor Needleman takes a book from her piano and shelves it. "Sing knows she should just come in when it's her lesson time. Work on the two Wolf songs for next time. I think those are good to keep in mind for your senior jury."

"Thanks, Professor." Lori slings her brown leather messenger bag over her shoulder and turns to Sing. "Sorry to run into your lesson. With the Fire Lake—oh, but you know all about it, right? See you later." She flashes a smile and swishes out.

There's nothing colder than an insincere smile, Sing thinks. A scowl or a hiss is an admission, a way to begin, but there's nothing to be done with a smile. Barbara da Navelli smiled a lot.

"So it's the understudy run-through tomorrow," Professor Needleman says. "How are you feeling?"

The understudy run-through. Sing has had butterflies in her stomach all week. She hesitates but decides on the truthful approach. "I'm not sure I can do it. I mean, I know all the music, but . . ."

The professor nods. "You know, that's not an unhealthy feeling. You have a right to be nervous. You'll be singing a major role for the first time in front of the Maestro and the whole orchestra and cast. It's a big deal."

"I'm not sure that made me feel better," Sing says.

"Maybe not. But there it is. Now, let's warm up." Professor Needleman sits at the piano, her black robes creasing as neatly as paper. Sing rolls her shoulders.

They don't pull out *Angelique* today. Instead, the professor gives Sing a Fauré song, gentle and lovely, and they read through it. It is one Sing knows but hasn't looked at in over a year. They start again at the beginning, but Professor Needleman stops playing after a few measures.

"You know this one."

"Yes, it was one of the first songs I did in recital."

"It sounds like it." The professor's voice isn't harsh, just businesslike.

Sing feels her shoulders droop. "I guess we should look at a different one, then."

Professor Needleman looks up, mouth curved down in an appraising frown. "It is particularly difficult to relearn a song your muscles already know. But I think we should keep at this one." Then, to Sing's surprise, she smiles. "We need to take you out of yourself, I think. You carry a lot of weight in your voice. I don't mean your tone, it's . . . something else."

Sing likes her teacher's smile. "I think I'd like to be taken out of myself, actually."

The professor nods. "Good. Now sing the beginning again, but this time do jumping jacks."

Sing is far too seasoned to question. But she laughs when her voice jolts and bumps along with the jumping jacks.

"Creative pitches aside, that was actually much better," the professor says as Sing catches her breath. "Now, singers do need to learn focus. You need to know what's going on physically and emotionally. Lessons are important; study is important. You can really damage yourself if you don't know what you're doing, no matter how sincere you are. But sometimes, too, we need to be distracted." She flips the music back to the beginning of the song. "*Your* body knows what to do, Sing. It *wants* to sing well. You have all the right instincts, but there's something missing. Something . . . flat. Not pitchwise, of course, just something that doesn't quite . . . sparkle."

Sing leans on the piano. "I think I think too much."

Professor Needleman looks at her. "We all think too much. Here, go grab that broom from the corner."

For the rest of her lesson, Sing sings while balancing a broom, bristles up, on her palm. Following the subtle, capricious swaying of the broom, not letting it fall, takes all her focus and energy. She feels herself getting out of the way of her own voice, peeling away a layer of resistance. It isn't perfect, but when she finally returns the broom to the corner, she feels energized rather than tired.

"Fauré would be proud," says Professor Needleman. "Now go do something else. And don't be late for your lesson again."

Forty-five

SING FINDS A SEAT NEAR THE BACK of the theater and stretches her legs out under the seat in front of her, annoyed that there isn't enough light to do her American lit homework. She'll be up too late again, slogging through *Moby-Dick,* actually missing her sappy orphan novels. And she'll be tired at the understudy run-through tomorrow.

She fingers the teardrop at her throat. It does nothing but rest against her skin, cool and lifeless, yet she can't bring herself to take it off.

The warm wood of the Woolly's polished stage glows under the lights where the singers are gathered. The Maestro perches in the orchestra pit, Daysmoor in a folding chair at his side.

Rehearsal begins with the villagers worrying about the approaching Felix. The chorus sounds fairly cohesive, although, as usual, there are one or two exuberant members whose exaggerated pronunciations make them look as though they're mouthing a message to a distant friend with poor vision.

The duet is next. Sing tries not to listen, but Lori and Prince Elbert have resonant voices. Without homework to distract her, there is only so much concentration she can devote to her fingernails, the chair back in front of her, and the shadowy, vaulted ceiling. Onstage, Prince Elbert takes Lori's hands and she smiles a sad, saintly smile. Sing rolls her eyes. A bit much for a simple orchestra rehearsal.

They skip the Silvain and Felix battle, which is too bad since it's the most exciting part. Sing has only seen it once. The second time she saw *Angelique,* of course, they never got to the end.

"Silvain, we'll go from your aria," the Maestro says. Charles takes center stage for his big moment. Lori takes a swig of water, a little flushed.

Charles, singing the aria in which Silvain wishes for Elbert's life over his own, is posing like an enthusiastic Hamlet and making sweeping gestures. Sing scrunches her eyebrows. At the end of his aria, Charles actually slumps over. Seriously? And Lori poignantly touches a hand to her lips. What is *with* everyone tonight?

The chorus sings their rousing final number. "House lights up," Mr. Bernard chirps from the front row. "Good job, everyone. Character is coming through!"

"Chorus, you can go." Apprentice Daysmoor's raspy voice is the antithesis of Mr. Bernard's chipper tenor. "We'll take ten minutes."

"Off book next week—lose those scores, people!" Mr. Bernard calls as the singers file off. "Where are the house lights?"

The lights come up. Sing unscrews the heavy plastic cap of her top-of-the-line water bottle, slides out of her seat, and means to head for the fountain in the lobby. But she is stopped by the sight of the back of a head in the third row: wavy dark hair more than peppered with gray; a crisp, excellent suit over round shoulders. She puts a hand on the seat in front of her.

Her father.

For once, she doesn't feel any eyes on her. Her famous father commands the attention in a room like a bomb going off. *What is he doing here?*

What will he say about Angelique?

Then, next to him, she sees the familiar shape of an expensive, bobbed haircut.

Zhin?

They have risen, and turn to make their way up the aisle toward Sing. Zhin sees her and rushes forward, squealing, to draw her into a bony hug.

"What are you *doing* here?" Sing says, unable to suppress a squeal of excitement herself. Their summer at Stone Hill seems so far away. Zhin looks different. Her clothes are a little more tailored, her makeup a little more refined. But her expression is the same—intelligent and alert.

"I asked your dad if I could come with him. Man, this place is *remote*." Zhin lets go of Sing and leans against one of the seats, already looking around with an air of authority. Warmth spreads through Sing's body at the sight of her, tension she didn't know she had being released.

"A surprise, eh?" Sing's father says, reaching them. "How are you feeling, *carina*?"

"*Bene,* Papà."

He smiles, sweeping her hair out of her face and tapping her nose. "You are looking beautiful, my dear. I think the conservatory is good for you, yes? Lots of opportunities."

She nods but has noticed a hardness in his eyes, a forced quality to the wide smile. Her muscles tense. If Zhin weren't here, what would he be saying right now?

His eyes don't stay with her for long, however. "Maestro!" he exclaims, voice jovial. Across the theater, Maestro Keppler turns, and Sing's father is off to greet him, rippling the crowd as he goes, glances turning to stares turning to whispers. *Ernesto da Navelli. The celebrity.* In a few moments, everyone in the Woolly will be watching him.

Everyone but Sing and Zhin, who settle into seats and grin at each other.

"So how is it?" Zhin asks, leaning forward and arching her smooth eyebrows. "Is it as rustic as it seems?"

Sing drapes an arm over the back of the seat next to her. "It's fine. The groups are good. Not *Fire Lake,* though, you know." She laughs.

Zhin smiles and rolls her eyes. "Oh, my God, it doesn't seem real, does it? You would not *believe* the money, and it's a lean year. But how are you doing? Your uniform is so cute. Don't you love those knee-high socks?"

Sing groans. "Oh, yes. I get to wear them every day."

Zhin laughs. "You look fantastic, by the way. Boys falling all over you, I bet!" The shadows of the house, even with the lights up, hide Sing's blush. Zhin goes on. "That's one thing about Fire Lake—the men are *old.* There's like one guy in his twenties—a trumpet—and he's married."

Near the stage, Maestro da Navelli is in conversation with Maestro Keppler, polite smiles on both sides. Daysmoor stands to one side, the only disinterested face in the theater. "So how's my father?" Sing asks.

Zhin shrugs. "Fine, as far as I know. I only see him in rehearsals, really. Hey, you know there's a New Artist vacancy? You going to go for it?"

"I don't have a shot," Sing says, hoping Zhin will argue with her.

Zhin never disappoints. "Of course you do!" She lowers her voice and leans in. "Look, why do you think your dad is here? Griss has him scouting it out. The board is going to be here for Gloria Stewart International, which means they'll be here for your performance, too. Word is, they're seriously considering infusing some fresh young blood into the opera. Fire Lake is hurting for cash, you know, and the crowd *loves* a prodigy."

"That's true," Sing concedes. "If they could have a ten-year-old wearing the Viking horns and riding in on the winged horse, I'm sure they would—the CDs would sell like crazy. But that's novelty. Fire Lake hires *talent. Class.*"

"Yeah, of course. I'm a case in point, right?" Zhin says, and they laugh. "But all I'm saying is they're, you know, trying to think differently. And an exceptional conservatory student would be a big hit with the masses. I mean, you gotta have the *pipes,* of course, but you *do,* Sing. I've heard you."

Diva-ness pulses in Sing's chest. "Still," she says, "they don't just hand New Artist spots out."

"Your mom got one, right? Sing Angelique. Bang, you're in."

It would never be as simple as *Bang, you're in.* But Sing allows herself to entertain the thought, with a mix of shame and glee. *Why not? Why shouldn't I capitalize on my mother's success?* Energized by Zhin's optimism, she tries out another doubt, just to see what Zhin does with it. "I'm not even the best singer at DC. You know I didn't get the lead, right? That I'm understudying Lori Pinkerton?"

"Who's Lori Pinkerton?" Zhin narrows her eyes and scans the room. "Never mind," she says. "Got her. Blondie over there, am I right? Yeah, she was the one hooting out Angelique, wasn't she?"

Sing looks. Lori is leaning against the stage, talking to friends. But she is not just part of a group. The friends are unmistakably *with her.*

"Typical," Zhin says. "Glitz and attitude. Loves the lifestyle, hates the work. Music is *work,* Sing. You know that."

"Sure." It is certainly work for Zhin, who practices five hours a day.

Zhin puts a hand on her hip. "Blondie's a big fish here, but she won't last five years out of conservatory. White teeth and a hot body may set her apart now, but girls like her aren't *dedicated.* Dime-a-dozen soprano. For every one onstage there are eleven more in the wings waiting for her to die. Forget her—Tori? Lori? Forget her."

"Yes, but she was cast," Sing says. "She's the one onstage. That makes me one of the eleven waiting in the wings, doesn't it?"

"You are *not* one of the eleven. You are a da Navelli. Lori?" Zhin leans back. "Politics."

Politics. Can it be that simple? Politics?

Everything is simpler with Zhin around. "You know," Sing says as the thought occurs to her, "maybe they didn't *want* me singing Angelique. Because of my mom and everything."

"Exactly." Zhin pulls a comb from her purse and runs it through her glossy hair.

"Maybe my dad even *talked* to them." Even as she says it, she isn't sure who *they* are—the Maestro? the president?—but her brain keeps churning. "Maybe he *knew* we were doing *Angelique* after all, and he told them not to cast me." It is ridiculous. Zhin makes her think ridiculous things sometimes, she knows, but she likes thinking them.

The lights flicker, heralding the end of the break. Zhin pauses midcomb. "You didn't tell him you were doing *Angelique*?" She whistles. "How'd he react?"

Sing grimaces. "I don't know. He must have found out tonight, I think, if he didn't know before."

"Wow." Zhin glances across the rows of theater seats to where Maestros da Navelli and Keppler seem to be finishing up their conversation. The lights dim. She turns back to Sing. "I don't think he wants you doing the understudy, but it's not what you think. Here he comes."

Ernesto da Navelli is making his way slowly across the house, stopping occasionally to murmur words of greeting and shake hands with excited students. He reaches Sing and Zhin, smiling warmly, and says, "Sing, my dear, come talk to your *papà*."

The lobby is empty now as rehearsal starts up again. The padded doors close softly behind Sing and her father, muffling the sounds from the theater. Maestro da Navelli fits perfectly with the deep red carpeting and gold walls, as though he lives there. He is not easily overshadowed by opulence.

"I will not ask why you kept the conservatory's choice of opera a secret from me," he says, smile gone. "I understand, *carina*."

She doesn't dare allow herself to feel relieved yet. "I'm sorry, Pap—"

"You probably thought I wouldn't allow you to participate. And I must tell you, Sing, it goes against my entire heart to think of you singing—this."

She looks at the floor, squishing the carpeting with her shiny black shoes.

He clears his throat. "But there is nothing we can do now. It is too late to change the program. If I had known earlier—but never mind. It is done. And perhaps it can be to our advantage."

To our advantage? Sing's stomach twists. Politics, just as Zhin said. The puppets and the strings. And somehow it's worse when your father has the strings.

"You may know already that Harland wants to stir things up a little at Fire Lake with this New Artist spot. There are any number of fine *soprani* who would be suitable for an audition, but he wants to try something new—a truly budding career. Someone we can really groom from day one, who will grow up right in front of our audience. A cocoon from which they can see a butterfly emerge! Wouldn't that be exciting?"

Sing tries to smile. She has trouble processing what she is hearing. Does he want *her* to be this butterfly?

He puts a hand to her chin. "It will be like Barbara da Navelli."

She doesn't know what to say. She looks away.

"But there is a problem." His voice is businesslike now. "Harland will only consider young singers who have performed at least one leading role. On this, he will not budge, and he is right, of course. Were *you* to show an interest in an audition for him, I'm afraid you would not qualify." He sighs and mutters, "I *knew* you should have sung Isis at Stone Hill! But I held my tongue. *Stupido!*"

Sing studies a nearly invisible seam where two sheets of gold damask wallpaper meet. She can hear singing from behind the padded doors. "I have to get back to rehearsal, Papà."

"Rehearsal? And what do you do there?" He throws his hands up. "Understudy for a run of one performance? You are useless. Oh, *carina,* don't be upset. I didn't mean it that way." He puts an arm around her shoulders, and she leans into his crisp suit. "You are *underappreciated.*"

"There's nothing wrong with being an understudy," she says, remembering his own words.

He kisses her forehead. "Certainly there is nothing wrong with it! Never forget that! But for one performance, my dear. Surely that is a lot of work for nothing, eh? For one so talented as my girl?" Sing shrugs. Her father goes on. "This Lori Pinkerton. She is not so wonderful, eh? Sometimes directors make mistakes, do they not? But mistakes are easily corrected."

Sing pulls away, heart beating forcefully just under the surface. "You would let me sing Angelique? After—after—?"

His face darkens. "We do not have much choice, do we?"

For just a moment, she sees everything laid out in front of her— the Autumn Festival, the conversation with Griss, the New Artist spot, Fire Lake, rehearsals with Zhin—

"No," she says quietly. "No, I can't."

"You *can,* my dear. Of course you can! You know the role already. You have been rehearsing it."

"It's not fair," she says. "It's not fair to everyone else. I—I want to do it on my own."

He pats her cheek. "You are a special girl, my little butterfly. Your voice is from heaven. I just want the world to hear it. Think about it, *carina.* I leave tomorrow afternoon. Think about it. Okay?"

And he is out the door and crossing the quad toward Hector Hall. Sing watches him go.

Angelique. This is what she has wanted her whole life. All it will take is one word to her father: *Sì*. Yet everything about it is wrong. What would Jenny and Marta say?

She pushes open the heavy door to the theater, makes her way down the dark aisle, and slides in beside Zhin. They are silent for a few moments, watching the rehearsal, which seems significantly more relaxed now that Maestro da Navelli is gone.

The teardrop is cold against Sing's chest. She leans in to Zhin and whispers, "What would you wish for, if you had one wish?"

Zhin laughs out loud, drawing attention. Sing slouches in her seat. Zhin whispers back, "Why wish for anything? There's nothing you can't have if you decide to go out and get it. Take advantage of every opportunity. You've got to learn that. There's no better feeling than going for what you want and grabbing it."

Sing remembers the exhilaration she felt after the Noble Call. After Ryan kissed her. But she didn't go out and grab either of those things—they just happened as she was pulled along through the life that seems to form around her.

But maybe there is a way to get that feeling again. Maybe it's as Zhin says—she must take advantage of every opportunity.

Like the opportunity her father is presenting her with now?

"You wanna go?" Zhin grabs her bag.

It's tempting. Another hour, at least, of Maestro Keppler's disapproving glares, of Daysmoor's scowl, of Lori's protruding lips. Of sitting unnoticed in the dark house.

"Look," Zhin says, "you want to be a diva? Stop letting people walk all over you. This is pointless. They are *making* you sit here in the dark for three hours just to watch somebody else sing what should be *your* role. Stand up for yourself, Sing."

Sing watches Maestro Keppler's back. He didn't turn around once during the entire first half of rehearsal. He probably can't even see into the house because of the stage lights. What is the point of her sitting here? Of all the understudies sitting here in the dark? It's not fair.

Could she go? Could she just . . . go?

What would Barbara da Navelli do?

"Okay," she says. "Let's go."

Zhin rises, and they make their way down the darkened aisle. "Seriously—where do *our* people hang out around here? I'm so done with this crowd. Did you check out hippie girl up there with the huge fairy necklace? Give me a break!"

Forty-six

Y EAH, THIS IS ABOUT IT," Carrie Stewart says, rattling the ice in her drink with her straw. "I don't know who'll show up tonight. Could be okay, could be dead."

Sing taps her foot to the Mountain Grill's live music—a circle of guitars, banjos, pennywhistles, drums, violins, and what look to her like weird little bagpipes. Quite a few customers are scattered, at the bar, snugged up to tables, pulling in extra chairs. Sing notices Laura and her friend from The Nature of Music sharing a plate of nachos in the corner and laughing. "I'm glad we didn't have to walk," she says. "Thanks for the ride."

"No problem," Carrie says. "That's what the Tomato is for." The temperature outside was dropping rapidly, and Sing and Zhin were grateful for a lift in Carrie's falling-apart red sedan.

"This is the only place open?" Zhin frowns in the direction of the music circle.

"It's the only place, period," Sing says. Zhin whistles quietly through her teeth.

Carrie sits back, her orange hair glowing in the low light. "They always do live music, though. It's all locals. Some of them have been coming every Saturday night for, like, forty years." The circle is playing something fast and folksy, and she taps her fingers on the table along with them.

Sing allows herself to sit back, too, despite Zhin's obvious, fidgety discomfort. She watches the circle—old people, young people, and a few bright-eyed children. One girl, who looks about ten or eleven, sits next to an older man who could be her grandfather. They are both playing violins—*fiddles,* she tells herself—and she can see the girl watching the man's fingers closely.

"She's cute and a half," Carrie says, following Sing's gaze. Sing nods.

Zhin peers across the room. "Choppy runs, awkward bowing, uneven tone. Sloppy."

"Well, I was pretty sloppy at that age, too," Carrie says, and Sing thinks her light tone seems a little more forced. "It's tricky when you grow a foot and your violin stays the same size."

"Yes, it is," Zhin says, sipping her drink. "You have to work twice as hard."

Carrie laughs. "I *always* work twice as hard. I'm just saying, it's okay to spend some time with your grandpa and have some fun. She's just a kid."

"That's fine." Zhin's gaze rests lazily on the musicians across the room. "But not taking your practicing seriously causes backsliding."

Sing has gone the occasional day without serious practice. Maybe it's different for voice students—after only a couple hours in the practice room, she is *tired*. But she studies Zhin's face—serious and flawless, just like her music. Zhin never gets tired.

Carrie mashes her ice with her straw. "There's nothing wrong with playing for fun. *All* playing should be fun. That's why we do this. I *love* to play, even if it's just scales. And a day off once in a while is good for you, too. I think it lets everything sink in."

Zhin winces as the musicians run off course a little. She turns back to Carrie. "For me, music is a career, not a hobby. I've fought to get where I am. I'm just saying, as a piece of friendly advice, it's never a good idea to lose your focus. If you want to get anywhere, that is."

Sing's stomach twists just a little as Carrie's expression grows noticeably frostier. "You know," Carrie says, "I am first chair at one of the most prestigious conservatories in the country."

Zhin smiles in a way Sing doesn't like. "Well, I'm glad all that commitment has worked out for you, then."

Carrie leans forward, her pixie face hard and pointed. "Don't talk to me about commitment."

The circle of musicians ends its song. Laughter bubbles over the scrape of chairs on the wooden floor and the thunk of sturdy glasses being set down on tables.

Sing says, "Carrie is Gloria Stewart's great-granddaughter. Isn't that cool?" Maybe Zhin will be won over by celebrity.

"You may be first chair among your teenage peers at this school," Zhin says, ignoring Sing, "but I'm contracted by one of the best orchestras in the world."

Sing feels her mouth open slightly.

Silently, Carrie gets up, throws a few dollars on the table, and walks out.

But Zhin is *right,* Sing tells herself, although she can't quite bring herself to look at her face. She knows the rigid expression she'll find there. Instead, she watches the young girl and her grandfather pick up their fiddles and start an easy jig. *You do have to fight for what you want,* she thinks. *You can't let your guard down. And that girl has sloppy articulation.*

"Great," Zhin says. "There goes our ride. What's her problem? It's not like I said anything that wasn't true."

"I don't know." Sing's stomach still feels weird. Maybe Carrie will come back once she realizes Zhin was only trying to be helpful. After all, there is no denying that as accomplished as Carrie is, she's not playing for Fire Lake. She should be grateful for Zhin's advice.

The door opens, but it isn't Carrie who steps in from the dark chill.

"Ooh, who's the fox?" Zhin says. "Is he from DC?"

Sing blushes. "Yeah. That's Ryan Larkin." *Tell her he's your boyfriend.*

But she doesn't. Suddenly she is afraid to say it out loud, as if he will disappear the moment she looks away toward the real world. Suddenly it seems too ridiculous to be true.

She watches Ryan, Aaron, and Teddy Lund scan the room, notice Zhin and her, and head toward their table. Aaron and Teddy might not be striking on their own, but Ryan makes them look important. Aaron seems lithe like a movie star, not skinny, and Teddy looks rugged instead of lumbering. Their entrance is clearly noticed by the Grill's other patrons—particularly the girls.

"Introduce me!" Zhin whispers as she and Sing slide their chairs to make room.

"Hey, girls," Ryan says. "Aren't you supposed to be at rehearsal, *Miss da Navelli*?" He sounds so much like Apprentice Daysmoor as he says her name that she laughs.

"Who's your friend?" Teddy asks, his cologne wafting over them. Zhin smiles.

"Oh, um, this is Zhin Fan," Sing says. "Zhin, this is Teddy, Aaron, and Ryan. From DC." Aaron leans forward, studying Zhin intently. Sing watches Ryan's face, but he displays only polite interest.

"Hi." Zhin's teeth are perfect.

"Nice to see you girls," Aaron says. "Now tell me—are you good divas or bad divas?"

Sing smirks. "We are queens of the land! Pay homage, and you may keep your heads!"

Everyone laughs except Zhin, who raises a thin eyebrow. "Sing, you are *Italian*. 'Divas' aren't queens. They're *goddesses*. You ought to know that." Sing forces a chuckle. "So," Zhin says to the guys, "what are your horns?"

"Oboe," Aaron says.

"Violin," Teddy says, which surprises Sing, who didn't wonder what his instrument was during their one unpleasant encounter at Carrie's party. As proof, he pulls a worn case from its bag under the table.

"And you brought it with you." Zhin's sweet tone covers just a hint of mockery, which Sing wonders if anyone else can detect.

"Teddy's going to play us a tune," Ryan says. "What, is there like one waitress? Don't worry, I've got this round." He rises. "You girls all set?"

Sing watches him head to the bar. Her tablemates are uncomfortably silent, but this barely registers as she studies the back of Ryan's head.

Finally, she hears Zhin say, "So?"

"So what?" Teddy says, and Sing turns back to the table.

"So are you going to play? Or are you all talk?"

Teddy's face flushes slightly as Aaron elbows him. "Okay," he says. "I've got a new tune this week, so don't make fun of me if it's not perfect." He clicks open his case and crosses the floor with the darkest, dullest violin Sing has ever seen; it looks as if he dug it up out of a bog somewhere. The local musicians, midjig, greet him with cheerful familiarity, and chairs squeak aside to make room.

The music ends as Ryan returns with the drinks, choosing the chair next to Sing's. Everyone at the table turns their attention to Teddy, lifting his violin to his chin amid scattered claps and shouts of, "Give us a tune!"

He closes his eyes and sets in on a tune, which to Sing's ears is virtually indistinguishable from the others she's heard tonight. But the tone of the dark violin is sweet and deep, the quick notes pattering pleasantly over the guitars and banjos like fat raindrops. The young girl watches Teddy intently—not his fingers this time, as with her grandfather, but his round face. Sing smiles. Ryan and Aaron tap the table in rhythm.

When the tune is over, the musicians bark words of praise and encouragement as Teddy's bashfulness adds color to his already florid cheeks. "A bird never flew on one wing," says the old man. "Give us another!"

Teddy is swayed and starts a strange, jerky melody. The others watch for a few moments, silently fingering the chords, then join in. The young girl apparently knows this one—she raises her violin and plays along, timidly at first, but becoming braver when Teddy notices her and flashes an encouraging smile.

Sing applauds along with the rest of the patrons as the musicians finish; Ryan whistles and Aaron pounds the table. Only Zhin seems too preoccupied with sipping her seltzer to notice the tune is over.

"Never heard that one," Aaron says as Teddy sits, carefully placing the dark violin on the table.

"It's just an old hornpipe my mum used to play on the pennywhistle."

"Really," Zhin says. "I liked the first one better."

"Oh, that." Teddy loosens his bow as the musicians begin another tune. "That's 'Saint Anne's Reel.' It's popular as hell, so I figured I'd better learn it."

"Yeah. I learned a few reels a while back as an exercise. My old teacher thought I should be familiar with folk ornaments." Zhin's tone is nonchalant, but Sing recognizes the underlying intent. She keeps her mouth shut.

Teddy says, "You know some reels? Go join in. They'd love it. You can borrow my violin."

"Yeah, let's see what you've got," Ryan says.

"Oh, no." Zhin leans back. "I wouldn't want to show off or anything."

At first, Sing thinks it is a joke and nearly snorts. But Zhin's expression is nothing but modesty.

By the time the tune is over, Zhin has been convinced to insinuate herself into the center of the circle. Young, beautiful, rich, and confident—clearly not a local—she drops the modest act as soon as she has the floor.

Sing has heard Zhin play many times and is not taken in by the reel, which is irrationally fast, extravagantly ornamented, and needlessly complex. But she watches the faces of the Grill's patrons and musicians. They are enthralled. If Teddy's notes were raindrops, Zhin's are ice shards—utterly uniform, cutting, glossy, cold, and hard. They are sharp, smooth perfection. And Sing realizes that nothing she has heard tonight can compare. It's as though each shining note Zhin plays illuminates a flaw in someone else. After a while, the guitars and banjos and strange little bagpipes are silent, and the room is filled only with the dazzling brightness emanating from the dark violin.

Zhin doesn't stop after one reel, or two. At one point, Sing realizes the young girl and her grandfather are no longer there, but she didn't notice when they left.

Forty-seven

THE SNOW STARTED JUST AFTER MIDNIGHT. Now, as Sing blearily crosses the quad with Zhin, the whole campus sparkles with fresh white radiance in the harsh sunlight.

"We should have gotten up earlier," Sing says. "I'm going to sound like crap. But at least I read my chapters in *Moby-Dick*."

"If they didn't stop serving breakfast so damn early, you'd be out here alone," Zhin says. "I'm going back to bed after this."

"I wish I could." Sing hopes the watery orange juice and watery eggs will wake her up. She and Zhin stayed up far too late talking and laughing before falling asleep in a heap of blankets on the floor.

"These socks are so cute!" Zhin admires her woolen calves. "Too bad you didn't have an extra skirt, too. I'll have to look for one."

"You're welcome." Sing's boots sound like yeti feet as they crunch along the newly shoveled walkway. She has to admit, Zhin's patent leather flats do look cool with the conservatory's regulation kneesocks, in what Jenny might call a sort of neo-retro-ironic way. But her feet must be freezing.

However, if they are, Zhin doesn't show it. Sing attempts to drag her own body into compliance, trying to emulate Zhin's confident stride and straight spine. *Today,* she thinks. *Today I sing Angelique for real.* She has no idea how she'll make it through American lit class. How can they schedule class before a run-through?

She frowns. "Is my father coming to rehearsal?"

"No," Zhin says. "He's having lunch with Maestro Keppler down in the village this afternoon. I told him I'd come along. Hope you don't mind."

Sing stops walking. "What? Maestro Keppler's not going to be at rehearsal?"

Zhin shrugs. "It's just a—" She shrugs again. "I don't know. I guess he has a lot going on. We're leaving today."

They start toward the dormitory again. "It's just an understudy rehearsal," Sing says. "That's what you meant."

It's an hour into American lit, and Sing can't stop doodling. But instead of her usual assortment of flowers, treble clefs, and cubes— and, lately, shepherdesses—she is drawing her own name. Over and over. Block letters, ornate script, tiny scratches, huge bubbles. *Sing. Sing. Sing.* Is it even her name anymore, or is it merely a word? An order? Given by whom?

Her father will be leaving soon to have lunch with Maestro Keppler and Zhin. Will she see him after the understudy run-through? Doubtful. He probably won't even come back to campus. Why would he?

Think about it, carina.

She has done nothing but think about it. Now, the soothing drone of Mr. Paul's weak baritone seems to create an insulated, timeless vacuum that contains nothing but herself, her thoughts, and the blond hair that glints as its owner takes notes from the chair-desk in front of her. It isn't Lori's hair, but it might as well be.

"What will happen?" asks Mr. Paul, his usually ruddy face approaching its natural pale hue in the chilly, cement-walled classroom. "Anyone? Miss da Navelli?"

"I don't know," Sing says. Some of her classmates chuckle, and the sound disrupts the vacuum. She looks up. Mr. Paul is frowning.

"Well, what do you think? You have read up to page 250, yes?"

She places a hand on the book on her desk. "Yes."

"So?" He extends his hands, palms up. He knows she wasn't paying attention.

Sing swallows, frustration pricking at her esophagus all the way down. She *read* the chapters. She *did* her homework. Why can't she just get a break?

Mr. Paul leans back against his desk at the front of the classroom, apparently deciding to take pity on her and repeat his question. "What do you think would happen if Ahab killed Moby Dick?"

Sing taps the book cover. She doesn't have the focus or brainpower right now to deal with this. "Um . . . the *Pequod* could go home."

"Yes, but what would happen to Ahab?"

After a few moments of uncomfortable silence, Sing hopes Mr. Paul will set his sights on someone else. She is relieved when the door opens with a metallic squeak.

An apprentice with long brown hair steps in discreetly. She surprises Sing by pointing in her direction, then curling her index finger into a *Come here* gesture. Sing mouths the word *Me?* although her silence is unnecessary; everyone is already looking at her. The apprentice nods, and Sing follows her into the hallway, closing the door behind her.

"Hey, Sing, right? Sorry to get you out of class."

"Not a problem. You saved me from Mr. Paul's *Moby-Dick* enthusiasm."

The apprentice laughs, her voice chipper and slightly shrill, but not wholly unpleasant. "For a minute, at least. Anyway, here you go." She holds out a folded piece of yellow paper. Sing hesitates but takes the paper; she draws her eyebrows in confusion. The apprentice says, "Oh, it's a write-up. You haven't gotten one of these before? Sorry, that didn't come out very nice! I mean, they're not that uncommon is all."

"A write-up? What did I do?" Sing unfolds the paper.

The apprentice shrugs. "Dunno. We're not supposed to read them, just deliver them."

WRITE-UP, the paper is severely headlined, though its hastily photocopied appearance isn't as intimidating as the pristine formality of a censure. Sing reads the description of her offense—leaving rehearsal without permission last night. The bottom is signed by the president's secretary and, unlike the censure, by the person reporting the offense.

She could just scream. "I've got understudy run-through this afternoon—our first one—and *Daysmoor's* giving me a write-up? *Now?* Like I don't have enough to think about!"

"Ugh, Plays-poor's the worst. He never even speaks to the other apprentices. Too good for us, I guess!" the apprentice says. "Anyway, the president likes write-ups to go out as soon as the paperwork's done, no matter what time it is. I think he tries to make it so people get pulled from class—that way everyone knows about it and it's more embarrassing. Sorry, I didn't mean to make it worse!"

An itching at the back of Sing's brain tells her she would probably like this girl some other time, some other place. But now, her mind is full of an imaginary conversation with her father, her voice high and bright. *Yes, a write-up. No, it's not the same as a censure. Yes, I've been misbehaving. I'm sorry. I haven't been doing what you sent me here to do.*

Sing doesn't collect her things or go back to class, and she doesn't stop marching until she has climbed up to senior floor of Hud, where Zhin's room is. She couldn't stand another minute of American lit, and Hud's empty lobby made her shiver.

Why am I freaking out about this write-up? she wonders, yeti boots thumping dully on the hard carpeting. *And why am I skipping class, which is sure to get me another one?*

But her gut answers her brain. It doesn't matter if she gets another one. One, two, ten, what does it matter?

What does any of this matter?

She needs Zhin now, the way Zhin puts everything in perspective.

The hallway is bright with sunlight streaming in generously through the large window at the end. Zhin is set up all the way down the hall from the stairwell in an unused room hastily made up for her visit. Sing calms down as she approaches. Zhin will have a few things to say about Apprentice Daysmoor, she is certain. And maybe she'll have more details about the New Artist vacancy, squirreled away from conversations with Sing's father.

Hardly anyone locks their doors when they're in, at least in Hud, so Sing isn't surprised when the handle turns. But, stepping into the dim room, she is surprised to find Zhin again tangled up in the heap of blankets on the floor, as she and Sing were last night.

Only it isn't nearly so innocent now, and it isn't Sing who is with her.

It is Ryan.

Forty-eight

SING'S HANDS ARE SHAKING, and it's not with cold or the thudding of her steps. She feels unbalanced, precarious, grasping. She is running across the snowy quad toward Hector Hall, where her father is.

Sì, she will tell him. *Sì. Yes.*

She has been stupid and childish. Zhin gets everything she wants, and always has. So does Lori Pinkerton. So did Barbara da Navelli. *Divas.* It's not a bad word or a good one. It's reality.

A winter breeze rushes down from the mountain. She has spent so much time wondering about the Felix and Tamino and the stupid teardrop around her neck, when she could have had her wishes granted anytime. The diva inside Sing is triumphing; pieces are falling into place to make a new picture of the world, even as part of the old Sing tugs at the corners, threatening to tear them back and reveal something ugly underneath. She doesn't care. She reaches Hector Hall with one word in her mind: *Sì.*

Ernesto da Navelli is in the lobby, reading a newspaper. He looks up, frowning, as the door slams, but his face softens as Sing rushes over. *"Oh, mio Dio, farfallina!* What is the matter?"

"Nothing, Papà—I just want to tell you yes—"

"You're crying! What has happened?"

"Nothing. Nothing! I just want to tell you yes!"

She feels the weight of his hands on her shoulders. "Calm yourself, *carina,*" he says. "Why are you telling me yes? What yes?"

She inhales; Hector's lobby smells musty and comfortable. "Yes about *Angelique.* I want to sing Angelique. I want to go to Fire Lake. I want—" She realizes she is speaking Italian and breaks off.

Her father smooths her hair and smiles. "I knew you would take this opportunity. Very well. Let me take care of it. Ah, and here is Maestro Keppler now. George!"

Maestro Keppler approaches from the staircase on the other side of the room. Sing sees his eyes dart to her, but he addresses her father. "Are you ready to leave already, Maestro? I thought—"

"No, no. I was just reading the newspaper, eh? And my little girl comes in to say hello." He puts an arm around her shoulders. "She has a run-through of *Angelique* today, yes? I couldn't be more proud. And I hear the production is coming along quite well."

Maestro Keppler's shoulders stiffen. "Yes, certainly it is. I'm very pleased."

"I am looking forward to it! A wonderful choice for the first production in the conservatory's new theater. Although perhaps the Autumn Festival should be called the Winter Festival with all this snow?" Sing's father laughs, and she ventures a look at Maestro Keppler, whose smile seems rather strained. "We have some fine *pianisti* coming for the competition," Maestro da Navelli goes on. "And the opera will be *magnifico,* yes? My esteemed colleague Signor Griss will be most interested. He would love to fill the New Artist vacancy at Fire Lake with a talented amateur. Someone who has performed a major role."

Sing senses the negotiation beginning. The first sign, though she doesn't know why, is always her father sprinkling the conversation with Italian words for which he well knows the English counterparts.

Maestro da Navelli gazes out the window. "You must be very

proud of the academy, Maestro. It is a beautiful campus. I'm suddenly tempted to take a walk. Do we have time before lunch?"

My cue to leave, Sing thinks, exhilarated.

It is done.

Sing grabs a box lunch and heads back to Hud.

"I did it, Woolly," she says, but isn't sure how to explain further. Woolly's smooth button eyes are friendly.

A knock. Sing covers Woolly with a pillow and says, "Come in."

"*There* you are." Jenny plops down next to her on the bed. Marta follows, lowering herself gracefully to the floor.

Sing takes a bite of fried rice. "Hey."

"Hey?" Jenny's stare pierces. "How about, Hey, where were you last night? You totally skipped out on rehearsal."

"Oh, sorry. My . . . friend is in town."

"Yeah." Jenny shoots Marta a glance. "We heard about your *friend*."

Sing puts her fork down. "Oh, yeah? What did you hear?" She notices an edge to her own voice.

"Nothing," Marta says quickly. "Have you been crying?"

"No," Sing says. "Look, I have to go to rehearsal."

Jenny scootches back and pulls her legs up onto the bed. "Not for a few minutes. Eat your lunch. Today's the big day, huh?"

Sing takes another bite of rice.

"Oh, I forgot about today!" Marta says. "That's right. Oh, you're going to be awesome!"

Sing looks at her. "Of course you forgot. Everyone forgets about the understudy run-through; or if they remember, they're just happy to have an easy rehearsal. We don't *matter*. Well, I'm going to show Maestro Keppler that I *do* matter."

"Fierce," Jenny says.

"Jeez, Sing," Marta says. "I'd be honored to understudy the lead. There's nothing wrong with that."

Sing pushes the rest of her lunch onto her bedside table. "That's easy for you to say. You got a role."

"Well . . ." Marta doesn't seem to know how to finish.

"Look," Sing says, "if I'm going to get anywhere, I have to start *acting* the part. It's what my—it's advice I've been given. Make an entrance. I'm going to show the Maestro he made a mistake."

Marta inhales, her wide eyes shining. "Wow! You're going to try to show up Lori?"

"Gutsy," Jenny says with approval.

"I don't think she'll like that," Marta says.

Sing crosses her arms. "I didn't like Lori telling President Martin I went into the woods. I didn't like getting a censure because of it."

"What?" Marta's jaw drops. "You got a censure?"

"So it's payback," Jenny says, still approving.

"It's not exactly payback," Sing says. "I just want to take what's mine. Angelique."

A brief but heavy silence dampens the room. "Well, technically, the role *isn't* yours," Jenny says.

Sing meets Jenny's gaze. "Like hell it isn't."

Jenny seems puzzled for a minute, then shrugs. "I mean, it's not like the Maestro is going to recast based on one rehearsal. You'll be great, don't get me wrong—you'll be better than Lori, I'm sure— but that kind of thing doesn't happen. As irritating as she is, Lori's paid her dues. She's a senior."

"Her mom and dad are coming to the performance," Marta says.

"You'll totally be in line for the lead next year," Jenny says. "Maybe even in the spring—Lori will be focusing on her senior recital, and—"

"I'm not talking about next year, or the spring." Sing stands. "I'm talking about *now. This* role. *This* New Artist vacancy. I don't care what the Maestro thinks. My father will *tell* him what he thinks, and I'll be *damned* if he or Lori Pinkerton or anyone else is going to get in my way."

Jenny crosses her arms. "Jesus, Sing, you're really doing this? You're using your dad to take someone else's part? Seriously?"

She's jealous. They're all jealous. Sing doesn't know where the thoughts come from. "It's not fair that I should be understudying Lori Pinkerton. I mean, do you *know* who my mother was?"

"Well." Jenny stands, and Marta follows suit. "Don't let *us* get in your way."

Sing hears Marta's "See ya" as the door clicks shut, but Jenny doesn't say another word.

Forty-nine

ONSTAGE, THE BELEAGUERED CHORUS sings the uncharacteristically sappy number that precedes Angelique's most famous aria. The orchestra is present and in tune, but Sing can't give them credit for anything more than that. *Just an understudy rehearsal.*

Normally, she would be mortified by walking in late to a rehearsal, particularly a full run-through. But today she strides up the center aisle. She took her time getting here. Let them wait.

She sees Daysmoor turn his head as he conducts, watching her out of the corner of his eye. Will he dare admonish her publicly, knowing it will just give her an opportunity to say where she has been? What she has been doing? *Securing her role.*

Or will he remain silent, aware that *the* Maestro da Navelli is here on campus? That would be just as much a victory, and everyone would notice. *I walk into rehearsal late and you have nothing to say about it.* Diva.

She sits in the front row and crosses her legs. She doesn't have her score with her.

The number ends and the chorus members shuffle off the stage and into the house. Daysmoor turns around.

"Are you warmed up?" he croaks at her.

This? This is what he has to say? She hates his gravelly voice. "Yes," she says, meeting his gaze with defiance. It isn't true, exactly, but under normal circumstances of course she would have come warmed up!

"Good," he says, turning back to the orchestra. "We started with act three. I'm sure you won't mind beginning with '*Quand il se trouvera.*' Remember your phrasing, please."

As Sing climbs the stairs to the stage, feeling Daysmoor's detached stare on her back, she begins to seethe. How *dare* he treat her like some novice? Sure, maybe she has gotten nervous a few times at rehearsal, which is natural, but that doesn't mean she doesn't know how to *phrase*. Anger obliterating any self-doubt, she throws her shoulders back and breathes.

The five-chord introduction swells. She watches Daysmoor conduct; his style is utilitarian, clunky, but authoritative. *It doesn't matter what he thinks, anyway.*

"*Quand il se trouvera . . .*"

The orchestra marches along, more responsive than her father's record player, which gives her a captivating feeling of dominance. She plays with a couple of phrases, stretching or hurrying the line when the notion strikes her. Daysmoor frowns but follows. She feels the rush of power.

Again she pictures the white dress, she imagines the blond ringlets. She finds herself moving her head and arms delicately, smiling a coy little smile. She understands, now, the dangerous, intoxicating quality of a leading role. It is as though she is the worst sort of dictator—callous and terrible and omnipotent. She wears the orchestra—Daysmoor—like a silk train, delighted by how he follows her own strong steps, perfectly attached. Her voice fills the theater.

And if it weren't for her anger, she might never have discovered this feeling!

When she has finished the aria, she looks haughtily over at Daysmoor, upright yet still managing to appear draped. His expression is inscrutable.

"Attitude isn't everything," he says after a moment. "In fact, it gets in the way of most things. I hope you will figure that out." Then he adds quietly, "But why should you, when your mother never did?"

Sing can't find words to respond. What does *he* know about her mother?

"All right," Daysmoor says. "Do it again." A murmur ripples through the orchestra, audible sighs from the singers in the audience.

"What?" Sing gapes at him.

The corners of his mouth are turned down slightly. "And this time, be a servant of the music, not your ego."

Scattered muttering from the house. Sing pulls her head back in surprise. "Excuse me?"

"Apprentice," the first chair viola says, a hand on his score, "we have a limited amount of time."

"You heard me." Daysmoor's voice is quiet but commanding, and Sing knows he is speaking only to her. "Do it again."

"This is ridiculous," the new diva inside Sing says. "What was wrong with it?"

Apprentice Daysmoor closes his eyes. "That wasn't singing. If I wanted people yelling at me, I'd burst unexpectedly into the girls' locker room. That aria had no shape and no support. It was angry shouting. It was garbage."

Sing gasps. A prickling feeling begins in her chest and spreads outward.

The first chair viola stands up. "Listen, man, don't call her singing garbage. Can we just move on?" He turns to Sing. "That was great, Sing. Night and day from a couple weeks ago."

Apprentice Daysmoor looks at Sing. "She knows I'm right."

Sing's face is hot. *Garbage.*

The ripple of murmuring throughout the theater has become a wave of nervous titters and expressions of shock. "That's cold," someone in the wind section says.

Apprentice Daysmoor straightens up, and Sing notices for the first time how tall he is. "I'm her coach," he says to the first chair viola. "It's my job to get the best performance possible out of her, not coddle her and tell her she's wonderful. Do you disagree?"

The viola sits down and flips the pages of his score. "Not at all, Apprentice Plays—ah, Daysmoor." He smirks. A few orchestra members laugh outright.

Daysmoor's face offers no hints about whatever emotion might be happening inside. He simply raises his baton, still as stone until the orchestra is focused, then gives the downbeat for the introduction to Angelique's aria.

Her face burning, Sing begins again. She will not be taken down. She will not be held back by an arrogant apprentice or ripped apart by the whispers of a jealous house. It is her role now. The aria is louder now, vainer, more energetic. She sings to the balcony. She sings like her mother.

Halfway through, Daysmoor cuts the orchestra off. "Miss da Navelli," he says, "if you're not going to take this seriously, then get out."

Fifty

B ARBARA DA NAVELLI HAS TAKEN to visiting Sing during the night. Sometimes the dream is a memory—the front door whooshing shut, the thuds of baggage hitting the hardwood floor, a loud coo, a present being thrust into Sing's small hands, the click of expensive shoes carrying her mother away again to recharge in some hidden place.

Sometimes the dream is Dunhammond, with Lori and Ryan and Apprentice Daysmoor and the Maestro scorched by Barbara da Navelli's radiance. In these dreams, Sing stands at her mother's side on the Woolly stage, afraid to move her feet lest she crack the shiny floor. "If you play a thing, you make it true," Barbara da Navelli says. She is dressed as Angelique, holding a magnificent golden crook.

"I'm only the understudy," Sing says, squinting at Lori's smug face in the shadows. Or is it Zhin's?

Her mother turns to her. Her eyes are catlike, her teeth elongated. Sing wonders if her mother can see the despair in her eyes, if she will shed a tear and grant her one wish. But her mother only says, "Impossible. You are a da Navelli. Take what is yours." She swings her crook, which crackles and hums so loudly, Sing covers her ears. The stage explodes with electricity. Zhin and Ryan clasp each other and shrink back into the darkness; the Maestro clutches his heart and turns his eyes skyward. Only Apprentice Daysmoor remains impassive, his black eyes fixed on Sing as though he is sitting in judgment of her.

This night, Sing wakes with a smoldering determination, her mother's words as fresh in her ears as if she had only just spoken them. *Take what is yours.* But in the dimness, Sing finds herself clutching not an electric, golden crook, but a soft, worn lamb with button eyes.

As her senses continue to awaken, she frowns. Something is glowing. A chill courses through her body, not from the air, but from what feels like an icicle driven into her chest.

The crystal.

She unclasps the necklace and holds the pendant away from her body, squinting at it in the dull gleam it is creating. She remembers the ashy smell of snow, trees as glossy as tar, and the gentle rustling of leaves.

Fifty-one

I *DIDN'T KNOW he was your boyfriend. You never told me.*"

Crossing the icy quad, Sing blinks away the memory.

"*You've got to know about him, Sing. How could you not know?*"

She doesn't want to hear it. Blink.

"*I thought we'd laugh about it. He's screwing around with that Pinkerton girl as well. I thought we'd make fun of her.*"

She kicks a chunk of snow out of the path. At least it is morning, and Zhin is gone. They are both gone. She doesn't need Zhin or her father anymore. She doesn't need Jenny and Marta. The clockwork has been set in motion. Once Harland Griss hears her at the Autumn Festival, once she has gotten the New Artist position, then . . . then . . .

She doesn't finish the thought. She doesn't know how.

Blink.

She should have done laundry last night, especially since Zhin took a pair of regulation kneesocks with her. She didn't even offer to give them back. Now Sing is on her last pair and she'll have to do laundry tonight, during the school week, when she should be doing homework. And she should really take a shower, as evidenced by her hair, shoved up into a messy ponytail. And the *crows*. She has to start thinking about her stupid report on the stupid *crows*.

As if to rub it in, they caw horribly as she reaches Archer. Part of her can't believe she is actually going to her coaching session after getting kicked out of rehearsal yesterday. But it doesn't seem to matter much, now. Not after everything has settled, flurries of emotion slowing and drifting into stillness. Not after—

Blink.

She pushes open the door to the little practice room.

Apprentice Daysmoor sits in the corner, head tipped back, eyes closed, mouth turned down in the smallest of scowls. His arms are folded and his legs crossed at the ankles, but his gray robes cover these bony angles in gentle folds.

She yanks up one of the rusty music stands to the proper height and tosses her *Angelique* score onto it. Then she sits down heavily at the piano and starts playing her warm-ups.

"Where's the little master?" Daysmoor murmurs after a moment, as though he isn't really interested. Sing doesn't turn her head, but she can see him out of the corner of her eye.

"Ahhhh-ehhhh-eeeee-ohhhh-oooo." That "ee" was flat. She stretches her neck, one side and the other.

The apprentice draws his arms out from his robes and crosses them behind his head. "Still abed? You want me to go fetch him?"

"I told him I'd eviscerate him if he showed his face. *Ahhhh-ehhhh-eeeee-ohhhh-ooooo.*" A little better. She moves on to arpeggios. *"La-la-la-laaaaa-la-la-la."*

Daysmoor doesn't say anything else, and he doesn't stir. It is nearly twenty past nine when Sing finishes warming up. She sits for a moment, looking at the reflection of her tired eyes in the piano's shiny music rack.

"I hear congratulations are in order," Daysmoor says. "For some unfathomable reason, Maestro Keppler has decided that you should sing Angelique at the Autumn Festival instead of Lori Pinkerton."

Sing's heart jumps. It has happened, then. She knew it would.

Even before her father's conversation with the Maestro yesterday, something in her knew it would happen; she's been groomed for two years to replace her mother. Yet it is still somehow unbelievable.

Unbelievable, and more real than she could possibly have imagined it to feel.

"So we have work to do," Daysmoor says. "And no sign of Mr. Larkin. Am I supposed to play accompanist as well as coach today? You tell me, since you're the one who decided to tell him not to come."

Before she can stop herself, she says, "Just give me another write-up, then." A mumble, barely audible. Why is she angry? *Now,* when she should be ecstatic. When the plan has worked.

It's his smirk, sitting under those cold, dispassionate eyes. *He probably won't say anything about my comment. He'll probably just shut his eyes and lean back in his chair, pretend he didn't hear—*

"*You* left rehearsal. Not me. And you did it again yesterday. I *should* give you another write-up."

"I only left yesterday because you were being a jerk," she says vehemently, yet bracing herself for the backlash. "And it didn't even matter that I left the other night! Nobody noticed!"

"I noticed," he says.

They are silent for a few moments. Sing slowly plays a scale with one hand.

"Would you rather have a different coach?" Daysmoor says.

Sing looks up. "What?"

The smirk is gone, but his voice isn't harsh. "You're obviously not my biggest fan. Would you rather have someone else?"

What kind of a question is that?

He sits up. "Well?"

Anger tightens her chest. "Well what? You don't even coach me." She didn't mean to say it aloud, but now that it is out there, she lets her hesitation drop away from her like a heavy old coat. "You don't give me any advice. Any *real* advice. Nobody does!"

"Would you listen if I did?" His voice hardens. "How could I possibly have anything useful to say to *Miss da Navelli*? How could anyone?"

"You don't know me," she hisses, rising.

He stands as well, a head taller than her, slouched, ungainly. "You don't know *me*."

She will not be intimidated. "I know you well enough. You gloom around this place like a dusty spirit. You actually *haunt*. You act like you're better than the rest of us. But you know what? You're a total hack and you know it. You're a hack amateur. You can't even play. That's why you're so critical and horrible and lazy. That's why you're not entering the Gloria Stewart competition."

He smiles coldly. "Tell me what you really think, Sing."

It is the first time he has called her by her first name. She doesn't like it. "What I really think? How about what Carnegie Hall thought when you tried to play there?"

His expression doesn't change. "You're attacking me for your own reasons."

Sing snaps, "Why don't you give me a censure, then? Give me two. Get me expelled."

"I'm not doing you any favors. You want to use your name to get roles? Go ahead. You're stuck with it now." His face betrays no emotion. *It never does,* she thinks. *Never more than a flicker, an edge.*

Fury bubbles up from her lungs. "Why can't you just leave me alone? You said yourself you think my singing is garbage." The words come faster now, *accelerando, appassionato.* "I can't help it if my father wants me to get ahead. What's it to you if I'm not a great singer? What's it to you if one stupid school production of *Angelique* is horrible because I couldn't do it?"

He raises his voice. "You want the truth? You say I don't know you. You're right. I *don't* know you. How can anyone know you? Are you the egomaniac your mother was? Sometimes I think so. Or are you a pathetic little mouse, afraid of your own father, your own voice? Sometimes it seems like that." Now he points at her, accusing. "And that's what you've done to your singing—it's constantly shifting between two extremes. Ninety-five percent of what comes out of your mouth *is* garbage."

She freezes, clutching the score, its dry cover chafing her fingers. He closes his mouth and turns away. For a moment, all she can do is stare.

Because it's true.

In the silence that follows, Sing's hot anger dissipates into nothingness. She doesn't say anything but slides the *Angelique* score off the stand and turns to the door.

Daysmoor is right.

"Where are you going?" His voice is cool again, detached. "You have a rehearsal."

Sing turns. "Are you serious?"

"This is a required coaching session. If you skip it, I'll have to report you to Maestro Keppler."

She leans against the door, cold metal against her forehead.

"Miss da Navelli. We have a rehearsal to run."

Her voice, when she finds it, is weak, and she doesn't look at him. "We don't have a rehearsal. Go ahead and tell the Maestro. Tell my father, too. The music world doesn't need me if all I sing is garbage, anyway."

"Stop feeling sorry for yourself." She hears him sit at the piano. "You can do it."

Something about his tone gives her pause. She remembers her first conversation with him, when she couldn't understand why the Maestro had cast her. *Someone he respects assured him you could do it.*

Could it have been Daysmoor?

She doesn't know what to think anymore.

"Anyway," he says softly, "I didn't say *all* your singing was garbage. I said ninety-five percent of it."

To her surprise, she laughs. She doesn't know why his remark makes her laugh, even as it seems her entire world is melting into oblivion. She can't help it.

When she looks up, she finds no malice in his eyes, only patience. "Well," she says, "as long as five percent is okay, I guess."

He is silent for a moment, then fixes her with that dark gaze. "That five percent . . . Sometimes, I think I see the real you. When you are listening—*really* listening. When you smile, always at someone else, of course. That five percent . . ." His gaze falls to the floor. "That five percent that *is* worth something," he says softly, "is the most beautiful sound I've ever heard."

Something in her gives a jolt at this. For the first time, but for just a brief moment, she thought she saw beyond those dull, black eyes to the feeling person within. And it is she who has made him feel something.

He extends his hand, and she looks at it for a moment in confusion before giving him the score.

"You know your sound is lacking something," he says. "That's why you've been parroting your mother's hot arrogance, or the cold, technical perfection that gets drilled into hungry young musicians."

She tries to see through his inscrutable stare, but a dullness at the edges of his eyes is keeping her out. There is something different about him as he speaks, though. A glint of wisdom beneath his hard face. And something else.

"What your sound is missing," he says, "is you."

Her shoulders slump. "I know. I try. I've never been good at acting."

"Listen to me," he says. "I'm not talking about acting. I'm talking about you."

She feels a familiar frustration stinging her throat. "My father is the one who said I was ready for this. I never asked—"

Now he stands and places a hand on each of her shoulders. "Sing da Navelli, look at me." She does, and something tingles her insides. "I'm not talking about your father. I'm talking about *you*."

She starts shaking. "I know, okay? You don't understand what it's like. My mother—"

"I'm not talking about your mother, or your teachers, or your friends. I'm talking about *you*."

"I get the point," she snaps. "All right? But what am I supposed to do? I've been at this school for less than three months!"

He grasps her shoulders more tightly. "I'm not talking about President Martin, the Maestro, François Durand, or goddamn Lori Pinkerton! *I'm talking about you*."

"Stop it!" She can't control her hands, her ribs—why won't they stop shuddering? She can't look at him anymore and drops her head.

His voice softens. "You can't even stand to hear that word, can you? I . . . you poor thing. No wonder you don't know who you are."

Without meaning to, she leans toward him, and he wraps his arms around her. His gray robes smell like the forest in winter.

"I never wanted to be Barbara da Navelli," she says, her voice muffled. "But, somehow, it became my only option."

"When did being Sing da Navelli stop being good enough?" he asks quietly.

"Sing da Navelli was never good enough," she says. "Not since I was little. Not since those afternoons with my father's record players. And definitely not since Barbara da Navelli died."

"Sing . . . ," he says tentatively. "You need to allow yourself to be better than your mother."

She straightens up, stepping away. "What?"

"Listen." He seats himself at the piano. Then he starts to play.

Eyes unfocused, staring at the floor, Sing hears those five famous chords.

Only they are different now. Instead of heavy, clumsy steps toward the grave, they bubble up from the dark heart of a deep lake. They are Angelique's ultimate anguish, knowing her prince will die in the forest. They are sung from the smallest, flattest, weakest, most shadowy place in the human heart.

They are the saddest sounds in the world.

Daysmoor has pushed up the sleeves of his robe and Sing sees his long, thin fingers. His eyes are open and calm, and he doesn't rock back and forth like Ryan. He just plays. He has swept his black hair back from his face, mouth serious.

Sing swallows and takes a step into the curve of the piano.

"Stand up straight and breathe," he says.

And she does.

"Quand il se trouvera . . ."

Daysmoor's words come back to her: *Be a servant of the music, not your ego.* She understands now. She lets go of fear, of showmanship, of the magic party mask. She has nothing to lose, now.

From the first note, it is different. It is all going to be different.

"That's better," he says. "Keep reinventing the sound. Every second. Keep re-forming the vowel. Don't let it decay."

"—dans la forêt sombre . . ." All the hundred little things she has to force herself to think about every time she sings just fall into place. Spine straightened, tongue relaxed, jaw loose, she lets everything drop away—the weight of years, the weight of self—

"More," he says.

"—il comprendra ce que c'est que d'être seul."

And the air. The air is amazing. Her ribs spread and stretch to let in what feels like every bit of air in the room, in the building, in the world.

"Legato," he says.

She has never sung it so quietly or meant it so much. When her last pianissimo has faded, she turns to watch Daysmoor play the end. He wears the same serious, almost blank expression.

When it is over, he turns to her and says, "That was good."

She can tell he means it. *That was good.* And she knows he is right.

He has been right all along.

The air that has been holding her up leaves her now, and she leans against the piano. Daysmoor stands, the sleeves of his robe falling once again over his hands. She looks up at him, face slack, eyes wide. To her surprise, his face lightens—he doesn't smile, exactly, but he loses his seriousness just for a moment. "It's Brahms that does that to me," he says. "I suppose that's enough for today."

Fifty-two

SING'S DRESS ISN'T READY for dress rehearsal.

It's still being altered. She's thicker than Lori, shorter. Lori is a swan. Sing is a duck.

She doesn't use the women's dressing room like everyone else; she doesn't have a costume. So she sits backstage on a metal folding chair, ready for the cue that won't come for at least half an hour. Other singers walk by, alone or in small groups, but no one speaks to her.

Marta flashes a weak smile as she passes but doesn't make eye contact. Lori Pinkerton doesn't show up.

I should be triumphant, Sing tells herself. Or maybe it is Barbara da Navelli telling her.

Eventually, Ryan finds her. "Hey." He pulls over another metal chair. His voice is flat, subdued. She looks at his round face. Without that mischievous smile, he doesn't seem quite as handsome. "Look, Sing," he says, "I screwed up."

Why is Ryan the only person talking to her? Is all this about her stealing Lori Pinkerton's role? Nobody even *likes* Lori Pinkerton.

Ryan stares at her, waiting for a response that doesn't come. "I'm sorry," he says. "You know what Zhin is like."

How can he say her name like that, so easily? Zhin belongs to Sing and Fire Lake and last summer, not to Dunhammond Conservatory. And certainly not to Ryan.

"Hey." He takes her hands in his. "I know everyone's mad about this whole *Angelique* thing right now. But I believe in you. You deserve this role."

She looks at him. The warmth of his fingers feels good. He smiles. "There you are," he says. "I knew you were in there somewhere."

"Everyone hates me," she says.

"Who cares about them? You're moving on to better things. You don't need them, especially not Lori."

Who do I need? she wonders. Her father? Harland Griss? Ryan? *And who needs me?*

Ryan pulls her fingers to his mouth. "Come back to me, Sing. I miss you."

On the other side of the thick velvet curtain, the overture begins with a flourish. Sing rises. "You'd better get out to the house," she says.

"But do you forgive me?" His voice is more urgent now. There is something new sparkling in his eyes; could it be panic? She remembers Lori's confident declaration: *I'll have him back as soon as Gloria Stewart is over.*

Ryan pulls her to himself. The familiar scent of his cologne envelops her. "Forgive me, Sing. Please forgive me."

"I'm on soon," she says, breaking away. "You need to go. I'm sorry."

Sing doesn't know how many people have gathered for the dress rehearsal. The glaring stage lights make it impossible to see into the dark house. She steps onto the set's second level, a faux stone balcony with narrow wooden steps leading down to the floor. The cast members already assembled onstage, farmers and merchants, look straight out of a fairy tale. Sing carries a prop pail of milk but wears her DC uniform, not the ruffly white gown that is still too long and slender for her.

What amazes her most about these first few minutes as Angelique is how well she knows the orchestral parts. Every time she has learned a role, she has become more than familiar with all the other facets of the opera—other characters' story lines and music, the preludes and interludes, the music's historical context, the designers' visions. It is what professionals do. Her mother never sang a role she hadn't studied for at least two years.

But this music is almost a part of her consciousness, like language. She knows the oboe part the way she knows her alphabet, effortlessly. She knows what the second horn is going to say before it says it. All of *Angelique* is a lush drawing she could produce entirely from memory, without even a thought.

This is how my father knows music, she realizes. *Every piece he conducts.*

But as she stands on the pretend balcony, a strangeness overtakes her. There is no Angelique now without her. Were she to shut her mouth and shut her eyes, the songs wouldn't come. The orchestra would play naked, without its mistress.

Maestro Keppler conducts magnificently. His artistry and command rival those of any of the celebrities she has seen, even her father. He cues her clearly. She starts to sing. They communicate with each other across the stage and the bright light, professional to professional, and Angelique comes to life.

It is easier in performance, or near performance. She is not nervous anymore, and she doesn't forget anything, not for a moment. The rehearsal is tiring, but her voice stays strong. She breathes. She stands up straight. She looks into Prince Elbert's florid face and wonders how on earth she could ever have let him intimidate her. Only Marta breaks the spell, ever so slightly, when they share the spotlight. She is not as good an actress as Sing thought; quiet frost radiates from behind her elaborate Tree Maiden makeup.

But for the most part, Sing's focus remains sharp. Even *"Quand il se trouvera"* goes well. It isn't perfect, but it is enough. It will be enough, in two days, to impress Harland Griss.

When the final curtain falls and the house lights come up, Sing collapses into the metal folding chair backstage. The performers chatter as they pack up and leave, the shiny beams of the new theater still ringing with Durand's glorious score.

But all Sing can hear is the five-chord introduction to Angelique's most famous aria, played not by a string section, but on a piano. By a master.

Fifty-three

SING LIES ON HER BED in the warm light of her dragonfly lamp. *Moby-Dick* and a stack of sappy novels sit untouched on her bedside table.

All she can see in her mind are Daysmoor's fingers on black and white keys. She can't think about *Angelique*. Something isn't right. Something she expected to happen today in dress rehearsal—didn't. But she can't even name it.

The cold teardrop rests against her throat, its chain bunched at the base of her neck. She puts a hand to it, wondering. *I wish . . . ,* she begins in her head. *I wish . . .* But she can't finish the sentence.

"Before, I was used to you being my only friend, Woolly," she says, giving him a squeeze. "But everything's all messed up now. I don't think I could get used to it again."

Woolly's dull button eyes seem sympathetic. Sing rolls onto her side, holding the worn gray lamb to her chest. He pushes against the teardrop and it digs into her skin.

"I think I know what Zhin was saying, now," she says to him. "About going out and getting what you want instead of wishing for it. I think a wish—a *real* wish—must be for something impossible.

Something unthinkable. Otherwise it's just you looking for an easy way to—to wherever it is you think you want to go." She looks into Woolly's placid face.

"That was the problem, wasn't it, with Barbara da Navelli? She had a wish granted she didn't need. The Felix would have just torn out her throat."

She turns off her lamp and tries to sleep, but her ears are filled with the dark introduction to Angelique's aria.

After an hour, she sits up. She must hear Daysmoor play again. Before time can move forward. His playing is the only thing that makes sense to her right now.

That means finding him, now, in the middle of the night. Sneaking into the apprentice quarters. And if she is caught, then what? Another write-up? Another censure? Expulsion?

But this is about music. No one could question her intentions. How could anyone hear Daysmoor play and not do anything to hear him again? Sure, he's a jerk, but after today—well, she feels . . . different.

She gets out of her soft pajamas and gathers the pieces of her uniform from the floor, feeling the familiar squeeze of the tight kneesocks, the itchy waistband of the skirt settling into place on her chafed skin. Not that wearing official attire would count for much if she got caught breaking rules again, but it has to be better than being caught out of uniform. She closes her door quietly and drapes a wool scarf over her coat.

She doesn't expect many people to be up and about this late during the school week, though there are always a few students who prefer practicing at night. It's too bad the practice rooms are in Archer, where Daysmoor's tower is, and she'll run the risk of seeing someone. But she can always pretend to be working on her pieces— she *could* have legitimate business there.

There is no one in Hud's lobby as she slips out, feeling like a criminal already even though there is nothing wrong with a student taking a nighttime stroll. The conservatory isn't a prison, after all. A few windows still glow in the dormitory and across the way in Hector Hall.

In the middle of the vast, dark quad, she imagines herself adrift at sea, the campus buildings as towering ocean liners. Light and warmth spill from the portholes in their black hulls, except for the massive ghost ship that is St. Augustine's, jagged and bleak in the gloom. She hurries by.

She can hear muffled music coming from some of the practice rooms as she reaches Archer's metal doors, glad to shut out the darkness at her back. Fluorescent lights flicker, the ugly gray industrial carpeting smells like mold, the world is real again.

She pads down the overly bright hallway. The only two rooms with decent pianos are occupied even now. The satin sound of a trumpet comes from within one of them—why does a trumpet need the good piano room? Still, most of the rooms emanate only silence.

It is easy to see the strange tower from the outside, not as easy to find it from the inside. But the door at the end of the hall is labeled NO STUDENTS, so it is as good a place to start as any. It is not locked, and within she finds an echoey stairwell with a hard rubber floor. Up is good.

Just as she steps through the doorway, a voice startles her.

"Sing?"

She turns, heart beating unreasonably loudly. Jenny is coming out of the room nearest her, clarinet in hand.

"Hi." Sing hopes Jenny doesn't notice the quaver in her voice.

Jenny eyes her. "What are you doing?"

Sing is at a loss. What is she doing? Sneaking into the apprentice quarters to find Apprentice Daysmoor, of all people? To ask him to give her a private concert?

She feels like a drug addict caught rooting through someone's medicine cabinet, embarrassed, no sane explanation. And determined to keep rooting.

"I . . . wanted to practice."

"Yeah, well, those are the stairs."

"Oh . . . yeah."

"You gonna practice on the stairs?"

"No."

Jenny gives her an unreadable look, then gestures. "The piano in this one's pretty good as long as you don't need the bottom octave. I'm done."

"Oh. Thanks." Sing closes the stairwell door and steps toward the practice room. "Um, see you tomorrow!"

"Sure." Jenny heads down the hallway to the main entrance. It wasn't exactly a friendly interaction, but it wasn't hostile, either. Sing watches her go.

When Jenny has left, Sing slips through the doorway and runs up the stairs on tiptoe.

Now is when she must be worried. If she meets an apprentice—or worse, a faculty member—she will have no excuse for her presence. Except maybe *I was looking for the bathroom.* Pretty weak.

She peeks out onto the second floor, identical to the first: the apprentice and faculty practice rooms. *They* probably have decent pianos.

The stairs end at the third floor, which means there must be a different entrance to the tower. The shadowy hallway has fewer doors than the other floors. The carpeting here is thicker and smells of detergent rather than mold.

Her breathing shallow, Sing creeps along the corridor. On each of the doors is a brass plate as in the dormitory, only they are etched with names instead of numbers. *Garcia, Hutchins, Wilson* . . . She steals from doorway to doorway, looking for a blank one or possibly STAIRS.

When she comes to the last door on the left, she is surprised to see *Daysmoor* written on the little plate. It is slightly difficult to read, tarnished and discolored.

The hall suddenly feels very quiet. Will her knocking on the door rouse the other apprentices? Would they report her?

Will *he* report her?

All the little thoughts she should have had before deciding to do this creep into her mind. What if he is asleep? What if he is angry? What if he gives her another censure, or mocks her, or tells her he will never play for her again?

All this she thinks even as her hand rises and raps three times on the door.

Nothing happens for what feels like a very long time.

What if he isn't home?

She has just about decided to turn away when the door opens and Apprentice Daysmoor is there. He is there, and she is there.

Only he isn't Apprentice Daysmoor right now. He can't be. Instead of stooping and scowling, he is standing comfortably straight and looking slightly bewildered. Instead of the requisite voluminous conservatory robes, he is wearing dark green sweatpants.

Only sweatpants.

Sing doesn't know how to feel about this. She remembers being held against his chest and her face starts to heat up.

What can she say to him? What was she thinking, taking such a risk to come here? This whole thing feels strange now. How can she just show up and ask him to play? Her eyes are drawn to an intricate tattoo of ivy tendrils winding up his left arm, wrist to shoulder. . . . Who *is* he?

He says, "Miss da Navelli. Um, hello." He glances down, apparently just becoming aware of his appearance, then looks along the hallway. "Why are you here? You're not supposed to be up here."

She finds her voice at last. "Are you going to report me?"

His face relaxes a little. "Did you come just to ask that?"

"No. I was . . . well, you mentioned you liked Brahms, and . . . I was wondering if you knew, um, the Intermezzo in A."

She is ready for the response. *You came all the way out here to ask me that?* or *What's the matter with you?* or *Why don't you go talk nonsense with your friends?*

But instead he asks, quite seriously, "Which one?"

"Oh! Oh, um, opus 118."

Stupid, she thinks. *Such a popular piece.* She should have mentioned one of his little-known works—that would have been more impressive—but she just blurted out the first one that came to mind. It has always been one of her favorites.

He looks at her a moment, considering, then says, "You'd better come up, then."

Behind him is a dark staircase. She follows him up, with only the most fleeting thoughts about vampires as she hears the door close with a soft hiss. They are in almost total blackness now, climbing to Apprentice Daysmoor's storied lonely tower.

She stumbles a little and hears his footsteps stop. "I'm sorry," he says. "I'm so used to these stairs at night. Here." She finds his hand, which isn't cold and clammy like death, as she'd imagined, but warm like a regular person's. As if to soothe her, though she has tried hard to hide her uncertainty, he says, "This used to be the president's quarters, this tower, before Hector was converted to faculty apartments. That's why it's a little different."

"Oh," she says, relieved to hear her own whisper, that she hasn't disappeared in all this darkness.

And then light. When they reach the landing, Daysmoor pushes open a door, and Sing is astonished to find not a crumbling, cobweb-covered relic, but quite a modern, cozy room with a high ceiling and a spiral staircase to one side. A small kitchen and fireplace, a comfortable chair, rugs, books; nothing particularly strange or hostile.

"I have three levels," he says proudly. She follows him up into a bedroom, spare and tidy. He grabs a gray T-shirt from a basket of folded laundry and pulls it on with a serious little throat clearing. Then up again to a large circular room with tall windows all around. It must be spectacular during the day, filled with sunlight, looking out over the campus and the forest—you could probably see all the way down to Dunhammond. Now it is lit by yellow sconces reflecting warmly off the window glass.

The room contains an old grand piano and little else except a couple of high-backed chairs and some stacks of music. Daysmoor gestures to a chair, and Sing sits. He is silent as he seats himself on the piano bench, but after he has looked at the keys for a moment, he says, "This is the one you mean?" and begins to play.

When the first notes sound, Sing no longer questions her request. Apprentice Daysmoor is not mocking this little piece, and he is not mocking her. He is just playing.

He doesn't play the intermezzo as though it is tired, as though it has lost its luster through too much exposure to the air. He plays seriously, attending to every note like a shepherd who refuses to lose even the weakest sheep. He plays with joy, the patterns of his breathing mimicking the depths and heights of the music.

He plays with devotion.

All this Sing hears as she sits in the high-backed chair. She watches his shoulders, the outline of his collarbone under gray cotton, the way his hair falls. She can't see his long fingers, but she remembers them.

But mostly she listens. Her eyes are open, but she doesn't see. Her mind is engaged, focused, but color, shape, and image are gone; the lines of the piece exist in time only, overwhelming all other dimensions, blotting them out, flowing over them like glossy ribbons. Tears well, induced not by thought or pain or happiness, but by the perfect sound that courses through her without design or name. And still she listens.

When he has finished, neither of them moves. Sing doesn't know how many silent minutes have passed when he finally rises and crosses the floor. He doesn't stand too close to her chair. His voice, when it comes, seems lower and more ravaged than usual. "Can I play something else for you?"

There is something different about his face, eyes lowered, muscles relaxed. She thinks she recognizes this awkwardness; he has revealed too much. The world has vaporized around him, and he is grasping at it, pulling it back.

"No." She rises and he nods, taking a step back. "But thank you."

She means it, and he smiles. She has never seen him really smile before and realizes he wears a party mask, too—a mask of arrogance and ugliness. And she understands why, because he is not wearing it now. Now he appears as he really is, competent and handsome—someone bigger than an apprenticeship, bigger than the conservatory. Someone out of place.

It is shocking. *Apprentice Plays-poor.* How could *anyone* who heard Daysmoor play fail to recognize his mastery, his passion?

But no one does hear him play, she realizes. *No one ever has.*

"Why . . ." She doesn't want to say the wrong thing, but she has to know. "Why aren't you entering the Gloria Stewart competition?"

He looks at her for a long moment. "I'm not allowed."

She doesn't know what she expected him to say, but it certainly wasn't this. She steps toward him, the night she met him in the forest coming back to her—a vision of the Maestro's arm firmly around his apprentice's shoulders, steering him back into the darkness. "It's something to do with a wish, isn't it?" She puts a hand to the teardrop at her throat.

He is silent for a moment but looks up with a puzzled expression. "I did make a wish, once." But he doesn't say any more.

The crystal is so cold, it slices. Sing pulls her hand away. "She cried for you," she says. "Did you know that?"

He frowns. "What?"

"The Felix," she says. "That's how she grants wishes. She—cries. The wish is a tear."

Daysmoor's eyes fix on the crystal. "This little thing?"

An image is forming in Sing's mind. "You're not allowed to play," she says. "Is it because . . . is it because *he* doesn't want you to play?"

The apprentice looks at her, his features shadowed. She expects him to feign ignorance. But instead he says, "You mean George."

Daysmoor closes his eyes for a moment. "He is a brilliant musician," he says, "and he was once a kind man. Kinder and more passionate than anyone I've ever met. But he has changed over the years."

She is taking a risk, but she can't help it. "He never wanted you to play, did he?" she says. "He wanted to keep you here. And something gave him the power to do it."

"You're assuming a lot." Daysmoor steps back, and Sing knows she has gone too far.

"I should go," she says, glancing back at the spiral staircase.

His focus returns. "You'd better take the outside stairs. It's safer. Don't want you getting in trouble again." He moves to an arched glass door, almost indistinguishable from the tall windows, and when he opens it Sing sees a wide stone balcony. She follows him outside, and he gestures to the narrow fire escape that zigzags down the tower. "Not too scary for you, are they?" His voice is easy now.

She clambers over the balcony railing in defiance and looks up with a smirk. He is leaning against the railing, closer than she anticipated, and for a moment there is nothing between them but silence and shadows and breath.

Her voice surprises her, seeming to come of its own accord. "Maybe . . . maybe you could play the intermezzo for me again sometime?"

He nods, inclining his upper body slightly, almost a bow. A strange light illuminates his face, and she realizes it is coming from the stone around her neck. She raises a hand to it, clutches it, and the light shines white and red through the cracks between her fingers.

She doesn't look up again as she descends the fire escape, the warm darkness rising over her like a pool. But she knows he is still there, watching. And somehow, a tiny bit of her insides, always shivering, *always* shivering, is quieted, and she knows it will never tremble again.

Fifty-four

As a matter of survival, the Felix nurtured within herself the discipline of shutting out the deaths of stars. She learned long ago that her terrestrial spirit could not absorb the enormity of such losses. When she first fell to earth, the new emptiness she felt at each exploded life was overpowering to the point of madness. But, gradually, she learned to open her eyes, to ground herself in the pattern of a tree's bark or the darks and lights of water. To block out the vast sky in all its beauty and bleakness.

But, cut off from the universe as she now was, a different kind of madness—savagery—began to settle over her. If it hadn't been for the Cat part of her mind, she would have torn out her own eyes and eaten her own legs. The Cat knew to sleep and hunt and drink and leave its scent. The Cat knew how to be alive here.

The Felix hasn't heard the call of the stars for a very long time, but she knows the sounds coming from the human place on the other side of the fence are something like it. Perhaps this is why her child continues to be drawn there, and why she herself feels the need to listen to the man-crow play his strange instrument on dark evenings.

Recognizing the draw that she and her child share has brought her dulled earth-senses into a new, vague understanding. She allows him to go to the fence now. Sometimes, in the new dawn, she waits in the underbrush and listens to the girl, and sometimes, when the stars rise, the child comes to hear the man-crow.

When the human place is quiet enough, the two cats venture closer to the tower. And when the sky is dark and the air is clear, the Felix can see the musician through his tall, yellow windows, seated at the instrument, hands moving purposefully. On these nights, she can see his heart, a purple, pulsating glow that surrounds him. It grows brighter as he plays and fades when he is done. Something about that vibrant purple glow shudders her insides with nameless regret and makes her long for the sky. It is in these moments she can almost touch the days before the hunger and fierceness; she can almost hear the stars again.

Tonight, she and the child hide on the white lawn, wearing the invisibility of night. The child is mesmerized by the glow of the man-crow's heart, his eyes bright with the reflection of it. The Felix allows her body to relax. They listen for a long time, until at last the sounds stop and only a fading purple haze indicates the now dark tower.

But the snow is comfortable and the humans are asleep except for a few hurrying blindly through the cold from shelter to shelter, so for a while, the Felix and her child rest in the silent, open air. She licks the stick-up fur between his soft ears.

Later, with a soft *chrrp,* the child raises his head. Even though the moon offers little light, the Felix senses what he has—that the girl is coming through the snow toward the tower building.

When the tower is lit again a short time later, they see the man-crow crossing to his instrument and the girl seating herself nearby. The beautiful sounds begin for the second time that evening, and the two cats listen contentedly, ears cocked forward, tails curled. The purple glow of the man-crow's heart is brilliant, rivaling its radiancy during the first few days of his transformation, so long ago.

The sounds last only a few minutes. The girl stands and they talk. Then the girl leaves, down the outside of the stone tower, and the man-crow watches her.

The Felix stares at him in confusion. Though he has long since stopped playing the instrument, the bright purple glow doesn't fade or even dim as he stands there. The Felix senses joy from her child—a thing she can still recognize but not hold. But as she watches the man-crow, his heart shining like a flame, she can think only of the bright deaths of stars.

Fifty-five

CROWS ARE MORE ATTRACTIVE IN WINTER, Sing thinks, studying vibrantly black, glossy bodies against the ashy trees and white sky. She leans against the fence with her notebook. The morning is soft and winter-warm, but she wears her coat out of habit.

Unfortunately, "more attractive in winter" isn't a valid scientific finding.

With all the people arriving for the Autumn Festival, it feels strange to be out here looking at crows. But as impossible as it seems, *Angelique* will be over soon, and her report will be due.

"*Caaaw!*" a crow calls from a high branch.

"I've got that one already!" she shouts up at him. He ruffles his wings. She can say anything to them now, do anything, and they don't care. She could probably climb up to the high branch and sit down right next to that crow and he wouldn't even budge. They don't mind Tamino anymore, either, even when he takes an occasional swipe at a low-hanging branch.

However, when Ryan and Lori Pinkerton saunter by, the crows scatter noisily.

"You are good judges of character!" she yells as they resettle. A few yell back at her. She sighs and taps her pencil against her notebook. "Good judges of character" doesn't seem particularly scientific, either.

"I am not a good judge of character," she says. "I'm wrong about everyone." The crows mutter and grumble. Was that a *chrrrp* amid the *rrawks*? Are ice-blue eyes watching her from between the fence posts?

Sing sinks onto a nearby picnic table. "Well, I was right about Tamino, at least." She inhales the fresh scent of snow. "But I was wrong about *them*."

She can still see them tangled up in the blankets, Ryan's green eyes wide, Zhin trying not to laugh. The time afterward was such a blur of anger and meaningless faces and *Angelique* and all the *pushing*.

Until yesterday, and the only clear thing.

"I was wrong about him, too," she says quietly, and the outside world disappears for a moment.

Until, *"Caaaw!"* A big crow squawks from a lower branch of Hud's maple tree. Sing squints over at it. Was it really *caaaw* that time, or was that just what she heard? What she expected to hear? Wasn't it actually more purry, less crackly? She listens.

Footsteps swish the snow behind her, and she turns to see Mrs. Bigelow approaching, wrapped in a puffy lavender coat.

A twinge of panic strikes Sing as she remembers her white tights.

Her whole laundry schedule was thrown off by Zhin, and she was one pair of kneesocks short this morning; she hoped no one would notice the white tights she'd substituted. As Mrs. Bigelow approaches, she pulls her skirt down as low as it will go.

"Doing your research, I see!"

Sing nods. *I hope she doesn't want to look at my notes.*

Mrs. Bigelow reaches her and looks up at the big tree. A few crows look back at her; others have fled to the edge of the forest. "How's it going?"

"Okay, I guess," Sing says. But something makes her add, "Not great."

Mrs. Bigelow looks at her. "You know, I don't think I was very fair to you when you chose this project. I thought you were just being defiant. But I've seen you out here, studying them. You've really put some effort into this. I was wrong, and I apologize."

Sing bends her closed notebook, curling it up, down, up, down. She doesn't know what to say. She *was* being defiant when she chose crows. But somehow, she thinks Mrs. Bigelow knows that.

"I've been doing a little research myself," Mrs. Bigelow says. "And I think you may have chosen a more difficult project than you anticipated. Have you written down 'caw' yet?"

Sing rolls her eyes and lets her head flop backward, and Mrs. Bigelow laughs. "Well, did you know that every 'caw' can be different?"

"I kind of figured that out." She is aware of how quiet the crows are right now.

"Caws can have different meanings depending on how loud or long they are, or how many in a row." Mrs. Bigelow looks up at the tree, her puffy jacket rustling. "And different groups of crows have different languages. It's pretty amazing, actually."

"*Caaaw!*" Sing says in her best gravelly voice to the crows on the lowest branch.

"Anyway, I just wanted to check up on you. And to let you know Maestro Keppler wants to see you."

Sing's stomach gives a lurch. What could the Maestro want?

His office is in the St. Augustine's annex, next to the president's office, behind an oak door. Sing hopes he's at lunch, but he answers her polite knock with a stern, "Come in."

He's at his desk, fingers woven together, pristine black robes ironed so meticulously, they almost shine. Not much else shines in the stuffy office, however. It reminds Sing of a Rembrandt painting—the Maestro's face sharp and illuminated yellow, the background merely a murky suggestion of furniture and curtains and objects.

Sing waits for him to say, "Sit down, please," which he does, his hard eyes focused on her face. She sits but keeps her gaze on the surface of his desk. His ornaments are spare but old-looking and ornate—a dark silver inkwell, photographs in heavy frames. She studies an old photo of a little boy, grinning and covered in mud, and a picture of the Maestro and Apprentice Daysmoor with—she squints—Gloria Stewart? No, she died twenty years ago. It must be someone else.

The Maestro doesn't speak for a few awful moments. Sing is aware of the pressure of the white tights on her waist and legs. *I should have known it wouldn't work,* she thinks. What is the punishment for being out of uniform? She can't afford another censure.

Finally, she says, "I'm sorry, Maestro. It won't happen again."

He sniffs. "You're right about that, Miss da Navelli." Sing detects a decidedly angry undercurrent and ventures a glance at his face. He looks much older than when she first arrived at DC. His jaw muscles are pulsating, his eyes narrow.

The Maestro doesn't say anything else, so she says, "Then— then may I go?"

Now, the lines around his mouth deepen in a way that almost resembles a smile. "Of course. You may go straight back to your room and pack your bags. I'm recommending to the president that you both be asked to leave the conservatory."

Sing's heart jumps. "What?" she cries. *Expelled?*

Wait . . . You both? Is he going to expel her tights as well?

"You can't possibly be surprised, Miss da Navelli," Maestro Keppler snaps, his voice still careful but beginning to lose its cool.

"But what about *Angelique*? The New Artist vacancy?" She knows he doesn't care about her future, but her words are faster than her brain.

"I think Lori Pinkerton will do just fine, don't you? I'm sure she'll impress the representatives from Fire Lake. You'll just have to explain it to your father. I'm sorry, Miss da Navelli, but you know the rules, and you broke them."

Sing's stomach twists. "But—but they're just *tights*! I loaned my last clean pair of kneesocks to Zhin, and I meant to do laundry yesterday, but it took so long to do the theory homework, and I—"

"*Tights?*" the Maestro roars, slapping his desk and rising. "You think this is about *tights*?" His hand still flat on his desk, he leans forward. He looks as though he has more to say, but nothing comes out.

And then, suddenly, Sing understands the real reason she has been summoned. It must show on her face, because the Maestro's body relaxes a little and he lowers himself back into his leather chair. "No, Miss da Navelli, we are not here to discuss tights. We are here to discuss what you were doing last night when you were supposed to be in your room. You weren't in your room, were you?"

Sing keeps her eyes on his desk. "No, sir."

"You were paying a clandestine visit to someone, weren't you?"

"Yes, sir."

"Who was it?" His voice is darker now, quieter, more dangerous. "Who were you with?"

Sing inhales. He already knows; why hide it? "Apprentice Daysmoor."

The Maestro is silent for a few moments. She doesn't look up, but she knows he is staring at her. Then he says softly, yet biting, "There are rules regarding inappropriate relationships between students and apprentices. I'm afraid you will both have to leave."

Reality sinks in. Apprentice Daysmoor, dismissed, because of her? As unappreciated as he is here, everyone knows the only thing that awaits disgraced DC apprentices is obscurity.

Sing's heart beats more quickly. "But it's my fault!" Her voice is high and crackly. "I went there on my own—he didn't ask me to. Please let him stay."

"He knew what he was doing," the Maestro spits.

"It's not like that." She is surprised at her own boldness and leans forward. "He didn't know I was coming—I snuck over there.

I just wanted to hear him play again, and he played for me. Just one piece. It—it was Brahms. That's all."

The Maestro's gaze is appraising now. He frowns and blinks.

"That's all," Sing repeats quietly.

The Maestro sniffs. "Why on earth would you sneak into the apprentice quarters in the middle of the night? Didn't you think of the consequences?"

The edge seems to be gone from his voice. Is he relenting? "I'm sorry, Maestro," Sing says. "He—he just played so beautifully at rehearsal and—and—" She doesn't know how to finish. It's all so ridiculous. Why did she sneak out? What was she thinking? She studies an ornate picture frame on the Maestro's desk, a nest of twisted metal tendrils.

When the Maestro speaks this time, she feels invisible. "He does play beautifully. There's such a—an *intelligence* there. Such intention. Such humanity."

She nods. "Yes."

Now his tone becomes focused and sharp. "Are you in love with him?"

Sing starts. "What? No! Of course not!" *What kind of a question is that?*

Her shock must show on her face, because the Maestro says, "All right. Well, I would hate to see a fine musician like Apprentice Daysmoor forced to leave the conservatory because of your poor judgment." He leans back in his chair. "So what should we do about this?"

Does that mean she's not expelled anymore, either? That she can still sing *Angelique*?

"It won't happen again?" She says it like a question, a suggestion.

He laughs coldly. "No, Miss da Navelli. Be sure that it doesn't."

Sing relaxes a little. Everything is going to be okay.

Maestro Keppler leans forward. "And to help make sure it doesn't happen again, I am giving you a censure for insolence."

Sing's stomach sinks, but she knows she has gotten off easy.

"Also," the Maestro adds, voice smooth, "from now on, I forbid you to associate with Daysmoor in any way. If you can do that, you may both stay. Do we have a deal?"

She is stunned. Does he mean at rehearsals, too, and coaching?

"Do we have a deal?" he repeats. There it is again in his voice, that hard undercurrent.

She has no choice.

She nods.

"Now," the Maestro says, "I see no reason to go to the president—or to Daysmoor—with any of this. But if I find you have broken our deal—if I find you have said as much as 'hello' to Nathan—there will be no second chances. For either of you. I don't care what your father thinks. Do you understand?"

Sing nods. *Blackmail.*

Maestro Keppler straightens up. "You have been performing adequately. Keep it up."

It is a dismissal. She starts to rise, but a knock stops her.

"George? Are you ready to go?"

At the sound of the low, gravelly voice, Sing's eyes meet the Maestro's. She freezes, but he smiles faintly.

"Come in!" he calls.

The door behind Sing opens, and she hears Daysmoor approach. "Oh, I'm sorry," he says, "I didn't know you were with a student. I'll come back."

Sing doesn't turn around as the Maestro says, "No, no, Miss da Navelli and I were just finishing up." His easy tone implies they've been doing nothing more than discussing favorite books or sharing recipes.

"Miss da Navelli?" Daysmoor rounds her chair. She is afraid to look up, afraid he will be the gloomy, distant stranger once again and that the night she will always remember never happened after all.

But when she sees his face, her fear dissolves. He has changed—or maybe *they* have changed, he and Sing. He is smiling—is it because of her?—and she smiles back.

He says lightly, "I didn't expect to find you here. Hello." She is taken in by him for a moment and starts to respond, but stops herself, glancing at the Maestro's face. The Maestro clears his throat, eyes as dull and hard as dry clay.

Not even hello.

She closes her mouth.

"What's going on?" This Daysmoor says to the Maestro before turning back to Sing, his face serious now. Sing shakes her head, almost imperceptibly. *Please understand.*

But there is no understanding in his face, only confusion. He returns his focus to Maestro Keppler.

"We've been discussing the opera, that's all," the Maestro says. Sing hopes he'll end it there, but Daysmoor's gaze is unwavering and he continues. "Miss da Navelli has requested a new coach."

Sing stares at the Maestro.

Daysmoor blinks twice. "Two days before the performance? We only have one session left. I—"

"Well," the Maestro says, "this is only the first performance of Miss da Navelli's time here. And, as she's already making quite a name for herself, she really deserves someone a bit more—accomplished."

Daysmoor turns to Sing and says softly, "Really?"

She looks at him but can feel the Maestro's threatening stare. She doesn't dare answer or even shake her head. She doesn't move a muscle when Daysmoor asks, almost in a whisper, "What did I do?"

"Don't put the girl on the spot, Nathan." The Maestro leans in to Sing and says gently, but loud enough for Daysmoor to hear, "I'm sorry this is uncomfortable, my dear, but I had to let him know eventually. I agree with you one hundred percent. Professor Hawkins is a much better match for you, more in line with the type of professionalism you're used to. We'll let the apprentices practice on the newer singers, eh?" He chuckles and turns back to Daysmoor, whose face is as still and dark as water. "Oh, come on, Nathan. You hate vocal coaching anyway. Isn't that what you said?"

He has said a lot of things, Sing knows. But she doesn't remember any of them now. All she can hear is the Brahms intermezzo, all she can see are his hands, his shoulders moving under a gray T-shirt, his sad, dark eyes. She watches him, unable to speak. The line of his jaw tightens for a moment, but then she sees a release. His whole body seems to relax just a little—not from relief, but because he is hurt.

Daysmoor turns and stalks silently from the room. And Sing, surprised to feel the wrench of her heart, knows for the first time what she would wish for, given the chance.

She would wish for him.

Fifty-six

Though there are warm bodies on either side of her, in truth Sing is sitting by herself at the Gloria Stewart International Piano Competition semifinals. The Woolly Theater, which has been hosting smaller events all day, has never been so packed. DC's Autumn Festival is really the theater's grand opening, and patrons and alumni have come from everywhere to be here. She hasn't spoken to her father, who must have arrived this morning. Their schedules have not yet coincided.

She didn't have to come. With the demanding performance of *Angelique* tomorrow afternoon, she technically has the night off. But the diva in her refused to curl up under a blanket in the dormitory; she has to keep everyone in her sights. It is exhausting.

Ernesto da Navelli sits in the front with Harland Griss and several other luminaries. Sing watches some of the bolder audience members approach them politely before the competition begins. The celebrities are gracious and cheerful, but two stern security guards hover nearby, ready for any commoner to put a toe out of line.

Sing can see Marta's frizzy hair across the room and assumes the apparently empty space she seems to be talking to contains Jenny, too petite to interrupt Sing's line of vision. Lori, Hayley, and Carrie Stewart are clustered at the back, laughing and leafing through programs. Sing starts to read through the biographies page again but can't stand Ryan's professionally photographed face smiling coyly up at her.

The competition has been going on all day behind closed doors. Those left standing in each of the three categories will perform tonight, with the final competition taking place tomorrow after *Angelique*. DC is abuzz with anticipation as one of its own, Ryan Larkin, is still in contention.

Why has she come? She scans the room again. Daysmoor and the Maestro are just entering, the Maestro taking his listless apprentice by the arm. Sing clasps her hands together; they are cold. She watches Daysmoor follow the Maestro to their seats, hoping he'll glance in her direction so she can try again to convey a silent message of . . . something. Apology? But the apprentice looks the way he did when she first saw him at her placement audition, eyelids lowered, movements sluggish.

The lights go down.

The heavy velvet curtains part to reveal a gleaming black grand piano. The Amateurs Under Sixteen are up first. A twelve-year-old boy pushes his way through a Bach fugue like a freight train; the notes reverberate coolly in the theater's well-designed curves and empty spaces. The audience coos and titters as a perfect little seven-year-old girl whose feet don't reach the pedals dances lightly through Mozart. They applaud politely for a somber thirteen-year-old girl in a stiff green dress who plays a busier Mozart piece with authority. Sing avoids looking into the children's tired eyes when they take their group bow.

The Amateurs Over Sixteen take the stage one by one. A red-faced, red-haired woman plays the strange first movement of Shostakovich's second piano sonata—alternately dark and playful—and Sing is captivated, though she knows this slightly mechanical performance won't hold up against Ryan's sparkling style. She sees her father lean in to Harland Griss, who nods.

Next is Ryan himself, striding onstage like a movie star and just as handsome in his black tuxedo. Liszt's coquettish *Valse-Impromptu* suits him perfectly. He wiggles his head along with the flashy runs and ornaments, and his copper hair shines. He shrugs his shoulders and rocks back and forth with the undulating tempo. He throws an impish look to the audience during a particularly frisky moment, making girls giggle. Sing's father will not appreciate this showmanship, but Ryan's skill is unquestionable. Harland Griss and the famous concert pianist Yvette Cordaro whisper to each other and nod.

It will take a truly extraordinary performer to beat Ryan. *He didn't really need me after all,* Sing thinks. Does that mean he actually *wanted* her? That he liked her? Or only that he *thought* he would need her influence to win?

She's surprised to realize she doesn't care.

The last performer is a serious bearded man with wild hair. He sits on the cushioned piano bench and, as the rest of the musicians have done, contemplates the black and white keys before him. When he is ready, he places his hands on the keyboard for a moment before depressing the first notes.

Sing gasps. It is Brahms. The piece Daysmoor played for her. Her throat closes. This man will play it with two or three of its brothers tonight, she knows; it isn't substantial enough on its own. It will need to be surrounded by glitter—this simple piece that any modestly talented pianist could play.

She doesn't allow herself a glance at the place where the Maestro and his apprentice are sitting. She doesn't need to; Daysmoor's profile is all she can see when she closes her eyes—the shadow at the corner of his eye, the way a lock of black hair curves in to the line of his jaw.

The rest of the audience seems pleasantly surprised with the performance. This piece is a favorite. Hum-able. Accessible.

Yet the man onstage doesn't do this Brahms justice. As the music winds on, Sing feels just the slightest tug embedded in the lines, an anticipation of the next thing. The wrong moments are savored, the wrong moments are rushed through. This man plays well, but he is not in love.

At intermission, she makes her way into the crowded lobby. She thought she wanted to know if Ryan would win, but now she can't imagine why. He is Prince Elbert, as he has been since the day she met him. Prince Elbert always gets what he wants.

He is in the lobby now, surrounded by friends and fans, mostly girls. But Sing doesn't go to him. Lori Pinkerton, at his side, shoots her a triumphant look. Lori has been strangely quiet since Sing was given Angelique, no fiery confrontation. Then again, Lori is a diva—ice and patience. Waiting in the wings for Sing to die.

Her father catches her as she is almost to the heavy double doors that lead outside. "Sing, my dear, a hello for your father!"

"I'm sorry, Papà." She turns to find him looking down at her, overly delighted. Harland Griss stands next to him, navy suit impeccable, dark hair neatly parted and greased, face clean-shaven but beginning to show the lines and folds that come with importance.

"Harland," Maestro da Navelli says, "you remember my daughter, Sing?"

"Of course." A soft hand is extended, and Sing takes it. "I understand," Griss says, "that you are to sing Angelique tomorrow? Impressive."

"Thank you, Mr. Griss." Sing doesn't look at her father for approval. *The mark of a professional—don't let anyone know who's pulling the strings.* "I have enjoyed learning the role. Angelique is a complex character."

Griss approves, launching into an anecdote about a recent Viennese production of the opera. Sing projects just enough confidence. She knows how to do this part, the schmoozing part. Barbara da Navelli was a master.

Then, over Griss's shoulder, she catches sight of coal-black hair and even blacker eyes. Daysmoor, across the lobby, with Maestro Keppler nowhere in sight. She stares. He doesn't look away.

If only she could tell him her silence is protecting them both, that the Maestro lied. But how?

Griss and her father are making small talk, but they are including her. She nods and smiles, willing Daysmoor to stay where he is with quick, furtive glances. His face disappears intermittently as the crowd between them shifts and swirls, but he keeps looking in her direction.

She nods at Griss again, laughing at a witty remark. Her hands begin to shake.

Intermission is nearly over and Daysmoor will join the Maestro again. Who knows what other lies Keppler will tell him?

If she were Barbara da Navelli, she would excuse herself, march up to Daysmoor, and tell him in a clear voice that she—that she didn't hate him, and the Maestro could go to hell.

But I am not Barbara da Navelli, she thinks, remembering the index card from her first day in Mr. Bernard's class. But now, rather than the sinking feeling that usually accompanies this thought, she feels just a bit of exhilaration.

Mind churning, she says, "Mr. Griss, I'm so happy you're coming to the performance tomorrow. Would you like to hear a sneak preview?"

Her father raises his eyebrows, but Griss seems amused. "Right now?"

"Of course." Sing's heart is thudding. She can't possibly do this. But Daysmoor is looking at her with uncertainty, not yet dislike, and she refuses to let this chance slip away.

Griss watches her with interest, hands in his pockets. Her father crosses his arms but remains quiet. Sing knows he has decided to trust her judgment. She doesn't yet know if he is right to.

"It would be bad luck to do something from *Angelique,* so here's a little *Magic Flute,*" she says. And starts to sing.

The first note, in the middle part of Sing's range, cuts through the low chatter of the lobby like a bell. She doesn't need to think about plot or character; she is Mozart's princess, grieving from misunderstood silence. By the time she reaches the first high note, everyone is watching her. Most people smile, some seem annoyed at having their conversations cut off, and some—mostly other sopranos, Lori Pinkerton among them—are plainly hostile. Her father, taking his cue from Griss, seems pleased.

But she doesn't care about any of them. She watches Daysmoor for a reaction, some kind of understanding. He wears his mask, but she sees through it now—it's astonishing that everyone can't see him for what he really is. The man who should have been playing Brahms tonight. The man who should be playing for the world.

From across the crowd, he watches her for the entire duration of the aria.

The aria ends not with wailing despair, but with low resignation. For Sing, tonight, it becomes a last entreatment. Across the lobby, Daysmoor's face is as impassive as ever. Amid warm applause from the spectators, he turns back to the doors to the theater and leaves.

The spell over her breaks. Blood rushes to her face as she realizes what she has done. She can't bear to look at her father.

"Brava!" Harland Griss says cheerfully. "Well done, Miss da Navelli. You would make a charming Pamina." Sing nods appreciatively before a woman steals Griss away with busy compliments and important questions.

People come up to her now with small words of praise, and she responds gratefully. A voice hisses in her ear, "It's always about *you*, isn't it?" but Lori Pinkerton is a yard away, leaving only the scent of roses, by the time Sing turns around.

A heavy arm corrals her shoulders and guides her out the front doors and onto the cold steps. She looks up and says, "I'm sorry, Papà. That was rude, wasn't it?"

Her father squeezes her shoulders. "They are lucky to hear you sing. I am—amazed at the progress you have made here. I am very pleased. Harland is interested. But your Angelique can speak for herself. You did not need special tricks to draw his attention."

She looks away. "It was a stupid thing to do."

"Never!" He takes her face in his hands. "Why do we sing if we do not love to sing? I'm very happy you're free with your gifts." He lets his hands drop and looks out at the snowy quad. Lights on posts and from windows illuminate the campus. People Sing doesn't know stroll the grounds in their winter coats. Her father sighs. "Sometimes you remind me so much of your mother."

Sing stretches and curls her fingers. It wasn't a compliment. Barbara da Navelli sought the spotlight with elegant ferocity. But Sing can't explain her real motives to her father; she can hardly explain them to herself. "I'll do better, Papà," she says.

With a burst of light, one of the Woolly's massive front doors opens and someone leans out, looking around.

"Can I help you, my dear?" Ernesto da Navelli says.

"Oh, Maestro da Navelli! I'm so sorry, I was looking for—oh, Sing, there you are." Marta emerges, silhouetted.

"*Bene, carina,* I will see you later, eh? Don't catch cold." Her father gives a little bow to Marta before heading inside.

Sing feels a rush of warmth that starts from her stomach and spreads to her shoulders. "Hi!" She grins. "I didn't think—"

"I'm sorry to interrupt you and your dad." Marta sounds sincere, but her voice has a flatness to it that pulls the grin from Sing's face.

"Oh. That's okay," Sing says. "Intermission is probably just about over, anyway. Though I think I'm just going to head back to Hud. You . . . you want to join me?"

"No," Marta says, but adds, "I, um, really want to hear the rest of this round."

"Oh."

"I just came to give you this." She holds out a glossy, printed page.

Sing takes it. "What—?"

"Bye, Sing." Marta heads for the doors. "Um. Have a good show tomorrow."

Sing's face falls. It isn't a plea for sympathy, just a natural reaction. But Marta notices. She bites her bottom lip and says softly, "I do mean it. You sound really good. You're going to get everything you want. I'm happy for you."

The door shuts behind her with a leathery thud.

Sing leans against one of the Woolly's fat pillars. Everything is so strange now. Only a few weeks ago, she and Jenny and Marta made shy conversation at the Welcome Gathering. *Angelique* was a lifetime away.

She looks at the folded paper, a page torn from tonight's program. She unfolds it to reveal a few words scribbled in pen over the print.

If you have something to say, meet me tonight at St. Augustine's.
I will leave the door unlocked. —Nathan

Fifty-seven

THE FELIX AWAKENS WITH A ROAR that shakes granules of dirt and snow from the rocks around her. She turns her gaze upward. The sky is black with night clouds.

It was a dream. Stars moaning, distorted, burning themselves out in spectacular, horrific displays of vivid golds and blues and purples. The whole of the night sky smeared with glittering, galactic death.

The Cat part of her mind has no time for this. It has already sensed what the Sky part is too distracted to notice—the child is gone.

This time, however, the Felix knows where he has gone. She feels the same inexplicable pull, toward the human place, that must have woken him.

An old wish is about to die.

Fifty-eight

Sing is certain someone will see her, that someone already sees her. Maybe Maestro Keppler, peering out from his dark office, scowling, or her father from his luxurious room in Hector Hall. Maybe Ryan, his head turned briefly toward the window of whoever's room he is in right now.

She inhales deeply, the frigid air stinging her lungs.

St. Augustine's looms in the darkness. It looms enough in the daylight, or when the windows are warm and bright for an evening rehearsal, but now, in the bleak, whispering cold, it seems to tower over the rest of the conservatory. Sing reminds herself she's not superstitious. Yet she thinks of Tamino—sweet Tamino—proof of either magic or madness, neither one of which is nice company in the middle of the night.

She finds the massive door unlocked, as Daysmoor said it would be. The door scrapes, but to Sing's relief its two-hundred-year-old voice is too tired for squeaks or squeals. She pulls it shut behind her.

Her footsteps do not echo; they are too small to affect the high walls or distant ceiling. Someone is playing the grand piano. It sings from the concert hall, vibrating the bones of the old building.

The music feels too loud, too noticeable. Surely the Maestro or the president will come striding in any moment. *No,* she tells herself. Hector Hall is all the way across the quad. No one will hear. No one will know.

Outside the hall, the reality of what she is doing—what she is doing *again*—hits her in the chest, and she stops. Daysmoor—*Nathan,* as he called himself in his note—is in there. His fluid, passionate notes are as distinctive as his own voice.

She pushes open the door. He is sitting at the piano on the other side of the hall, but he rises quickly when he hears her. She looks at the shiny old floor as she crosses the room. The golden light from the piano lamp leaves most of the hall in shadows, illuminating only a small, safe haven around the piano.

He watches her uncertainly. She suddenly wishes it were not so late and lonely and that he were wearing his voluminous, stodgy robes instead of, *of all things,* the gray T-shirt—the one he grabbed out of the laundry basket in his bedroom that night. She doesn't want to see the outline of his shoulders so clearly, remembering what they looked like without the T-shirt covering them. She wishes he were scowling, slouching; but that was Apprentice Daysmoor, and he has cast off that persona. This young man standing before her, his black eyes deepened by the shadows around him, is Nathan.

And she has no idea who he is.

"Um," she says, taking off her coat and draping it over a chair, "I got your note."

He puts his hands in his pockets. "This would be quite a coincidence otherwise."

She stifles her annoyance. He has a right to be huffy with her. She inhales. "You've really . . . helped me. I—still need you. I need your help, I mean. I just couldn't tell you that in front of the Maestro . . . I'm sorry."

The corners of his mouth turn up just a little, and her insides feel strange. "Well, it's nice to be wanted," he says, "even in the middle of the night."

Do not think about wanting him in the middle of the night, she tells herself, and says, "I'm nervous about tomorrow. I was really disappointed we didn't get our last coaching session."

"You'll do fine." He clears his throat. "But I'm glad you want my advice. I mean—I guess what I mean is that I'm glad you came back." His eyes glint. "And I liked your secret code."

Sing is glad for the shadowy room as she feels a blush creep into her cheeks. "I didn't come back. I didn't leave in the first place. The Maestro made all that up. He knew I went to the tower. He gave me a censure and said he would kick us both out if I talked to you again."

Nathan's face darkens. "He would say that. But he's not going to kick me out anytime soon."

"*The Magic Flute* was the only way I could think of to explain." Sing realizes how easily she is speaking to him, with the familiarity of a—a what? A peer? A friend? And that he seems to be speaking to her the same way. Nathan is so different from Apprentice Daysmoor.

"I should have known," he says, and sighs. "I'm sorry."

Relief tingles her chest. "What were you playing just now?" she asks. "Are you going to play for me?" Why did her voice sound like that—perky and amused?

Oh, my God, she thinks. *I'm flirting. Stop flirting.*

"Well, I have been practicing." He sits at the piano.

She is all politeness. "I don't think you could play the Brahms any better."

A hint of color rises in his face, and she wonders how often he receives compliments. "I haven't been practicing Brahms," he says.

"What have you been practicing?"

He raises his eyebrows mischievously. "Liszt."

Liszt. Why does the word embarrass her? "Oh," she says.

"I hope you'll indulge me." He moves his hands to the keys with a flourish, and before Sing has even lowered herself into one of the folding chairs, the concert has begun.

He plays nothing like Ryan. Ryan played Liszt with a wink, with conceit. With "fast little notes," Sing remembers Nathan saying. But Nathan plays Liszt as he does Brahms—with exhilaration and precision. This piece, the *Totentanz,* which Sing remembers her father playing, begins with low, dark, angry shouts. But it has more to say. Sounds flash and zip and cavort as Daysmoor's long hands rush along the keyboard like water. Then it becomes pensive. Sing hears the famous eight-note *Dies Irae* repeated, over and over, but there is no wrath in Daysmoor's performance. Only life.

He plays magnificently. She's cascading through space.

At last he stops, and she can hardly believe it when she looks at her watch to find he has played for only fifteen minutes. They both laugh, though Sing doesn't quite know why. His eyes, which she once thought so hard and arrogant, are now vibrant.

"There, I've given you another private concert. Be careful what you wish for," he says. "But you wanted to sing. Isn't that what this is about?"

What is this about? she wonders.

He opens an *Angelique* score. "Where shall we start?"

The question gives her pause. She doesn't know where to start. What will it be like tomorrow, in front of the whole conservatory, her professors, her father? Is she ready for this?

"Are you all right?" he says after a moment, and she realizes she's been standing there, staring at nothing. She looks at him.

"Look," he says. "You have something to prove. I get that. I . . . I'm sorry I haven't been understanding about it. I'm not always very understanding. Let's just sing this through first, okay? This first aria." He begins to play, and she rolls her shoulders.

She sings through the aria. Somewhere in the middle, she realizes the light, resonant tone coming out is—well—

Is what she sounds like.

She, herself. Her real voice. Because of Nathan.

The tension in her shoulders subsides a little. "Wow," she says after the last note. "That was okay."

Nathan laughs. "That *was* okay."

She grins at him, a warm sense of comfort spreading out from her core.

"All right, let's go back," he says, turning the pages. "From the beginning, and we'll work."

Sing feels even better about it this time. It is as if until now she has been on the verge of reaching a plateau—sometimes gaining a sure handhold, sometimes slipping back—but now she is *there,* the ground solid underneath, no longer struggling against gravity. The overall physical exertion hasn't changed that much, but now as she sings, she is simply *sustaining.* She is in a place of resonance and air, and the sound makes her whole face tingle. Invincible.

Nathan stops playing. "That part was very good. But let's see if we can get some more harmonics in there. Here, find the space right here—" He demonstrates, placing his fingers on his throat. "Got it?"

Sing feels the underside of her jaw, runs her fingers down the sides of her own throat, pushes in to find her larynx.

"At the top, just here—you see?" he says, prodding his throat and rising.

"You mean my larynx? Or—"

"No, here," he says, suddenly very close to her. He places his fingers on her throat now, finding the space below her jaw. Sing closes her eyes, hardly breathing. She is used to being prodded and manhandled by her voice teachers; it's part of the process. And a coach as knowledgeable as Daysmoor—as *Nathan*—has certainly prodded and manhandled lots of singers. But she wills her heart to stop beating so quickly. He can probably feel her pulse. "See?" he says. "Keep your larynx low and you won't have to work as hard. Feel that?"

He takes her hand and guides it to the space below her jaw. She doesn't look at his face, but her eyes trace the ivy tattoo until it disappears under his gray shirtsleeve. She feels the warmth of his graceful fingers on her own, his breath on her forehead.

But she realizes his touch is no different from that of Professor Needleman, or Maestra Collins, or any of them. This closeness they are sharing will be over in a moment. It isn't real—it only has the shape of truth. He is interested in her cartilage, not her skin; her trachea, not her neck; her consonants, not her mouth.

Still, she wants so badly to feel her face close to his, the way it was on the tower balcony. A month ago, maybe even an hour ago, she would never have dared look up. But her voice is giving her strength. She feels liberated by her own identity.

She meets his gaze.

"You—see?" He falters a little. "The . . . the space here . . ."

His voice has never faltered before, she thinks with a shiver of exhilaration. Is he nervous? Is she making him nervous?

He doesn't finish his sentence, and he doesn't look away. She wondered in the past if Apprentice Daysmoor had any feelings at all. Now, she wonders if, maybe, he has feelings for her.

Is it possible?

The voice in her head sounds like Jenny. *There's only one way to find out.*

She leans in. Her lips brush against his. He inhales deeply, and for a split second, the tips of his fingers slide upward from her throat, finding her face.

But then he steps back, clearing his throat. Her stomach leaps; her body tenses. She was wrong, she was wrong. Her mind turns frantically. How to undo it? How to take back the last ten seconds? It is impossible. What has she done?

His shoulders look stiff. "Sing—"

She backs up, words shooting out. "I'm sorry. I made a mistake. I'm so sorry. I don't know why I did that." But, looking at his face in the muted light of the piano lamp, she knows exactly why she did it. "I'm sorry," she says again, taking a step away into the shadows on the periphery of the lamp's glow.

"No—don't say that." He puts a hand to his forehead. "Forget it." He sits at the piano and begins to plunk out something vapid and simple. "This was a crazy idea. You need sleep, not more singing." She watches him, almost silhouetted. Only a short time ago, he was playing Liszt for her. Now they will probably never be friends again.

If only he really were Apprentice Daysmoor, haughty and talentless, someone she'd be glad to be rid of. If only he weren't Nathan.

The cold teardrop crystal around her feels so heavy. She looks down to find it shimmering through her white shirt. Nathan's eyes flick to it as well.

"This thing weighs on me," she says, undoing the clasp. He stares at the teardrop but says nothing.

She takes a step closer, holding it out. "It isn't mine." When he doesn't move, she takes his hand and presses the tear into it.

He closes his fingers and considers her. "It's mine, isn't it? All this time. It should have been mine." She wants to leave but finds herself watching him, waiting for more. After a moment, he says, "It's like George's entire life is about keeping me here. He's let himself turn to dust. His music, his dreams, gone. All that burns in him now is a—a fierce scrabbling. I don't know how to describe it. He's clutching. At me, at this magic, maybe at his own existence."

Sing listens to his low, ragged voice. There is something familiar about it, she realizes. *Who is Nathan?*

A faint glow pulses from between his fingers. Sing feels lighter without the crystal and its strange sadness around her neck. "You have the tear now," she says. "You can leave. Do anything you want. Enter the Gloria Stewart competition. It's not too late. My father could arrange it."

He puts the necklace into his pocket. He doesn't seem to be speaking to her. "It makes me . . . afraid." Now he looks at her. "Do you really think your father could help me?"

As she studies his tired, lean face, there are two things about which she is certain. One is that she will never forget the kiss they almost shared. "Yes," she says. "I'm certain my father could get you into the competition."

Nathan's face brightens a little. "That would be—"

A scrape-groan muscles its way into the quiet hall. The outside door.

"What—?" Sing begins, but Nathan puts a finger to his lips. He leans in and whispers, "George. He comes here at night sometimes, to play. We have to get out of here. He can't find us."

His urgent tone startles her. She looks to the door, but he shakes his head. They would certainly meet the Maestro in the hall if they tried to get out that way. Nathan takes her hand and leads her to a small wooden door behind the platform on which the piano sits. His fingers reach for the lamp cord as they pass, but he seems to decide against turning it off. Sing agrees; better to let whoever has come in think the lamp was left on accidentally, in case its light was visible from the outside.

The door, which Nathan locks behind them, leads to a narrow, twisting, wooden staircase. In utter darkness, they start to climb. The air grows colder as they ascend. Nathan doesn't let go of Sing's hand until they reach a little landing and he whispers, "We can sit here until he goes away."

The stairwell smells like metal and dry old wood, but Sing can't see anything. She sits next to Nathan in the blackness. After a few minutes, they hear the piano—a flowery piece Sing doesn't recognize.

"It's him," Nathan whispers. "Don't worry. He's probably antsy about the performance tomorrow and can't sleep. He'll play for a while, then go to bed."

They are silent for a moment. Sing pulls her coat closed and, realizing, whispers, "You don't have a coat."

"I left it in the hall," is the reply.

"Are you cold?"

"Damn right I'm cold."

Sing can't help a whispered giggle at this, to which Nathan mutters, "Oh, *thanks*." She listens to the busy, muffled music coming from the hall below them. She hears Nathan rub his hands together and resists the urge to put her arms around him.

"I come here sometimes when I need to settle down," he says. "To think."

"The *stairwell*?"

He laughs quietly. "The roof."

She gives him an incredulous look he cannot see. "The roof!" she hisses. "Aren't you afraid you'll fall off?"

"The peak is actually flat." He sounds amused. "And there's a pretty wide ledge the gargoyles sit on."

"Still—it's a long way down. And the gargoyles!"

He pats her leg. "Believe me, there's nothing less dangerous than a stone monster, ready to save the place from flooding or whatever it is they do. And our gargoyles are especially artistic. They've been soaking up good music for a lot of years."

He hasn't moved his hand from her leg, a warm weight in the chilly darkness, and she doesn't want him to. She puts her own hand on top of his. His fingers seem to tense for just a moment, but he doesn't move. They sit, silent, in the blackness for a while. Maestro Keppler has started playing Bach.

Eventually, Nathan whispers, "Now will you tell me what the Felix wanted with you?"

That night. Those violet eyes. She hesitates. "I'm not sure. I think it has something to do with—well, I met someone in the woods. A cat. A little one. I mean, he's *big,* but—I think he might be the Felix's baby." Sing finds it easier to talk in the dark. "He likes me. I named him Tamino. He follows me around sometimes."

"The Felix is a dangerous enemy," Nathan murmurs.

"I know," Sing says. "But Tamino—he likes to hear me sing. I think the Felix was angry about that." She traces a circle on the floor with her shoe. "Thank you for saving me that night."

She hears Nathan exhale. Then he squeezes her leg. "Well. I like to hear you sing, too."

Feeling braver, Sing whispers, "Will you tell me what you wished for now?"

He doesn't respond at first. She wishes she could see his face, worried she has offended him. But after a moment, she hears him sigh, feels the movement of his shoulder against hers as he does so.

Then he says, "I wished to be human."

Fifty-nine

ALONE IN ST. AUGUSTINE'S CAVERNOUS HALL, George plays. Sometimes, when it's Bach or Schubert, it seems to him almost as though Nathan and the crystal don't matter. It is like when he was a child, playing his grandmother's tinny upright piano for hours at a time. No one disturbed him when he was focused on music. Not even the day his brother drowned, when George should have been with him at the river. But George had been captivated by Beethoven and spent the day crawling clumsily through his piano sonatas. The family let him finish them before they broke the news.

Lately, it has been more and more difficult to lose himself in music, at the piano or in heady dreams of conducting glorious pieces. He used to allow himself to be consumed by music. Now something else consumes him. It *feels* like music, but it looks like Nathan Daysmoor.

And now, ever since the crystal disappeared, he feels the weight of his overdue years pressing him from all sides. It has driven him nearly mad. But it has puzzled him as well. Nathan has no knowledge of the crystal. Why would he steal it, even if he could?

Then, today, he *saw it.*

On the da Navelli girl, the one following in the entitled footsteps of her mother. She had it on a chain around her neck at the Gloria Stewart competition, when she was singing in the lobby. She didn't see him watching her. Neither did Nathan.

He *knew* something was going on between them. He saw how Nathan looked at her during rehearsals. Tonight, he watched Nathan cross the snowy quad, using the shadows to hide his progress. George wouldn't have seen him if he hadn't been looking. And the da Navelli girl followed a while later.

George comes to the end of a Bach invention, pauses, then starts on another.

Now they are hiding from him. Nathan's black coat is thrown over one of the chairs at the back of the hall. They must be in the stairwell.

He feels like playing a bit longer. It doesn't matter. The crystal is here, and he will have it back soon.

Then no one will take Nathan away ever again.

Sixty

Y OU'RE NOT . . . HUMAN?"
Sing's body tenses. Nathan takes his hand from her leg.
"Not really," he says. "I mean, I am human, yes, physically. Men-
tally. But my soul—my essence—is something else."

Does she believe this? Here in the dark, she feels she could believe anything. And wasn't she the one to tell him the tiny crystal
was a Felix tear? His wish?

She touches his shoulder.

"When the Felix caught me," he says, "I was a crow. But I had
discovered the beauty of human music. I longed for it more than
anything, and it broke my heart that I could only make ugly sounds.
So she granted my deepest wish, to become human."

Sing doesn't want to believe it. It's too crazy. But suddenly, she
realizes why his voice sounds familiar. She remembers the ugly
caws and crackles from the snowy branches of the big tree. "I can
hear it," she whispers. "You sound like them."

Her eyes are growing more accustomed to the darkness, and she
can just see him turn toward her. "Yes," he says. "She didn't—or
couldn't—change my voice. It's much lower now, of course, but it's
the voice I've always had."

Carrie's conspiracy theories come back to her, the mysterious, ageless Apprentice Daysmoor. "You knew the Maestro when he was young, didn't you? And you've been here all this time?"

He seems to consider this. "I was just about to enter my second autumn when I was changed. That is where I have been frozen. Time doesn't pass for me as it does for you."

"You're immortal?" She has fallen into a fairy tale. The cold space of the stairwell makes her dizzy.

"I don't think so," he says. "I don't know. You see, I'm not supposed to be who I am. I was supposed to live for a short time, many years ago. There isn't a place for me—for Nathan Daysmoor—here and now. I have to cheat."

Sing stares at the darkness in front of her. All of this is starting to make an improbable kind of sense. "Why couldn't she just make you a human?"

"I've thought about that," he whispers. "I think it's that humans—all living things—don't just appear out of nowhere. To make me truly human, the Felix would have had to create a space for me—parents, grandparents, all the way back. Or find a space somewhere I could fit into. Maybe it would have been too much, even for her." He is quiet for a moment, but she waits. "She didn't mean to hurt me. It was George who did that. He kept me here, away from the world and people who would have loved me. I told myself it was for the best, resigned myself to this existence. I couldn't even take comfort in time passing, because it—didn't. I know that doesn't make any sense."

Sing imagines Daysmoor, alone in his tower, year after year, giving exquisite performances no one would hear.

She senses him turn to her. "But when you came," he says, "when I heard you sing, it drew me back to this world. Made me remember why I gave up everything to be here."

She can see him a little now. He tips his head back, arms propped behind him. She can see his chest rising and falling slightly as he breathes. "Do you want to wear my coat for a little while?" she asks.

He looks in her direction and she thinks his eyes scrunch into a smile. "No. I'm okay."

She pulls her cold hands into her coat sleeves. "Nathan, I'm sorry about tonight. I shouldn't have tried to . . . well, I just didn't know I—wasn't your type." She says it with a bit of a laugh. *I probably don't have enough feathers for him.*

And she actually feels a little better about the whole thing. There is something comforting about clarity, even unhappy clarity.

When she turns her head, he is still looking at her. "Sing," he whispers, "you know there are a hundred reasons why what almost happened tonight shouldn't happen. Ever. Starting with the fact that I'm an apprentice and you're a student."

"I know," she whispers.

He hesitates. "But if I told you one of the reasons I didn't kiss you was that I didn't want to—I'd be lying."

She is silent. Of all the confessions he has made in this cold, black stairwell, this seems the most incredible.

"I was afraid, I think," he says, his fingers touching her face in the dark. It is his left arm, the one with the intricate ivy tattoo that starts at his wrist and snakes its way to his shoulder, a twisting bridge across the space between them that she can't see but knows is there. "You are so lovely, and your voice—I thought you were arrogant at first. I was wrong. I know now that someone has hurt you." Sing doesn't know who he means. He says, "But I've been Apprentice Daysmoor for so long, I couldn't talk to you, even if I had dared. And you only had eyes for Ryan Larkin."

She doesn't—can't—move. Her heart thuds. She remembers the night of the attack, with Ryan, the dark shape of Daysmoor watching them from the window. "I don't mind," she whispers. "You know. The not-human thing."

He laughs at this. She has rarely heard him laugh, and it warms her. Then, without a word, he pulls her to him and finds her mouth in the blackness.

For a moment, she doesn't dare believe the invisible phantom whose lips press against her own could be Nathan. She closes her eyes and slips her arms around his neck, remembering the look of his unkempt black hair as she touches it. At first his movements are slow, careful, but she leans into him, returning the kiss, assuring him. His embrace strengthens. He winds his arms around her, under her coat. She feels his fingers on her skin just over her right hip, where her shirt has come untucked from her skirt. They make her shudder, and not just with their chill.

Something else he does better than Ryan.

She becomes aware of light and opens her eyes.

"I—," he starts, pulling away, straightening his shirt. "Oh, God, I'm sorry."

"No, it's okay," she says. "I just noticed the glowing."

He looks down. The teardrop in his pocket is shining through the fabric, dully illuminating their small landing. "Oh," he says. "I think it . . . reacts to me. To my emotions."

She smiles. "So you weren't pretending just now."

He laughs again, mostly with his eyes, now lit by the strange, soft light of the crystal. Then he takes her hands. "Sing, there are very, very few people who can make me feel the way you do. Most of them are dead. And none of them can do it without an orchestra."

She kisses him again.

"Or a piano," he adds, his words muffled by her mouth. She laughs.

Suddenly, she feels his body tense. And before a question escapes her, she realizes what he has realized—the hall below them has gone quiet.

"Is he gone?" she whispers, wondering how loud they let their voices become just now.

"I don't know," Nathan says. The crystal's light is fading, and they cast their eyes and ears into the darkness. Silence. Then—

Footsteps. In the hall, coming closer.

Sing wraps her arms around Nathan's arm. Is Maestro Keppler going to come up into the stairwell? It's absurd. Yet the footsteps continue to approach.

The door at the bottom of the stairs gives a rattle. Someone is unlocking it.

Nathan finds Sing's hand and leads her skyward. They climb quickly, and Sing is relieved to hear the creak of the roof hatch and see the less-dark of night spill in from above. They pull themselves onto the cold, gray roof and Nathan closes the hatch without a sound. He puts his arms around her as they back away from the hatch, as a gesture not of affection, she realizes, but of protection. On both sides of the long, flat apex on which they stand, the slick roof slopes sharply down. Far below, the concrete walk cuts through the snow like a dark river.

The wind drives stinging cold across their faces. She feels him shiver. "Take my coat," she says, slipping it off. The cold hits her like a plunge into icy water. He doesn't take the coat, but she can see his shivering intensifying. "Don't be an ass," she says, thrusting the coat toward him. "I have a sweater vest, at least. Just for a minute."

He drapes the woolen coat around his shoulders. It won't close in the front, but she can see the relief in his face. "Thanks," he says.

Sing looks out over the campus. Even now, when the buildings are dark with sleep, there are dots of light everywhere—lampposts, security lights, the odd illuminated window. And the blazing Woolly, where the Gloria Stewart semifinals reception must still be going on. She casts her gaze farther, over the fence, all the way up to the icy summit of the forbidden mountain behind them. The forest is black, changing to gray above the tree line where the exposed snow contrasts with the darker sky.

The cold scrapes at her skin, and she moves closer to Nathan. "He won't come up here, will he?" she asks.

"I can't imagine why he would. Probably heard a noise in the stairwell. Once he sees there's no one there—"

But at that moment, the hatch flies open, landing with a thud on the tiled roof.

Sing feels Nathan inhale sharply. He puts an arm around her, drawing her close. It is instinctual, and exactly the wrong thing to do if they are to have any hope of defending their innocence, but she can't make herself pull away.

Despite the mechanics of climbing up through the hatch, Maestro Keppler manages to storm onto the roof. His face is drawn, his hair unkempt.

Sing flinches. She waits for the shouting. But it doesn't come.

"Nathan," the Maestro says, "you shouldn't be up here. It's freezing." He doesn't address Sing. He doesn't even seem to notice her.

"I'm fine," Nathan says. "Go to bed."

The Maestro scowls. "I know what you're plotting, Nathan. Leaving me here to rot. After—after—"

"Don't be ridiculous."

"I know you! What do you have in your pocket?" The Maestro lurches a step closer.

Sing inhales. Nathan releases her, putting a hand into his pocket. "This is mine," he says.

The Maestro holds out his hand. "It's not. It's *mine*. Give it back, and I will forgive you."

To Sing's astonishment, Nathan takes a step toward him. "Nathan," she says, "what are you doing? Don't give the tear to him!" Nathan hesitates.

"Give me the crystal, Nathan," Maestro Keppler says. "It is the only way I can keep you safe."

Nathan's fingers close around the necklace. "You have never kept me safe. You've kept me prisoner."

The Maestro is silent for a moment, robes fluttering like the wings of a trapped bird. It is hard for Sing to read his expression in the weak light that reaches the roof from campus. When his voice comes, it is calm. "Is that what you think?"

STRANGE SWEET SONG   273

"George," Nathan says gently, "you know I—"

"It doesn't matter." The Maestro's tone is suddenly hard. "Give me the crystal, Nathan. Do it now, and we can go home."

But Nathan shakes his head. "No. I can't do this anymore. There's a way for me to enter the Gloria Stewart after all. I have to do it, George. It's time. It will be all right."

"No!" the Maestro screeches, startling Sing, who presses closer to Nathan. "It will not be all right!" He inhales deeply and seems to regain himself. Then, with a detached deliberation that sends sparks through Sing's body, he pulls an object from his pocket. Even in the dimness, the dull, narrow gleam is unmistakable.

He points the gun at Nathan's chest.

"Maestro!" she shrieks, her voice carrying across the campus and into the forest. Birds rustle the woods.

"Damn it, George, are you out of your mind?" Nathan steps back, positioning his body between Sing and the Maestro.

Even with the stinging breeze whipping his robes, the Maestro's arm retains the steadiness of a seasoned conductor. Sing watches him. He seems much older now, and withered, eyes sunken in their sockets like those of a corpse. There is something inhuman in his gaze, greedy and ferocious.

"I would have protected you, Nathan, if you'd let me," he says. "But it's better to end it here than lose you to the world."

He's going to do it, Sing realizes. The night presses in on her—the harsh, icy air, the rattling of the forest, the glare of stars, the silent menace of the slate roof angling sharply down on either side of her, and Nathan, inches away, with a gun pointed at his chest.

Without thinking, she wraps her arms around his waist and pulls him down to the cold slate. The monstrous noise of the pistol strikes her ears.

At the same moment, she is aware of a rush of warmth that swishes between herself and the Maestro. A heaviness dampens the air, like the wake of a rocket. She looks up to see glistening orange fur hurtling toward Keppler.

"Tamino!" She tries to rise, but now Nathan holds her. She hears Tamino's menacing growl for the first time, the click of his claws running across the slate.

A second gunshot, and all is silent again.

A mass of glittering orange and violet slides down the slippery roof. Nathan can't hold Sing back any longer; she dashes forward, half staggering to her feet at the same time.

Tamino falls through space.

Before he hits the ground, he has dissolved into a million golden sparks, which crackle and arc their ways into the blackness in every direction. It would be beautiful, were it not for the image now indelibly seared into Sing's mind—a glimpse of lifeless blue eyes as he fell.

Numb, she lets Nathan pull her back from the edge.

"What the hell was that animal?" The Maestro is visibly shaken. "What *was* it?" He looks at the pistol in his hand. Here and there on the campus, lights flick on.

You killed Tamino. The words don't come out.

Nathan doesn't let go of her. He is shaking. Her coat has fallen off him and lies like a huddled animal, several yards away on the narrow apex of the roof.

"George, listen—," Nathan says.

Maestro Keppler seems to regain his frayed senses. He raises the gun to Nathan's chest again. "I don't want to do this, Nathan. But you must stay here. You mustn't go to the river."

"Okay. Okay." Nathan raises a hand. "Just hang on."

No, Nathan. Sing doesn't dare speak, even if somehow she could. The Maestro *cannot* get the crystal now. All she can see are Tamino's vacant eyes.

But Nathan is reaching into his pocket, sliding the necklace out. The crystal is a tiny, glimmering star.

Sing finds her voice. "Nathan." *No.*

He doesn't look at her. Instead he says, "I won't leave. I won't play. But she sings tomorrow."

What? "Nathan, don't be ridiculous," she says. "One stupid opera doesn't matter!"

The Maestro seems to notice Sing for the first time. *"Her?"* He sounds familiar now. "The da Navelli girl? She's never singing again, my boy. She is expelled. We don't need her."

Expelled. Sing exhales mirthlessly at the absurdity of it. How can that word have meaning? Here, with Nathan and the Maestro and the gun and the memory of Tamino?

Nathan closes his fingers. "Then you're not getting this."

The Maestro's arm quivers. His gaze never leaves Nathan's face. "Very well."

Sing pulls Nathan's arm. "No! What are you doing?"

He turns to her. "Do you know what it will mean if you're expelled? He can ruin you. It doesn't matter who your father is—he's not as influential as the conservatory. George can ruin your career. And he will."

Sing can hear people now, talking out there in the dark. But no one hurries to St. Augustine's; they are not certain where the loud noises came from. They are not looking to the rooftops.

"Just give me the crystal," the Maestro barks.

"I'm not afraid of him!" Sing says. "Nathan, take the crystal and we'll leave. Together. I don't care about *Angelique* or this damn conservatory!" The heaviness of the night is starting to overwhelm her. *Tamino is gone.*

Now Nathan reaches for her hands. His skin is cold, but his hands are gentle. "You *have* to care about music, Sing. It's who you are."

She doesn't know how to respond. Nathan turns, holding the necklace out to the Maestro, his fingers tightly closed. "We have a deal. I give this back, and Sing doesn't get punished?"

Maestro Keppler's eyes narrow, but he nods.

"Don't, Nathan," Sing whispers. "You'll be trapped here."

Nathan looks at her and smiles. "Then only one thing will have changed." And he opens his fingers.

The Maestro snatches the necklace and peers at it. The gun falls and skitters down the sloped roof. Nathan picks up Sing's coat from where it has fallen and drapes it over her shivering shoulders. She leans against him, suddenly exhausted. He kisses the top of her head. Somewhere below, a light flicks off.

"But it's just going to continue."

They both look to the Maestro, still contemplating the bright teardrop in his hands. His voice is soft now.

He looks up as if surprised by their presence. "It's going to continue, isn't it, Nathan? You love her. . . . That's so strange."

Nathan's tone is careful. "What's going to continue, George?"

"I can't keep you here, can I?" The Maestro's face is so forlorn, Sing almost wants to comfort him.

"I'll stay," Nathan says.

George sighs. "You don't *want* to stay."

Nathan is silent. Sing watches his face, but she can't read his expression. Maestro Keppler is looking at them, brows drawn, mouth curved in a pensive frown. He lets the crystal fall, and it clatters on the slate.

"Good-bye, Nathan," he says, lifting one of his gleaming leather shoes.

There is a moment of quiet confusion. Then, ugly comprehension dawning, Sing and Nathan rush forward at the same instant.

They are too late. The rigid heel of the Maestro's shoe slams down onto the slate with an icy crunch. Sing and Nathan freeze. The Maestro lifts his shoe again to reveal a tiny, glittering splatter of shards.

"What have you done, George?" Nathan says, eyes wide. "We *need* the crystal."

George smiles. "I only needed you, Nathan." And he is frozen, still smiling. His eyes lose their sheen, then their intelligence. Sing gasps as the Maestro seems to grow hollow before her eyes. She clutches Nathan's arm. After a moment, Maestro Keppler sinks slowly to the slate rooftop like a macabre, deflating balloon. Sing sees again her mother's white dress, collapsing onto the stage, the woman inside it just as dead.

She lets out a cry and buries her face in Nathan's chest. But he, too, is disappearing.

"Nathan!" He can no longer stand. She helps him lie down on the slate. "Nathan! We can fix this. I'll find the Felix. I'll—"

He looks up at her, weak but bright-eyed. "It's all right."

Her tears are ice sliding down her cheeks. She doesn't want them to fall on him. She gathers him in her arms. He feels so light now.

His mouth is against her cheek, his breath still warm. She squeezes her eyes closed and grips him tighter. But suddenly, there is nothing to grip.

She looks down to find a mass of lustrous black feathers scattering in the wind.

Hold on to them. Gather them. Get him back. Hold on. She scrabbles at the air. *Grab them, grab them,*

"Grab what?" Ryan says.

Sing realizes she has been staring vacantly at the red-and-gold-leaf design on the Woolly lounge's lush carpet. "What?"

Ryan's expression is puzzled yet amused. "You just said, 'Grab them.'"

"Oh." She studies the carpet, trying to remember. She didn't intend to stay this long at the reception; she must be overtired. Her father and the president are still in conversation across the room. She thought she'd lost Ryan to the famous pianist Yvette Cordaro and a string of giggling girls, but apparently he has found his way back to her.

The golden leaves on the carpet seem to swirl. She has a strange, overpowering desire to scoop them up in her hands and clutch them safe. "I think I meant the leaves," she says. "On the pattern, there." *Is that what I meant?* The shape of it is right. But something tickles her brain.

"Well," Ryan says lightly, extracting a glass of something from her hand, "I don't think you'll be needing any more of *these*." His green eyes are as alert as ever, but slightly shadowed by the late hour. He puts Sing's glass down on the tray of a passing server and takes her arm. "Here, it's getting boring. I'm going to play some waltzes to celebrate my impending victory." He steers her toward the shining grand piano in the corner.

She watches the golden leaves in the sea of red carpet float by as they walk.

Sixty-one

Morning sun digs its fingers into Sing's closed eyes, causing her to groan and pull a pillow over her head. Her head aches. Why does her head ache? What time is it?

She peers blearily at the clock on her bedside table: 9:24. She'd better get up if she's going to be in good voice for *Angelique* this afternoon. Harland Griss will be there. The New Artist vacancy is at stake, perhaps more than she would like to admit. Her father's influence is important, but she knows he doesn't wield it the same way her mother did. If Griss chooses to look elsewhere for his new butterfly, Ernesto da Navelli will leave it at that.

No one is using the bathroom at this hour on a Sunday. Students with something going on today were up long ago, and those who had something going on last night won't be up for a while. The tile floor is cold on Sing's bare feet. She takes her time brushing her teeth, trying not to think about what she will do with the hours before the performance. She squints at her reflection, face tilted so close that the mirror traps clouds of breath on its cool surface.

Her eyes are shadowed, her skin pale. She steps back, studying. Something pricks at her mind. Something isn't right.

She shuffles back down the hallway in her bathrobe. Voices

emanate from behind the closed door across the hall—Jenny and Marta, still in their room. They have nothing to worry about today. The performance of *Angelique* will come and go, they will do their parts, onstage and in the orchestra, and then school will continue. School, homework, practice, performance, boys, drama, self. Sing, trying to bring her own future into focus, is surprised to find herself longing for their company.

Who are they? Barbara da Navelli would say. *You'll be leaving this school soon. Why do you need them?*

Sing puts a hand to her door but doesn't go in. She stands for a long moment in the empty hallway, listening to the muffled voices behind her. It's not often she feels the *girl* inside her—not a child, not an adult, but the part of her psyche that longs for validation from her own kind. Ryan feeds this part of her—*Ryan,* that's why her head aches, the semifinals reception that ran far too late into the night—but she needs friends, too.

Barbara da Navelli wouldn't understand. She fed only two parts of herself, the professional and the strategist. Never the girl. "I need them because I'm not you," Sing says aloud.

"That's it?" Jenny says. " 'Sorry'?"

Sing shrugs. "That's all I've got." She strokes the yarn mane of a glittery stuffed Pegasus.

"Her name is Belinda," Marta says.

"I shouldn't have taken you guys for granted the way I did," Sing says. "And I shouldn't have played the celebrity card on you. It's . . . embarrassing. I don't really have an excuse, I guess. New schools are hard."

Jenny eyes her. "Yes, well, some of us manage it."

"I know," Sing says. "I'm sorry. Please . . . don't do a tawdry exposé on me for *The Trumpeter.*"

Jenny snort-laughs. "Oh, it's *tempting.* But the thing is, Sing, we do love you, really, even though you can be kind of an entitled bitch, there I said it. And it's hard to stay mad at you for screwing

Lori Pinkerton since she's just about the most irritating person there is. I secretly love that she's finally getting what she deserves. Just don't make a habit of it, okay?"

"My mother made a habit of it," Sing says. She and Marta are seated on Marta's bed, while Jenny sits nearby in a rolling desk chair, the lazy light of the free Sunday morning drifting in through the ancient beige curtains. Jenny is still in pajamas, while Marta wears flowing, embroidered garments that are possibly also pajamas. "It's easy to get caught up in the superficiality of it," Sing says. "How a thing looks."

"Oh, right." Jenny swings her legs and spins slowly in the desk chair. "Makeup and eyebrows and hair. Like you need to worry about *that*. Ryan may be a jerk, no offense, but he is definitely the cutest guy on campus. And, *and*, you stole him from the resident diva. So it's not like you're going to curl your hair and put on lipstick and he'll be like, 'Oh, my God, Sing, how could I not have seen how amazingly hot you are? Let me dump my popular cheerleader girlfriend for you.' Because that's *already happened*."

"She's not talking about that," Marta says. "She means wanting the lead just because it's the lead, not because it's right."

"It *is* right. It's what I've always wanted." Sing winds the Pegasus's yarn tail around her fingers. "I just . . . I think I need to feel *normal* today. I don't know why."

"Of course you know why," Jenny says. "Everything is riding on this performance. You're wondering if you're good enough. Honestly, you're pretty damn good."

Sing pulls her hair into a ponytail with one hand. *Zhin would tell me I'm the best,* she thinks. Then, surprising herself, she says it aloud.

"Psh," Jenny says. "I'll tell you one thing—you do *not* need her."

"I know," Sing says. "She's just . . . she's like . . ."

"Like what? Underhanded? Egotistical? Betray . . . erous?"

"She's a lot like my mother."

Jenny arches a brow. "Vell, zen," she says with a thick accent that is possibly trying to be German, "I sink ve're getting shome-vhere!

Zat vill be vun hundred dollars. Next veek ve disguss your boy-froind."

Sing laughs. "Oh, God, let's not."

"I don't know how you forgave him, by the way." Jenny flops back in her chair.

Forgave him. There's something fuzzy there, in Sing's mind. Ryan cheated on her with Zhin. And probably with Lori. Heck, he probably cheated on Lori with Sing. But she forgave him, right? At the reception last night, after the Gloria Stewart semifinals. Something about it feels so unreal.

The door opens and Carrie Stewart pokes her pixie face in. "Hey, guys, I just saw Mr. Bernard!"

Jenny's expression is flat. "Oh, my God."

"No!" Carrie breathes. "Maestro Keppler *died* last night!"

During its busy Sunday lunch hour, the Mountain Grill smells like beef stew, onions, cinnamon, charcoal, woodsmoke, and ladies' perfume. The window is cheerful but cold, and Sing snuggles into her sweatshirt, grateful to be out of uniform. Midday sunlight illuminates the details of the wood grain on the tables and floor, as well as the smooth, silver lines of Marta's mermaid pendant as she leans forward, mouth open slightly.

"What did he say?"

Sing found her father in Hector Hall surrounded by faculty, apprentices, and a couple of quick-out-of-the-gate reporters. He managed to speak to her briefly, with Jenny and Marta waiting for the details. "Heart failure," she says. "Around midnight. Discovered in his bed early this morning by Apprentice Garcia. The ambulance or whatever, the hearse, I don't know, has been and gone. That's it."

Jenny frowns, crossing her arms. "And the performance is going on? The man is *dead*."

"Well, they could just tell everyone to go home, I guess," Sing says. "But there's been so much put into the Autumn Festival, it would be a shame." *Maestro Keppler is dead. Heart failure.* Why does that seem . . . *wrong?*

"Will your father conduct?" Marta asks.

Sing's stomach squirms. "Yes."

"Wow!" Marta says. Jenny raises an eyebrow at her, but she goes on. "I know, I'm sorry the Maestro died. But it was his time." Sing resists the urge to roll her eyes; Jenny doesn't. "But I may never get the chance to sing under Maestro da Navelli again. It's kind of incredible."

"It will be interesting." Sing keeps her voice low, even though their booth is fairly insulated from the Grill's other patrons. "My father's never conducted *Angelique.*"

"Really?" Marta is aghast. "But he must know it!"

"Yeah," Sing says. "He knows it."

Despite Jenny's efforts to hide it, Sing catches the movement in her shoulder as she elbows Marta under the table.

"No, it's okay." Sing smiles and actually feels it inside as well as outside. "It will be good for him. And a treat for the audience. Well, I guess 'treat' is kind of a horrible way to put it."

The waitress brings their lunches in thick ceramic dishes that clatter against the wooden table. "Not really," Marta says. "We can't help it the Maestro died." She dips a spoon into her tomato soup.

"He was like a *hundred,*" Jenny says. "Honestly, what was holding that man together? I think we were his last stop, honestly."

Sing scrunches her eyebrows. "His last stop?"

"Well, he's been haunting the Orchestre de Paris for so long, I didn't think anyone could peel him off the walls and shoot him stateside again. This 'homecoming performance' always felt less like a publicity stunt and more like a grand finale."

"That's awfully cynical," Marta says.

Sing studies her hamburger. Again, that strange prickly feeling starts at the back of her mind. She saw Maestro Keppler only last night, at the Gloria Stewart semifinals. He was there with his assistant, Apprentice Garcia, the doughy-faced young man who turns Ryan's pages at rehearsal. Did the Maestro seem sick? She doesn't think so. But then, you can't always tell with hearts.

"I still think we should be allowed a crazy, campuswide snowball fight instead of the performance." Jenny pokes at her potatoes with a short fork. "We could use the woods! It would be epic! And, you know, healing."

"Not very mournful," Sing says. *The woods.* She pictures their ashy smell, their sharp chill. The night she escaped there, after Carrie Stewart's party. She can remember the woods with pristine clarity. Or can she? In some of her memories, there is a strange vagueness. A dark cloud.

"I don't think a snowball fight in the woods would be very safe." Marta's eyes are wide and her mouth curls into a slight frown. "You could get attacked by a bear."

Jenny chews a potato. "Don't bears, like, hibernate? Or something? When do they do that?"

"They stop hibernating if you hit them with snowballs." Marta's tone is so serious that Jenny and Sing laugh.

"Or if you call them!" Jenny says. "I've been working on my bear call with Professor Needleman—what do you think? *Figaro! Figarofigarofigaro, feee-gah-roh!*"

They laugh at Jenny's poorly executed opera reference, even Jenny herself, who snorts.

A blond head pokes around the side of the booth. Pretty eyes glint charmingly, and pink-glossed lips coo, "You girls are having a good time over here."

Sing freezes.

"Hey, Lori," Marta says, sipping her water. "What's up?"

"Just enjoying the day, looking forward to the Gloria Stewart finals tonight." Lori looks pointedly at Sing. "I've got an easy afternoon."

Lori's party gets up to leave as Sing and Jenny sit in silence. Aaron slides out of the booth, followed by Carrie Stewart and—

"Ryan?" Sing doesn't mean to say it. He turns around and for the briefest of moments looks more than a little uncomfortable. But it passes in a flash, and he smiles broadly.

"Hey, Sing. Hey, girls. Looking lovely today, I see."

Marta blushes. Sing doesn't know what to say. *Ryan, here with Lori? Were they eavesdropping? Did I say anything embarrassing?*

"Oh, hi, guys!" Carrie says.

"We won't keep you from your lunches." Lori pulls on a cream-colored knitted hat. "I know you've got a big day. Especially you, Sing. Good luck with *Angelique*."

Don't take the bait. Sing smiles as artificially as she can. "Thanks."

Lori returns the fake smile. "Special father-daughter performance, I hear! Won't that be fun."

Ignore it.

"Even though, you know, it's *this* role." Lori pulls on a beige leather glove. "I'm sure no one will mind."

Sing feels her jaw stiffen. She can't ignore it. Not now. Not if it's what everyone is thinking. "What's that supposed to mean?"

Lori's gaze hardens. Ryan pulls his jacket on. "We'd better go," he says brightly. "You girls—"

Sing stands. "Do you have a problem with me, Lori?"

Lori raises her eyebrows, and for a second, it seems like she is going to feign innocence. But her pink smile disappears with a derisive huff, and she cocks her head. "It's not *me* you need to worry about, da Navelli. I'm going to enjoy watching you crash and burn out there today in front of Harland Griss and everyone else."

"That's right, it *will* be me out there." Sing can't believe the words coming out of her mouth. Everyone around them is quiet. "Do you think you could sing it better?"

Lori pauses. When she speaks, all the coo in her voice has dried up. "It doesn't matter. It was *my role*."

She turns, and Sing lets her have the last word. The whole party is gone in a few short moments.

Jenny and Marta watch her as she sits down.

"Stop," Jenny says, raising a hand. "We can analyze the last thirty seconds for the next two hours, I promise, but please can I order another soda before we begin? I have a feeling I'm going to need my strength."

"I'm not analyzing anything," Sing says. "Whatever."

"Lori's trying to undermine your confidence," Marta says.

Jenny scrunches her napkin and puts it on her plate. "I don't blame her. No offense."

"Ryan was just having lunch with friends," Marta says. She raises her ceramic bowl and tips the last drops of tomato soup into her mouth.

"Ryan can do what he wants," Sing says. "It's no big deal. Sheesh. I—" She can't make herself finish the sentence: *I trust him*.

Jenny smiles slyly. "What Ryan *wants* is you, Sing da Navelli. Much to the chagrin of the female population of DC. They'll have to see if another Prince Charming appears out of the ether next year, I guess."

"Not Prince Charming—Prince Elbert!" Marta says, and giggles.

"I prefer Prince Charming." Sing swirls a French fry in the remains of the ketchup lake on her plate. Then she voices what seems to just have occurred to her, but as she speaks, she realizes it is what she has always known: "Prince Elbert doesn't love Angelique for who she is. She's a trophy to him. That's the only thing wrong with the opera."

Jenny just shrugs and says, "Men. Man opera. Written by men. Whatcha gonna do."

Marta is staring at Sing, who can almost see the gears in her mind turning. "Maybe it's not *wrong*," she says, absently stroking the heavy silver pendant around her neck. "Maybe it's just a tragedy. Only it doesn't feel like a tragedy at first, because you forget about him."

Sing frowns. "Forget about who?"

Marta blushes. "Angelique's true love, of course. Silvain."

Sixty-two

THE NIGHT ZHIN STAYED AT DC, she and Sing laughed and ate microwave popcorn until two in the morning. And even though Zhin would betray her the next day, Sing can't remember that night with anything but fondness.

She sat here. Sing places her folded blanket at the end of her bed. Only it wasn't here; it was in Zhin's identical room on senior floor. Sing remembers her in her sea-green pajamas, cross-legged, a pillow wedged between her torso and the wall, both of them giggling as though they were ten instead of seventeen. Sing liked that Zhin.

She sits on her bed, reaches for one of the novels on her nightstand, and, instead of taking it, lets herself be drawn downward by the weight of her outstretched arm. Another hour before she has to be at the Woolly to sing Angelique. She closes her eyes.

"It was my role," Lori said. Zhin would have something to say about *that*. Something about a mistake that never should have been made, about Sing's talent, about all those dime-a-dozen sopranos not worth her time. Maybe that was why Ryan had been drawn to Zhin. She made you feel you were worth great things.

Zhin wasn't afraid to talk about things, either. *"Sometimes I hate my name,"* Sing told her that night as they sat with their popcorn bowls. *"It's too heavy to drag around."*

"You shouldn't be dragging it," Zhin said. "You should be waving it like a flag. That's what your mother did. She knew how to get ahead." Then, surprisingly, Zhin leaned over and rubbed Sing's shoulder. "And she wanted the best for you."

"I'm not sure we have the same definition of 'the best,'" Sing said, but she felt a little better.

"Music is the best," Zhin said. "And she named you Sing."

Sing stirred the kernels in the bottom of her bowl with her finger. "Yeah, but what if your parents had named you Play Violin? Even though you love playing violin, it's a lot of pressure."

Zhin snorted at this. "*My* parents would never have named me anything so interesting. We have rules, you know. We actually have our family tree written in a book that goes back a gazillion years, and there's this poem in there about flowers or something, and every generation has its own character from the poem that has to go in everyone's name. I'm going to name my kids Potato and Chip just to watch Grandma's head explode."

"I'd rather be Chip than Potato," Sing said, laughing.

Zhin tossed a pillow her way. "Too bad. You're Potato."

Sing threw the pillow back, which upset Zhin's popcorn bowl, and they both covered their mouths to stop their laughter from waking the other students on senior floor.

"All right," Zhin said. "You can be Sing, a star."

Sing sighed. "I don't know if I'll ever be a star."

Zhin's face relaxed into an expression Sing had never seen before, unguarded and young. *"Sing,"* Zhin said, only it sounded different now. It wasn't quite *sing;* it was thin and strange and lovely. "It means 'star' in Chinese. Like in the sky. See? You just have to look at your name differently, that's all."

Sing smiled. "Really? That's pretty cool." *Star.*

"It's not a perfect match. There are lots of words in Chinese that sound a bit like it. But that's the one I'd think of first."

Not a command after all. Star. "Thanks, Zhin."

Zhin shrugged. "Well, it's that or 'gorilla.'" They laughed. Sing wanted to hold on to this Zhin, the one who disappeared as soon as other people were around.

Now Sing lies alone in her shadowy room and thinks of stars. Not artificial stars, who shine only in comparison with lesser beings, who revel in their own glory like Barbara da Navelli. Like Zhin. No, Sing imagines the diamond scattering of real stars, burning cold and fierce across the infinite blackness, fixed and alone and complete.

Sixty-three

THE WOOLLY THEATER DOESN'T have special accommodations for principals. Sing arrives at the women's dressing room well before call time, but even so, she is not alone.

"Lori," she says to the blond hair seated in front of the long lighted mirror.

Lori turns around. "You surprised I'm here? Well, I always come two hours early. And yes, I'm still in. I'm in the chorus. Sorry." She faces the mirror again, hair swishing.

Jealous, Barbara da Navelli would say. No, would *think.*

Sing doesn't speak to Lori. She sits at the other end of the mirror and does her stage makeup. After a while, she leans back to make sure it reads from a distance. Sweet. Natural. It is only when she leans in close that the exaggerated darks and lights become clear—severe stripes of black and white, strange rounded reds and pinks. Up close, she looks like a monster.

Other cast members start to arrive, chatting, staking out territory with their bags and coats, but none of them speak to Sing.

The dress fits perfectly. She can't even tell which pieces have had to be shortened or lengthened. She takes the carefully curled blond wig from its perch on a Styrofoam head and pulls it over her own hair, held in place with a cap. A few dark strands poke out from the shining gold. She shoves them back under. Perfect.

And there she is, in the mirror. A beautiful girl in a ruffly white dress, golden ringlets cascading over her shoulders.

Angelique.

Sing studies her face—serious, haughty, commanding. She frowns. This isn't the naïve shepherd girl she had anticipated. Where is the innocence? The radiance? All Sing sees are hard eyes and a shadowy, lined face. Barbara da Navelli.

Maybe it's a tragedy, Marta suggested.

There, in the background of the reflection, over her shoulder— the busy dressing room and, beyond, the open door. That's what's wrong. The drab, dusty backstage, the asymmetrical shadows. And the faces. Lori.

There is so much beyond the reflection of the beautiful girl. The mirror catches only the dress, the hair, the smile. But beyond is the world the mirror doesn't see, the world the audience doesn't see. Maybe Angelique could have lived in this mirror, but not in the world beyond.

Singing Angelique doesn't bring her to life. She should have known. For all her elaborate costumes, Barbara da Navelli was always Barbara da Navelli. Sing could never take Angelique back from her mother, because her mother never possessed her.

Is that what she wanted? To take Angelique back? And then what?

Sing feels her shoulders collapsing. Her heart grows heavier. *It isn't real.*

Now anger. *You said playing a thing would make it true.* She stares at her reflection, her mother staring back at her, eyes cold. "I can't make it true," she hisses. "And neither could you. The only true thing you ever did was die."

She puts a hand to the soft blond curls. They slip off easily, just two pins holding them on. Barbara da Navelli was wrong. Playing a thing doesn't make it true. Not really. Not at all.

Sing turns around. "Lori. I—"

"Whatever it is, I don't care." Lori crosses her arms. "Whatever. Have a good show."

"I'm sorry." Sing places the wig on the dressing table.

Lori turns away, applying a final layer of mascara. She looks like a Barbie doll. "You don't need to be sorry," she says. "You won."

"It's not a game."

Lori turns back now and smiles sadness in a way that makes Sing ache. "Yes. It is."

Sing unzips the white ruffly dress. She feels as though she is committing a terrible betrayal as it slides to the floor, but she is not sure who she's betraying. "Then I quit," she says.

Her reflection is still haggard, but it's *her* again. Barbara da Navelli is gone.

Barbara da Navelli is gone.

"*Carina,* are you sure?"

She can't read her father's face. He should be angry. He *is* angry, but there is something else there, too, which makes her less afraid. "I don't think it's right for me to sing today when I wasn't cast. I know you spoke to Maestro Keppler."

Orchestra members filter into the cushy musicians' lounge on the Woolly's second floor. Some glance Sing's way, but most talk or grab snacks from the buffet table. Ernesto da Navelli shrugs. "Yes, of course I spoke to him. He agreed with me."

"Well, he *would* agree with you. You're a celebrity."

Her father frowns. "I do not use my status to tell people what to do."

Yes, you do. She doesn't say it. Instead, "I appreciate what you and Maestro Keppler did for me. But I'm not singing today. I hope you can forgive me."

"Forgive you?" He raises his voice enough to cause a few more glances to fall their way. "My dear, you are only hurting your own career!"

She toys with the teardrop pearl around her neck and looks at the floor. Her father pats her shoulder; she can tell he has realized he went too far. "Sing, *farfallina,* this is your decision. And if you will not sing, I can't make you." He sighs. "But you would have been a lovely Angelique."

A great, dark pressure seems to seep out of her chest and dissipate into the busyness of the lounge. "I will be, someday," she says.

Sixty-four

THE BRIGHT ADVERTISEMENT FOR the Autumn Festival seems more incongruous on this weathered old beast of a door than anywhere else on campus. Maybe this is why Sing has come to St. Augustine's. It feels as separated from the loud, vibrant Woolly Theater as she does.

She puts a hand to the edge of the advertisement. These posters have been staring at her for so long, it seems incredible they will be gone after today. True, they will only be replaced by the next big thing, but at least it won't include a hundred *Angelique*s dotting the campus like painful subliminal messages.

Because it *is* painful, she thinks, nudging open the heavy door, which gives a labored creak. The chill follows her into the dim, gaping hallway, but she pushes the door shut and the air quietens. She will not sing Angelique today, and maybe not ever. She will not be given the New Artist position at Fire Lake. This is as it should be, but—

But.

But she had thought, for a little while, that both of these things would happen. Had she not been given that hope, it wouldn't matter. But to love something for a lifetime—even a small lifetime—to wish for something so passionately and then to have *hope* of it, only to have that hope taken away again—that is the worst part.

To wish for something. Her mind's eye flickers to life, just for a pinprick of a moment.

She shuffles down the empty hall. The president's office door is ajar, but she knows he is at the performance with everyone else. Strangely, the sight of the door comforts her. Despite Dunhammond Conservatory's formal air and spattering of draconian regulations, she has always found its doors unlocked. She runs a finger along the backs of the long wooden benches that line the wall. Afternoon sun diffuses through the stained glass, dappling the hall like a summer forest.

The next door she passes is closed, and she realizes with a shiver that it leads to the late Maestro Keppler's office, a guest space set up to accommodate him during his residency this semester. *The last time I was in there, the Maestro was alive,* she thinks. *Now, he—*

She pauses. It was a strange thing to think. Although she imagines a shadowy room, silver-framed pictures, ornaments, she knows she has never been in the Maestro's office.

Her plans in coming to St. Augustine's this afternoon were vague, a simple attempt to be somewhere everyone else wasn't. But she starts down the hallway again with the idea of playing the beautiful grand piano in the concert hall. It is not forbidden for students to play it, but she has never dared. Her rudimentary skills would seem inadequate, even offensive, on such a fine instrument. Today, though, with the hall empty and echoing, maybe her playing will be good enough. Maybe her modest efforts will be better than silence.

She has never really appreciated the beauty of the concert hall before. Sturdy stone columns flare into arches like the lotus pillars in *Osiris and Seth.* Winter light peeks with bright eyes through the tall, narrow windows at ground level and floats lazily near the small stained-glass panels just below the ceiling. The floor shines, warm orange wood.

Her spirits rise as she takes in the room, and for a moment, she feels more at home than she ever has. But when she removes the dustcover and sits at the piano, sadness overtakes her. It is nothing she can explain, separate from the dull disappointment that has settled over her body since she left *Angelique*. Sharper, more urgent. Staring at the black and white keys, she feels as if she has just awoken from a vivid dream—the details are so close to the surface, but somehow utterly lost at the same time. Her reflection in the music rack offers no clues.

She plays a little. A minuet, which she manages to butcher despite its simplicity. The notes echo off the high walls. After a while, she starts humming along. *It really is amazing what a few months can do,* she thinks, not of her clumsy fingers, but of the effortlessness with which she now calls forth her own voice. Professor Needleman is a good teacher, despite her stern exterior, and Sing knows Mr. Bernard's acting classes were part of the reason dress rehearsal went well this week. Even Mrs. Bigelow and the crows have helped her become a deeper musician. And—

She stops playing. *And?*

Again, as when she thought of the forest earlier today, there seems to be a vagueness in her mind. She closes her eyes, willing the amorphous clouds of her memory to solidify into something real. Snatches of images. Where do they come from? *Long hands. A gray T-shirt.* And sounds—the Brahms intermezzo she has loved so much lately.

That is one piece she will never have a hope of learning. But, giving up on the minuet, she starts to pick out Brahms's melody. Three notes, six notes. The first four phrases. She tries to construct a spare bass line, which stumbles as it goes. Slowly, her bare-bones version begins to resemble the music in her mind.

Nathan.

She pulls her hands off the keyboard as though it has burned them.

The vague cloud is *Nathan.* It is as if an explosion has torn through her mind—no, not as scattered as an explosion. A flower of memory, closed tightly, has burst open. She can picture him clearly now, his black hair and blacker eyes, his straight nose and sharp features, his hands. The way it felt when he kissed her.

How could she have forgotten him? What happened? He was here last night; they hid from Maestro Keppler in the stairwell—was that a dream?

Her hand finds the teardrop pearl around her neck. It is wrong; this is the necklace her mother sent for her tenth birthday, from Austria. But this pearl should have been put away, flung to the back of the little drawer in her bedside table. There should be a real tear in its place. Nathan's wish.

It comes back to her now, the roof, the cold, the gun, the black feathers swirling upward and away from her outstretched hands. All the lives extinguished last night—Tamino, the Maestro, Nathan. Did they ever exist? Or did she dream it all?

She pushes back the piano bench and runs to the door, shoes squeaking. She *has* been in the Maestro's office, and there was a photograph of Nathan in there. She saw it the day the Maestro summoned her. Would it still be there?

The door is not locked. Unable to find a light switch, she stumbles to the little window and pulls open the curtains. The large desk is covered with papers, scores, and pictures. She snatches one silver frame after another, holding them to the light.

Here. The photograph she remembers. She picks it up, and a jolt of disbelief snaps through her. The Maestro is there as before, looking reasonably happy, and next to him is the pianist Gloria Stewart. But Nathan isn't there.

She peers at the faded picture. Could his image have been erased? It's possible. She puts a hand to her forehead. *Could I have invented him?*

The cantankerous scrape of the outside door startles her. She replaces the photograph and hurries to the hallway. It's probably not a good idea to be found snooping around a dead man's office.

President Martin is just coming in from the cold and leans against the door with a grimace. As it creaks shut, he looks up at Sing, who stands guiltily at the other end of the hallway.

"Miss da Navelli?" His voice is strong and deep. "Are you all right?"

"I was just playing the piano in the concert hall," she says, answering the question she expected him to ask.

He stamps the snow off his shoes. "Come into my office. Come on, hurry up. You're not in trouble."

She follows him into the spacious office. Her instinct is to stand on the carpet in the embrace of the mahogany baby grand, but she joins him at his desk instead.

He rummages around in the top drawer and pulls out a small plastic case and bottle. "Contact lenses are bothering me," he says, popping out the lenses one at a time and shaking them off his fingers into the case. "Sit down." He seats himself in the puffy leather chair behind the desk. Sing sits. He said she wasn't in trouble, but she wonders.

The president puts on large, gold-rimmed glasses. "I've only got a few minutes," he says. "It's intermission."

She doesn't know what to say. He's looking at her expectantly, but it was *he* who told *her* to come in here.

The president taps his fingers. "I was expecting to see you on-stage today, Miss da Navelli."

So that's it. She finds her voice. "I'm sorry, sir. I . . . wasn't."

"I see." He raises his eyebrows. "Is everything all right?"

She sees the concern in his lined face. *No,* she wants to say. *Everything is not all right.*

She should tell him about her father's conversation with Maestro Keppler, about how she stole Lori Pinkerton's role and gave it back again. And how that doesn't make her a better person. But instead, she finds herself saying, "Can I ask you something, sir?" On the wall opposite, a small clock with a pretty frosted glass cabinet chimes a tiny proclamation.

"Certainly," the president says.

Still unsure whether this is a good idea, she asks, "Who lives in the tower? At Archer?"

If he finds her question strange, he hides it. "That used to be the president's quarters, until they renovated Hector in the twenties. No one lives there now. Sometimes we'll have a gathering on the upper floor, but the rest is storage." He shrugs. "It's not off-limits, you know. You can have a look around if you'd like."

I'm not crazy, she thinks, willing it to be true. *There was a spiral staircase, a basket of laundry next to his bed, yellow light.* Her memories are so vivid. "Do we have an Apprentice Daysmoor?"

He leans back, frowning. "Daysmoor? No, we don't. Daysmoor. There's a Daysmoor School for Boys not far from here. Maestro Keppler is a graduate, I believe. *Was,* I should say."

"He's tall," she says, her voice starting to fail her. "Apprentice Daysmoor is tall, with black hair and long fingers, and he's the best piano player DC's ever seen."

"Miss da Navelli." He rises, and she thinks he's going to scold her, but he pats her shoulder. "It's been a difficult start for you here, hasn't it? I understand. We want our students to be excellent musicians, and we make you work for it. But you must take care of yourself." He heads for the door. "Look, intermission is half over; I have to get back. But you can always come and talk to me, okay?"

She nods.

"Good," he says. "Take your time. Play my piano if you want to."

She means to say *thank you.* He nods a farewell, but Sing can't figure out if he wears a look of friendliness or pity. She leans forward onto the president's large desk and sits for a moment, her head on her arms.

Nathan smelled faintly of pine. You couldn't tell the black of his pupils from the black around them. He played Liszt better than Ryan, probably better than Yvette Cordaro. Maybe better than Gloria Stewart.

With new energy, she springs from the chair and rushes into the hallway. In no time she is sprinting across the bright quad toward

Archer. As the wintry air pushes at her, she realizes she forgot her coat. But she keeps running.

She doesn't open the front doors. Instead, she veers right, crunching through the snow around to the back of the tower. The air is cold in the tower's dark shadow, and the fire escape creaks as she runs up it.

The stone balcony is covered with untouched snow, pristine and silent. It is deep here, having drifted off the roof, and her steps are awkward as she crosses. She presses her forehead to the glass door, blocking the bright sun with her hands so her eyes can adjust to the gloom beyond.

The shape of a piano under a dustcover. Two chairs. No stacks of music.

She tries the door, which surprises her by swinging open. She steps into the dimness and pushes the door closed against the gleaming snow.

It's a trick. President Martin lied to me. Nathan is here.

No sound or light comes from the corner of the room where the spiral staircase descends into the lower tower. Sing pulls the dustcover off the piano. In what she feels is her memory, the image of him sitting at this piano is so clear. She sits on the bench and flips up the fallboard.

The first and only key she depresses sends a tinny rattle into the shadows.

This piano hasn't been played in years.

Sixty-five

A VOICE OVER THE INTERCOM says, "First call," as Sing steps inside the Woolly Lounge onto the red-and-gold carpeting. The orchestra and cast begin to file past her, back down to the stage area.

The rest of Daysmoor's tower was as bleak and lifeless as the topmost room, but her conviction that he existed only grew stronger with each echoing step. She needs to find someone who believes her.

"Carrie!" She pushes her way against the tide of irritated musicians. Carrie Stewart stands by the water cooler, paper cup in hand.

"Sing!" she says. "What's up? Why aren't you singing today? I have to go play, but catch me after, okay?"

"No, wait!" Sing puts a hand on her arm, and Carrie pauses. "I have to ask you something."

Carrie crumples her cup. "Shoot."

"Do you remember Apprentice Daysmoor? Please think." Sing bites her lip.

"Apprentice who?"

"Daysmoor. He lives—lived—in the tower at Archer. You and your brother thought he'd been here longer than everyone said.

You said nobody ever heard him play." She stares into Carrie's eyes as though by sheer force of will she can make her remember.

Carrie looks to the doorway. "Sorry, Sing. I don't know any Apprentice Daysmoor. I wish I could help you out." The intercom calls out final call, and Carrie smiles her good-bye—the same ambiguous smile the president wore.

They think I'm losing it.

A last spark of hope still prickling her chest, she hurries out of the lounge and down the stairs to backstage. The women's dressing room is crowded since the chorus isn't onstage now. She finds Marta at the far end of the room on a couch, reading a magazine in her Queen of the Tree Maidens costume.

Marta looks up, branches twisting outward from her head. "Are you okay?"

Sing sits next to her and speaks with a low voice. "You remember talking about the Felix with me, right?" *Please.*

Marta puts her magazine down. "Yeah. What's this about? Are you all right?"

"Do you remember me showing you my necklace?" Sing holds out the teardrop pearl. "This necklace, only it didn't have a pearl in it. It had a—a crystal. You thought it was a Felix tear."

"A Felix tear? Like, a wish tear?" For a moment, Marta seems like she might continue, but then she closes her mouth.

Sing inhales. "Do you remember Apprentice Daysmoor?"

The look on Marta's face is all the answer she needs.

I'm not crazy, she thinks again. She knows it's true. But now she knows something else as well.

Nathan is gone.

A sadness consumes her so suddenly and so fiercely, her stomach lurches. How could she have forgotten him? She hates the Maestro, now more than ever. Not only did he take Nathan's life, he took him from humanity's collective memory. He took Nathan's music from the world. *He has never existed.* A crow simply lived out its short life all those years ago, its heart broken because of its love of human music. No one ever knew.

Sing's heart has wanted to cry many times over the past two years, but her eyes and her lungs haven't complied very often. But now she feels as though her insides are just an expanding void, a terrible, devastating nothingness trying to push its way out through her chest, her face, her throat.

"Sing! Oh, my goodness, what's wrong?"

She feels Marta's arms around her, branches and leaves scratching at her hair and face. Others are gathered, watching, mostly silent but occasionally cooing words of comfort. But she can't stop crying. *Nathan is gone.*

Yet through this violent, rocking anguish, she realizes with a strange, pricking clarity—this is what the Felix saw in Nathan's eyes in that other, lost reality. This is utter despair.

And she knows she must find the Felix.

Sixty-six

THE FOREST HAS LOST THE OTHERWORLDLY glitter of first snow and has settled into a dark, freezing grayness. Sing trudges up the mountain, acutely aware of the muted rustles and cries around her. She doesn't know where the Felix lives, and part of her mind still insists that none of what she thinks she remembers was ever real. But the deepest part of her heart insists otherwise.

Nathan. She clutches his memory.

Maestro Keppler will never get the better of her again. He is dead.

The snow becomes deeper and more biting as she ascends. The Felix will be near the summit. Durand told her so in *Angelique—La bête se cache en haut.* The beast hides itself above.

The mountain isn't enormous, but it is steep. She pulls herself up tumbles of snowy rock and pushes stiff branches out of her face. There is no path here—there are no paths anywhere in this forest—but she just keeps going up.

Eventually, the trees thin and finally disappear. She can see the conservatory below, closer than she imagined. Dunhammond is already close to the clouds. It didn't take much to reach the tree line.

The low sun gives the mountain a golden haze but is not yet setting the snow on fire. The Felix probably lives not on the open summit, but in a sheltered place nearby. Sing peers around her. For the first time, she has doubt. Although the summit is smaller than she expected, there are many places for a cat to hide—even a big cat. She heads toward some small ledges. Their embrace would leave a cat safe from the elements, and the view from their shoulders is spectacular.

It is the perfect place for the big cat to live. She should expect—or at least be prepared—to see it.

But when she clambers down into the shelter of a small over-hang, she gasps at the sight of the massive, otherworldly creature sleeping there.

The Felix is bigger than she remembers, though in truth she remembers very little about the night she was attacked. The great cat's fur is brilliant reds and violets, with tiny dots of white scattered throughout like stars.

For the first time, Sing considers the fact that if the Felix chooses not to grant her wish, she will instead tear out her throat.

The cat raises her head. She wasn't sleeping after all.

There is no point to running away, so Sing takes a step closer.

The Felix rises, evening sun rippling her fur like water. Her head is level with Sing's own. Then a low noise begins in the cat's throat and pushes itself out past her yellow teeth. Sing can smell decay and bad meat.

This was not a good idea.

The low noise becomes a growl, and Sing tries to edge away. The Felix presses closer, however, not with feline slink but with menacing purpose, tail swishing. Sing feels her back scrape against the ledge and hardy bushes behind her. One strike from a heavy paw, one tear of her jugular, and everything will be over.

The Felix cocks her ears and catches Sing in an unwavering gaze. Sing could not move now even if there was a chance she could escape this creature. Her hands shake. She remembers the black-violet eyes that now hold her, but the eyes in her memory are different somehow—colder, fiercer. These eyes, the shimmering nebulae surrounded by coarse, fiery fur, stare listlessly into Sing's own eyes without judgment or wrath. Sing's breath freezes in her lungs. *Please,* she thinks. *Please help me. Please bring Nathan back. You must see my pain.*

The nebulae lock on to her gaze, burning her mind.

And then, without ceremony or fireworks, a single tear escapes the massive cat's eye, slides over the red fur, and falls with a small warmth into Sing's hand. She looks down, transfixed. The tear sits in her palm, shivering and glowing.

A wish.

Nathan once asked her what she would wish for, given the chance. She had to think about it then. But the wish in her hand isn't filled with beautiful possibilities. It is a solitary lifeline to the thing she wants more than anything in the world. *That is what a wish really is,* she realizes.

Then, to her amazement, a second tear falls into her hand.

She stares at it, shining and pulsating next to the first.

Two wishes? Why has she been granted two wishes? Is this Fire Lake after all, then? Can she have Nathan *and* her career?

When the third tear falls, she finally looks up. The Felix is staring, eyes filling again, until a fourth and fifth tear fall into Sing's outstretched hands. Then a sixth. A seventh. Sing watches her palms fill with glittering diamonds, twenty, thirty, a hundred, until the tears start overflowing onto the frozen ground in little glowing heaps. Enough wishes to grant Sing everything she could ever desire for the rest of her life.

But she returns her focus again to the Felix's eyes. And something happens that has never happened in the history of the world, though the Felix has stared into the souls of countless creatures.

Sing stares back.

She looks beyond the sheen of sadness, beyond the black-violet nebulae, into the broken heart of the great cat.

"I'm so sorry," she says. "I . . . I didn't even think about the fact that you lost Tamino."

The Felix's gaze becomes more present now, and she seems to study Sing's face. Sing lets her hands fall to her sides, tears scattering over the ground. She feels the last of them drip off the ends of her fingers and knows they are all gone, drops of water seeping into the mountain.

"I can't grant your wish," she says. "I can't do magic."

The Felix looks at her a moment longer, then slowly turns her head away and retreats into the shadow of the rocky overhang.

Sing looks out across the snowy landscape. The sun is approaching the horizon, spreading a fiery veil over the quiet spaces of the forest.

I can't do magic.

Only . . . only maybe that isn't true.

Didn't she cast a spell that drew Tamino from the forest? There were no crystalline wishes or ethereal bargains that night. There was only a song. Maybe, now, a song will be enough.

She starts to sing.

She sings the first song that drew Tamino to her, Angelique's most difficult aria. Her voice cannot cut through the vastness of the mountain sky, but it spreads and carries, drifting among needles and seeping under rocks. She feels the Felix watching her.

The words haven't changed, but she hears new meaning in them now. *When he finds himself in the dark forest, he will know what it is to be alone.* She always thought Angelique was imagining Elbert's fear, but now the song feels like a warning. Prince Elbert had power and wealth, but no one to go with him into the dark forest.

When the last note has died, everything around her is still for just a moment before the rustles and crunches of lives being lived return. She stares into the woods. So does the Felix. A small breeze ruffles Sing's hair, icy but not unkind.

Then, deep among the trees below them, a light appears. A little spark, golden and steady, which seems to wind its way in their direction. A jolt of electricity shoots outward from Sing's heart. Could it be a piece of Tamino, coaxed out from the ether by the music he loves? The Felix emerges from the shadows, eyes fixed on the spark.

But just when the spark reaches the tree line, it seems to drift away, as though it has lost its focus. Sing senses the Felix glance at her.

He can't find us unless I sing, she thinks, and starts again.

This time, she sings the *farfallina* song. Before long, the spark finds its way to them and remains, hovering, near the shadowy overhang. The Felix watches it intently.

"Ecco, ecco, a trovata. Bianca e rosa, colorata . . ."

Other sparks find their way to the overhang and cluster there. She sings as many verses as she can remember, as more and more sparks arrive from every direction. They seem to bring warmth with them, and her voice grows.

"Gira qua, gira là, fin che posa su papà." As Sing finishes the last verse, she realizes she hasn't thought of that final line in years—the moment when the little butterfly at last comes to rest on its *papà*. Her father used to hold her hands as he sang, making them flit here and there and finally come to rest on his heart.

The sparks have gathered into a single bright shape that illuminates the ledges and the dusky forest around them. Sing and the Felix watch as the light gradually dims, settling into a solid form. Orange fur. Bright eyes.

Sing exhales, letting her body fall back against the brackeny ledge. She is exhilarated. It *was* magic.

The Felix rubs her head against the orange fur and licks the fuzzy ears. Tamino says, *"Chrrrrp!"* Sing catches his eyes, and he closes them. She feels *thank you*.

Twilight settles over the mountaintop, but the two cats do not retreat to the shelter of the rocky overhang. Sing watches them turn and start to make their way up the ledge toward the summit, their dusky forms glittering rust and deep lavender. She knows she will never see them again. It is like the end of an opera, whole but bittersweet.

But just before they disappear completely, Tamino looks back and closes his eyes in a last cat-smile. Then, the golden light still clinging to his fur expands, washing over the landscape like a great exhalation, causing the trees to bend and the snow to drift. Sing feels it pass through her with a warmth. She feels something change.

She watches their vague forms disappearing up into the darkness. And she can't be sure, but it seems as though once they reach the summit, they just keep going.

Sixty-seven

MARTA AND JENNY ARE SITTING on Sing's bed. Marta holds Woolly, which, unexpectedly, doesn't bother Sing at all.

"Where have you *been*?" Jenny crosses her arms and scowls like someone's tiny mother. "Do you know what time it is?"

Sing would laugh if it weren't for the genuine concern in Jenny's face. "Eight thirty?" she hazards.

Jenny glances at her watch. "Well, yes. It's about eight thirty. Which isn't so late. But still. Where have you been?"

"Are you okay?" Marta asks.

Sing throws her coat over her desk chair. She pulls the chain on her Tiffany lamp and switches off the garish ceiling light. "I'm okay," she says. "Sorry to scare you guys."

"Marta told me you lost it earlier," Jenny says.

Marta inhales, eyes wide. "I didn't use those words!"

"It's okay," Sing says. "I had a hard day. *Angelique* and Fire Lake and the Maestro and . . . and everything. I'm sorry for freaking out."

Jenny plays with a bit of thread on the quilt on Sing's bed. "Well, as long as you're having a bad day, we might as well tell you—"

"No!" Marta says. "I mean, at least wait!"

Sing takes her boots off and throws them in the corner. "Tell me what?"

Marta taps Jenny's knee forcefully, *tap tap tap*. "Jenny—"

"Ryan's back with Lori," Jenny says. "She sang well today, you know. At the performance. That guy from Fire Lake was talking to her." They both look at Sing.

Now Sing does laugh, despite her friends' serious faces. It's an unconscious reaction, her body jolting with sudden emotion that could easily have been a sob. *Ryan.* How ridiculous it seems now that she ever worried about what Ryan thought.

"Don't lose your marbles, Sing," Jenny says.

"Are you okay?" Marta asks.

"I'm fine. Stop asking if I'm okay." Sing finds her sneakers, one under her chair, one under the desk. Jenny and Marta are still look-ing at her. She tries not to think of Nathan, whom she alone in all the world still keeps. She thinks instead of Tamino, and the last cat-smile he gave her. "I'm fine. I mean . . . I'm going to be."

Sing, Jenny, and Marta cross the quad toward the Woolly, feet crunching the snow in and out of the circles of lamplight. Although Sing's body would rather sleep, her mind wants stimulation. Or dis-traction. They are too late to hear the finals of the Gloria Stewart competition, but the after-party promises to be good.

Sing is secretly glad she won't have to listen to Ryan play, though she can tell the others would have liked to go. Marta rattles off the names of the finalists in each category. Sing barely listens, her nostrils tingling with the cold, her woolen hat itchy against her forehead.

"Wait," she says, and Marta pauses. "Who was that last one? Keppler?"

"Yeah," Jenny says, a little out of breath from keeping up with them. "Amateurs Over Sixteen. Gave Ryan a run for his money, I'll tell you that. My money's on him to take it all."

"He was *amazing*," Marta says.

"Not—" Sing isn't sure how to phrase it. "Not *Maestro* Keppler?"

"Um, no." Jenny's voice is flat. "Maestro Keppler, besides not being an amateur, is dead. As of yesterday. You do remember that, right?"

Sing remembers. But just for a moment, she wondered. She has been thinking about that last golden wave of light that Tamino sent out from himself. It felt as though the world changed with it, but she doesn't know how. "Yes," she says. "Sorry."

"Sing means Apprentice Keppler," Marta says. "Yeah, it was him."

"*Apprentice* Keppler?"

Jenny sighs. "Um, yeah. Your voice coach? Maestro Keppler's nephew, or grandnephew, or whatever? You really have had a bad day, haven't you?" They reach the broad steps of the Woolly. The light from the theater's large windows deepens the darkness outside. Jenny pauses at the door. "Are you sure you're up for this party? Did you hit your head?"

Sing puts her mittened hand against one of the pillars that frame the theater's entrance. *Your voice coach.* She doesn't remember any voice coach other than—

No. She can't get her hopes up. When Nathan was erased from history, of course things had to be filled in. She had a voice coach this year. Apprentice Keppler. Maestro Keppler's grandnephew. She will probably "remember" him when she sees him, if that's how these things work.

Her head aches. She sees herself scrabbling at swirling black feathers. Part of her wishes her memories had changed with everything else, but it seems she clutched them too closely, and nothing could take them from her. It is a strange comfort.

The competition is over and the party has begun. There are a few people gathered in the lobby, talking and sipping champagne. Sing, Marta, and Jenny slide off their puffy winter jackets and make their way to a set of white leather double doors. Jenny tugs at her tight navy dress with silver sequins and leads the way up a marble staircase. Laughter and the sound of a solo cello drift down from the upstairs lounge as they ascend.

Halfway up the stairs, Sing hears a familiar voice. Two familiar voices. Jenny and Marta seem to recognize them, too, because they exchange looks. A moment later, Ryan and Lori come into view, his arm around her waist.

"Oh," he says, pausing. "Hey, Sing."

Sing stops. "Hey."

"Taking off?" Jenny says innocently.

Ryan shrugs. "Win some, lose some." His voice is easy, but his eyes are dull. "That Apprentice Keppler, well . . ."

"He's no big deal," Lori says.

Ryan laughs mirthlessly. "Lori," he says, "he's a big deal."

"Nice job today, Lori," Marta says. Lori doesn't say anything. She seems preoccupied with the fringe on her slinky white dress.

For the first time Sing can remember, Ryan seems at a loss for words. He flashes a smile, but it appears hollow. He looks at Sing for a long moment that gets more awkward as time passes. Eventually, he attempts to speak, but Sing interrupts.

"See you around, Ryan." And she starts up the stairs again. Jenny and Marta follow. She hears Ryan and Lori continue down the stairs, but she doesn't look back.

"So Keppler did win," Marta says. "I knew he would. That's him playing now, I bet." The solo cello beyond the doors has stopped, and now someone is playing the piano.

They reach the doors to the lounge. *"Well,"* Jenny says.

Marta and Sing hang their coats on a rack. "Well what?" Marta asks.

"It looks like *somebody* didn't get offered the Fire Lake vacancy after all." Jenny's smug expression makes Sing laugh.

"You don't know that," Sing says.

"Oh, you're right," Jenny says. "I'm sure Lori was just being polite.

There's no way she would have wanted to rub something like that in your face."

Could it be true? Maybe Harland Griss wasn't impressed with Lori after all.

No. Sing pushes the thought from her mind and steps through the doorway.

At the sight of so many beads and brooches, she is glad Jenny persuaded her to wear her black formal dress. Marta looks customarily out of place, but in a more elegant way; her strange, flowing garments flow with a little more style.

"Ooh, boys in tuxes," Jenny says. "Let's mingle."

Sing smiles but doesn't feel it. "I'm hungry. I'll catch up." She heads to a long table set with platters of tiny food, but when she reaches it, she just stands there. *Nothing would be worse than being alone with your thoughts right now,* she tells herself. Still, she wonders how she will endure this exercise in decorum when the rift in her heart threatens to swallow every word and every smile. She takes a miniquiche. The swirling red-and-gold-leaf pattern of the carpet makes her dizzy.

The music comforts her a little, at least, a tasteful piano-cello duet. The piece is nothing extraordinary, but they are excellent musicians. For a moment, she almost makes herself believe it is Nathan himself playing, and she looks to the piano. But the crowd pressing in on the performers hides them from view. She glimpses the cellist, a shriveled faculty member with curly yellow hair. Then the crowd parts for just a moment to reveal the pianist, but he has his back to her.

It doesn't matter, though. He may have Nathan's black hair, cut short instead of long, but his shoulders don't look right. And no ivy tattoo winds down his left arm from his rolled shirtsleeve.

"Miss da Navelli, there you are!" A voice from another lifetime draws her attention.

"Mr. Griss. How are you?" The party mask she adopts now seems so foreign, a gaudy weight she must hold up on a stick rather than a silken chameleon skin. "I hope you've enjoyed the Autumn Festival."

"Very much." Griss's fleshy face is unusually animated. "Though I was disappointed not to hear your Angelique in performance. Especially after that excellent sneak preview. Your father tells me you were ill; I'm glad to see you're feeling better."

Sing clings to her fake smile. She still can't believe she embarrassed herself like that, showing off in the theater lobby. And for what? For Nathan, who is gone? Who, now, wasn't even *there*?

No more, she decides, and lets the mask dissolve. Maybe Griss doesn't even notice, but Sing's body relaxes. Now that Barbara da Navelli has released her, there is no need to try to be like her anymore. "I wasn't sick, sir. I decided not to go on. I—I had kind of stolen Lori's role." She doesn't meet Griss's eyes. "I wanted a shot at the New Artist vacancy. More than that, I just wanted to sing the role. But it wasn't right for me to go through with it."

Now she dares venture a glance at Griss's face. He nods, businesslike. "Well," he says. "There are two things you should know about Fire Lake, then. One is that we frown on that sort of infighting."

"Yes, sir." She looks around the glittering room. People talk and eat, clinking glasses onto plates.

Griss goes on. "And the other is that we are exceptionally ruthless when it comes to casting. There are no dues to be paid, no ladders to climb. It doesn't matter if someone has been doing roles for one year or twenty. You sing what we want to hear you sing, when we think you're ready to sing it."

"Yes, s—" Sing stops, her mind frothing. Can he possibly be saying what she thinks he's saying?

"*Carina,* Harland has found you, I see." Ernesto da Navelli strolls over to them, shedding admirers as he comes. Sing follows his funny, fastidious steps, examines the fall of the designer suit over his round shoulders and rounder midsection, and something in her warms.

"Well," Griss says good-naturedly, "I was just getting to the part where we offer Miss da Navelli the New Artist spot."

Sing feels her eyes widen and her jaw drop, like a cartoon character. She never knew people's faces actually reacted like this, but she can't help it. She can sense people on the periphery of their conversation speaking in low voices and trying not to look.

"I know this is a bit unusual," Griss says. "But I think you are an excellent choice. And I feel that my stipulation that the candidate must have taken on at least one leading role has been fulfilled, despite the fact that you didn't sing the final performance. You may argue this if you'd like, but I would advise against it."

Her father gives her a crinkly-eyed smile. "You were not expecting this, eh? What do you say, my girl?"

She looks at her father, then at Griss. "But you haven't heard me!" *More politics, more puppetry. How many deserving young singers are being passed over right now?*

"I heard all I needed to," Griss says. "I heard a Pamina who broke my heart."

Sing can't seem to control her breathing. Her father puts his hands on her shoulders. His face is serious. "You are the *best choice,* Sing. I have always told you you sing like an angel, but you do not believe me. Believe me now, *carina.*"

His smile is wide. He is so proud. She wants to be worthy of his pride—it's a new feeling for her. She inhales, *sì* poised on her tongue.

The first three notes of a melody capture her attention. The pianist in the corner has started to play Brahms, opus 118, Intermezzo in A Major.

Just as her music drew the million broken pieces of Tamino together again into one shining whole, the sounds from the piano seem to gather the shards of her shattered heart. And without the party mask, there is nothing preventing her from throwing her arms around her father and saying, "Papà."

Her father chuckles, but when she pulls away, she sees a cloudiness in his eyes. "What is it, *farfallina*? Are you all right?" She has pulled every drop of his focus away from Griss and the soiree happening around them.

She smiles. *"Sì."* The music expands in her ears like foam. Then she looks at Griss and says, "I would be honored to accept the New Artist position."

"Wonderful!" Her father extends his hand, and Griss shakes it heartily. The murmuring around them grows in intensity, but all Sing cares about is Brahms.

"When I graduate from DC," she finishes.

"That's not how it works." Griss's calm voice reminds Sing of her mother's lawyer. "We fill the openings as they arise. New Artists only tend to stay for a year or two. So you'll be settling in as soon as you can. As soon as this term ends."

Sing takes a breath. For a long moment, she doesn't know what to say.

"What is the matter, Sing?" her father asks.

All her life, she has never really been sure she's in the right place. Certainly not that first evening at DC, when she stepped out of her father's Mercedes into the shadow of the cold mountain. Would Fire Lake be the right place now? She imagines missing this once-in-a-lifetime opportunity, and shivers of nausea course through her. But is she ready? Her father was right about DC, but is he right now?

Maybe DC is where she belongs, now, for the first time. She thinks of Jenny's voice and Marta's gaudy necklaces, of Professor Needleman's pristine robes and Mr. Bernard's ugly sweatpants. She thinks of President Martin's baby grand piano. She remembers the songs of crows.

She smiles at her father. "Thank you for helping me, Papà." Now she turns. "Mr. Griss, this is an amazing opportunity. But I'd like to finish my studies here before coming to Fire Lake. Often your New Artists are in their twenties or early thirties—I don't think nineteen will be too old."

Her father clears his throat. "It is not your place to make demands of Mr. Griss, Sing. Accept the position and be grateful, or do not."

But she holds Griss's gaze. "I am grateful. Incredibly, mind-bogglingly grateful. But it's not charity you're offering me—I can give Fire Lake something back. You want something from me. You believe in me. All I'm asking is for you to keep believing in me until I've graduated." She takes a deep breath. "At first, I wasn't sure I belonged here at DC, but—I do."

Silence falls over the room as the Brahms intermezzo ends—or did the pianist cut it off in the middle?

Griss crosses his arms. Sing can tell he is unused to hearing anything he doesn't like, and she finds the speed at which his face goes from friendly to calculating unnerving. She knows she may be throwing away something irretrievable, and it makes her light-headed. Her father says nothing.

After a moment, Griss gives a curt nod. "Okay."

Sixty-eight

A FIRM HANDSHAKE. *We'll be interested in your progress here, Miss da Navelli.*

A hug. I'll see you soon, farfallina. Break is coming up. Do you want me to get tickets to the new production of— Oh? Well . . . well, that would be nice, wouldn't it? We haven't been to the beach house since you were little. I'll have them open it up.

Sing steps back from the mirror on her dresser. "What do you think, Woolly? Diamonds or hoops?" She squints at the reflection of her ears. "You're right. Neither. Maybe Marta has something I can borrow."

Mr. Bernard's private screening of his favorite movie musical will not be a formal affair, but Sing thinks earrings are appropriate. After getting up early to say good-bye to her father and Harland Griss, she welcomes any accessory that will draw attention from her baggy eyes. It felt like the Autumn Festival was nothing but receptions and after-parties, and now she has to drag herself to a final Opera Workshop get-together. At least there are no classes today.

She slides open a dresser drawer. There is no way she's wearing her uniform. Her pajamas' green stripes move with her in the dresser mirror, and she thinks of the green-striped cabana that her parents used to set up on the sand in front of the beach house in St. John. Maybe she'll invite Zhin to come with her and her father over break.

She remembers Barbara da Navelli on the beach. Perfect makeup. A string bikini that looked fantastic but never went near the actual water. Eyes searching for cameras and celebrities, not interesting shells or disgruntled crabs.

Maybe she'll invite Jenny and Marta instead.

Knock, knock. "Hello? Sing?" It's a voice she doesn't recognize. She glances at her pajamas. "Who is it?"

"Apprentice Keppler," the voice calls from behind the door. Chipper.

Apprentice Keppler. Her voice coach. She puts a hand to the dresser and lets it support some of her weight. She can't picture him. Everything else in this strange new *now* has settled into a kind of reality, but not him. Not this person who has taken Nathan's shape—coaching Opera Workshop, turning Ryan's pages, playing Brahms. He is still a stranger.

"Miss da Navelli?" he says, his voice muffled. "I just wanted to say good-bye."

"Oh." She flexes her fingers. "Good-bye."

A pause. "I've got some engagements. And Yvette Cordaro wants to introduce me to a few people. You know, because of Gloria Stewart International." Another pause. "I'm getting representation."

Sing looks at the closed door. She forces a smile he can't see. "Oh. Great!"

Another knock. "Sing?" It's Jenny. "Are you in there?"

Keppler says something Sing can't make out. Then Jenny's voice, lower. "Through the door? Is she sick?" Now louder. "Are you sick?"

"No," Sing calls.

"Naked?"

"No!"

The door opens and Jenny steps into the room, hands on hips.

"What is with you? You're a hermit now or something? Doing something illegal in here?"

But Sing doesn't answer her. She stares at Apprentice Keppler, who is still standing in the doorway. His shirtsleeves are rolled up, as they were last night, revealing tattoo-free forearms. His hair is cut neatly, his shoulders narrower than they should be. But he has the blackest eyes she's ever seen.

Jenny looks at Sing, then at Apprentice Keppler. "Well. Well, Sing, you have a very strange look on your face. I will . . . see you around." She backs out of the room. Sing hears the door across the hall open and close, and after a moment, she can hear Jenny and Marta laughing. But she doesn't take her eyes from Apprentice Keppler's face.

It *is* him, isn't it?

Or is it?

"Nathan?" she says at last.

"Yes?" Politeness.

"You look . . . different."

He tilts his head. "Different?"

She pushes off the dresser and lets herself be propelled to her desk. Gravity presses her into the chair.

"Are you okay?" he asks.

"I'm tired of people asking if I'm okay."

"Sorry." He leans on the doorframe. "How am I different?"

She pushes her hair back from her forehead. "You're just . . . you look like . . . Never mind."

He studies her. She looks back, trying to see Nathan Daysmoor. Nathan Keppler's eyes are dark and lovely, but they stare with courtesy. She remembers the arresting, almost intrusive gaze that caught her breath at her placement audition.

Sing can't stand this new Nathan looking at her. She lowers her eyes.

He puts his hands into the pockets of his jeans. "I traded in my robes for people clothes. Maybe that's what's different."

"Maybe." She wishes he would leave.

But he just stands there with his hands in his pockets. She looks out the window at the bright gray sky, then back to his face. The straight nose, the angular contours. The black hair cut too short to curve into his jaw the way she knows it would.

After a moment, he says, "I look like Nathan Daysmoor."

She looks up sharply. "What? How do you—"

"Sing," he says quietly, "don't you recognize me?" He starts to continue, but his words sound like "Unghf" because of the force with which Sing throws her arms around his neck. He wraps his arms around her, kisses her cheek, her eyes, her lips. Then he laughs.

Eventually, she asks, "What happened?"

He steps back, his arms still around her waist. "I have a place now. Tamino found me a place."

"Who are you?" she asks. "Are you Daysmoor or Keppler?"

"I'm Nathan Keppler," he says. "Just as my great-grandfather was."

"But what *happened*? How are you here?"

He shuts the door. "The strangest thing. You see, my great-grandfather almost drowned when he was just a boy. But the story that's been handed down in my family is that he was saved by a great orange cat who dragged him from the river."

She hugs him. She can't stop hugging him. It occurs to her to ask, "Do you remember everything?"

He rests his cheek on the top of her head. "I remember too much everything. I remember Daysmoor. And every moment that passes, I remember more of this new life. I *feel* as though I have—well, a life, and a home. I remember piano lessons with a woman who wore sweatshirts with puppies on them. I remember my human parents. It's strange. I imagine I'll see them soon." He laughs. "I imagine they're proud of me."

Sing looks up at him. "But . . . but you're leaving. That's what you said."

He hesitates. "It's better that I do."

"It's not better for *me*."

"Well," he says, "you'll just have to come hear me play. I might even get you a backstage pass. Ha ha! I'm kidding. No violence! Anyway, you've got a lot to do at DC. You need to get ready for Fire Lake." He takes her hands. "Congratulations."

Sing wonders if they were really together in that dark stairwell or if those memories are merely phantoms. Is this new reality creating itself around them? Are all these people and relationships as new as they feel? Or are the past few months a trick of her mind now, seamlessly replaced by a solid chain of events that has always existed?

Nathan smiles. "Thank you. For wishing for me."

She looks down. "I didn't. I mean—I would have. But Tamino did this on his own. There was no tear. There was only this warm light."

Nathan steps to Sing's bed and sits on the edge. She sits next to him. He says, "There doesn't always have to be a tear."

The light from Sing's window is white like the snow and the sky outside. She rubs her thumb along the inside of Nathan's forearm. "Your tattoo's gone."

He weaves his fingers with hers. "You sound disappointed. Should I get another one?"

"I'm pretty sure there's a tattoo parlor in the village," she says.

"Well," Nathan says, leaning in, "I suppose I could leave tomorrow instead of today."

She tries to decide if this kiss feels like the first one or if, in this reality, they have already done this. But it doesn't really matter.

"Wednesday at the *latest*," Nathan says.

The door opens, but Sing doesn't even open her eyes. She hears Marta giggle. Then Jenny's voice. "I *knew* it!"

Sixty-nine

THE FELIX DOES NOT KNOW how long she has been on earth. She felt little of its rotations and orbits, of the rise and fall of mountains. She was aware of time as one who is not a sailor is aware of the sea.

But she knew about forever. She knew that death was forever for the creatures around her, those she devoured and those who simply stopped breathing for their own reasons.

Yet here is the child, back from death.

For the first time since her fall, the Felix is joyful.

And she will choose to spend the rest of forever in the sky.

ACKNOWLEDGMENTS

Thank you to everyone who made this book possible, especially—
My mom (who only sings karaoke), my dad, and Mr. K; Ammi-Joan Paquette; S. Jae-Jones and Mollie Traver at St. Martin's Press; Beatrice Clerc, Sarah Ellis and Leda Schubert, Katie Bayerl, Liz Cook, Alicia Potter, Laura Sanscartier, the Pathfinder Academy junior high, Dr. Jiahao Chen, Piero Garofalo, the Thunderbadgers, Alan Cumyn, Ellen Howard, Blessy Alancheril, and the VCFA community.